The house was like the *Mary Celeste*, living and breathing but empty of life. No master or mistress, no children or grandchildren, no butler, cook or parlourmaid, not even the kitchen cat.

The stranger didn't let that worry him . . . he set out on a tour of inspection, fingering the ornaments, testing the armchairs, picking out a pom-tiddly-om-pom on the piano, helping himself to the sugared almonds, poking up the fire with the air of a man who was perfectly entitled to poke up the fire if he wanted to.

As, indeed, he was, because the house that had been home to Tassie since the day she was born wasn't her home any more. It had just passed, with virtually everything else her family possessed, into the hands of this total stranger.

Reay Tannahill was born and brought up in Scotland, and is a graduate of the University of Glasgow. In addition to four previous novels, she is the author of two bestselling works of non-fiction which have been translated into seven languages. *Passing Glory* won the Romantic Novel of the Year Award, and *Food in History* was the winner of the Italian gastronomic award, the *Premio Antico Fattore*.

ALSO BY REAY TANNAHILL

Fiction

A Dark and Distant Shore
The World, the Flesh and the Devil
Passing Glory
In Still and Stormy Waters

Non-Fiction

Food in History
Sex in History

RETURN OF THE STRANGER

Reay Tannahill

ORION

An Orion paperback
First published in Great Britain by Orion in 1995
This paperback edition published in 1996 by Orion Books Ltd,
Orion House, 5 Upper St Martin's Lane, London WC2H 9EA

Copyright © 1995 Reay Tannahill

A CIP catalogue record for this book is available
from the British Library.

ISBN: 0 75280 284 4

Typeset by Deltatype Ltd, Ellesmere Port, S. Wirral
Printed in Great Britain by Clays Ltd, St Ives plc

This book is dedicated,
with affection,
to Vi and Tommy Tomlinson,
long-time friends

CONTENTS

PROLOGUE

April
1894

April 1894

PROLOGUE

I

To the stranger paying off his hansom in the damp,
chilly April dusk, everything about the solid, grey
stone villa spoke of prosperity, warmth and welcome.
He smiled as he waited for someone to open the door
and ask him in.

No one did.

He glanced through the window. There were bowls
of pink hyacinths on the sill and flames dancing in the
marble hearth. Brass lamps with green glass shades
shone down invitingly on a pair of small fireside tables
cluttered with china ornaments, lacquered boxes, and
crystal dishes full of sugared almonds. The only other
light in the room came from an opal-globed gasolier,
turned low, but even the shadows whispered of money
– the middle-class kind of money that didn't make a
parade of itself but didn't undervalue itself, either. The
curtains were opulently swagged and fringed, the
cornices intricately moulded, the oil paintings dark and
rich in their gilded frames. The hands of the mantelshelf
clock – a pretty, expensive toy smothered in ormolu
spires, enamelled garlands and painted flowers –
showed the hour as six precisely.

Turning back to the door, the stranger hauled on the
polished brass bell pull, but the jangling rose and fell
and slowly died, raising no answer beyond echoes in the
mist that had begun to glide in from the sea. After a

moment, he stepped back to scan the upstairs windows for signs of life, and raised his voice. 'Hello? Anyone there?' And after another moment, again, 'Hello?' Then, his smile fading, he took two strides forward and raised his hand to the knocker.

But before he touched it, the door swung open smoothly, silently, and of its own accord.

2

Thirteen-year-old Tassie, lurking in the shrubbery, choked back a hiccup of laughter. It was just like the beginning of a ghost story. All that was needed – and *why* hadn't she thought of it! – was for some horrid apparition in a droopy white sheet and cobwebs to leap out from behind the door and frighten the stranger into fits. With luck, he would have dropped dead on the spot.

It was the fate he deserved.

But Tassie was a realistic girl and recognised, with regret, that any such scheme would have been doomed from the start. For one thing, St Andrews didn't run to a Spooks' Outfitters shop, and the domestic linen at Graceholm *never* drooped – was, indeed, so fiercely starched and ironed that it could have stood up on its own. Nor was there the dimmest, remotest, most spider-inviting corner that wasn't swept and garnished daily. Tassie sometimes thought that, even if the house had been lucky enough to have a really, truly ghost of its own, her mother wouldn't have allowed it out without making sure that one of the servants gave it a good wash and brush-up first.

In any case, it seemed to Tassie that the stranger was the kind of gentleman who would give short shrift to any horrid apparition foolhardy enough to get in his way. Although from her dank and leafy lair she could see only a stalwart back and a glimpse of profile, the

4

force of his personality carried all the way across the wide, sweeping curve of the gravelled drive. She found it rather unnerving.

If the behaviour of the door had given him pause, he showed no sign of it but, with only a faint shrug, pushed it wide, crossed the threshold and vanished from Tassie's sight. The sound of another, 'Hello? Anyone there?' floated back to her through the dusk.

But there was still no answering voice and by then he must have guessed that there wouldn't be. The house was like the *Mary Celeste*, living and breathing but empty of life. No master or mistress, no children or grandchildren, no butler, cook or parlourmaid, not even the kitchen cat.

The stranger didn't let that worry him, either. Within seconds, he was sauntering into the drawing room, unbuttoning his thick, dark overcoat and tossing his soft felt hat down on a chair – a rather shocking hat, in the view of a schoolgirl who knew no other sartorial code than the one that prevailed in St Andrews. A bowler might have been acceptable – just – but only Bohemians and piano tuners wore soft felts.

Tucking the ungentlemanly hat away for future consideration, Tassie raised hopeful eyes to the new-comer's face, to discover with frustration that, because of the way the light was falling, all she could see was a study in contrasts, like a bleached-out photograph or an old woodcut. She could be sure of nothing more than that he was dark of hair, probably not above thirty years old, cleanshaven – another affront to convention – and possessed of a jaw, nose and eyebrows that confirmed her impression that their owner was the kind of person who wouldn't stand any nonsense from anybody.

It was deeply disappointing not to be able to see his expression as he set out on a tour of inspection, fingering the ornaments, testing the armchairs, picking out a pom-tiddly-om-pom on the piano, helping himself to the sugared almonds, poking up the fire with the air of a man who was perfectly entitled to poke up the fire if he wanted to.

As, indeed, he was, because the house that had been home to Tassie since the day she was born wasn't her home any more. It had just passed, with virtually everything else her family possessed, into the hands of this total stranger.

3

Even her mother, the gentlest and least critical of women, had been provoked into saying that she couldn't imagine what Tassie's late papa had been thinking of, leaving a Will that had allowed such a thing to happen. No, she had no idea who the Mysterious Heir might be, nor did she wish to know. And no, she had no intention of staying to make his acquaintance, although she would – naturally – ensure that the house was left in perfect order for him, a courtesy she would accord to any guest, even one whom she suspected of being no better than a Pharisee.

'You mean Philistine,' Tassie had said helpfully. 'Aren't you curious about him? Not even a little bit?'

'Not even a little bit.'

It had been clear to Tassie where her duty lay. Whatever her mama might say about not wanting to know, she was going to be dreadfully disappointed if no one made any effort to find out.

4

Which was why she was crouched in the shrubbery with a spotted laurel dripping down the back of her neck, suffering an unexpected reversal of feeling.

To begin with – and alone of the family – she had reacted to the provisions of her father's Will with unqualified excitement. Mystery, melodrama and the promise of change were unheard-of delights in the sedate and ordered world of St Andrews. She had even indulged in dreams of the Mysterious Heir turning out to be Prince Charming in disguise – a temporarily misguided Prince Charming who would prove perfectly willing to be enslaved by her and shown the error of his ways. In her dreams, he had assured her that the matter of the inheritance had been a dreadful misunderstanding, and that he would, of course, give back to the family *instantly* everything he had stolen from it.

How lovely, she had thought. What fun!

But now, as she watched the dark, formidable gentleman with the ungentlemanly hat laying possessive hands on the materials of her life, on all the familiar, disregarded things that had formed the background, and more than the background, to the thirteen years of her growing up, she discovered that it wasn't fun at all – especially since, as Prince Charmings went, the stranger was quite the wrong kind of person. Lively though Tassie's imagination was, it didn't stretch to seeing him enslaved at her feet. It didn't stretch to seeing him volunteer to give the inheritance back, either.

For the first time, she found herself wondering why her adored papa had done what he had done. And wishing he hadn't.

5

She had no difficulty in charting the stranger's progress as he moved through the house, exploring it from top to bottom, turning up the gas in one room after another and leaving it triumphantly blazing as if it were Queen Victoria's Jubilee all over again. She had just reached the stage of reflecting, with gloomy relish, on the probable size of his gas bill when a loud rustling behind her made her jump, and her small nephew's voice squeaked, 'Tassie, where are you? Ow! Oooh! Something scratched me!'

'The holly,' Tassie hissed back. 'And watch out for the bamboo. Really, Bazz, what are you doing here? There isn't room for two of us.'

'Beastly prickly things!' he complained, massaging his wounds. 'Mama sent me to say she's tired of waiting for you and if you don't come straight away she'll tell John Coachman to drive off and leave you. The moon's clouding over and it's going to rain soon.'

'Oh, bother!' Tassie was annoyed but not surprised, because it was just like Selina to rate her own convenience above the mission on which her sister was engaged. 'I don't want to have to walk all the way to Seamount in the dark. Where's the carriage?'

'Round the corner by the church. And if you . . . Eeek!'

All the light had been blotted out so suddenly and completely that Tassie thought for a moment she had gone blind. But it wasn't that. Instead of an excellent view of the brilliantly illuminated house, her spyhole between the evergreens now afforded, in alarming close up, an even more excellent view of a broadcloth torso, complete with gold watch chain and fobs. Related to the torso was a pair of hands, one of which, armoured in a good thick leather glove, was holding back a holly branch, while the other was reaching out towards her.

Bazz stayed not upon the order of his going, but Tassie, hampered by some bramble canes that had attached themselves to her tweed knickerbockers, was still furiously struggling to free herself when the hand lunged.

It missed her by a hair's breadth.

A dark brown voice with an accent she couldn't identify said, 'Damnation! And who may you be?'

Afterwards, Tassie wondered whether the voice

hadn't been more amused than sinister, but at the time she felt no passionate urge to stay and find out. Tearing herself free of the brambles, she gasped with instinctive – if somewhat misplaced – politeness, 'I'm so sorry. We didn't mean to intrude. We must be going. Goodbye!' and bolted for her life along the gardeners' path through the shrubbery, emerging at the drive gates to find Bazz waiting for her, hopping up and down with impatience, and Selina's carriage already rounding the corner from the church.

6

'Goodness, you look like the ragtag and bobtail!' Selina scolded as they scrambled aboard. 'Tassie, how could you let Basil get so dirty? And, Basil, my pet, what are those horrid scratches on your hand? Let me look. Monty, move over and make space for your brother. Go and sit beside Granny Grace.'

Monty, sighing ostentatiously, did as he was bid while Grace Smith, a slender, elegant forty-nine who didn't look in the least like a granny, gathered in her fashionable, prune-coloured skirts to make space for him, then turned her limpid green gaze on her younger daughter and waited.

She didn't say, 'Well?' because she wasn't supposed to be curious.

Tassie took a deep breath. 'Well . . .' she began.

PART ONE

1894 —
1898

April–September 1894

CHAPTER ONE

I

The terms of Josiah Smith's Will, when they had first been revealed to his family some months previously, had come as a severe shock to those of its members who, unlike Tassie, found nothing at all pleasurable in the prospect of having the established order of things turned upside down.

It had been a lovely summer's afternoon, the sun penetrating even the dim mahogany office in South Street, when the situation had been explained to them by Joss's solicitor, a stout gentleman with flappy ears and steel spectacles who (or so it seemed to Tassie) regarded any sentence of less than a hundred words as an offence against the majesty of the law. As he droned on, and on, and on, his mouth opening and closing with the regularity of a metronome, she had watched the dust motes dancing and found herself drowsily puzzling over why his beard should be so luxuriant when his head was completely bald. Perhaps exercise had something to do with it.

The essence of what he had said was that there was nothing singular about the deceased's testamentary dispositions. Indeed, the late Mr Smith had acted as many another gentleman would have done in his place. Not having been blessed with sons of his own and anxious to ensure that his female relicts continued to be protected from the contamination of too much contact with the world, he had elected to bequeath his entire estate – comprising the jute mills and factory, the house, various parcels of land and the bulk of his investments – to his nearest male relative. In the lawyer's opinion, it had been a wise decision.

'I am sure you are right,' had said the widow after a dazed moment, while her younger daughter wondered mutinously why everyone seemed to think it perfectly proper for a gentleman, even when dead, to go on sheltering the females of his family whether they wanted to be sheltered or not. Personally, Tassie thought contact with the world sounded like quite an interesting thing.

'But,' Grace Smith continued, 'I was unaware that my late husband *had* any near male relative.'

'Not "near",' the lawyer corrected her. 'Nearest.'

Whereupon he had revealed that the 'nearest male relative' was a cousin so distant that no one in the family had ever heard of him. 'A Mr J. M. McKenzie.'

'Mr Who?' Grace Smith's luminous green eyes had widened.

But before the lawyer could answer, he was forestalled by a scandalised Selina, who hadn't been invited to the meeting but had insisted on coming, anyway – to give her mother moral support, she said, though Tassie knew it was because she was terrified of missing something.

'A *cousin*!' she exclaimed. 'A cousin no one's ever heard of, when my sons have a *far* better entitlement!'

Even Tassie knew that they didn't. Although she herself was the daughter of Grace's marriage to Joss Smith, Selina, sixteen years older, had been born of Grace's first marriage, which meant that her sons weren't related to Joss Smith at all, except by courtesy. And there had been precious little of that, where Selina and her stepfather were concerned. Tassie sometimes thought it was in order to get away from Joss that Selina had rushed into early wedlock with the Dreadful Dudley. She must have had *some* reason for marrying him and Tassie had never been able to see that he had anything else to recommend him.

'Not in law, Mistress Fitzalan,' the solicitor said repressively. 'They are not blood relations to the late Mr Smith.'

'Anyway, they're only little boys,' Tassie chipped in brightly, earning a glare from her sister and a reproachful look from her mother. Schoolgirls were supposed to be seen and not heard.

'Well? Their father could manage things for them until they grow up, couldn't he?'

And that, Tassie thought, was what her own father must have been afraid of. The idea of big, burly Dudley, with his loud voice, high complexion and even higher opinion of himself, trying to direct one of the leading heavy textile businesses in Dundee, would have been enough to make anyone shudder. Even the boys' boarding school he ran at Seamount would have reverted to primeval chaos long before if it hadn't been for Selina's fondness for telling people what to do and making sure that they did it.

The lawyer pushed his steel-rimmed spectacles firmly back on his nose. 'Possibly. However, as I say, blood relations take precedence over step relations in law and also, in the present case, by the testator's own considered decision. Now, if we may proceed?'

It had taken him a good ten minutes to proceed to the next bombshell, whose effect was muffled, as everything else had been, in such a profusion of polysyllables that it was a moment or two before his hearers grasped its full import – which was that the deceased expected his heir to take over not only the estate, but all the more direct and personal responsibilities associated with being head of the family.

Three stunned pairs of eyes had fastened themselves

on the lawyer's face and three mouths opened in horrified astonishment because, well intentioned though the idea had no doubt been on Joss Smith's part, it was a proposition that entirely failed to recommend itself to his female relicts, who didn't in the least want an unknown cousin taking up residence at Graceholm and ordering everyone about.

They were not convinced even when the lawyer pointed out that the fact of Mistress and Miss Smith not being compelled to leave their home or worry about financial security could be construed as full compensation for having to live under the rule of a stranger.

Tassie had no idea how the fate of female relicts was usually resolved but, observing her mother's expression, felt quite strongly that her papa ought to have found a less earthquaking way of ensuring her own and her mother's continued wellbeing.

2

Resilient by nature, however, she had very soon begun to view the future in a rose-coloured light. It would be an adventure, and she'd never had an adventure before. Not for a moment did she consider the possibility of the Mysterious Heir turning out to be an undesirable kind of person. Mysterious Heirs were romantic by definition.

But then, just a month ago, with the painters already at work on the best spare bedroom, the mysterious Mr McKenzie had written to the lawyer to say that, according to his understanding, taking over the duties of head of the family had not been a legal condition of the bequest. It was a pleasure he therefore intended to forego. As far as he was concerned, the entire inheritance was personal to himself – mills, factory, land, investments, Graceholm and all. Which being so, he proposed to take possession four weeks from today, if that was convenient.

Though the language of his letter was perfectly formal, it had somehow managed to convey that Mr McKenzie didn't care tuppence whether it was convenient or not.

Joss's lawyer, confronted this time not only by three genteel female relicts but six feet of incensed Dudley, had conceded that possibly the Will had been insufficiently binding on the point, the late Mr Smith not having foreseen such a betrayal of trust on the part of the beneficiary. In his professional opinion, however, there was nothing to be done about it.

'Rubbish!' Dudley had declared. 'Of course there's something to be done about it. There's always something to be done about it. Never give in! Even if the other fellow's twice your size, grit your teeth and go for the ball! That's what I always tell my boys.'

'Indeed.'

Suspecting – rightly – that he was being patronised, Dudley had flushed an even darker red. 'Yes, "indeed". And I'll tell you this. It's my view that old Joss was of unsound mind when he made his Will . . .'

Tassie's gasp of outrage was lost under her mother's uncharacteristically sharp, 'Dudley, that is *quite* untrue.'

'No, it isn't. I mean, if he chose to employ a useless fellow like him' – he gestured contemptuously at the lawyer – 'he *must* have been of unsound mind. Stands to reason. Means the Will's a dud. We'll contest it, that's what we'll do.'

'That is your privilege,' said the lawyer with an affability that would have served as a warning to anyone other than Dudley. 'But I would not recommend it.'

3

Afterwards, as Dudley had handed his mother-in-law into her carriage, she had tried gently to dissuade him from a course of action that seemed to foreshadow endless complications. Not until long after was Tassie to understand that the matter of the Mysterious Heir had suddenly begun to appear to her mother in an entirely new light – not as a source of trial and tribulation but of release from a world to which, in her heart, she did not belong.

Grace said, 'Dudley, my dear, I don't in the least wish to seem ungrateful, but what a very unsettling notion. Should we not just submit to the inevitable? Yes, I *quite* see that, if the Will were overturned, Tassie and I could stay at Graceholm – *and* without having to suffer the intrusion of Mr McKenzie – which is of course what we would both like. But, if it should be upheld . . . I do feel that we ought to give some thought to where we are going to live if we must leave Graceholm. How long is the case likely to take? What are we to do while everything is in the air?'

Dudley, of course, couldn't see that there was any difficulty. His mother-in-law and Tassie, he replied in a lordly way, would come to Seamount as his and Selina's guests until everything was sorted out. He had not the slightest doubt that his own lawyers would make dashed sure that the courts found in the family's favour, and in double-quick time, too.

Naughtily, Tassie murmured, 'Ooo-oo-ooh!' Nothing in which Dudley was involved ever turned out to be swift or simple, though she knew her mother would never dream of saying so. She was far, far too polite; far, far too dutiful.

During Joss Smith's lifetime, Grace had been the perfect wife, conscientious and submissive, sincerely believing that he, as a man, was by definition superior to her, as a female – a belief that had been bred into all women of her generation and which she had never seen any reason to doubt. Tassie couldn't remember her mother ever making a decision of her own except in matters of housekeeping or fashion, and even then she had needed Joss's approval before she felt truly comfortable in a new hat or blouse.

Which had been perfectly proper for a married lady. The trouble was that she was still so much in the habit of deferring to gentlemen that she even deferred to the Dreadful Dudley. Tassie hoped it wouldn't last.

'I see,' Grace said. 'Yes, I am sure you are right, Dudley. Come along, Tassie. Robertson shall drive us straight home. Goodness, but I *am* looking forward to a nice cup of tea after that horrid, stuffy office.'

4

And so it had come about that Graceholm, in the damp dusk of an April evening, had been abandoned to the stranger.

Concluding her report as Selina's carriage rattled and bounced its way towards Seamount, Tassie said, 'And he left *all* the lights blazing. But I was thinking, perhaps he doesn't know about gas bills. He had some kind of accent, so he might be a foreigner. Perhaps foreigners don't know about hats and beards, either.'

Selina, knotting off the handkerchief with which she had been bandaging up her younger son's scratches, said pettishly, 'A foreigner? No, really! That would be beyond the pale!'

'I didn't mean *foreign* foreign. Anyway, he couldn't be, could he? Not if he's a cousin. I just meant not from Scotland. Perhaps not from England, either.'

Despite everything, they were still completely in the dark about Mr McKenzie's background and origins. All the lawyer had felt able to tell them – though it wasn't clear whether his use of the word 'able' reflected honest ignorance or professional reticence – was that the gentleman's credentials were incontrovertible and that communication with him was carried on through a valued associate in London. Tassie, who couldn't see how the stranger's credentials *could* be incontrovertible if the lawyer didn't know what they were, would have suspected him of telling untruths except that her mother said no one was allowed to be a lawyer unless they were of the highest moral character.

For the first time, Monty, a bumptious eleven-year-old who wasn't accustomed to being ignored, raised his voice. 'Probably a Colonial,' he drawled.

There was silence except for the clatter of carriage on cobbles as his grandmother surveyed him pensively and then, clutching at the handstrap as one of the wheels hit a pot-hole, said, 'I wonder . . . Tassie, could he have been from Australia? Your late papa did have a cousin – Agatha, was it? – who married and went to Australia in about 1860. A *most* peculiar thing for a wellbred young woman to do. I never met her. I wonder if this Mr McKenzie might be a son of hers?'

It was a question that only Mr McKenzie himself seemed equipped to answer, but no one was given the opportunity to ask it. Because although he moved into Graceholm the very next day, he made no attempt at all during the weeks that followed to establish contact with the cousins he had dispossessed.

5

It was on a Sunday evening towards the end of May when Tassie's mama, coming to her room to see that she was tucked up in bed, said consideringly, 'You know, my love, I think perhaps that our staying here at Seamount is not an ideal arrangement. While one perfectly accepts that noise, argument, rushing about, fresh air and cold baths are inseparable from boarding school life, I confess that I find it trying to have to hesitate every time I venture outdoors for fear of being knocked senseless by a cricket ball or swept away in the hundred yards dash.'

Tassie giggled. It was so like her mother not to mention all the other hazards of living at Seamount – the stodgy food, the howling draughts, the lumpy mattresses, above all Dudley and Selina's idea of conversation, which consisted largely of elevating molehills into mountains and then arguing about the height of them. Their current preoccupation was the defection of the school matron, who had just announced her intention of leaving to Take Up A Post Elsewhere – and not just *any* Elsewhere, but at Goshawk Hall, whose cricket eleven habitually defeated Seamount's by anything up to an innings and forty runs.

'So,' Grace went on, 'I think we should go to Dunaird until things are more settled.'

Tassie bounced up in bed again. 'Can we? Oh yes, *please*!'

Dunaird was her mother's girlhood home in the Highlands and although Tassie had heard a good deal about it, she had never been there. Neither had her parents, not even on a flying visit, in the whole of the twenty-seven years since they had moved to St Andrews to live.

One reason was that Dunaird House itself had been gutted by fire at some time in the 1870s, so that only the shooting lodge, half a dozen miles away, remained. This had given Joss Smith, neither sportsman nor country lover, an excellent excuse for saying, 'No,' on the increasingly rare occasions when his wife suggested a visit. Nothing, he swore, would induce him to go vagabonding off to the end of nowhere to sit watching the rain from a poky little lodge with, he dared say, scarcely more than a dozen rooms to bless itself with. He had never liked the Highlands, anyway – nothing but moors and lochs, mountains and midges, and not a soul for him to have a civilised conversation with for fifty miles around. Since civilised conversation, to Joss, meant shop talk about jute or, at a pinch, cotton, it was an argument no one could gainsay. His wife had given up trying.

Tassie demanded, 'Do you mean it? How lovely! Though Selina and Dudley are going to be *awfully* offended if we go. They'll think we don't like it here.' She giggled again.

But her mother merely smiled and said, 'Settle down, darling. Shall I blow out the candle for you?'

6

At supper the following evening, Tassie was feeling less than her usual buoyant self after a horrid day at school and the cold, blowy three-mile bicycle ride back from St Andrews. Moodily contemplating her cottonwoolly salmon, she barely heard Dudley and Selina moaning about the matron, being more concerned with whether her mama really meant it about going to Dunaird. Selina was sure to try and put her off and she wasn't very good at standing up to people.

'Base ingratitude,' grumbled Dudley for the tenth time, 'and I told the woman so in no uncertain terms.' With a nasty, scraping noise, he swept the remains of the salmon onto his fork and popped it in his mouth.

It was then that, quite without warning, Grace seized her moment. '*So* tiresome for you,' she murmured, laying down her own knife and fork. 'Poor Dudley! It seems to me that you and Selina have more than enough to worry you without having to put up with Tassie and myself as well, so I have been thinking that it would be best if we went to Dunaird.'

There was a disorientated silence.

After a moment, Dudley resumed chewing while he adjusted his mind and then, swallowing, said, 'Well, you must do as you choose,' and turned back to Selina. 'Anyway, as I said to her, if you expect me to give you a character reference, you're very much mistaken. Not after the way you've let us down. And if . . .'

'Oh, do be quiet, Dudley!' Selina looked quite distressed and Tassie thought that she probably was. 'Is your room not comfortable, mama? I know that the rooms at the front do tend to be draughty when the wind's in the east. Would you like me to move you to the back?'

'It isn't anything like that, my love. Truly! It's just that, even if Dudley succeeds in having the Will overturned, it will be months before we can move back into Gracehólm and I don't think we should impose ourselves on you for so long.'

Dudley, lighting on the only point that interested him, said, 'There's no "if" about it. I know old Joss thought he could do what he liked, but I'm dashed well sure there's some law against bequeathing things to distant cousins when you've a pair of perfectly good grandsons right here at home.' And that, apparently, was that. Squaring up to a plate of spring lamb and turnips, he instructed Tassie to pass the condiments.

Obediently, she passed the little silver-plated tray of salt, pepper and mustard pots, desperately willing her mother not to give in to the objections Selina was preparing to launch.

'But you can't possibly,' Selina began, 'mean to stay at the Lodge, when it's been empty for years? It must be riddled with damp and rot. *Dreadfully* unhealthy. And you're not as young as you were, mama.'

The state of the Lodge, the rigours of the journey, the insalubrious Highland climate, the isolation, the impossibility of finding respectable servants in the middle of nowhere . . .

Grace said nothing but allowed Selina's voice to flow on and on, unchallenged, until she had argued herself to a standstill.

It was only when her mother finally spoke that Tassie

23

realised – though Selina fortunately didn't – that she must have had the Dunaird plan in mind all along, because although she should have dismissed all the Graceholm servants when they abandoned the house to Mr McKenzie, it now turned out that she hadn't.

'I couldn't bear to,' she said. 'So I sent them up to Dunaird. You are quite right, Selina, my dear, about the Lodge having been neglected, and I thought they could make themselves useful in getting it warmed and aired and made habitable again.'

'You sent the servants up to . . . Mother, *really*, how extravagant of you! You should have dismissed them! You know you should. Or the lawyer could have arranged for Mr McKenzie to keep them on.'

'Yes, I thought of that, but Murdo told me he spoke for all the servants – well, all except the new tweeny – when he said they would prefer not to be abandoned to the new owner, who might not know how to treat servants. And I must say, it seems to me perfectly possible. One might, I suppose, excuse Mr McKenzie for regarding the inheritance as personal to himself. One might even excuse him for having chosen not to take up the duties of head of the family. But there can be no excuse for his not having had the courtesy to send me so much as a note of thanks for leaving the house in perfect order for him. It merely confirms my impression that he is not a gentleman.'

Tassie was still reflecting on the mystery of why hats, beards and thank-you notes – or lack of them – should be such an infallible guide to breeding, when Dudley said, 'Don't recall if I mentioned it, but I'm told the fellow's moving into the Cross Keys while he has some alterations made to the house and gets it properly staffed.'

His wife and mother-in-law stared at him, and Tassie, watching them, thought how alike they suddenly looked. Although they had a good deal in common – both being tall, fair, green-eyed and enviably slim – the resemblance was rarely striking, because their personalities were so different. Grace had a calm elegance that had escaped Selina and wore her pale blonde hair, now edging towards silver, in smooth Grecian coils, while her classically untroubled, fine-boned face was remarkable, even at forty-nine, for its complete freedom from lines and wrinkles. Selina, on the other hand, affected a pert modernity, and Tassie thought perhaps that was why, whereas their mother was beautiful, Selina was no more than pretty with the kind of prettiness that didn't altogether distract the eye from its flaws – the tip-tilted nose, the over-full lips, the two deep little lines already etched on her brow beneath the fashionable row of corkscrew curls. She could be really quite attractive when she felt like it, but she didn't often feel like it. It was the great sadness of Tassie's life that she and Selina had never got on.

She sighed inside, envying the two of them their slenderness and blonde fragility. Looking as if the lightest breeze would blow them away, they could always be sure of gentlemen standing aside for them, picking up their handkerchiefs when they dropped them, offering to carry even the smallest of their bags, laying cloaks over puddles so that they could cross without getting their feet wet. Even a hovering gnat was enough to bring chivalry charging to the rescue with a fly swatter.

Tassie herself was on the sturdy side of fragile and her hair was closer to red than fair. Not even the boy who lived next door had ever volunteered to carry so much as her school slate for her. It was very dispiriting.

'Dudley, you are impossible!' Selina snapped. 'No, you didn't tell us what That Man was up to. How dare he make changes to Graceholm!'

Her mother looked thoughtful. 'It does sound as if he is *sure* of his right to do so. Well, we must just wait and

see. In the meantime, I have spoken to Tassie's head-
mistress, and she has no objection to her missing the last
few weeks of term. So I think we should set out on
Thursday next.'

7

Tassie spent the next few days in a fever of anticipation,
continuing to pray that her mother wouldn't change her
mind, listening to her advice about long sleeves and
scarves to protect against the midges, laying out such
other clothing as she imagined to be suitable, and filling
her papa's old Gladstone bag with sketch blocks,
pencils, brushes, pots, paint rags, and a brand new box
of Winsor and Newton's watercolour cakes which had
used up almost all the pennies in her moneybox.

She even spent a whole, heavenly Saturday morning
at Gow's in Dundee, hopefully inspecting – just in case
she should need them – every single exotic item of
fishing tackle in the shop. The assistant kindly found a
suitable rod for her and showed her how to cast, so that
she felt quite guilty when, in the end, she had to confess
that all she really needed at this moment was a pair of
good, stout waterproof boots.

Her mother, of course, would never have allowed
her to mislead the young man like that, but her mother
had been too busy to go with her.

It was a busyness that left Tassie utterly bemused.
For someone who had spent the better part of thirty
years relying on her masterful husband to make all but
the most minor arrangements, her mama was showing
an extraordinary talent for organisation. Even the
Duke of Wellington might have learned a thing or two
about marshalling troops and supplies over the two-
day, two-hundred-mile journey that would take them
to Dunaird, a journey involving four changes of train,
a twenty-mile stage by pony cart, and three more

26

miles on foot over the roughest of rough ground.

And as if that wasn't enough, her mother's decree that they should take a few small comforts with them resolved itself, before Tassie's startled eyes, into six trolley loads of supplies including not only a wide variety of comestibles in tins and jars but two full dinner services, a canteen of cutlery, a huge miscellany of pots and pans, household linens, towels, bedding, and a pair of hip baths complete with ewers for filling them.

Tassie said, 'But . . . but . . . but' and wondered what on earth was going to happen when they reached the last stages of their journey and had to leave the railway porters behind.

Teasingly, her mother told her, 'You'll find out.'

8

Tassie had never been further than Edinburgh before, and by the time the train reached Perth had given up trying to behave like a well brought up young lady and was rushing excitedly back and forward from one window of the carriage to the other, gasping and exclaiming as fields of oats and turnips gave way to birch-clad hills hazed with young green and then to low ranges of mountains coloured purple and brown and still embroidered here and there with snow.

The waterfalls were stupendous, and with every mile the scenery grew wilder and grander, until by the time the train had snorted its way to the ·top of the Drumochter Pass, Tassie had run out of exclamations.

It was then that her mother said, 'This is nothing, my love. Wait until you see the mountains of the west.'

She was smiling but there was a trace of tears in her eyes and Tassie, mystified, demanded, 'Why are you crying?'

'I'm not, or not in the way you mean. It's just that it's lovely to be going home.'

'But St Andrews is home.'

Her mother smiled again, and shook her head a little.

It was late but still quite light when the train reached Aviemore, where their carriage had to be uncoupled and recoupled to a different train, which took them to Inverness in time for breakfast. And then there was a third train, to Dingwall, and a fourth, that hooked back to the south-west along the line to Strome Ferry.

The weather began deteriorating at Dingwall, and it was in a torrential downpour that they descended from their last train at Achnasheen, a bleak place of railway tracks and rough stone cottages and rainswept winter-yellow grass.

Tassie scarcely noticed. All she saw, with damp delight, was the welcoming committee that awaited them, a committee consisting of Murdo, the butler; wee Jamie, the footman; McFie, the gardener; Robertson, the coachman; and four unknown, expressionless, middle-aged men with clay pipes in their mouths, beards down to their black serge chests and woolly tam-o'-shanters on their heads.

There were also a wagonette and seven box carts drawn by sturdy little dun-coloured ponies with high-peaked harnesses.

By the time they were loaded up and on the road, Tassie thought gleefully that they must look exactly like a picture she had once seen of an expedition setting out for the Arctic. Only the huskies were missing.

She wasn't sure whether it rained in the Arctic, but in the west of Scotland for the next two hours it did nothing else. It was as if someone had tipped the sea on end. The carts and carriages would have been completely awash, like half-sunk rowing boats, if it hadn't been for the gaps between the floorboards, gaps which Tassie at first took for a sign of poor workmanship. But her mother said no, they were designed like that to let the rain drain away.

It wasn't a very encouraging thought, but Tassie knew that her mother's beautiful complexion was a result of having been rained on so much in her youth, so it was a good thing really.

And then, quite suddenly at about five o'clock, when even waterproof capes and knee wraps and hat covers were giving up the unequal struggle, the sky lightened and the rain went off and the sun came out.

One, two, three! Just like that!

Tassie's mother said, 'The tide must have turned. The weather often changes at the turn of the tide.'

It was the most astounding transformation Tassie could have dreamed of, because a completely new world stretched out before them. The mountains emerged from their mists and she could see, for the first time, the narrow road winding downhill ahead of them, picking its way like some dainty-footed animal round the skirts of hills whose profiles, on either side of the road, were as perfectly matched as parts of a jigsaw. Tassie could almost visualise them being pulled apart, long, long ago, by a pair of giant hands – just a little, just enough to clear a path for travellers.

Close by, the hills were clothed in raindrop-sparkling new green and old amber, but ahead they merged, hazy purple and indigo, into a bright blue sky that was advancing with unbelievable speed from the west, sweeping the clouds before it like some hasty celestial housemaid with dustpan and brush. There was a stretch of water in the distance, shining in the sun. Loch Maree, her mother said; no, not the sea, not yet.

Over to their left, curving from one mountain peak to another, was a complete and perfect double rainbow.

Tassie was gazing at it, open-mouthed in wonder, when her mother chuckled. 'They've put up a triumphal arch for us,' she said. 'That's where we're going, right between those peaks.'

9

They had to leave the wagonette and carts, because there was no road to Dunaird Lodge, only three miles of foot track.

'I am afraid you will have to walk, my love,' her mother said as, with one of the tam-o'-shantered men holding her mount for her, she hitched herself up to perch sideways on the bare back of one of the ponies, winding her fingers into the little animal's mane as if it were something she had been doing all her life. Her black straw bonnet was slightly askew, its three bedraggled green plumes looking positively rakish. 'But tomorrow Robertson will begin teaching you to ride.'

Tassie, a child of the bicycle age who had never learned to ride anything else, said, 'Yes, please'.

'In the meantime, the men will carry what baggage we need tonight. They can return for the rest in the morning.'

Thinking in terms of valises and carpet bags, Tassie nodded, but the nod turned into a blink of disbelief as one of the hip baths went striding off into the heather on black serge legs, followed by Wee Jamie, with a huge bundle under each arm and half a dozen assorted cooking pots dangling from a string round his neck, and Murdo, wearing some towels as a shawl and the big enamelled stewpan as a hat.

It had been far and away the most thrilling two days of Tassie's life – and certainly the fullest of surprises – but although the sun obligingly stayed out, it seemed a very long three miles over sodden hill and waterlogged dale, through squelching bush and dripping briar, to the Lodge that was their destination.

She saw it, at last, only through a haze of weariness – a long, plain, slate-roofed, two storeyed house sitting on a natural grassy platform at the base of a hump-shaped hill above a loch, bowered in silver birches and gigantic Scotch pines that looked as if they had been there for centuries. It was built of a rich, almost salmon-coloured sandstone sugared with quartz that sparkled in the sinking sun.

All Tassie was able to think of was bed.

But her mother, with a stamina her daughter had no idea she possessed, stayed up long after, speaking appreciatively to each of the servants in turn, thanking the men who had acted as porters, hearing from Murdo and his wife Mary, the cook, the saga of their steward-ship over the previous few weeks and finally, privately, flitting from one to another of the downstairs rooms, a figure as ghostly as the rooms themselves under the rising moon.

When she retired upstairs at last, she stood gazing out at the star-laden sky and the gleaming loch and the dark chiaroscuro of the mountains for a long time before she went to bed, and no one could have told what thoughts there were behind her smooth, untroubled brow.

10

Next morning, Tassie erupted into the big, warm, whitewashed kitchen at the disgracefully slothful hour of nine o'clock, ravenously hungry and demanding to know what was for breakfast and where she was to eat it.

'Ye'll eat it here,' said Mary. 'The breakfast room isn't fit to live in yet. Ye can start on your porridge, and Murdo caught some fine trout this morning so I'll do one in oatmeal for you, unless ye'd rather have kidneys and scrambled eggs. Whatever your ladyship requires.'

'Sumptuous!' exclaimed her ladyship, plumping her-self down at the scrubbed deal table and beaming back. 'Can I have the trout first and kidneys afterwards?'

'No, ye can not.'

Mary was the best kind of cook, rosy and round-faced, a cheery soul who took life as it came and didn't let anything worry her. She wasn't exactly stout, but she always looked it beside Murdo, who was tall and cadaverous and smiled only once in a blue moon. Mr and Mrs Jack Sprat, Tassie thought, happily dipping her spoon into the warm, creamy milk and then into the porridge.

Half an hour later, blissfully replete, she ran her mother to earth in what turned out to be the parlour.

After an early glimmer of sunshine, the heavens had opened again and the rain was sluicing, like moiré, down the windows so that they seemed less a barrier against the weather than a direct link between the sodden bleakness without and the decrepit splendours within.

'Ugh,' Tassie said with an exaggerated shudder.

Her mother's green eyes twinkled. 'I thought you were supposed to be the imaginative one. No house can be expected to look its best after twenty-seven years of neglect, but it only needs a little work to make it perfectly delightful again. You'll see.'

'I'm supposed to be the artistic one, too,' her daughter objected, eyeing her surroundings with revulsion. The red velvet curtains were disintegrating, the Turkey carpet was threadbare and the plasterwork crumbling. The window frames were mouldy and rotten, and there were huge chalky streaks and water-marks on walls and ceiling. The wallpaper was a repellent patchwork of faded pink and garish red, where pictures had once hung, and it was patterned all over with Prince of Wales feathers in gold. It looked terrible.

Her nose twitched and she sneezed.

'It's the damp.' Her mother gestured towards the big, black cast iron fireplace, currently occupied by a pile of soot and what appeared to be the decaying remnants of several birds' nests, and said, 'Having the fires lit will soon take care of that.'

'Y-e-e-s,' Tassie agreed doubtfully.

'Truly! I remember when my father used to have guests here for the stalking and my mama and I came over from the House for a few days. It can be the cosiest place. Nothing could be more enjoyable in weather like this than to settle down by the fire with one's stitchery or a magazine or the solitaire board or even a book. No, it will be lovely again. You'll see.' She sounded easy, cheerful and confident.

Tassie, puzzled, couldn't understand it at first, but then wondered suddenly whether this new decisiveness on the part of someone who had always been lost without a gentleman to guide and support her might have something to do with being home again at Dunaird, *her* Dunaird. Perhaps, here, she felt in command of her own life, as she had never been at Graceholm, where everything had revolved around her husband's needs, comforts and commands.

Tassie had loved her father very much, but she found it worrying to think that, by being a gentleman and the kind of gentleman he was, he might have stopped her mother from being the kind of lady *she* was.

Tucking the matter away for future consideration, she declared, '*Of course* it's going to be lovely again. Now, the first question is – where's the nearest wallpaper shop?'

II

The nearest wallpaper shop turned out to be in Glasgow, which was two hundred miles away, and one went there by sea or not at all. The only alternative was to do everything by letter and it soon became necessary for Angus the Post, a peppery individual whose round of sixty miles was covered entirely on foot, to be

33

appeased on his twice-weekly visits with a good, strong dram to make up for the weight of patterns, samples, catalogues and estimates he carried in his home-made leather pouch.

During the first few weeks, when nothing much could be done but write letters, measure up, and write more letters, Tassie made two discoveries about herself.

The first was that she enjoyed living in a state of chaos, free from the restrictions of tidy home, tidy town, tidy society, tidy life. At Dunaird, no one – least of all her mother – minded if she was late for meals, or came in with her boots muddy or her hair escaping from its ribbon. She wasn't even expected to change into something prim and proper for supper and, when darkness fell (which wasn't until after ten), was encouraged to stay up and watch when Mary put out bread and milk for the badgers.

The second thing she discovered – something that was to influence the whole course of her future life – was that her painting mattered far more to her than she had thought. She had always had a natural talent for it, but a talent that had never been stretched. Now it was, and it was a salutary experience to be confronted with a challenge she couldn't meet.

Having succeeded in coming to terms with Hughie, a Highland pony with a stripe down his back and a skittish disposition, she set off with him to look for a view that wouldn't be too demanding for her amateur brush. It took them a week to find one, mainly because their early forays were hampered by Tassie's craven desire to scuttle back home as soon as they were out of sight of the Lodge. The vast emptiness of the Highland landscape made her acutely uneasy, so that, more often than not, she found herself looking over her shoulder as if sensing some unseen presence. For the first time it occurred to her that people who believed in fairies might not be as silly as she had always thought.

Once she had overcome her fears sufficiently to give her full attention to the scenery – which was far more dramatic than anything she had ever seen in the undulating lowlands of Fife – she could only marvel at the vistas that presented themselves at every turn, at the constantly changing light on loch and river, at the mountains forming a living backdrop of amethyst and emerald. It was grand and magical and majestic. It was just begging to be painted.

But not, it soon became clear, by Tassie Smith.

Hughie whiffled sympathetically when she confessed that she wasn't getting on very well, that watercolours were too weak a medium for such splendour and, if he didn't mind being dragged away from that nice patch of grazing, she thought they might perhaps go and look for a waterfall or a tree or something, because a good, strong image in the foreground would help to push the mountains into the distance, so that it didn't matter if they looked a bit wishywashy.

By the time another week had passed, waterfalls and trees were beginning to pall and she found herself wishing something more interesting would come along, something living, for preference, but sufficiently obliging to stand still while she tried to paint it. She wondered how on earth Sir Edwin Landseer had managed with *The Monarch of the Glen*, because presumably the stag hadn't just stood there with its antlers up for hours on end while Sir Edwin said, 'Hold it like that. No, head back a little. And slightly to the left, please.'

Even a few ruins would be nice, she thought, but her mother, when consulted, said, 'I can't think of any. Though, I suppose . . . There must have been something left of Dunaird House after the fire. It's about six miles away, on the coast. We might ride over one day.'

12

The 'one day', however, was indefinitely postponed by the arrival on Mr MacBrayne's S.S. *Claymore* of four men from Wylie and Lochhead in Glasgow – accompanied by ten crates of tools, papers, paints and fabrics – to spend the next two months hammering and sawing, painting and paperhanging, and driving everyone to distraction by constantly whistling the new song that everyone in the West seemed to be daft about, 'Speed, bonny boat, like a bird on the wing . . . Over the sea to Skye'.

The men were fed at the Lodge and bedded at the nearby farm, but Tassie's impression was that, when the weather permitted, they spent most of their nights out poaching. Mary, more concerned with what they might get up to when the weather didn't permit, locked the Lodge maids ruthlessly in their rooms every night before she herself retired to bed.

Just to add to the fun, scarcely had the workmen embarked on stripping walls and ripping out windows when Monty and Bazz turned up, sent by Selina to keep their grandmother company and advance their education in gentlemanly sports. Monty, supercilious brat that he was, declared himself astonished that the Lodge should be lacking not only in architectural distinction but in such run-of-the-mill country house amenities as a croquet lawn, tennis court and putting green, while Bazz had the time of his life making all the noise he wasn't allowed to make at home.

Two or three energetic days of induction into the arts of stalking and fishing sufficed to remind the boys that learning about gentlemanly sports was only the secondary purpose of their visit and should not be permitted to outweigh their primary one of 'keeping their grandmother company' – which they interpreted to mean lolling by the fire and getting in everyone's way. It hadn't occurred to them that their grandmother, whom they knew only as sweet and yielding, might have other views, one of which was that fresh air and exercise were healthy and character-forming.

So out they went. By the end of another two or three days, however, they had begun to develop an amazing talent for getting wet even when it had scarcely rained at all. Time after time they returned from the hills, woeful and soaked, so that every functioning fireplace in the Lodge was soon fronted by racks of sodden clothing, steaming busily, and the smell of damp wool would have been all-pervading if it hadn't been for the competing smell of the mustard baths their grandmother decreed to ward off colds and chills.

Tassie, who didn't trust Monty an inch, began to suspect that he was up to something and her suspicion was confirmed when, one day, rounding a corner of the hill just where the Dunaird burn launched into its last descent to the loch and became a full cascade, she found Monty and Bazz standing beside it, twirling in the spray.

'Don't you *dare* tell!' Monty said.

She wouldn't have told, anyway, bound by the playground code of 'Tell-tale-tit, Your tongue shall be split!' but there was something about his expression that she didn't like at all. She said stoutly, 'If you go on doing it, I will.'

Fortunately, the situation didn't arise, because their mother arrived the very next day and, greeted by two pathetic small boys, one with a suddenly acquired racking cough and the other with an equally sudden and revolting sniffle, promptly diagnosed pneumonia. She was deterred from sending for the doctor only by the discovery that the nearest doctor lived fifty miles away.

It was, she said, just as she would have expected. What with the discomforts indoors and the insects outdoors; the lack of such ordinary, basic conveniences as gas lighting and plumbed-in baths; the distance to the village; the need to write away even for the merest trifles – well, really, it was an object lesson in what the world must have been like in the days before civilisation.

From now on, her darlings must stay indoors, and that was that.

Monty waited until her back was turned and then threw Tassie a cocky grin and strolled off to find the cards for a noisy game of Snap.

After supper that evening, having reported that there had been no progress in the matter of the Will, Selina added with a disparaging glance around, 'Though I see I shall have to do something to hurry the lawyers along. I cannot imagine how you can bear to live here. And for goodness' sake, Tassie, give that sewing to me! I have never seen anyone so unhandy with a needle.'

So Tassie abandoned her stitchery and embarked on a series of watercolours recording the transformation of the Lodge, in the course of which she discovered that she was much better at interiors and figures than she was at landscapes.

13

When the summer drew to its close, there was still no news of the Will.

Although Tassie had known that her mother must have been giving some thought to where they were to live if Dudley failed to have Graceholm returned to them, it came as an unpleasant surprise when she said that they might have to make Dunaird their permanent home. It would be necessary to exercise economy, she explained, and being economical in the Highlands, where they already owned a house, was more practicable than being economical in St Andrews, where the demands of everyday intercourse were a severe drain on one's purse.

Tassie was filled with foreboding at the prospect of a winter – of many winters – living miles from anyone and anywhere. Perhaps she resembled her late papa more than she had thought. She had already begun to suspect that, when all the bustle of redecoration came to an end, she would find that she wasn't a country sort of person and was sure of it when Selina and the boys departed, followed soon after by the workmen, their ten crates empty, their tools and personal possessions crammed into satchels spangled with salmon scales and smelling powerfully of fish.

Despatching one of her sketches to her best friend, Poppy Marr, she wrote, 'Everything's finished now, and looks lovely, especially my bedroom. It's all done out in this new, flowery kind of chintz. You asked when we were coming back to St Andrews but I'm afraid I don't know. My mother's plans are rather fluid just now. Please give everybody my love. I do miss having you to talk to, especially now that everyone's gone and the house feels empty. It's weird.'

It was true. The Lodge seemed to have changed character, to have turned in upon itself as if emptiness were its natural and preferred state.

Something must happen soon to change things, she thought. Surely something must happen soon?

14

Something did happen, although Tassie didn't recognise it at the time.

It was a lovely day in September when her mother said unexpectedly, 'Shall we ride over to the coast and see whether the ruins of the House are paintable?'

The air was balmy and the sky a soft blue over mountains clad in green moss, blue-green myrtle and purple heather, splashed with gold where the bracken was turning colour. Here and there on the slopes a rowan tree in full berry stood tall, straight and scarlet as a guardsman, while thickets of birch and beech were taking on the pale flame of their early autumn livery. All that was lacking was the sea, and after three miles they came within sight of it, a shining azure touched with silver.

It was like entering another world. The Lodge, its location dictated by the haunts of deer, stood in an enclosed glen where the loneliness of the surrounding hills was intensified by their very nearness. The coast, too, was empty, without sign of human life or habitation, but Tassie felt no sense of isolation, of exile. With surprise, she thought that she could live here easily, with only the sea for company.

'We'll ride along the sands,' her mother said, 'and look for whatever remains of the House from where I always see it in my memory.'

The sands were firm, white and starred with shells, but on the green cliff top on the landward side Tassie could see no sign of anything that might once have been a house. She began to worry, not because she any longer wanted to paint its ruins but because she had come to suspect that her mother felt very much more deeply about the home of her youth than she chose to show. If there was nothing there, it would be awful for her. Like having her past life stolen away. As bad as – worse than – it had been for Tassie, watching a stranger take possession of her own childhood.

And then they rounded a curve in the beach and she gasped aloud. Rising sheer out of the sands was a rocky promontory, soaring high as the heavens, and on its grassy summit was a tall stone tower. Tassie didn't even notice, at first, that the tower had neither roof nor windows, so powerful was its impact on her imagination. What it had was strength, simplicity, and the arrogance of something that had been there for six hundred years past and would be there for six hundred years to come.

It was awe-inspiring.

It couldn't be the house they had come to look for.

She had already steeled herself for disappointment when her mother said, 'There it is. Dunaird House.'

'But it's a *castle*!'

They had reined in their ponies and with the cessation of movement could hear the lapping of the water, the hum of insects and, faint and far off, the seabirds' song.

Her mother said abstractedly, 'No, not really. It was a watchtower once, centuries ago. Then watchtowers and fortifications went out of fashion, and one of my ancestors, somewhere in the 1600s, incorporated the tower into a new, "modern" house he was building for himself. It looks as if most of that must have gone in the fire.'

Tassie had been pondering this for weeks. 'Didn't you know? Didn't you *want* to know? I can't understand why you and papa didn't come up to see how much damage had been done.'

'You know how your father disliked the Highlands. We were told that the House was no longer fit to be lived in, and that was all that mattered. After the fire your papa sold off all the land except for the few acres surrounding it. He kept the Lodge only because, with stalking becoming so fashionable, its value was bound to appreciate. He decided to wait for the best price.'

Indignantly, Tassie demanded, 'But why did you let him sell the land? Wouldn't you rather have kept it? I mean, it was yours, wasn't it?'

'No. The law was different in those days. Everything a wife owned before marriage became her husband's property, to do with as he wished. In fact, Dunaird would have become part of my first husband's estate except that there was a family trust which barred me from inheriting until I was twenty-one. By then, I was a widow. When I later married your papa, it became his, but he made a gift of it to me – or what remained of it –

shortly before he died, so it is mine again. Come, let us climb up. There's a track over there.'

15

Of the seventeenth-century house, nothing at all remained beyond the stone line of the foundations, lying flush with the grass, which showed that it had been built round a three-sided courtyard with the tower at one corner.

There was something odd and it took a moment or two for Tassie to identify what it was – the grass was as beautifully swept and garnished as a kitchen floor. Nowhere was there a trace of rubble or debris. 'Where has everything gone? All the fallen-down stones and things?'

Her mother laughed. 'Into Donnie McRae's new barn, or Jock Fraser's new sheep pen, or Peter McLeod's new cottage. No one in the Highlands can bear to see good, masoned stone going to waste. That's why you haven't found any other ruins to paint.'

The tower itself was sound. Carefully testing each foothold, Grace and Tassie climbed the circular stone staircase until they reached the fourth and highest floor, open to the sky.

The view was breathtaking – the wide, sweeping bay with its fringe of pure silver sand; the sea stretching clear to the horizon, as if only the curve of the world prevented them from seeing all the way to America; the scattering of islands, hazy blue and amethyst in the noon light; a sky as vast as the vaults of heaven.

'Don't be deceived,' Grace said. 'It's not always like this. The sea can be very wild.'

It was an appealing thought. However rough the sea at St Andrews, it was always tidily rough. Never wild.

Crossing to the landward side, Grace leaned her elbows in the window embrasure. 'I can still see them all. My father and mother strolling in the garden. Jamie and Alasdair waving up to me. Great-aunt Lizzie basking in the sun with one of the cats in her lap . . .'

'Jamie and Alasdair?'

'My brothers.'

Tassie, completely taken aback, exclaimed, 'I didn't know you had any! What happened to them? Did you lose touch?'

'They were both older than I. Jamie died when he was eleven and it broke my mother's heart. Then Alasdair joined the 78th Highlanders and was killed at Cawnpore in the Indian Mutiny.' She sighed faintly. 'Jamie, then my mother, then Alasdair. It was too much for my father. He died soon after.'

'How absolutely terrible!' Tassie, who had always loved her mother more than anyone else in the world, was astounded and ashamed to discover how little she knew about her. Tragedy after tragedy, and yet she had never once harked back to them, had kept her private griefs just that – private.

Tranquilly, her green eyes as clear and pale as those of a water sprite, Grace said, 'It is the way of things.'

Tassie was still struggling to accept such fatalism when, descending the staircase again, her mother spoke again with a touch of regret in her voice and, for the first time in her daughter's memory, a trace also of Highland sibilance. 'If it was only possible. Though the roof and the windows would be but the start of it.'

'You mean rebuild it? But it would cost a fortune!'

'Yes. Too much, too much.'

She was dreaming, Tassie thought worriedly. Castles in the air.

Since no other solution presented itself, she gave her an enormous hug and said bracingly, 'Never mind. It would be sinful to rebuild it. Because it makes an absolutely spiffing ruin!'

16

A few days later, after all the months of waiting for something to happen, a letter arrived. Not from Dudley, not from the lawyers, but from Mr McKenzie himself.

He was anxious to make the acquaintance of his new family, he said, in language that suggested his letter had been drafted by a solicitor. It looked as if it might have been written by one, too, because the handwriting was in a neat and clerkly style that didn't seem, to Tassie, to match the gentleman she had spied on from the shrubbery almost six months before.

Whatever the case, Mr McKenzie wondered whether Mistress and Miss Smith would do him the honour of being his guests at Graceholm during the second week of October.

Curiosity won, although it took Mistress and Miss Smith the better part of a day to compose a suitably lofty acceptance.

CHAPTER TWO

I

The door of Graceholm was opened to Mistress and Miss Smith by a butler who, for the last twenty years, had been the jewel in the crown of Isabella Murray's household at Broughty Ferry. Wondering how in the world Mr McKenzie had contrived to lure him away from the notoriously possessive Isabella, Grace said, 'Good evening, Johnson. I hope you are well?'

'Yes, moddom. Thank you, moddom.' Johnson's native woodnotes were purest Glasgow, but when he was on duty he always spoke as if he had a hot potato in his mouth. 'This way, please, moddom and miss.'

Grace, with many years' experience in the wellbred art of noticing everything while appearing to notice nothing, marked the changes that had taken place in her formerly elegant hall. The occasional chairs, once tastefully disposed, had been pushed back against the wall in a regimented line. On a side table stood a specimen of that newfangled instrument of torture, the telephone. The air smelled strongly of cigars; there were no flowers to be seen; and a pair of pretty little paintings of Highland cattle had been removed, leaving an empty space on the wall. Grace would have expected them, in what was so obviously a bachelor establishment, to have been replaced by sepia photographs of the new owner with a gun in his hand and his foot on a tiger, or as one among a sea of small faces memorialising some school rowing eight or cricket eleven. But there were no such mementoes of Mr McKenzie's past.

Unlike her mother, Tassie had little attention to spare for such details. It wasn't only that her curiosity – which had been growing by leaps and bounds during the previous few weeks – was about to be satisfied at last. She was also feeling unnaturally self-conscious.

Never before had she worried about what kind of impression she might make on a stranger, although, thinking about it, she recognised that there had been very few strangers in her life, mostly business associates of her father who had addressed her as 'little girl', hesitated about patting her on the head and then ignored her. Strangers they had certainly been, but they hadn't *mattered* to her. Mr McKenzie mattered very much. She loathed him – of course – but felt obscurely that this made it all the more necessary for her to look her best.

Resigning her serviceable travelling cape to Johnson's care, she discovered that the weight of its shoulder mantle had flattened the leg-o'-mutton sleeves of her best white blouse and was busily absorbed in tweaking them out when a warm, deep, slightly nasal voice said, 'Mistress Smith. Miss Smith. It is a pleasure to welcome you to my humble abode.'

Tassie looked up, startled. *My* 'humble' abode, indeed! What sauce!

And then she saw that there was a smile on Mr McKenzie's face, a smile that took all the offence out of his words, a smile that was at once rueful, conspiratorial and heartstoppingly charming, a smile that said he perfectly understood how embarrassing the situation was and hoped they would forgive him.

Tassie smiled back at him, her eyes like saucers. She would have forgiven him anything.

The thick overcoat in which she had first seen him had been deceiving. Without it, he looked taller, and muscular rather than heavy, although the square forehead and jaw could never have belonged to a man born to be thin. Under the newly barbered dark brown hair, his complexion was brown, too, as if from exposure to a warmer sun than ever shone on Scotland.

Absorbed in the smile that seemed to be swallowing her up, Tassie barely noticed what he was wearing, save that everything from high-buttoned black morning coat to dark grey trousers, from tall, starched white collar to grey ascot cravat, looked spankingly new. There was a pin in his cravat that glittered suddenly in the gaslight. It looked like a diamond but Tassie didn't know enough about precious stones to be sure; it might only have been cut glass.

Having bowed to her mother who – less susceptible than she, merely inclined her head in acknowledgement – he turned consideringly back to Tassie.

'I think we've met before,' he said. His eyes were a very dark brown, the colour of peat.

She hadn't dreamed that he would know her again and, aware of the blush surging to her cheeks, blurted, 'No, we haven't. How did you guess it was me? It was dark. You can't possibly have seen me well enough to recognise me.'

'I didn't.' The lingering smile blazed out into a grin. 'But by all the laws of probability, if there was someone watching from the bushes, it had to be someone connected with the family. You've just told me who.'

'That was cheating!'

Most improperly, he winked at her. 'It was, wasn't it?'

And then her mother cleared her throat slightly and Mr McKenzie at once became the perfect host. 'My apologies. Your elder daughter, Mistress Fitzalan, arrived some time ago and has gone to her room to change for dinner. Would you like to go straight upstairs? I gave orders for your own rooms to be prepared for you, and one of the maids will bring a tea

47

tray up immediately. You must be tired after your journey.'

Slightly mollified, Tassie's mother said, 'That would be most kind. Perhaps Johnson would see to it that our baggage is sent up right away?'

No china, no cutlery, no pots, pans, towels or tin baths . . . Not this time. Only a leather trunk and a valise, enough for a few days' stay.

Tassie hadn't foreseen how strange it would be to find herself a guest in her own home.

2

Selina was looking strikingly pretty in a dinner dress of pale pink moiré taffeta, with huge pink velvet sleeves and satin bows catching up the velvet ribbons festooned round the hem. Her cheeks, too, were pink – unnaturally so – and she looked as if there was powder on her nose and round her eyes, which was shockingly fast of her. But she was in one of her captious moods and, when Tassie asked, as they went downstairs for dinner, 'What's the matter?' replied offhandedly, 'The matter? Nothing. What should be the matter?'

She couldn't think why she had come. She had better things to do. And – so tiresome – there was no moon, so she couldn't drive back to Seamount after dinner and would have to spend the night at Graceholm.

She made it sound as if Tassie shouldn't have needed to ask.

Partly because of the difference in their ages, she and Tassie had never known each other well or cared for each other much. Tassie could still remember the day when, as a frustrated four-year-old, she had stamped her foot at Selina and screamed, 'You don't love me. You're s'posed to love me. Why don't you love me?' And an impatient Selina had replied, 'Don't be silly. You're my sister. Of course I love you'. A douche of ice water would have been more encouraging.

When she was older, her mother had tried to explain. 'Your papa is a loving father to you and a loving husband to me, but he is not a man who has love to spare for others. Selina, as his stepdaughter, feels left out.' Tassie had been relieved to discover that Selina didn't dislike her for herself, and had even succeeded in feeling sorry for her sister – though only until the next time Selina had ticked her off for something.

It had all been a terrible disappointment, because Tassie would dearly have liked a sister or brother she could be be close to. It was so *limiting*, feeling like an only child.

3

Dinner proved to be a formal affair, all crystal and damask and shiny new knives and forks and spoons, so heavily chased that even Tassie's surreptitious eye couldn't find the markings to show if they were sterling silver or just plated.

The conversation was formal, too. Sitting silently through what began – and continued, and ended – as a gruesomely polite and impersonal duologue between her mother and Mr McKenzie, Tassie wondered whether it might be worth copying it all down and trying to get it published as a cure for insomnia. It was like being at a meeting of the St Andrews Monuments, Buildings, Golf Courses and Rusack's Marine Hotel Admiration Society.

The food was almost as uninspiring – veal broth, fillets of cod in caper sauce, roast beef (badly overdone), braised partridges and custard pudding – the menu of a bachelor who liked food he could get his teeth into. Most gentlemen were like that, of course, but most of them had wives who made sure that the tastes of their lady guests were catered for, too.

Perhaps Mr McKenzie *did* have a wife, somewhere. Perhaps he had two wives. Perhaps he had a harem.

Tassie hoped the conversation wasn't going to go on like this forever, otherwise they would leave Graceholm as ignorant about Mr McKenzie as when they had arrived.

Who was he? Where did he come from? What did he do? Why had he invited them to visit him? What did he want?

Making a desperate effort to discount the charm, which wasn't easy, she had spent the preceding two hours convincing herself that he was just an orthodox, commercially-minded businessman like her father – which meant that he was the kind of gentleman who would never dream of putting himself to trouble merely for the pleasure of establishing social relations with a parcel of unimportant females.

So he must want *some*thing. The question was, what?

4

They moved to the drawing room for coffee, and found it unchanged. Even the knicknacks were set out as they had always been, right down to the dish of sugared almonds. For a giddy moment, Tassie wondered if they could possibly be the same ones as six months before, feather dusted daily along with the Mauchline-ware boxes and the Staffordshire figurine of Bonnie Prince Charlie.

The St Andrews Admiration Society seemed to have run out of steam and in the ensuing lull Tassie found herself, for the first of what were to be many times in her life, observing the scene as if she were detached from it, an audience of one waiting for the play to begin.

On stage, the winged chair to the left of the fireplace was occupied by her mysterious cousin, his square, competent hands resting on its arms, his eyes slightly wary as they scanned the semicircle of women facing him, uniformly fair of skin, green of eye and fine of bone. Two of them were blonde and willowy, while the third had hair that was nearer red than gold and a fullness of figure that the wide sash and puffed sleeves of thirteen-year-old fashion did nothing to diminish. Tassie's mother said she would grow out of it, and Tassie hoped she was right.

The first two pairs of feminine eyes were, respectively, noncommittal and resentful. Tassie, realising that her own were wide and expectant, took a deep breath, dropped her lashes, and did her best to look grown up and demure.

Why didn't somebody say something?

5

It was her mother, stirring the coffee in her Crown Derby cup, who broke not only the silence but the rules governing polite conversation by asking an outright question.

'You have travelled a good deal, Mr McKenzie?'

Almost imperceptibly, Mr McKenzie relaxed. Tassie knew how he felt. Nothing was more nerve-racking than having to make polite conversation when you couldn't think of anything to say.

'I guess I must have been born with an adventurous disposition,' he replied. 'I ran away from home and joined the Navy as a cabin boy when I was fifteen. Then I went looking for diamonds in South Africa and, a couple of years ago, when I heard rumours of a new gold strike in Australia, I tried my luck there.'

So it must be a real diamond in his cravat pin.

'Australia,' Tassie's mother repeated with a hint of satisfaction. 'An interesting country, I believe.' There was nothing to indicate to Mr McKenzie that 'interesting' was the word she always resorted to when her personal views seemed in danger of clashing with the demands of civility. 'Though I imagine it is all perfectly well ordered and law-abiding now that education is more widely available. Do children have free elementary education there, as they do here?'

One of Mr McKenzie's dark brows rose. 'I'm sorry, I have no idea. I was past the age of being interested in schooling when I arrived in Australia.'

'But I thought . . . Agatha . . .'

'Who?'

'My late husband's cousin Agatha,' Grace explained with the dawning of a frown. 'She married and went to Australia in the sixties. I assumed you were her son.'

The ensuing pause lasted for what seemed a very long time.

Then, 'No,' said Mr McKenzie.

And, after another intent moment or two, 'Well, isn't that a b . . .'

It came out as a sudden burst and was bitten off abruptly, as if he had been going to use a word he shouldn't. Tassie had the feeling he might not be used to ladies' company.

'No, I was born here in Scotland,' he went on in a more controlled tone. 'I'm a Highlander. If I don't sound like one, it's because I've mixed with men from all over. You pick up other people's accents like you pick up their turns of speech.'

Still looking thoughtful, he rose to his feet, used the steel and brass tongs to put some more coal on the fire, then began pacing the room, his hand going to the inside pocket of his coat but being withdrawn again, empty.

With thirty years' experience of marriage behind her, Grace had no difficulty in interpreting the gesture. She said, 'In the circumstances, I have no objection if you wish to smoke.'

'I'm obliged to you.'

Extracting a thin cheroot from his cigar case, he lit it with a spill from the fire and drew the smoke in gratefully.

Then, his eyes still on the glowing tip, he said, 'Well, at least that answers one question. *You* don't know who I am, either.'

6

'Either?'

It was Selina, who had been uncharacteristically silent all evening.

'Are you trying to tell us that you yourself don't know who you are? I don't believe a word of it. You must have some idea. And you must certainly have some idea why my father should have bequeathed everything to you instead of to his grandsons, who have a far better entitlement!'

Trust Selina, Tassie thought, to ignore the 'step' in 'stepfather' when her own or her sons' advantage was involved.

The ticking of the gilded and enamelled clock on the mantelshelf sounded unnaturally loud in the interval before Mr McKenzie turned his emotionless gaze on Selina and said, 'You can believe it or not, as you like. All I know is that I was reared by a foster mother who told me no more than that I was distantly related to Josiah Smith, the Dundee jute manufacturer, but could expect no generosity from him. It was all she knew herself.'

Tassie, whose first recorded word, after 'mamma' and 'dadda', had been 'why?' – or so her mother always teased her – couldn't hold her tongue any longer. 'But didn't you try to find out?'

'No. Before I ran away to sea, I was too young, and afterwards . . . Well, when you're down a diamond

53

mine in Kimberley, there isn't much scope for doing research into your family history.'

'I suppose not. But how could you *bear* to ignore the whole thing when so much depended on it!'

'My dear young lady, if you've been listening, you should know I wasn't aware that anything depended on it.' The easiness of his tone didn't take the edge off his words but, almost at once, he added, 'Sorry. That was uncalled for.'

'It's all right,' Tassie said stoutly. 'When you're thirteen, people are always ticking you off. I just thought you might have asked the lawyers.'

'Oh, I did!' The peat-brown eyes gleaming suddenly, he linked his hands over his stomach, sat well back in his chair, puffed out his lips judicially, and said, 'Our instructions from the deceased – ahhh – were that you – ahhh – might best be described as the – ahhh – cousin – whom Mr Smith elected to name as his legatee.'

Tassie giggled, but her mother's cool gaze suggested that she, for one, was not amused. In Grace's view, Mr McKenzie was sending out too many conflicting signals. His dress and manner might be respectable, but his accent was several hairs'-breadths short of cultured and his speech altogether too free and easy. She didn't know what to make of him.

'No doubt the truth will emerge in due course,' he said. 'But, now, ladies, I have a favour to ask. I've spent these last months beginning to get acquainted with the jute business, and I reckon it's now time for me to meet with my fellow manufacturers. I also need to introduce myself to the trade press. They already know, of course, that I'm the new proprietary partner of Josiah Smith & Co, but . . .'

'Do they, indeed!' Selina interrupted rudely. 'Well, I don't know how you have the impertinence to behave as if everything is settled. And if the newspapers puff you off as the sole legatee, you're going to look very silly when my father's Will is overturned.'

Mr McKenzie didn't snap back, which Tassie thought was nice of him. He merely said, 'Maybe. However, since each of you ladies still has a personal share, however small, in the business, I hope you'll see the benefit of presenting a united front. There's a fellow from the *Textile Trades Journal* coming to interview me tomorrow afternoon and I'd like you to be present.'

'*What?* To lend you countenance? When we scarcely know a thing about you? Really!'

'Selina!' said her mother in gentle reproof.

Selina tossed her head. 'Well, I shan't be there. I shall go home to Seamount in the morning and I strongly advise you and Tassie to come with me.'

Although her private reservations about Joss's legatee might remain, Grace said, 'I see nothing wrong in what Mr McKenzie asks of us. If he believes it to be important . . . Gentlemen always know better than we do about such things.'

Her younger daughter, who had watched her mother doing very well for the last five months without any gentlemen to know better, felt a twinge of exasperation – and more than a twinge when it occurred to her that she herself had already, and equally instinctively, accepted that Mr McKenzie *did* know best.

He smiled. 'Good. Tomorrow should be an interesting day.'

7

It turned out to be a much more interesting day than anyone could have foreseen.

Soon after breakfast, Mr McKenzie was standing in the hall, top hat in hand – someone must have told him about hats, Tassie thought – while the ladies finished buttoning their gloves and the carriage waited outside to set Mr McKenzie down at the station; go on to the Largo road, where Mistress Smith and Miss Smith were to visit a friend; and finally convey Mistress Fitzalan home to Seamount. The horses were fresh, tossing their harnesses and pawing the gravel, so that no one heard the other carriage arrive.

The effect was all the more dramatic, therefore, when the front door flew open to reveal Dudley Fitzalan on the threshold, a Dudley whose complexion, high enough at the best of times, now put Tassie forcefully in mind of the new Turkey carpet at Dunaird.

Mr McKenzie, with no idea who Dudley was, raised his strongly marked brows and snapped, 'What the hell . . . ?'

'Are you McKenzie?' Dudley bellowed, ignoring his wife's demand to know what was the matter. 'I want a word with you'. Then, without so much as a by-your-leave, he marched past the open-mouthed little group into the drawing room, Selina at his heels.

Mr McKenzie, suddenly hard-eyed, placed his top hat carefully on the hall table and turned to usher Grace and Tassie through to join them.

Dudley was already ensconced on the hearthrug, arms akimbo, looking as if he were on the school touchline and not just ready but actively thirsting to knock his pupils' heads together.

'Ha!' he burst out. 'Well, we know now, don't we? And if you'd said so in the first place, you'd've saved us all a deal of trouble. Never struck you, I suppose, that I've better things to do with my time and money than waste them on lawyers? Well, the cat's out of the bag! Only because I made a dashed good case for Monty and Basil, mind you. I know old Joss thought he could do what he liked, but I've always said there must be some law against bequeathing things to cousins no one's ever heard of when you've a pair of perfectly good grandsons right here at home. Left them without a leg to stand on, I did. I tell you . . .'

Not for the first time, Tassie wondered how Selina had managed to live with Dudley for more than a dozen years without murdering him.

'I'd be grateful if you would,' Mr McKenzie ground out.

Dudley, arrested in full flow, stared at him. 'Would? Would what?'

'*Tell* us! Tell us what the f . . . Tell us – what – you – are – shouting about.'

Tassie saw her mother's concerned eyes move back and forth from one man to the other. Graceholm wasn't accustomed to the sound of raised voices. Graceholm wasn't accustomed to gentlemen making exhibitions of themselves within its wellbred portals.

Tassie wasn't either, which was perhaps why she was secretly rather enjoying it.

'I'm not shouting,' Dudley bellowed. 'And I'm talking about who your parents were. What else?'

There was a vibrating silence while, oblivious, Dudley blundered on. 'The lawyers said old Joss had forbidden them to tell, unless it was absolutely necessary to prove your entitlement, or some such rubbish. Well, I sorted them out there and no mistake. Joss said he had – what was it, now? – reached his decision for "personal and commercial reasons". And no wonder. Absolutely scandalous, I call it! I should think . . .'

Mr McKenzie's jaw muscles were standing out like cords. He was two inches shorter than Dudley and muscular rather than burly, but he looked much the more dangerous of the two.

It was Grace, however, who put an end to Dudley's ranting. 'Perhaps you would come to the point,' she said quietly. 'Who *is* Mr McKenzie?'

'He's no more a McKenzie than I am. That's only his

foster mother's name. His real name's Smith. John Maximilian Smith. He was old Joss's son on the wrong side of the blanket.'

8

It was the kind of revelation that took a moment to sink in.

Then, 'I *knew* it!' exclaimed Selina. 'I'm sorry, mama, but I'm not in the least surprised that Joss should have played you false. It would have been just like him!'

Grace's fine skin, always pale, had turned ashen. 'I don't . . .' she gasped. 'I don't . . . I must sit down.'

Tassie rushed to help her to a chair and began fanning her with the previous day's *Dundee Courier*, the only thing ready to hand, but almost at once the tension in the atmosphere dragged her eyes back to Mr McKenzie's face.

'And if Joss Smith was my father,' he said carefully, though without any great show of surprise, 'who was my mother?'

Selina snapped, 'Someone no better than she should be,' but no one paid any attention.

Everyone was looking at Dudley. Afterwards, Tassie realised that they had all been expecting him to say one of the parlourmaids or mill girls, the local sempstress or the woman who ran the sweetie shop. But he didn't.

He said, 'Your mother was the lady who *later* became his wife. The lady sitting there before you. The lady who was then Mistress Grace Lindsay and is now Mistress Grace Smith.'

9

Grace looked as if she were about to faint clean away.

But it was Selina who, gasping 'What?' put a hand to

her forehead, swayed, and before Tassie's astonished eyes, *did* faint clean away.

Neither of the men even noticed.

Tassie, her gaze flying from mother to sister and back again, abandoned her mother and ran to Selina, collapsed half on the floor and half on the sofa, and tried to lift her.

She wasn't strong enough. Exclaiming, 'Help me!' she glanced up.

But Mr McKenzie's eyes were almost incandescent and his lips caught between his teeth as if he were holding back a yell of exultation. He wasn't even looking at her. He wasn't looking at Dudley, either, when Dudley's rage and resentment at last got the better of him and he swung an uninhibited fist at Mr McKenzie's jaw.

Mr McKenzie dropped as if he had been poleaxed, his arm trailing discordantly over the piano keys as he went.

But he was up again instantly and – with Tassie distractedly shrieking, 'Stop it! Stop it!' – laying into Dudley with every evidence of enthusiasm and, as far as she could see, no holds barred. At one point, he even took Dudley by the ears and bounced his head off the marble mantelshelf. In no time at all, Dudley, too, had joined the insensible figures strewn around the room.

Whereupon Mr McKenzie brushed himself down, settled his coat back over his shoulders, shot his cuffs, and turned to Tassie with his hand extended and a huge beam on his face.

'Since it appears that we are brother and sister,' he said, 'you may call me Max.'

10

Three hours later, Graceholm having been restored to normal with the departure of Dudley and a pallid

Selina, Mr McKenzie tapped on the door of his mother's room and was invited to enter. He found her resting on a chaise longue with Tassie in attendance.

Tassie didn't rate a glance. All his attention was on Grace, just as all hers was on him. They stared at each other across the room as if neither of them knew how to handle the situation.

Then Grace held her hands out. 'I still cannot believe it,' she said. 'I thought I had lost you forever.'

He didn't hurry towards her, nor did he hug her when he reached her. Instead, he took her hands in his and, after a barely perceptible hesitation, bent to kiss her cheek. 'I don't know what to say.'

Tassie, who was still fizzing with excitement and convinced that her new brother must be, too, offered brightly, 'You could try saying, "How nice and what *fun*".'

It was the wrong note to strike. His voice and smile were perfunctory as, drawing up a chair, he replied, 'So I could. But before I commit myself, I would prefer to be told – among other things – whether my mother "lost" me accidentally or on purpose. It makes a difference, you know.'

Grace was still pale and physically drained, though that was because all her resources had been concentrated during the last hours on coming to terms with a shocked heart and ravaged mind, on preparing, too, for a scene that she knew would be as difficult as it was inevitable.

There had been many tragedies in her life, but she had been sustained, and would always be sustained, by the fatalism that had been born into her, the fatalism that was her strength. Others, the kind of people who sought to control their own lives, who didn't accept that fate was immutable, saw it as weakness. Studying her lost son, his compelling presence filling the room, she knew that he would be one of those. He wouldn't understand. Nor did she allow herself the luxury of hoping that he would forgive. Child of hers though he might be, there was no personal affection between them – not yet – to aid in the forgiving. They were two adults, tied by blood and nothing else. He was a stranger to her in every way, and perhaps always would be.

She said, 'I can't answer you in such simple terms. There are things you must hear first, but I think Tassie should leave us. It is not a story for such young ears.'

Tassie couldn't believe it. '*Mama*! You can't! It's not fair! You mustn't shut me out.'

After a long moment during which her eyes were far away, her mother sighed. 'Perhaps not. You will have to know it all some day, I suppose, although I would have preferred it not to be until you were older and knew what marriage meant.'

'I know about the birds and the bees,' Tassie assured her.

'That's not quite the same. But very well. You may stay.'

11

Taking a further moment to gather her thoughts, she turned to her new-found son and began, 'As Dudley said, I was still married to Selina's father when you were conceived . . .'

He frowned and she stopped, surprised, until she remembered that he probably thought Selina was Joss's child, too. Selina, the evening before, had referred to Joss as 'my father' and the subject of her parentage hadn't been touched on in the course of Dudley's revelations.

Reassured, she resumed, 'Simon, my first husband, had been in America on business for several months and Joss – well, Joss had developed an obsession about me and wasn't the kind of person to be diverted from anyone or anything he had set his heart on. I think you and he may be very alike in that.'

If she herself had been a different kind of person, living in the kind of world where it was permissible to utter such thoughts, she might have tried to exonerate herself by asking this grown son of hers, outright, if he had ever forced a woman, thinking himself justified by the strength of his own desire. She might have asked him, too, if he had considered the woman's feelings, or the consequences. As it was, she went on quietly, 'I make no excuses. Although the choice was not mine, I was ashamed then, and I am ashamed now. However . . . I had been carrying you, Joss's child, for three months when news came that my husband had died in a sailing accident.'

She stopped for a moment. She had been very young, and she had loved Simon very much in a young, romantic way.

'Joss and I were married, privately, soon after. Joss insisted that both the marriage and the child be kept secret from anyone one who might guess that the child could not be Simon's. There were a good many such people. Simon had a wide acquaintance.'

It was impossible to explain, to the son who had been sacrificed almost thirty years before to the gods of conventional morality, how important it had all seemed at the time, but she tried. 'It wasn't only my reputation that was at stake, you see. It was Joss's, too, because everyone in Scotland's business community knows everyone else, and he couldn't afford a scandal. People can be very rigid and disapproving. It matters, in business.'

Mr McKenzie's – Max's – face showed nothing and there was no sound or movement in the room beyond the flutter of the flames in the fireplace. Tassie, her mother saw, was sitting chin on fist, totally absorbed but with a trace of anxiety in her wide green eyes. She was such a loving, trusting child, and Grace prayed that she would not be too much hurt.

'So we went away. We went to Dunaird House and stayed there until after you were born. You were the loveliest baby.' Grace smiled slightly, to herself, not to her son.

'Dunaird is very isolated. If we had been able to stay longer, so that there was time for you to grow up a little, everything might have turned out differently. It is easy for outsiders to judge the age of a baby to within a month or two, but it becomes less easy as time passes. Joss wouldn't agree. He was someone who did not like having his plans upset and he was anxious to see his new business established. He couldn't afford to waste two years or more. And we could not appear with a new baby when everyone knew that Simon had died less than nine months earlier.

'So Joss arranged for you to be sent to a wet nurse in Ullapool, and by the time the Dunaird servants would have expected you to be brought home again, we had closed up the house and come here to St Andrews. We never went back.'

Tassie, two or three times in her life, had seen her mother weep, mildly and sentimentally. There were no tears, now, but neither was there any mistaking the pain.

Hesitantly, she said, 'Mama . . .' But that was all. She was only thirteen, inexperienced, ignorant of any but the simplest sorrows. She could barely guess at what underlay her mother's seemingly calm chronicle of events; could think of nothing to say that would not be clumsy and insensitive.

There remained only the one, unavoidable question, and since her new brother showed no sign of asking it, Tassie did. 'What about the baby?'

Despite the look in her eyes, there was no furrow on

Grace's wide, clear brow. 'I was never told, although I guessed that Joss had arranged to have him adopted. He said he had taken care of everything, and it was better that I shouldn't know. I was to put the whole thing out of my mind.'

Tassie gulped. 'But . . . How *could* you?'

'One can do anything, if one must.'

12

Tassie had loved her father very much and he had spoiled her unmercifully, but she had always known herself to be lucky. He hadn't been nice to many people, and was stubborn as a mule when his mind was made up about something. Tears pricking behind her eyelids, she found herself able to understand, with her mind if not entirely with her heart, that her mother had had no choice – calm, gentle Grace, whose habit had always been to bend so that she shouldn't break.

It suddenly became very important to explain to Mr McKenzie – Max – about Joss and how impossible it had been to stand up to him. But having opened her mouth to speak, Tassie closed it again, because her new brother didn't appear to be in the least angry or upset. She supposed that, long ago, he must have got used to the idea that his parents hadn't wanted him. Hadn't loved him. Had abandoned him.

Amiably, he said, 'Well, he didn't have me adopted. He just left me with Jeannie McKenzie, the nurse, and sent her an annual allowance for my bed and board. My education, too, though I wasn't so keen on that. The only condition was that the local minister sent Mr Smith's lawyers an annual report on my progress. And there was a proviso that we weren't to make any attempt to approach him or his family directly.'

Tassie was trying to remember something he had said the previous evening that didn't quite seem to fit when he stopped abruptly and exclaimed, 'Damn!' Drawing a gold hunter from his pocket, he said, 'It's after one. We must agree on what to say to the fellow from the *Textile Trades Journal*.'

'What about?' Tassie asked.

'About all this, of course.'

'Do we have to say anything?'

He grimaced at her. 'I'll thank you, young Tassie, to remember I'm your big brother now. You're not supposed to question what I say. But the answer is, yes, we do have to say something. We've just had an object lesson in the complications that ensue when you try to keep secrets.

'You do see, don't you,' he went on, turning to Grace, 'that I have to be acknowledged as your son? If we're going to live here together as a family – because you and Tassie obviously must come back to Graceholm – we can't go on trying to kid people that I'm only a distant cousin. They'd get suspicious and the gossips would have a high old time. We have to cut the ground from under their feet, because Mr Smith – my father – was right about one thing. Business and gossip make uneasy bedfellows. And, in fairness,' he paused briefly, 'the family owes it to me. It's time I was acknowledged for who I am.'

They had known him for less than twenty-four hours, and it was the third or fourth occasion on which he had smiled to take the edge off something he had said. Each time, what he had said had been justified. Tassie thought he must be the kindest and most forgiving person on earth, to take it all so well.

But to insist on being acknowledged? He couldn't possibly mean to make the whole story public. He couldn't possibly mean to throw her mother – his mother – to the wolves.

Grace, her shock betrayed only by the slight fixity of her gaze, said, 'I understand how you feel, and you must do as you think best. But, my dear, is it really necessary? For everything to come out? All those long-ago sins . . .'

'Not *every*thing!' Tassie interrupted, hopping up to give her mother a reassuring hug. 'We'll think of some way of getting round it. *Max* will think of some way of getting round it.' And then, warmth and excitement and a passionate, newborn trust in her stranger-brother coming suddenly together, she rushed on inconsequently. 'It's all so wonderful I can't believe it. I'm so thrilled at having a real, live brother. Oh, Max, aren't you thrilled, too?'

Drily, he said, 'Well, not at having a brother,' and she felt a little dashed. For the first time it occurred to her that having a close family might not be a new experience for him. 'Did Jeannie have children of her own? I mean, do you have foster brothers and sisters as well as Selina and me?'

He wasn't paying attention, preoccupied with his thoughts. 'What? No.' And then his eyes came into focus again and lit up and he snapped his fingers in jubilation. '*Yes*! Now, that *is* an idea!'

Tassie, in receipt of an approving and wonderfully boyish grin, felt a glow inside, though she didn't know what she had done to deserve it.

'Clever girl!' he said. 'Now, don't worry your head, mother. Just listen.'

Moving to the window, he stood with his fingers tapping rhythmically on the sill, thinking things out even as he spoke. 'There are three points that have to be gotten round. First, that you and Joss weren't married when I was conceived, which means keeping quiet about the date of my birth.' He turned. 'Can I pass for twenty-six rather than twenty-seven?'

'Yes,' Grace said, 'though twenty-five would be better.'

'I'll only be specific if I have to. Secondly, why didn't my family know I existed? Young Ginger's given me the answer to that.'

'Who, me?' Tassie had never been called 'Ginger' before and wasn't at all sure that she liked it. 'Have I?'

He turned back to the window. 'And thirdly, why have I suddenly been translated from cousin into son?' His tone changed. 'Hell!'

Tassie wondered how soon her mother was going to break it to him that using bad language in the presence of ladies was a shocking sin.

'That's the station carriage coming up the drive,' he said. 'It must be the journalist fellow. He's early.'

Hastily crossing the room to the mirror, he smoothed down his hair and applied the clothes brush to his lapels, saying, 'Can you both come downstairs as soon as you're ready? The quicker the better. Leave all the talking to me and, whatever I say, don't look surprised.'

Catching Tassie's eye in the glass, he grinned. 'Especially you, young Ginger. Those big, innocent eyes of yours are easier to read than a book.'

October 1894

CHAPTER THREE

I

Francis Rivers, owner, editor and sole reporter of the *Textile Trades Journal*, looked around him with interest as the station fly approached Graceholm. More than once, in the past, he had interviewed Joss Smith about the state of business, the latest technical developments, the costs of materials and plant, and all the other things journalists routinely interviewed manufacturers about. But such meetings had always taken place at the factory in Dundee.

So why, Francis wondered, should the new proprietary partner have suggested a cosy little chat at home?

It was no surprise that 'home' should be in St Andrews. Almost without exception, the men whose indecently large incomes were provided by the dirty, disagreeable, smelly but enormously profitable jute industry of Dundee preferred to live in more salubrious surroundings, some in Broughty Ferry – reputedly home to more wealth per square yard than anywhere else in Scotland – others in this stately little backwater across the Tay, with its ruins, its golf, and its ancient university.

Francis was looking forward to meeting the mysterious Mr Max McKenzie, who had inherited thirty-one of the thirty-four shares in Josiah Smith & Co. In the original press announcement, there had been little that was specific about the new owner's back-ground or experience, and his name had meant nothing to Francis, even though his knowledge of the textile trade was encyclopaedic. He found it a matter for concern that the future livelihood of Smith's three thousand employees should depend on the character and business acumen of this one unknown and possibly untried man.

'Welcome aboard, my dear fellow!' exclaimed the object of his thoughts, giving him a cheerful clout on the shoulder. 'Lovely day for so late in the season. Come in, come in. Did you have a good journey?'

It made a change. Francis was more accustomed to being ushered into spartan offices, peopled by large, solid, humourless men who were reluctant even to raise their heads from their desks to answer the impertinent questions of a mere journalist, the lowest of the low. Unless, of course, they wanted him to blow their trumpets for them over their latest business coup.

'Thank you, yes,' he said, and stepped into the hall.

McKenzie was younger than he had expected, only a few years older than himself, his looks striking, his eyebrows sitting like a thick dark bar over eyes that were themselves so dark as to render the pupils invisible. It made them appear oddly expressionless in a face otherwise remarkable for its vitality and charm. Old Joss had been a rough diamond. Time would tell whether the assured gentleman who had succeeded him was diamond or only diamanté.

After half an hour during which Mr McKenzie – whose classless accent, Francis sensed, owed more to art than nature – said scarcely a word to the point, Francis could have done with less of the easy self-confidence and more in the way of hard facts. And then his host said, 'Mistress Josiah Smith and her daughter should have finished luncheon by now. Let's go and join them over the tea tray. Never been a man for luncheon myself, or not beyond Madeira cake and a glass of sherry, but I'm never averse to a cup of tea. The drawing-room's this way.'

He sounded perfectly natural, open and innocent, but an open and innocent businessman was a contradiction in terms. If they were going to be playing Happy Families, there was a reason for it and the only one Francis could think of was to make it even more difficult for him to discover how much, or how little, Mr Max McKenzie actually knew about the jute industry. Convention had it that business, politics and religion were not fit subjects for a lady's ears, although it was not a convention to which Francis personally subscribed – or not when he was in pursuit of a story.

Joss Smith's widow was a surprise, considering what a tough old bird her husband had been – a delicately handsome woman and unmistakably wellbred, even if she had something of the wilting lily about her. The daughter, still a schoolgirl, looked by far the more vital of the two, though Francis wasn't sufficiently interested to notice more than that she had pretty auburn hair and an air of uncomplicated hopefulness that made him think of a jaunty little puppy or kitten.

'Are you familiar with St Andrews, Mr Rivers?' enquired his hostess, and Francis wondered how many conversational balls she had set rolling over the years with that same question, uttered with the smile that suggested she was genuinely interested in the answer. She struck him as a remarkably nice woman.

Courteously, he submitted to being fobbed off with empty chatter for the better part of fifteen minutes, and was just coming to the resigned conclusion that, if he wanted an opening, he would have to make it himself, when Joss Smith's widow did it for him, saying with the kindliest intent that her late husband had always found the *Textile Trades Journal* a most interesting publication and very well-informed.

'Thank you,' he replied. 'That's the kind of compliment I appreciate. With everyone who matters in the jute business having been born and bred in it, I live in perpetual fear of being exposed as the merest Johnny-come-lately. I take it you're a newcomer yourself, Mr McKenzie? I wonder how the industry strikes you, entering it from an entirely different background? As I presume you do?'

2

Tassie had thought Mr Rivers awfully attractive until he started putting Max through the hoop.

He wasn't at all what she had expected, though of course she didn't know enough about journalists to make comparisons; they weren't the kind of people one met socially. But in her previous and admittedly limited experience, a newspaperman was always one of two kinds, the elderly and mildewed kind with soft hats and scruffy shoes whom the *Dundee Courier* habitually sent to report on the laying of foundation stones by important visitors (a regular occurrence in St Andrews), and the young and impudent kind, with thick Fife accents and chewed pencils, sent by the *St Andrews Citizen* to cover school prize givings and egg-and-spoon races. The *Citizen* prided itself on being a truly local paper.

Mr Rivers, though still quite young, was very different from either of these. Admittedly, his black hair was not only ruffled but badly in need of a trim, while his shirt, unstarched and with a turned-down collar, spoke of the most complete disregard for convention. But he had a patrician, almost arrogant air about him that suggested money, education and breeding. His voice, pleasant and even, was so slightly accented that Tassie took him for English rather than Scots, and she couldn't imagine it raised in anger.

He wasn't the kind of person who would need to get angry.

He was also either not very polite or extremely single-minded because, after the first few minutes, he paid no attention to her mother or herself. He was interested only in Max, with whom, all too clearly, he wanted to find fault. It wasn't fair. Max couldn't be expected to know all those things about the business after just a few months.

Not for years was she to discover that it was single-mindedness that made Francis Rivers such an effective journalist and such an infuriating human being. At the time, she was aware only that, although Max might have been able to charm his way through an interview with someone less knowledgeable, there wasn't a single one of his evasions that escaped Mr Rivers's notice. Mr Rivers didn't even bother to hide it.

3

It soon became apparent to Francis that his host had an adequate, if basic, grasp of manufacturing methods and a better than adequate grasp of figures, though only the impressive ones like the invoice totals for the millions of sacks Josiah Smith & Co. exported to the Americas for the meat and grain of the prairies.

Francis's disingenuous mention of the *frigorificos* of Argentina, however, elicited no other response than an equally disingenuous diversion into whether Mistress Smith was warm enough, or would like the fire poked up. The huge world market for post office mailbag strings, negligible-seeming but highly profitable items, produced an admittedly entertaining anecdote about a letter lost in the Australian bush. And a question about the problems of shipping thousands of army kitbags and haversacks to inaccessible places in unknown Africa brought an instantaneous and startlingly fluent diatribe against the Boers.

'The sooner they're put in their place, the better,' McKenzie concluded. 'Take my word for it. I learned everything there is to know about them when I was in the diamond business in Kimberley.'

It was too good an opportunity to miss. Francis, who had been intending to test him next on his knowledge of Dundee as the money and management centre of one of the largest cattle ranching operations in America, swiftly changed tack.

'That's interesting. I'd like to round out my article with something about your personal history and how you came to inherit your controlling interest in Josiah Smith & Co. You don't mind, do you? Readers enjoy that kind of thing. But can I first confirm a couple of points about your background? As I recall, you are a distant cousin of the late Joss Smith?'

He had been moderately sure that the chatty Mr McKenzie would not, like most mill owners, tell him snappishly that his private life was his own affair, but he hadn't expected the opposite reaction. It looked as if he had asked the very question McKenzie had been hoping for.

4

Settling comfortably back in his chair, Max said, 'Not a cousin. A son.'

And that, Tassie thought, had startled clever Mr Rivers, even if the only sign of it was a momentary silence and an odd look in the deep set grey eyes. After a moment, he smiled sardonically. 'Indeed? Do I scent a journalistic scoop?'

'You do. Although not, perhaps, of the kind you are expecting. Shall I begin at the beginning?'

'What an admirable notion.'

Tassie, remembering Max's instructions about not looking surprised at anything he said, took a deep breath and waited. She still didn't know how Max was going to tell the story in a way that didn't reflect too badly on her mother, and her blind faith in his ingenuity was beginning to waver, just a little, in the presence of the formidable, cynical Mr Rivers. She prayed that Max would find the right words.

Max said, 'In actual fact, Joss Smith was my father, and my mother is the lady seated in the chair facing you. Soon after I was born I was given into the care of a wet nurse – a common practice in the late 60s and still, I am told, fairly common today.'

And that was the first hurdle over. It was the truth, too. Without a trace of hesitation, Max went on, 'The wet nurse, as it happened, had an infant of her own, an illegitimate son called Robbie, and the story really starts when, soon after I was put in her care, little Robbie died.'

Goodness! Tassie thought, leaning forward non-chalantly to replace her cup and saucer on the table and missing it completely.

Picking up and mopping up, she smiled weakly at Max and sat down again, this time with her eyes firmly fixed on the hands folded in her lap.

'All right now?' Max enquired with a trace of sarcasm, before turning back to Mr Rivers. 'I don't know if you know anything about life in the Highlands . . .'

Mr Rivers nodded.

'. . . but it's hard for a woman to survive there without a man to work the croft. Partly for that reason, and partly, I suppose, because she was distracted by grief, my foster mother looked at me and saw me as a substitute for the child of her own who had died.' He sighed, his brows drawing together. 'The upshot was that she sent a message to my parents telling them *their* son had died.'

Her brain reeling, Tassie thought that Max must have been reading too many cheap novelettes. Stealing a glance at Mr Rivers, she saw that his eyes had narrowed. But before he had time to say anything caustic, Max went on, 'You find it hard to believe? So would I, if I hadn't known Jeannie. But a poorly educated woman, well past her first youth, living in a turf cottage – a Black House – in an in-turned little town like Ullapool, with no income, no husband and no prospect of one, will do strange things.'

'Yes. I appreciate that,' Francis Rivers said, transferring his gaze to Grace. 'But – forgive me, Mistress Smith – I find it equally hard to believe that you and your husband accepted your bereavement so readily. Quite apart from anything else, it occurs to me that you might have wanted to bring your son's body home for burial?'

Max took the question to himself. 'Robbie was drowned,' he said flatly, 'and the body was never recovered, so the question didn't arise. My parents moved away from the district soon after. Came here to St Andrews, in fact.'

Then, ignoring the expression on Mr Rivers' face – which said very clearly that there was still something wrong with this saga that he couldn't quite put his finger on – he resumed, 'Anyway, Jeannie brought me up to believe that I was her own son by some itinerant father. A road mender, she said. I think she had even convinced herself of it. But when I was fifteen, I rebelled against the hardships of life on the croft and ran away to sea. I'm ashamed of it now, but at the time it seemed the only answer. I won't bore you with my subsequent adventures . . .'

'There's no danger of that,' murmured Mr Rivers, but Max ignored it.

'I soon learned that I hadn't been cut out for life in the Navy. After a couple of years, I jumped ship and lit out for Kimberley, where I was modestly successful. Then, when I heard rumours of a new gold strike in Australia in '92, I decided to try my luck there. Coolgardie first, and then I was in on Paddy Hannan's discovery at Kalgoorlie. But the surface gold soon petered out and mining the rock is a hard way of earning a living. Besides, I'd made enough profit to satisfy me and by the end of last year I was beginning to be homesick for Scotland.'

Although Tassie was relieved to find that they were back on firm ground again, she was all too conscious of the fact that Max hadn't had time to tell her and her mother what had happened when he actually arrived back in Scotland. It meant that she didn't know whether what came next was going to be the truth, or whether he would be making it up as he went along.

Making it up, she guessed when, producing his cigar case, he looked enquiringly at her mother and was granted permission to smoke. It seemed that he needed a few moments to arrange his thoughts because, Mr Rivers having politely refused to join him, he made rather a performance of trimming, lighting and drawing on his cheroot.

His voice, when he resumed, was fractionally less fluent than before. 'Anyway, to conclude, by pure chance I arrived back to find Jeannie – my mother, as I still thought – ill and close to death. She was much relieved to see me. She had read in some newspaper that the jute manufacturer, Josiah Smith, was mortally ill and had realised that, by keeping me to herself all those years before, she had robbed me of my inheritance. It was then that she told me who my real parents were.'

It sounded all right. Tassie risked another quick glance at Mr Rivers, but his face told her nothing except that, if he was moved by this affecting tale, he was keeping it to himself. All he did was murmur, '*L'hasard, c'est seulement l'effet connu des causes inconnues.*'

Max said, 'What?'

' "Chance is but the known effect of unknown causes." Or, to put it another way, what a remarkable series of coincidences.'

Max didn't pursue it, but his voice grated slightly as he resumed. 'Possibly. In any case, she wrote to Josiah, telling him the truth. When my father died, it turned out that he had believed her to the extent of remaking his Will in my favour.'

Beguiled by the neat way in which Max had knitted everything together, Tassie decided it didn't sound nearly as far-fetched as she had first thought. He was terribly clever. If she hadn't known that Robbie was a myth, she would have believed the whole thing.

Mr Rivers, gently stroking the edge of his thumb across his upper lip, murmured, 'But, despite that, it was publicly announced that you were "a distant cousin"?'

Max tapped an inch of ash off his cheroot. 'Obviously, in such a situation, a certain doubt remained . . .'

He *couldn't* have run out of invention.

And then Grace came to his rescue. 'It was for my sake,' she said quietly. 'My husband wished the lawyers to be quite sure that Max really was Max before anything was said, even to me. He thought that, if I were to believe that my long dead son had come to life again only to find, perhaps, that he was not my son after all, it would be more than I could bear.'

5

When Francis Rivers had departed, Tassie said, a little shyly, 'Max, you were wonderful,' but he didn't hear her. He was much too busy waxing furious about the insolent young pup who had done nothing but patronise him with his mailbag strings and friggicose

77

and foreign quotations. 'No one talks to me like that and gets away with it. Cheap little hack!'

It was a very queer description of someone who might well be a hack but was six feet tall and looked to Tassie as if he carried rather a high price ticket. She had never met anyone like Mr Rivers before and wasn't sure that she wanted to meet him again. He had made her feel dreadfully insignificant.

When Max paused for breath, she tried again. 'Max, you were wonderful. And it doesn't matter about Mr Rivers, does it, as long as he believed the story you told him? And Mother, you were wonderful, too. In fact, you were quite inspired. You seemed to put an end to all his doubts.'

'Your father was very protective towards me,' her mother said. 'I had no need to invent. It's exactly what he would have done in such circumstances.'

Tassie wrinkled her nose. 'The only thing is, it all sounded so convincing that I'm not sure what's fact and what's fiction any more. I almost began to believe in Robbie. There wasn't *really* a Robbie, was there?'

'What?' Max grinned unexpectedly. 'No, of course not. You gave me the idea yourself. Remember?'

'Did I? I suppose I did. And the turf cottage – the Black House – and being poor and ignorant? They can't have been true, either.'

'Nope. Jeannie wasn't very bright, mind you.'

Tassie became a sudden prey to doubt. She had always had a weakness for fairy tales, but that wasn't the same as telling people something was true when it wasn't. 'Are you absolutely sure we can get away with it?' she asked uneasily. 'What if anyone finds out? What if the lawyers deny it?'

'I only meddled with the truth at the very beginning and the very end. And the lawyers won't talk. They're supposed to respect their clients' confidence.'

'Or what if mama lets it out by mistake? She's not awfully good at keeping secrets.'

'She kept *me* secret for twenty-seven years.'

And that was true enough.

'Don't worry about it,' Max went on airily. 'The trick is to forget what really happened and tell yourself that the story I gave Rivers this afternoon was the truth, the whole truth, and nothing but the truth. Then you won't make any mistakes.'

Grace said, 'Max, my dear, you mustn't undermine everything I have ever taught Tassie about truth and morality! Hiding a sin from other people is one thing, lying to oneself about it is quite another.'

Although Max's expression didn't change, Tassie had the feeling that he wasn't awfully pleased, but he said nothing as Grace, smiling now, went on, 'Why not ring for Johnson? It has been the most exhausting day and I think we deserve a small restorative. A glass of sherry, perhaps.'

Tassie bounced to her feet. 'I'll do it!' Then she turned exaggeratedly yearning eyes on her mother.

Grace laughed, actually laughed, twenty-seven years of private grief washed away in a matter of hours. 'Very well,' she agreed. 'Your education has been much advanced today, hasn't it? You won't be a schoolgirl for much longer and I suppose it's time you entered the grown-up world.

'Let us drink a toast to that, but not until we have first drunk one to Max, my dear and long lost son.'

6

'Long lost son? Fiddlesticks!' declared Abigail Rivers. 'Sentimental twaddle. Grace Smith was a silly, spineless creature before she ever met Josiah and I do not imagine she has improved one iota since. Mark my words, if Josiah had any hand in that farrago you have just told me, you may be sure that there is very much more to it than meets the eye. Did you tell them who you were?'

'No. Why should I?'

Francis, lounging against the bookcase with his hands in his trousers pockets, yawned uncontrollably. Unlike his mother, he was not at his best first thing in the morning and resented being dragged in to her expensively panelled, chintz-curtained office at the mill before he was properly awake, before he had even had breakfast, in order to satisfy her curiosity about the new proprietary partner in Josiah Smith & Co.

Since he was a very small boy, he had known that his mother loathed Josiah Smith with a loathing intense and profound. Some of it had even rubbed off on him, so that he had always been ambivalent about old Joss. But he had never discovered what was at the root of it. All he knew was that, before Grace Smith had become Joss's wife, she had been the wife of Abigail's twin, Simon. She had been widowed within two or three years of the marriage and, afterwards, she and Abigail had lost touch.

Abigail herself – then Abigail Graham – had been widowed at much the same time, wedding her second husband, the quiet and unworldly Professor John Rivers, two years later, and presenting that surprised gentleman with three sons in rapid succession, of whom Francis was the eldest.

'The name Rivers didn't mean anything to them,' he went on, 'and if I had told Grace Smith we were related, however distantly, I would have had to put up with an interminable inquest into family history. No, I was in St Andrews purely and simply to interview Mr Max McKenzie, who now intends, I should tell you, to be known as Max McKenzie Smith. He's going to change the company's name from Josiah Smith & Co. to McKenzie Smith & Co.'

'Good,' said his mother grimly. 'That ought to set

Josiah revolving in his grave. It would be too much to hope, I take it, that you discovered the young man's date of birth, which would be of far more interest than all this fustian about wet nurses and the rest.'

Abigail had the most amazing vocabulary of synonyms for the word 'nonsense'. Francis sometimes wondered whether she made a secret hobby of collecting them.

'No, I didn't discover it,' he said. 'I didn't know you wanted me to. And I doubt if I'd have succeeded, because the gentleman told me with great charm everything he wanted to tell me and not much that he didn't. Except in the matter of the business, of course, where he didn't know enough to be able to cover up convincingly. It's worrying, in its way, because there's nothing more dangerous than an ignorant man who won't admit it. The best I can do for you in the way of birth date is the late 6os.'

'Useless.'

'Why do you want to know, anyway?'

'Never you mind. Just find out.'

He straightened up sharply. 'No! And there's no use glaring at me. I have better things to do with my time than spend it ransacking New Register House for the birth certificate of someone called Smith. *Smith*, my God! If it's so important, you can send David or Jonny.'

'David is too busy. We're having problems with the new Jacquard looms. And as for Jonny – well, really!'

Her thin lips twitched. The youngest of her sons was a dashing, highly strung and blindingly handsome army subaltern who had been absent without leave on the day when brains were being handed out. The idea of relying on Jonny for anything involving mental effort would have been enough to make an undertaker laugh.

Francis grinned back. His relationship with his mother seldom ran smoothly, because Francis was one of the few people who stood up to Abigail Rivers – on principle, more often than not – but, fight though they did, they both had the same, saving sense of the ridiculous.

'Oh, all right,' he said. 'I'll ask a few questions here and there, if the opportunity happens to arise. But don't bank on my finding any answers.'

7

Francis was pleased when the national press picked up his scoop on Max McKenzie Smith, although they didn't bother to read between the lines. They saw it simply as a great human interest story.

Max was even more pleased. 'Long lost son inherits' looked very arresting in 48-point bold capitals.

'Got 'em!' he exclaimed elatedly. 'I never dared to hope it would be so easy. The public are gluttons for barefoot-boy-makes-good stories, so the papers'll *have* to follow my progress from now on. Well, I'll give them something to write headlines about.

'But not until I'm ready. And that's where you come in, young Ginger.'

CHAPTER FOUR

I

Highland schoolboy, naval cabin boy, diamond miner, gold digger.

Max had led a varied and exciting life, but it was a life that had left him ignorant of the social and business conventions that were second nature to the deeply conservative manufacturers of Dundee. As he said to Tassie – back in residence at Graceholm with her mother, the servants, most of the china and linen, some of the pots and pans, but not the hip baths – he was a bit like a wolf who wouldn't be accepted unless he dressed up in sheep's clothing.

She giggled. 'Well, I've never seen a wolf *looking* so sheepish.'

'Careful, young lady! No one insults me and gets away with it. I'm a believer in tit for tat, diamond cut diamond. I always pay back.'

'It was a joke! I meant you looked so respectable that no one would ever guess you were a wolf in disguise.'

He had known she was teasing, of course, and he grinned at her. 'Well, that's one hurdle overcome. But it's only the beginning. It's easy enough to look right. I damn' well have to talk right, too.'

It was a perfect opening. She said, 'Rule number one, never use bad language when there are ladies present.'

'No? Can I use it when there are gentlemen present?'

She didn't know.

Laughing at her crestfallen expression, he put an arm round her shoulders. 'Diamond cut diamond, young Ginger! This time, I was the one who was teasing. We're quits, now.'

2

During the months that followed, a glorious new world opened out before Tassie as Max became for her not only a brother, entitled by blood – as Selina was – to the lip service of love, but a brother who, warm, funny and companionable, was someone to be loved for himself – as Selina was not.

Blithely shedding the years that separated them, he joined in all the adolescent pleasures of her life, going on picnics with her, to funfairs, on blackberrying and bluebell gathering expeditions according to the season. On crisp, moonlit winter evenings he wandered with her through the romantic ruins of the cathedral; on sunny spring Sundays along the wide golden stretch of the West Sands; talking occasionally about his ambitions, more often listening intently as she told him everything she knew that would be of help to him, and trying, not altogether successfully, to take his general education in hand because there were some things in which he was shockingly weak.

She had thought, at first, that it was only his way of talking that needed attention, his occasional slanginess and habit of using short, blunt words rather than the long and pompous ones to which she remembered her father's business friends being addicted. But then she had discovered that he couldn't spell, either.

'I don't have to,' he said when she broached the subject. 'I've secretaries and assistants to do that for me.'

'I suppose so. But they can't help you with the other things you don't know about.'

'Such as . . . ?'

'Music, painting, history and literature, for a start.'

'For God's sake! I'm trying to be a jute manufacturer, not an aesthete.'

'It matters, though,' she told him earnestly. 'Really it does. Dundee and St Andrews are bursting at the seams with music and literary societies and people can be awfully sniffy if they think you're ignorant about such things.' She chuckled. 'I can't imagine what papa would have said. All that money he sent Jeannie McKenzie for your education, and you can't tell Shelley from Shakespeare.'

'I was never one for book learning. And who the devil was Shelley, anyway?'

'*Max!* You mean you really don't know?'

They had strolled from the harbour onto the pier that, on Sundays, was vivid with the traditional procession of scarlet-gowned students but today was empty, grey and windy, a long, narrow stone bulwark against the North Sea rollers.

Tassie stopped, strands of hair whipping out from under the knitted green tammy and wrapping themselves round her eyes, the spray from the sea gusting over the breastwork and raining on her upturned face as she stared at her new brother – handsome, dark and powerful in looks, with the kind of presence that said he would never be in doubt about anything. Would never be wrong about anything.

And that was the problem.

Summoning up every ounce of tact she possessed, she raised her voice against the wind and said, 'It's like looking up the encyclopaedia. If it's wrong about something you happen to know about, it destroys your faith in all the other entries on things you *don't* know about.'

'Really? Do you often find yourself knowing better than the encyclopaedia?'

'No, of course not, though there's a children's one at school that's absolutely full of mistakes about St Andrews. What I mean is . . .' She didn't dare mention Mr Rivers. 'I mean, you're so impressive, you've such assurance, such an air . . .'

'Thank you.'

'. . . that if you make mistakes about things everyone else has learned at school . . . well . . . I mean . . .'

There was the purest amusement on his face. 'What a tangle you're getting yourself into! What you're trying to say, I take it, is that my impressiveness will crumble at a touch if people find out I've never heard of this fellow Shally, or whatever his name was.'

'Shelley.'

'In other words, schooling matters more than what you've done with your life since?'

'It sounds awfully silly when you put it like that but, yes.' She gave it a moment's frowning consideration. 'I think perhaps people are suspicious if you're obviously clever but don't know about the things they've been brought up to regard as the foundations of civilisation.'

'Oh, well! We can't have them being suspicious, can we? Not about anything.'

Tassie knew what he meant, because it had lain behind what she herself had just been saying. Max *must* not transgress the code. *Must* not raise questions about his past. Otherwise he – and, more importantly, their mother – would suffer.

'But I tell you here and now,' he went on, 'that I've better things to do with my brains than clutter them up with poets and painters. Don't worry your head about that kind of stuff, young Ginger. Leave it to me. I'll manage.'

'I don't know how,' she said doubtfully.

It was to be a while before she found out because, although in the meantime Max willingly accompanied their mother and herself to many of the social events which occupied the long winter evenings in St Andrews, he rarely opened his mouth at them.

Everyone, of course, had read the newspaper stories about him, and Tassie was conscious, more than once, of an almost irresistible urge to giggle as she observed the good impression he was making by not putting himself forward. Respectable society was wary of people who got their names in the papers and thought it entitled them to give themselves airs. But Max was discretion personified.

It meant he didn't have to utter a word even when awkward subjects like the Amateur Dramatic Society's new production of *Twelfth Night* cropped up. He just smiled warmly and appreciatively.

Tassie knew that he couldn't – and wouldn't want to – keep it up forever, but for the time being it worked very well.

She would dearly have liked to know whether he was following the same general strategy at the mills, but she was given no opportunity to find out. When her father had been alive, she and her mother had sometimes gone to his office after a shopping trip in Dundee so that he could escort them home. But Max had put his foot down about that. He was still settling in and he didn't want them there.

In fact, he barely mentioned the business for months on end. It was as if the interview with Mr Rivers had taught him such a salutary lesson that he was determined not to risk exposing his ignorance to anyone, ever again. Tassie couldn't decide whether it was endearingly silly of him – after all, she and her mother knew less about it than he did – or rather sad, that he didn't feel safe even at home.

Then she thought, no, it couldn't be that. After even such a short time, she knew him well enough to know that he liked doing things with a flourish and guessed that he was shutting everyone out while he learned so that, at the end, he could present his new proficiency, not as the result of months of plodding but more like a conversion on the road to Damascus.

4

Almost as soon as Tassie and her mother returned to Graceholm, life settled into a pattern – a pattern which Max insisted should be exactly the same as the one laid down by Joss Smith during his lifetime. 'What *could* be more respectable than for me to model myself on my father!' he said to Tassie, adding with a gleam, 'For the time being, anyway.'

'You'll have to try harder. I mean, papa would *never* have flopped in a chair in the parlour and undone his collar stud and said, "Whew! That's better!" '

'Wouldn't he?'

'Papa,' she told him austerely, 'was a business gentlemen through and through. Papa was a business gentleman *even at home*.'

Her brother grinned at her. 'More fool he!'

The only real difference under the new dispensation was that, now, instead of revolving around Joss, the household revolved around Max.

Waking every morning at 6.30 am after a regular six hours sleep, he dressed formally in stiff white shirt, braid-edged black wool morning coat and waistcoat, twilled black trousers, black cravat, and black shoes with pale grey spats. Then, having breakfasted on porridge, followed by kippers or kidneys or eggs, with morning rolls and butter and marmalade and strong black tea, he armed himself with top hat, gloves and stick and, waved off by Grace and Tassie, was

88

driven to the station by Robertson to catch the Dundee train.

Returning at 5.30 pm, he was welcomed home again by Grace – who had spent her day supervising the household, shopping, paying visits or playing bridge – and Tassie who, as one of the senior pupils at St Leonard's, had been put in charge of preparing the Assembly Hall for meetings and functions and felt herself bowed down under almost as many duties and responsibilities as her mother.

Since Max disliked being kept waiting for his food, high tea was expected to be on the table within five minutes of his walking through the door, which gave him just sufficient time to take off his hat and coat and wash his hands. It was a full tea, of course – fish pie or veal galantine or a meat loaf stuffed with hard-boiled eggs, and a substantial spread of bread and butter, jams and honey and cheese, oatcakes, scones, shortbread, sponge sandwich, gingerbread, currant cake . . .

Mary, the cook, complained that she did nothing but bake, bake, bake all week, and what a blessing it was that Mr Max condescended to have a civilised late dinner on Saturdays and Sundays. Mr Max, of course – whose inexpertly chosen staff had been generously remunerated and gently dismissed the moment Grace took up the reins of the household again – had no trouble making his peace with Mary. All it took was a few warm and entirely sincere superlatives about her shortbread and Dundee cake.

Evenings usually saw Grace playing the piano or sewing, Tassie working at her lessons, and Max reading the papers, although sometimes they played cheerful, childish games of cards, and once or twice a week went out to the kind of early-evening function that allowed them to be home by Tassie's nine o'clock bedtime.

Soon, it began to feel as if life had always been like this. Tassie found it reassuring at first, but then it made her fidgety. It was good sense, she knew, to appear to be *tediously* respectable, but what had happened to the adventure Max's arrival had seemed to promise? She wished the future would begin to happen.

That, perhaps, was why she found herself occasionally fretting over the one thing she didn't quite like about life with Max. Although Grace – by temperament, upbringing, and the habit of three decades of marriage – seemed perfectly resigned to subordinating her own life to that of her son, Tassie belonged to a different generation and was unable to approve. It might be all very well with husbands but, in her view, sons should defer to their mothers, not the other way round. Even Max. He was unfailingly loving and polite to Grace, but not exactly considerate.

And then she would think, with a shudder, of what her long lost brother *might* have been like. He might have been stuffy, or ugly, or a bully. He might have been *boring*. Max's imperfections were negligible by comparison, although it didn't make them any the less irritating. Meditating on how it was possible to love someone very dearly while yearning to hit him over the head with a poker, Tassie came to the conclusion that nearly all his faults arose from the simple fact of his being a man.

One couldn't grow up in the 1890s without knowing about the doctrine of 'separate spheres', which held it as a law of Nature that it was a gentleman's duty to look after the material needs of his womenfolk, and his womenfolk's duty to look after him. Max subscribed to this doctrine wholeheartedly. Tassie didn't.

It wasn't that she minded waving him off in the mornings and generally running around after him; she quite liked it. It was the *principle* she objected to.

But almost invariably, just as she reached the exasperated stage of wondering whether the women's suffrage movement accepted schoolgirl members, Max

would smile at her conspiratorially, or pay her some
teasing compliment on a new dress or a new way of
doing her hair and she would find herself, much against
her better judgement, smiling gratefully back at him
and feeling warm inside.

5

And then, suddenly, everything changed again and the
future did begin to happen.

The first hint that Max had learned all he needed or
wanted to know came in the late summer of 1895,
though it didn't have anything directly to do with the
business. It was more in the nature of a final experi-
ment, a way of proving to himself and others that he
was now able to carry almost anything off.

Being Max, of course, he failed to warn his
conventionally-reared sister that he was about to make
everybody sit up and take notice.

The first Tassie knew of it was at a church soirée
where the names of Bach and Beethoven, Botticelli and
Bruegel, were being bandied about with disquieting
fluency. Halfway through the evening, suddenly aware
that Max's eyes were on her and that there was a glint of
mischief in them, she felt a small shiver run down her
spine. Then, with horrified disbelief, she saw him smile
consideringly at the group of people surrounding them
and heard him say, 'You may be right, but I feel,
myself, that our modern preoccupation with dead art
and dead music is sadly unrewarding. In my view, the
songs of today offer far more valuable insights into the
human spirit. Yes, even "Abdul the Bulbul Ameer",
even "Ta-ra-ra-boom-de-ay"! And in the case of art, I'd
be prepared to argue that a furnishing firm like Maples
adds more to the sum of human happiness than the
entire contents of this fellow Tate's proposed new
gallery.'

There was a stupefied silence.

Then, 'Really, now, that goes too far!' protested one of his hearers, and a babble of other voices immediately followed, prefacing the liveliest confrontation in the Town Kirk since the days of John Knox.

Tassie felt quite faint and Selina, who also happened to be present, murmured, 'How utterly shaming! What has one done to be saddled with such a brother!'

But Max got away with it.

Tassie had supposed, at first, that her own inability to resist his charm was natural to their relationship. He was her brother and she adored him. She had scarcely been able to believe how lucky she was to have found not only a brother to be close to, but a brother who was the answer to any sister's prayer. Except Selina's, of course. Selina could barely be polite to him, but Selina was never polite to Tassie, either, so it didn't count.

As time passed, however, she had come to see that he possessed the most amazing knack of making other people feel good, too, so that even the merest acquaintances blossomed in his warmth – marriageable maidens, critical matrons, even crusty old colonial administrators who never so much as signed their name to a birthday card without putting 'Indian Civil Service, Retd.' after it.

Now, he proved that the force of his charm and assurance were sufficient to let him get away with opinions which were outrageous by anyone's standards, and he continued to get away with them in the weeks and months and years that followed. He never put a foot wrong – except on one dreadful occasion when he let slip that he thought Chaucer was a sculptor.

6

Exactly a year after he had come back into their lives, Max decided they ought to have an anniversary celebration. With champagne, but without Selina and Dudley.

So Grace and Tassie dressed up in their best, and Mary got the Crown Derby and the crystal out, and Murdo gave the silver an extra polish, and Max amused them throughout dinner with tales of his travels, the nearest he had ever come, despite all their coaxing, to telling them the story of his life.

Afterwards, rising to his feet, he gave every indication of being about to make a speech. A proper one. Like the Lord Provost addressing the Dundee Corporation.

'I swore last year,' he said, 'that I would give the newspapers something to write headlines about, and I meant it. Well, now I'm ready to start. I know the business, and I know where I'm going. I've decided that, from now on and under my general direction, of course, the manufacturing and administrative sides will be the responsibility of Bruce Goudy and John Bell, while I myself . . .'

Grace, who had developed a knack over the years of only half-listening to what she thought of as 'gentlemen's talk', murmured pensively, 'Dear Mr Goudy. Such a nice man and such a devoted husband. Nine children, is it? The eldest must be twelve or thirteen by now and the youngest – let me see – about three.'

Max turned a reproving eye on her. 'You're behind the times, mother. The youngest was a year old yesterday.'

Tassie, who thought ten children was carrying husbandly devotion altogether too far, exclaimed, 'Really! How on earth can poor little Mrs Goudy find time to think about anything else, with a brood like that to look after?'

'I don't know,' replied her brother through gritted teeth. 'May I go on? Thank you. As I was saying, I know now that my own talents lie more in the realms of

93

ideas and sales. You'd be surprised how many ideas I have . . .'

'No, we wouldn't,' Tassie said, but her interruption so obviously came from the heart that Max laughed. 'Some of them are dashed good ones, too! Now . . .'

Tassie was interested. 'What kind of ideas, Max? I remember papa always said that industry was one per cent inspiration and ninety-nine per cent perspiration. He said that what was called inspiration was very often just an intelligent development of an idea suggested by the people who worked the machinery. He said . . .'

'*Did he?*'

'Sorry,' she murmured, and twiddled her thumbs, a picture of wide-eyed innocence.

'Why I am telling you this,' resumed her brother in carefully modulated tones, 'is because I shall be away a good deal from now on, looking for contracts, making deals, getting to know people who matter . . .'

Tassie sighed enviously. 'How exciting! Where will you go?'

Max glared at her. Then, sitting down with a thud, said, 'I give up! I shall choose my audiences more carefully in future. All right, I'm going to London first. With war looming in South Africa, I want more army contracts. Goudy tells me that, now the recession's over in Europe, the Indian jute producers will be trying to break into our traditional markets and I want to get things settled before they start undercutting our prices.'

Grace said, 'We shall miss you, my dear.'

'And I'll miss you. But never mind. Look on it as an investment in the future. Some day, soon, you'll be proud of me. Some day, soon, the newspapers are going to be calling me, "the millionaire raised in a Black House in the Highlands". Pick up your glasses and let's drink to it.'

He was so full of belief in himself that Grace could only smile back at him. She couldn't say it was an ambition that she believed to be impossible of achievement.

And then she thought, perhaps she was wrong. Perhaps he *could* do it, this unknown son of hers. He had two attributes that were very rare in the safe and stolid world of the 1890s, the force of personality he had inherited from Joss and the extraordinary power to charm that was entirely his own.

It was a charm which he never failed to exercise on his mother, and Grace wished she weren't so conscious of it. But it would have been too much to expect, after twenty-seven years of separation, that they would fall into the instinctively loving and rewarding relationship that might have existed if they had never been parted. True intimacy couldn't be imposed. It had to develop, carefully cherished, throughout the long, sensitive process of growing up. Grace was a little sad, but not surprised or disappointed that Max couldn't be wholly and spontaneously natural with her. It might not, even, be in his nature to be spontaneous or to confide. She didn't know. She didn't understand him very well. Perhaps she never would.

It was the irrepressible Tassie who objected, 'But, Max! Papa always said that, though jute was profitable, it was awfully unreliable. It was nothing but boom and recession, boom and recession, he used to say. I mean, you can't be *sure* of becoming a millionaire.'

Then, being a fair-minded girl as well as an adoring sister, she added, 'Though if anyone can do it, you can.'

He laughed and threw his arms wide, champagne bottle in one hand and glass in the other.

'There's *nothing* I can't do!'

7

He was away a good deal after that, usually for a week or two at a time, sometimes – especially during the summer, the sailing season – for two or three months, which enabled Grace and Tassie to go to Dunaird.

Max was as little interested in Dunaird as his father had been. When Grace had first suggested that he might like to accompany them, he had shuddered extravagantly. 'The Highlands? I was rained on and blown at for all the first fifteen years of my life, when I didn't have a choice. Now I do have a choice, and the answer is, no thanks. I've been spoiled by Africa and Australia. But you go, by all means, as long as you're here when I get back.'

He detested being at Graceholm on his own, as if his mother, sister and the house together formed an anchor for him in a life that had never before known stability.

Dunaird was Grace's anchor. With every visit, Tassie saw more clearly how her mother, tranquil as she always appeared, was only truly at peace when she was there, sitting on the cliff or the sands below the tower, a figure in a landscape that, harsh or gentle according to the season, was the landscape to which in her heart she belonged. An exile come home. Tassie didn't know whether to be sad or happy for her.

She herself, adaptable by nature, enjoyed being in the West Highlands – where they were, indeed, rained on and blown at, though not all the time – but felt no such sense of belonging, only the kind of romantic, almost sentimental attachment that, she was to learn in time, all Scots had for that remote, majestic, infinitely beautiful wilderness.

In truth, a few weeks were long enough and she was always secretly relieved when the time came to return to St Andrews, where she could be reassured that the world was still turning. She missed not only liveliness and people but something else, too. In the process of emerging from the chrysalis of adolescence into young ladyhood, in the process gaining two inches in height and losing four in circumference, she had left St

Leonard's school for girls and begun attending classes at 'The Studio', where the Misses Munro gave instruction in drawing and painting to the select few whom they considered worthy of their teaching. Both her mother and Max thought it was just a hobby, but it wasn't.

When she was at Dunaird, she missed 'The Studio' almost as much as she missed Max.

Passionately, she envied Max his trips to exciting places like America, though he assured her that it was hard work, because the Yanks were real go-getters and you couldn't afford to relax for a minute when you were trying to sell them something.

And yes, of course the visit had been worth it. He had come back this time with a five-year contract to supply sacking to the Chicago stockyards.

Tassie, who was becoming not only a little older but a little wiser every day, said, 'You're getting awfully good at it,' adding perceptively, 'I suppose you sell yourself first, and McKenzie Smith's products second?'

'What?' It was the only time she had ever seen him look startled. And then he said, 'Ah, I see what you mean. Well, selling's like bird-trapping. First charm the birds from the trees and then grab 'em and shove 'em in your game bag.'

Whatever the reasons for his success, his business reputation grew by leaps and bounds. More and more often, Tassie overheard him being referred to, at whist drives and golf matches and church fêtes, as 'the coming man' and the firm of McKenzie Smith mentioned as a model for industry in the new century that was soon to dawn.

Even the *Textile Trades Journal*, which Max occasionally brought home and which Tassie took private care to glance through – having met the editor once in person and more than once in her dreams – was taking a less ambivalent view of him. It actually commended one of his coups and remarked favourably on the volume of new business he was bringing to Dundee.

It didn't change Max's view of Mr Rivers, whom he still viewed with the deepest loathing.

Tassie wished that that superior gentleman would come and interview him again, because there would be no question, this time, of him catching Max out on anything.

8

It was three days before Tassie's seventeenth birthday when Max telephoned from London to say that he was not going to be able to get home to celebrate it with her. But she had scarcely had time to feel disappointed when he went on, 'So, instead of me coming to you, you'll have to come to me!'

Max had always been good at surprises, and not only the kind that had kept Tassie on the *qui vive* until she grew up enough to recognise that decorum and 'the done thing' weren't necessarily the yardsticks by which she wanted to measure her life. This, however, was something quite out of the ordinary.

Thinking she had misheard, 'What?' she screamed through the crackle of static on the line. 'What did you say?'

'I've arranged a party for you!' he shouted back. 'In London. Supper at the Carlton. New place. Very smart. I've invited some friends. You and mother can catch the train tomorrow night. And don't, for God's sake, bring any of those terrible provincial party dresses of yours. You can buy something more dashing when you get here. I've booked rooms for you at my hotel. See you on Wednesday.'

With which he rang off.

Tassie had never been to London. She had never

worn anything dashing. She had never dined in a smart hotel.

She couldn't believe it.

9

Two evenings later, slightly above herself, she waved an airy hand and said, 'I can't believe it. A life of wine and roses!'

It was true, within limits, because the dominant features of the table, as of most other tables in the restaurant, were a bowl of suffocatingly scented hot-house blooms and three bottles of a wine which had been recommended to Max by no less a personage than M. Ritz himself.

M. Ritz, formerly of the Savoy, now presided – off and on – over the very new, very fashionable and very expensive London Carlton, which was green painted, softly lit, deeply carpeted, forested with palms and filled on this December evening with sweet music and famous people. Tassie, more than a little awed, guessed that their supper for six wouldn't cost Max a penny less than £3.

Her brother grinned. 'I thought you'd like it.'

Grace, who had been unobtrusively scrutinising the other diners, said in a low voice. 'Max, that can't be Lillie Langtry at the next table, can it?'

'Where? Yes. Not her husband with her, though. Don't know who the fellow is. And there's Horatio Bottomley over there and John Lubbock directly opposite us.'

'Who?'

A low, amused, faintly foreign voice broke in. 'Max, my dear, you cannot expect your mother to be thrilled by financiers and Members of Parliament. Why do you not leave it to me to point out the interesting people to her?'

Mrs Naomi Merton.

Tassie had disliked her on sight.

The lady was a widow, perhaps a year or two older than Max, and possessed of the kind of charm that might have been deliberately designed to make other women feel small. Her looks were striking, her dark hair smoothly and perfectly coiffed, her brown eyes, which held a faint, perpetual smile, levelly set under arched brows, and her lips, the lower one unusually full, of a warm pink that Tassie refused to believe was natural.

The dress she was wearing was the height of sophistication, a clinging confection in black satin and sapphire blue, its deeply decolleté bodice draped in the latest mode to emphasise the bust, its princess skirt outlining an admirably slim waist. The scarf of spangled black gauze wasn't, Tassie thought grimly, doing much to keep her warm.

She looked very cosmopolitan, and Tassie felt more than ever like a mobile meringue in her frothy new white blouse and pale yellow, ribbed silk skirt – *le dernier cri* according to the modiste, and the only thing she and her mama had seen during their hurried expedition to Bond Street which Grace had considered sufficiently demure to be worn by a young lady just turning seventeen. The knowledge that she was dressed every bit as modishly as Mrs Merton, if rather more youthfully, was no consolation at all. Mrs Merton wouldn't have been seen dead in white frills.

Max had introduced the lady as if she were merely an acquaintance. 'Mrs Merton is very well-informed about jewellery, and has been advising me on the quality of the pearls we've recently started taking on consignment from India as a sideline. I'm told everyone who is anyone will soon be wearing pearl dog collars, though why ladies should want to get into high collars just when men are getting out of them escapes me completely.'

It had sounded perfectly plausible, but Tassie, whose training at 'The Studio' had done a good deal for her powers of observation, had the feeling that Max and Mrs Merton knew each other better – very much better – than Max pretended. They couldn't, she wondered daringly, be lovers?

Could they?

Of course not. No gentleman would introduce a woman of that sort to his mother and sister.

Mr Algernon Vale, the fifth member of the little party, was also introduced as a business acquaintance. Max had invited him as an escort for Grace and Tassie couldn't think why. Limited though her experience was, she knew enough to mistrust gentlemen with finger-waved hair, fat handshakes that lasted longer than was strictly necessary, and an avuncular mode of address. He was vulgar. Max should have known better.

Mrs Merton's seductive voice was murmuring, 'That is Mr Edward Elgar on the other side of the dance floor, beside the palm. And Mr H.G. Wells by the window. Miss Marie Tempest, the actress, is at the table being served by the small waiter with the long neck. Oh, and the lady just coming in is Clara Butt, the contralto. Now, who can her escort be, I wonder?'

Amiably, the young gentleman on Tassie's right enquired, 'Ever heard the Divine Clara sing, Miss Smith? No? She's dashed good. Sends my sister Genevieve into raptures. You should ask Max to take you, if you have the time.'

'Genevieve? What a pretty name.'

Tassie was relieved that Mr Freddy Pelham, despite the extraordinary plumminess of his accent, was turning out to be a normal human being, chubby and cheerful, his tufty hair and the shape of his head making her think of a ribboned Easter egg or Humpty Dumpty with a toothache bandage tied on top.

She had been momentarily nonplussed when Max introduced him as 'the son of Sir Leoday Pelham', as if that said all that needed to be said, but Mr Pelham had beamed engagingly at her.

'Don't worry, Miss Smith. The pater don't rate more than a couple of dozen lines in Debrett. No reason for his name to mean anything to you. Spiffing place this, what? Ah, we're going in to supper now. May I offer you my arm?'

Debrett! Heavens above! Tassie had never met anybody related to a title before.

10

It was the first time Max had ever arranged such a party, the first time Tassie or her mother had met any of the new friends he had made during his absences from home. Although Grace had suggested on several occasions – as mothers were prone to do – that Max might like to bring some of his new friends to Graceholm on a few days' visit, he had always smiled and said it would be too much trouble for her, afterwards remarking to a slightly offended Tassie that an antiquated villa in St Andrews wasn't quite what his new friends expected of him.

Ever since his telephone call, she had been consumed with curiosity about her fellow guests and, now that it had been satisfied, thought them a very ill-matched trio. But they turned out to have at least one thing in common, a way of discussing the affairs of the nation as freely and knowledgeably as the inhabitants of St Andrews discussed the vagaries of the weather or the price of fish.

It made her feel dreadfully parochial. She wasn't used to hearing Lord Salisbury's prime ministerial record and political future dissected as if he were just some ordinary mortal; still less to having the Prince of

Wales's lady friends talked about and compared as carelessly as if lady friends were perfectly respectable things for him to have. Worst of all was that the conversation was so studded with words, names and phrases that meant nothing to her that she began to feel as if they were talking a foreign language. Chemmy, the Automobile Club, Liechtenstein, the Dingley tariff, wireless telegraphy . . .

And there was Max, not only entering into the conversation but taking a leading part in it, as to the manner born.

Four summers previously, during a few weeks in the then unfamiliar surroundings of Dunaird, Tassie had learned more about her mother than during the whole of her previous life. Then it had been a case of the past illuminating the present. Now, watching Max in other, equally unfamiliar surroundings, she found the present casting a light on the future.

Seeing him so completely at ease in a place where almost everyone seemed to be either rich or famous or both, she realised that, although she had been immensely proud of the reputation he was making for himself, she had been unwittingly guilty of diminishing him in her mind by slotting his achievements into the only business context she knew, that of St Andrews and Dundee.

Now, with all the force of revelation, she saw that both his talents and his ambitions went far beyond the provincial.

Some day, some other Mrs Merton was going to be dining in some other grand hotel and murmuring to some other country cousin, 'And that's Mr Max McKenzie Smith, the great industrialist, over there by the window . . .'

11

She was so busy feeling awed about Max and ignorant about everything else that it was some time before she noticed that the one thing missing from all this highly informed table talk was any reference to the arts. Remarking on the presence of Miss Clara Butt and Mr H.G. Wells was the nearest anyone had come to acknowledging that the theatre, music, art or literature so much as existed. It was a sure sign that Max was manipulating the conversation.

Tempted, she succumbed. After all, he deserved to be paid back for leaving her and her mother out of things. At the first pause in the conversation, therefore, she said, wide-eyed and ingenuous, 'Max, you're the expert on music. What *is* that tune they're playing?'

There probably wasn't another soul in the room who hadn't recognised Mozart's 'Eine kleine Nachtmusik'.

But Max was equal to anything. With scarcely a moment's hesitation, he replied, 'That, my pet, is a question you should never ask. Don't you know the story about Her Majesty graciously summoning the bandmaster at Windsor to her presence to ask him the name of the sad and beautiful melody the band had just played? And he was forced to confess that it had been "Come where the booze is cheaper".'

It was neatly done, and Tassie laughed with the rest. Max's eyes were gleaming at her and she murmured, 'One to you!' They still played tit for tat, diamond cut diamond, each of them honour bound to retaliate for any teasing or any affront, large or small, offered by the other. It had become a habit.

Laying down his knife and fork, Max gave a sigh of contentment. 'That was excellent. There's nothing I enjoy more than chef-cooked food, good wine, and good conversation. Beats life in a Black House any day.'

'Oops!' Tassie thought.

But the Black House didn't come as news to his guests. Some reference to it was nearly always attached to Max's name when the newspapers made mention of him as, increasingly, they did. In cold truth, as Tassie now knew, his foster mother had lived in a neat little cottage in the once thriving fishing port of Ullapool until the simultaneous arrival of Max and his maintenance money had enabled her to move to an equally neat but very much larger and more comfortable cottage thirty miles to the east, on the Inverness road. But the Black House – the ancient turf and drystone dwelling – made his rags-to-riches story sound a lot more romantic. The trouble was, Tassie sometimes thought, he was beginning to believe it himself.

'I'll never forget old Jeannie,' he went on. 'By God, she was strict with me. We might live at the back of nowhere but I had to wear my shirt and tie and jacket – my one and only jacket – every time I sat down to table, and she'd test me all through the meal on dates and spelling and mental arithmetic.' At least he had the grace to avoid Tassie's eye when he mentioned the word 'spelling'. Reflectively, he went on, 'Mince and tatties it usually was, or fish stew and tea like tar. I was always half starved. Jeannie had no income except for what she earned taking in washing from the people at the shooting lodge. It was a hard life.'

Tassie, conscientiously guarding her expression, wished he wouldn't invent so many colourful details, because he never remembered them afterwards. Minor detail was one of the few things he was careless about. Why should he bother? he said. Other people never remembered, either. Which wasn't quite true, though if anyone questioned something he had said, he nearly always got away with it simply by denying any inconsistency and declaring with bland and total conviction that it was his interlocutor's memory that was at fault. But it was a dangerous game. Tassie never forgot – though, nowadays, Max sometimes seemed to – that he held not only his own but Grace's reputation in his hands.

'Well, you've risen above it, old fellow,' said Freddy Pelham. 'Breeding always tells.'

'True, true.' Max twirled the stem of his glass between his fingers and beamed beneficently at his mother and sister. Tassie, remembering the day when they had first found out who he was, the day when he had insisted that he must be acknowledged, had the feeling that deep down he still saw them as guarantors of his legitimacy. It was funny to think of the self-confident Max needing that kind of reassurance, but it was the only rational explanation Tassie had ever been able to think of for his insistence, even after he had made a place for himself in St Andrews and Dundee society, on Grace and Tassie accompanying him to every party or reception to which he was invited. He, of course, said it was because he was proud of them. He liked to show them off. They did him credit.

Tassie was just deciding that it might be desirable to change the subject when Mrs Merton murmured, 'It sounds as if your Jeannie was a remarkable woman. It takes great strength of character in this modern world for a woman to survive on her own.'

Max merely nodded, but Tassie sensed some kind of undercurrent between them.

And then it occurred to her that it might be a subject on which they disagreed. Mrs Merton sounded as if she might have advanced views about the position of women in society. All too well, Tassie knew that Max had views, too, although 'advanced' was the last word she would have used to describe them. In the jute industry, women outnumbered men by three to one and were *very* independent-minded. Max said women in business were nothing but trouble.

The question popped out almost of its own accord. 'Are you a supporter of the suffragette cause, Mrs Merton?'

She had scarcely spoken before she regretted it. The only suffragettes she had ever seen had been plain-looking, intense ladies in serviceable tailormades and clumping boots. Mrs Merton didn't qualify on any of those counts.

'The suffragettes? *Grand dieu, non*! When one is uniquely capable of making one's own way in the world, why struggle for the vote when all it offers is the privilege of being reduced to a single voice among millions?'

'Millions of *women*, though.'

'Women, men, what does it matter? To be one among millions, that is of no interest. Believe me, my little Teresa, as an attractive young woman you will soon discover that feminine wiles may be relied on to achieve a great deal more for you than the exercise of the vote, if it should ever be granted.'

Tassie, taken aback by the unexpected compliment, still didn't think Mrs Merton's attitude was very proper. She confined herself, however, to saying, 'My name isn't Teresa, actually. It's Anastasie. The name has been in the family for centuries, but I couldn't pronounce it when I was small. "Tassie" was the nearest I could get.'

'But that was most clever of you. To invent such a charming and unusual name!'

Sternly, Tassie suppressed her objection to being patronised. There was something she had been wanting to broach with Max for weeks, but she knew he wasn't going to like it and had never succeeded in finding the right opening. She didn't know if this was the right opening but his obvious approval of the self-possessed and successful lady seated on his left inspired her with a sudden, rash courage.

Swallowing hard, she said, 'Names are awfully important. Max will tell you. With a surname like Smith you *need* an unusual Christian name. I mean, he's much more memorable as Max than he would be as James or John, and – and – I think Tassie is going to be much more useful to me when I become an artist than if I were just Mary or something.'

Stopping as abruptly as she had started, she smoothed out the napkin in her lap and tried to pretend she wasn't aware of her mother's questioning green gaze or Max's frowning scrutiny.

Freddy Pelham bounded amiably into the breach. 'Going to be an artist, are you? What a ripping idea! Dashed hard work, though. Look at poor Beardsley. Friend of mine, and I can tell you, he's worn to a thread.'

Her mother smiled. 'Tassie doesn't mean she wants to *work* as an artist. That would be out of the question for a lady.'

Max said nothing.

'But I do mean it,' Tassie offered hardily. 'I want to attend classes at the Glasgow School of Art and learn properly, instead of frittering away my time on genteel little sketches of flowers and birds and things.'

'Do you, indeed?' Max said at last. 'Well, you can forget that idea. I forbid it.'

It was what she had been afraid of, even while she had hoped that, in front of his friends, he might have been more amenable.

She swallowed again. 'You can't forbid me. I'm over sixteen. If I'm old enough to get married without your permission, I'm old enough to go to art school.'

'Ah, but are you old enough to pay for it?'

And that, of course, was the question.

He was smiling now, teasing her, and she could see that everyone else at the table – except the detestable Mrs Merton – perfectly understood and approved his attitude.

No one was taking her seriously. She knew what they were all thinking. Ladies didn't have careers. And, most certainly, ladies didn't have careers in art. Artists weren't respectable.

With an attempt at brightness, she said, 'I see! It's all right for Mrs Merton to make her own way in the world, but not for me?'

Max, ignoring Mrs Merton's murmured, '*Touché*, I think, my dear Max?' said drily, 'Mrs Merton didn't expect me to fund her progress. No, Tassie. Firstly, education is wasted on women. In another year or two, it'll be, "Oh, Max, dear Max! Will you pay for my wedding, please?" Secondly, mother needs you at home. Thirdly, you are too young. And that is final.'

Her chin up, she said, 'I'm not too young.' They could hear midnight striking. 'Listen to that. It means I'm seventeen now. I'm grown up.'

She couldn't understand why Max was grinning broadly and everyone else was beaming warmly upon her.

And then a procession of waiters appeared, one of them bearing a cake with seventeen candles, and the orchestra struck up, 'Happy Birthday to You', and glasses were being raised to their table from all around the room.

Inside her head, a voice cried, *Max, Max*!

It was almost as if he had known.

But there was nothing she could do other than blush, and smile, and blow out the candles and try to hold back the sweet-sour tears.

12

Drearily, in the darkness of that night, she saw the future stretching before her, a future of keeping diaries full of watercolours of birds and flowers and children playing on the sands; of painting tasteful pictures for birthday gifts; of labouring over sweet little shell boxes and embossed leather bookmarks for bazaars. It was what 'artistic' ladies did. She didn't want to be an artistic lady. She wanted to be an artist.

Max didn't really understand, she told herself, and it was only to be expected. She had been just a schoolgirl at the time of his thrilling advent into her life, but he had already been shaped, a fully formed human being. Things would have been different if they had known each other always, because despite the disparity in their ages, they would still have shared at least a little of the rough and tumble of juvenile intimacy. If he had watched her growing up, he would have understood her instinctively; as it was, they had become the very best of friends without quite bridging the gap of years and experience.

It was perfectly natural that he should have been too much concerned with his own affairs during these last few years to make a special effort to understand her as a person, to discover what she thought or felt. He probably thought that being a loving brother was enough. As, until now, it had been.

He had a great deal on his mind.

He hadn't meant what he'd said.

He was teasing her. Diamond cut diamond. He was paying her back for being mischievous about Mozart.

He would understand when she explained it all to him properly.

It would be all right – really it would.

13

Two crowded days later, during which Grace and Tassie saw the Changing of the Guard, the Tower of London, Madame Tussaud's, the ducks in Hyde Park and the bookshops in the Charing Cross Road, they were on their way home again. No one had said another word about Tassie's ambitions.

By the time they arrived back in St Andrews, she had reached the conclusion that she would have to Take Steps. If nothing else, the near-quarrel with Max – the first quarrel they had ever had – had driven it home to her that, unless she could find a way of earning her own living, she would always be dependent, first on her brother, then on her husband and, eventually, on her sons. It was a prospect that didn't appeal to her in the least. She wanted to be dependent on herself.

She would start as she meant to go on. Somehow, she would *earn* her art school fees and lodging bills.

Her mother, subjected to an edited version of these reflections, didn't take them altogether seriously. All she said, gently, was, 'But, darling, I don't think you should disobey Max, should you?'

'Yes, I should,' Tassie said firmly.

14

The very next morning, therefore, she removed the trimmings from her grey alpaca costume and matching winter cape, donned her plainest hat, and set off for the factory at Dundee, to coax John Bell, who was in charge of administration and ledger accounts, into giving her a job.

She had known him, off and on, for ten years, ever since the day her father had taken her to see the mills and the factory for the first time. By coincidence, it had also been the day on which John Bell, aged twenty, had joined the firm. They had met no more than half a dozen times since, only in the office and only in passing, but there was a bond of sympathy between them. Tassie sometimes wondered whether Mr Bell had been as overcome by his first day at the works as she had.

She could still remember it, could still remember clinging to her father's hand as he led her, in her trim little yoked and gathered cotton frock and the hat with the goffered frills, from batching shed to hackling shed, weaving shed to finishing shed, showing the works off to her, or her to them. She had never been sure which.

Everything had combined to numb her brain, so that she had barely been able to distinguish one machine from another, one process from another. The noise was nightmarish, the clacking, rolling, flapping, thumping of all the different machinery merging into a volume of sound so huge as to suggest, to a small girl accustomed to the peace of the town across the Tay, that the end of the world was nigh. Even the air was an assault on the senses. High though the sheds were, it was thick with dust and fluff and particles of fibre, with smells of hot metal and engine oil, batched jute and steam and effluent from the privies. Tassie, deafened, sneezing, her eyes stinging, hadn't even seen the people who worked the machines except as automata, bloodless, feelingless figures of men in caps and women in aprons.

In the years between her seventh and seventeenth birthdays, the noise hadn't diminished nor the air cleared. Nothing had changed.

But she had. The people were real human beings and she didn't know how they could stand it.

15

John Bell was still the chirpy young man he had always been, with a mobile face, a wicked streak of humour, and a knack of appearing to be very much too clever for his own good, though her father had always said he was efficient and wholly trustworthy.

He looked innocently surprised and pleased when she walked into the dark and dusty office with its high stools and high desks, though only until she told him the reason why she was there.

'D'ye want me to lose my job?' he yelped. 'Yer brither 'ud murder me!'

She had come prepared for that one. 'Why should he? I'm a shareholder in the company' – well, she did have one lonely little share – 'so you have to do what I tell you, don't you?'

'We-e-ell . . .'

'I mean, it's not for you to question my motives, is it?'

'We-e-ell . . .'

'And I'm quite good with figures. And he's away until the beginning of next month. If I'm properly settled in by the time he comes back he'll look awfully silly if he kicks up a fuss, won't he?'

'Whooh!' John Bell's cheeks, normally no more than a brief hiatus between high brow and long, pointed chin, inflated and deflated themselves like a pair of badly tied balloons. 'There's many an adjective I could use about yer brither, but "silly" isny one o' them. As our Yankee chums would say, he's a tough customer.'

'Is he?'

'O-o-oh, aye. Keeps us all on the hop. *He* knows exactly what he's doing, but we don't. Ye never know where you are wi' him. One day he'll see you on request. Ither times ye have to wait a week. One day he's nice as ninepence to you. Ither days . . . Aye, well!'

Tassie knew all about Max keeping people on the hop – especially Miss Tassie Smith – but she couldn't see him as a tyrant, which was what John Bell was implying. She said, 'You're exaggerating!'

It was a mistake because, overtaken by discretion in the presence of the boss's sister, he looked momentarily uneasy before he reverted to normal and grinned at her. 'Maybe. It doesny do us any harm, anyway. And he's got some great tricks wi' the opposition.'

Tassie said, 'Such as?' She knew perfectly well that John Bell was trying to put off answering her, but saw no reason not to benefit from it by learning something about a side of Max she didn't know at all.

'Och, well. In a place like this, ye're aye being bombarded by suppliers trying to sell ye things. Anything from accounts books to haversack buckles. Sometimes they're things we need, sometimes not. Anyway, yer brither makes a habit of keeping the salesmen – and a pushy lot they are, I can tell you – waiting for exactly fifteen minutes, and after a few visits they begin to cotton on. And then they try to be clever and turn up fourteen minutes late for their appointments. And when they do, yer brither's secretary says, what a pity, Mr McKenzie Smith's engaged now and won't be free for the rest of the day. Fair warms yer heart, it does.'

Tassie, who had never met a pushy salesman and knew nothing about the tactics of dominance, asked after a moment, 'Is that all?'

His eyes ascending heavenward in search of divine rescue, John Bell said, 'Aye. And since ye ask, we've only the one vacancy, and that's for an office boy.'

'All right,' Tassie said. 'I'll put my hair up under a cap and wear one of those smock things.'

'Ye'll have to talk to Goudy.'

Not for a moment did Tassie believe that anyone as senior as Mr Goudy, the chief accountant who was in overall charge whenever Max was away, made a habit of wasting his time interviewing lowly office boys, but she said, 'All right. Can he see me now or will I have to wait for fifteen minutes?'

Mr Goudy didn't pretend to understand why Mr McKenzie Smith's sister should wish for employment but, himself the father of seven hopeful daughters, was well aware that young ladies often took inexplicable notions into their heads. On the admitted grounds that she was a shareholder, and the unadmitted grounds that a week should be enough to cure her of her ambitions, he agreed to take her on as a very junior clerk. She would be gone, he thought, long before her brother returned.

16

She was spared, as a female, most of the induction tortures devised over the years for new employees of McKenzie Smith & Co, although on her first day John Bell's assistant despatched her to the Town Clerk's Office for a poetic licence, and the man repairing a broken window sent her to the workshop to fetch him a glass hammer. She was quick to learn, however, and held her own successfully until the fourth day after Max's return from London.

On each of the four mornings she had skipped out of the house while he was dressing and in the evenings had lingered in the office until she was sure he had left.

She knew it wouldn't be long before he found out what she was up to, but had no passionate desire to hurry the day of reckoning. She was *perfectly* entitled to do what she was doing. But . . .

It was a few minutes before noon on the Thursday when he sent his senior clerk down with a request that his sister join him in his office for lunch. At twelve precisely. Sherry and Madeira cake.

The invitation arrived at an inauspicious moment, just when Tassie was drying off the import department's letter book. Although the firm employed two typewriting ladies, most correspondence was still done by hand, and it was Tassie's duty to take copies by placing each letter in contact with one of the damped tissue pages of the book and then putting the whole thing in a screw press to transfer the impression. Afterwards, everything had to be dried out again in front of a gas jet.

Distracted at the crucial moment, Tassie succeeded in setting the letter book on fire, destroying the only

115

copies of the department's entire correspondence for the previous six months.

That was the sole reason, she told herself, why she was shaking as, raising a cursorily washed hand to knock on her brother's door, she noticed that she was still wearing her celluloid cuffs, smoke-stained and filthy. Whisking them off, she crushed them into her pocket. There were probably smuts on her nose, too.

'Come in.'

She wasn't sure that she was going to be capable of uttering a word, even if Max gave her the chance. The only consolation was that, although he might say a good deal, he couldn't *do* anything beyond sacking her.

It was a large office, and the big mahogany desk was positioned in the window at the far end. It meant that anyone summoned to an interview with the proprietary partner – in business terms, a kind of lay version of God – had a long, intimidating walk towards a dark figure sitting with his back to the light, his face shadowed and unreadable. It was a dull and overcast day, which didn't help.

Tassie hadn't been summoned to an interview, she reminded herself. She had been invited to lunch.

So, stiffening her spine, she smiled gaily in Max's general direction, glanced round to see where the tray of sherry and cake had been set out, and went and sat down beside it.

'I haven't disobeyed you,' she said without preamble. 'You didn't forbid me to look for work.'

'I didn't think it necessary,' he replied at last. 'Ladies do not take up paid employment.' There was nothing to be deduced from his tone.

'It's the affront to your dignity, isn't it?' she went on chattily, and then, as he showed no sign of moving, poured herself a small glass of sherry and proceeded to cut herself a slice of cake. 'You're afraid people will think you've no sense of propriety. Or that the business isn't making enough profit to pay for your sister's hats. Or that you're a horrid skinflint.'

In for a penny, in for a pound. Might as well be hanged for a sheep as a lamb. She who rides a tiger . . .

The Madeira cake was light as a feather, but dry. Pursuing an errant crumb, she waited for him to say something. Almost anything would have done.

In the end, he moved so quietly that she didn't realise he had moved at all until he was at her side, looming over her. Insouciantly, she popped the crumb in her mouth and it went down the wrong way.

She was still coughing and spluttering when Max sat down in the chair opposite and said with the greatest cordiality, 'What an abominable girl you are. I can't think what I did to deserve you as a sister.'

She remembered Selina saying much the same thing about having Max as a brother. 'You mean . . .' she gasped. 'You mean you don't mind?'

'Of course I mind. And don't gulp your Amontillado like that. I can't have my clerks getting tipsy.'

'I'm quite good at it,' she assured him. 'At clerking, I mean, not getting tipsy.'

'So I hear. Observant, Goudy says, and quick to learn.'

'Well, being observant is all part of being an artist, you see, and . . .'

'All right, all right!' Max raised his hands in surrender. 'It's blackmail, of course, and don't *ever* try anything like this with me again. You won't get away with it twice. But I was testing the strength of your wish to go to art school and it seems I underestimated it.'

He stopped, while Tassie waited, trying not to tremble.

'So, as a reward for your undoubted spirit of enterprise, and because the firm can't afford to employ arsonists' – how on earth had he found out about that already? – 'I will pay your fees for the first year. After that, young Ginger, everything will depend on how you get on.'

He had risen again and was smiling down at her. It wasn't his ordinary, everyday smile but the special warm, conspiratorial one that raised his brows and carved deep new-moon creases in the shadowed circles under his eyes; the smile that drew her into a private alliance that always, at the time, seemed to matter more than anything else in the world.

Jumping up on tiptoe, she threw her arms round him and gave him an ecstatic and prolonged kiss on the cheek. 'Max, *dearest* Max! You're the most wonderful brother I could possibly have, even when you try to tease me into thinking you're not. Thank you!'

He didn't hug her back. To her surprise, he almost resisted her and it was a moment before she realised that he must be startled, because embracing him was something she had never done before, or not with such impassioned spontaneity. He was so much older and more worldly wise that hugs and kisses had always seemed out of place. It was a queer, unexpected thought, considering that during the last three years or so she had been finding it progressively more difficult to remember what it had been like *not* to have a brother.

She dropped her arms, and he stepped back, his smile a curious mixture of distance and self-derision as he flipped the lid of the silver sovereign purse that hung from his watch chain and slid out one of the lovely golden coins from under the spring.

His thumb caressing it, he said drily, 'How much of my heart's blood do you need?'

17

Everything in the world was wonderful, except that the relationship between Grace Smith and her long lost son had progressed scarcely at all since the day, four years before, when he had come back into her life as an adult, as a stranger.

Grace loved him for being her son. She knew that 'gentlemanliness' was less to do with nature than nurture and that time would make of him what he should always have been. And time, of course, would bring them closer, too, until in the end he would feel able to offer her a warmth deeper and more heartfelt than the surface warmth of his charm. So she told herself. But she was not wholly at ease.

It wasn't apparent. Even Tassie, sensing it once or twice, thought she was imagining things.

PART TWO

1899 —

1901

December 1899 – October 1900

CHAPTER ONE

I

As the son of a mother who had made it a principle never to mollycoddle her children, and a father who had made it a principle never to argue with his wife, Francis had learned in infancy to be impervious to cold. Despite the rawness of the December day, therefore, it was a chill more intellectual than physical that caused him to shiver as he stood listening to Sir James King declare Glasgow's new School of Art building officially open.

Francis had known its sometimes volatile, sometimes morose architect, Charles Rennie Mackintosh, for years; had listened so often to him laying down the law about spatial values, austerity of line and economy of colour that he could have faced a stiff examination in the Modern Movement without even having to think about it.

Mackintosh had given him a private tour of the new premises a few days before, but Francis's main impression had been of frenetic last-minute activity – decorators whitewashing the walls, carpenters sanding down finishes, removal men bringing in statues, students rushing around with pictures and embroideries for hanging. It was very different today, the guests as subordinate to their surroundings as the congregation in a cathedral, silent intruders in the purity of space, secessionists from simplicity of line, dissenters from the despotism of white and green. The electric lamps were pitiless and the light from the huge, north-facing windows grey and chill.

Francis didn't think he liked it much. On the other hand, it was new, original and stimulating, and he'd promised Mackintosh four pages of pictures and editorial. Until now, the thirty-one-year-old architect had been a classic example of the prophet who was not without honour save in his own country, a modernist highly regarded in Germany and Italy but virtually ignored at home. Mackintosh hoped the School of Art was going to change things, and Francis, although privately doubting it, was prepared to back him all the way.

Moodily contemplating a marble St Cecilia and wishing Sir James would stop blethering, Francis found his eye caught by a splash of colour beyond the statue, a head of glowing red-gold hair under a ridiculous little toque of yellow roses. He couldn't think why there was something familiar about it. Certainly, he didn't recognise the face underneath, which belonged to a slim, goodlooking girl of about eighteen or nineteen.

As if aware of his glance, she turned her head towards him and smiled uncertainly. But then her eyes shifted and he wasn't sure whether it was him she was smiling at, or the young man two along from him who was hissing, 'Miss Smith!' and beckoning her to join him. Apparently, she didn't regard an improved view of the platform as sufficient inducement to move, and shook her head, half reprovingly, before transferring her glance – this time unmistakably –back to Francis.

Only then, his mind racing back through the years, did he make the connection, and remember Grace Smith, and see the subtle resemblances, and identify the girl as the daughter with the bright hair and the tendency to drop teacups at inopportune moments.

Max McKenzie Smith's sister. She had improved a lot.

He smiled back.

2

The speeches over, Francis canvassed a few of the more distinguished guests for their opinions, keeping a weather eye on Miss Smith the while. She was one of a group of young people, and he saw them talking to Fra Newbery, the School of Art's velvet-jacketed headmaster, with a ready familiarity that suggested they might be students.

It gave Francis a useful idea for killing two birds with a single, well-aimed stone.

Without haste, he strolled over to join the little group, which fell silent as such groups always do at the approach of an outsider. But Francis, seasoned journalist that he was, had expected the reaction and knew how to deal with it.

'Don't let me interrupt,' he said. 'What was it? State secrets, or the Lady Provost's feather boa?'

They all smiled politely and he went on, 'I'm a journalist and you're art students, I take it? So you can help me. What colour should I call it? The feather boa, I mean.'

'Heliotrope. Isn't it awful?' replied a plain, cheerful girl with mousy hair, a cut-glass English accent, and a mud-coloured outfit that Francis vaguely identified as being in the Aesthetic mode.

And then Miss Smith found her voice and introduced him to her friends. 'I think Mr Rivers must be ragging us,' she concluded. 'I can't imagine readers of the *Textile Trades Journal* being interested in anything as trivial as a feather boa, whatever its colour. Black serge or bombazine is more in their line.'

'I'm not so sure about that,' Francis replied.

Appearances were deceptive and he would have been prepared to bet that at least some of the *Journal*'s most worshipful and straitlaced subscribers would be very interested indeed in feather boas – though only if the wearers happened to be wearing nothing else. 'But I should tell you that I have expanded my empire since we last met. I still own the *Journal*, but I am also proprietor and editor of the Glasgow *Enterprise*.'

'Oh, the new weekly?' exclaimed the plain young woman, whose name was Norah ('with an h') St John. 'It's rather good. You've got the right ideas. I say! I'd like to have a word with you about the women's suffrage movement, because I think it's time the newspapers paid a bit more attention . . .'

Inwardly, Francis sighed. A novelist friend of his swore that every chance-met acquaintance could be relied on to say, after about five minutes, 'You know, I've often thought I could write a book, if only I had the time'. Journalists had much the same problem, except that in their case every chance-met acquaintance could be relied on to have an axe to grind and plenty of time for grinding it.

'Of course.' He stopped her expertly. 'But, if you'll forgive me, just at this moment I have architecture on my mind and a deadline to meet. If Miss Smith doesn't object, I should like to borrow her to give me a student's-eye view for tomorrow's edition. I'll return her to you in good order.'

3

She conducted him along every corridor, up and down every flight of stairs, in and out of every room, explaining how beautiful it all was in its economy of style and how practical. The white walls reflected and purified the daylight; the electric lamps in the studios could be adjusted over every easel; the antique tapestries and cases of art curios on the upper floor weren't museum pieces but teaching tools.

'Yes,' he said dutifully, and 'Yes', again, many times, as if he hadn't had it all explained to him before. At one stage, Mackintosh himself went past with a party of local worthies in tow and, overhearing, raised mystified eyebrows at Francis, who returned him his blandest smile.

They were descending the stairs for the last time, the tour over, when Francis casually asked after the health and wellbeing of Miss Smith's brother. 'I've been following his career with interest over these last five years.'

And not just with interest but sheer bloody annoyance at the fact that Mr Max McKenzie Smith had been so quick to make a name for himself.

Miss Smith's face face lit up. 'He's been doing marvellously well, hasn't he? The business has expanded enormously. Did you know he switched one of the mills to linoleum production last year? He's convinced that there's going to be a huge expansion in the domestic decoration market now that people are moving into the new residential districts and have more money to spend. It's very exciting.'

'I'm sure it is. Though I gather that Nairns don't relish the competition. They've always had everything very much their own way in the linoleum market.'

'I *know*,' she chuckled. 'And the competition's scarcely even begun yet! Max says business isn't any fun unless you play to win. It's a game, he says, just like cricket or chess – only with more blood.'

'It makes journalism sound like a rest cure.' There was no mistaking that the girl thought her brother was wonderful, and who was Francis to deny it? It had been instinct tinged with prejudice that had made him distrust the gentleman in the first place and Max's knack of attracting favourable publicity had done nothing to change his view. That was the trouble with being a cynic born and bred.

With a deadline looming, he didn't have time to enquire further into Max's business philosophy. Instead, he said, 'There's one thing you haven't shown me. An example of your own work.'

She grimaced – very fetchingly, he thought. She had a distinctive face with high cheekbones and a straight nose that might have appeared autocratic if it hadn't been for the wide, generous mouth and big, expressive green eyes which were almost translucent in the austere whiteness of the light. She seemed a nice girl, and rather sweet.

'That was deliberate. We're all convinced, when we come here, that we're destined to be great artists, and the first thing we learn is that most of us are never going to be more than craftsmen. Oh, all right. There's something in one of the corridors off the hall.'

He would have expected a piece of the flowing Art Nouveau embroidery which Jessie Newbery had made a speciality of the school, but what Miss Smith deprecatingly showed him was a small wooden panel in painted gesso filled with two dreamlike female figures arched round a single rose.

It wasn't bad at all. 'Oh dear,' Francis said. 'You're a nonconformist, are you? No straight lines. No wide open spaces. No white and green.'

She wasn't, it seemed, used to being teased about her art and he felt a momentary guilt, because she was still rather young and didn't know how to handle it. 'The rose is the school's symbol,' she said defensively. 'And this isn't a factory, you know. We don't have to work to a formula. Oh, hello, Norah.'

'Good. You haven't gone!' Norah St John, a practical young woman, finished tying the rain cover over her hat and said, 'Tassie, it just occurred to me that perhaps Mr Rivers might like to come to our Christmas party on Saturday. Why don't you, Mr Rivers? Tassie and I share digs, and there are about a dozen of our fellow students coming. You could learn all about the joys and sorrows of being aspiring artists. It would make a jolly good article. We could even pretend to be sinful Bohemians, if you like.'

And we could fit in a puff for women's suffrage, too, Francis thought. But he had an axe of his own to grind. 'I'd like that,' he said. 'Where and when?'

'Gosh! You'll come? Ripping! Any time after six. We're at 23 Hillhead Street.'

Miss Tassie Smith entered an embarrassed caveat about Mr Rivers having better things to do with his time, but her friend ignored her. 'So what do you think of our work?' she demanded. 'Our talents are pretty varied, you know. That's one of my things over there, the design for a stained glass panel of Joan of Arc. We're allowed to do almost anything we like, even the mere females among us!'

'I imagine it would be a brave man who tried to stop you.'

She grinned. 'Rather! We all had to fight like billy-o before our families would let us come here at all – not the thing, you know! – so we've learned to be pretty strongminded. Even Tassie here. Don't be misled by that bit of frivolity on her head into thinking she's not a New Woman. Because she is.'

'If she came out victorious over that redoubtable brother of hers, I can well believe it.'

Miss Smith said lightly, 'Oh, it wasn't as bad as all that.' Though it had been at the time, she remembered, even if two years had taken most of the edge off that first – and last – quarrel with Max. It seemed longer, because she had grown up since then, pitched into a world where no one remembered her as a child and didn't therefore still think of her as one, a world where no concessions were made. The Glasgow School of Art didn't believe in pampering its students.

She smiled at Francis Rivers. 'My brother didn't approve at first, but he's resigned to it now. He rather likes people standing up to him.'

Mr Rivers failed to hide his scepticism, an expression that seemed very much at home on his lean, patrician features. Tassie found it irritating, especially as he'd been a model of detached courtesy for the last half hour and hadn't said a word out of place. She supposed he must still – though she couldn't think why – have reservations about Max, despite the fact that Max had very publicly overcome the deficiencies Mr Rivers had so ruthlessly exposed during their interview five years before. Perhaps journalists were just suspicious by nature.

It was ridiculous, she knew, for her to feel this indignation, this need to defend her brother, who had nothing whatsoever to be defensive about. It was of no interest to her what the disturbing Mr Rivers thought. She wished Norah hadn't invited him to their party.

He probably wouldn't turn up, anyway.

4

He did turn up, although he didn't stay for very long because, Christmas or no Christmas, he had work to do, a story to cover for next week's paper. He was an easy guest, and even listened for almost ten minutes to Norah talking about votes for women, a subject on which he seemed to be already quite well informed.

When Tassie saw him to the door, he said, 'Perhaps I might repay your hospitality by inviting you out to tea some time?'

'Oh. Thank you. Yes. That would be nice.'

She had thought that by 'you' he meant herself and Norah, but when the invitation came it was addressed to Miss T. Smith, and Miss N. St John didn't rate a mention.

'*No*, I won't go without you!' she declared to Norah. 'He terrifies the life out of me.'

But Norah, predictably, said she had never heard such nonsense. For a New Woman to be terrified by a mere male! Tassie should be ashamed of herself.

Tassie wasn't in the least ashamed of herself, but she went. She wanted to go.

He took her to tea at Miss Cranston's, and nothing could have been more sedate or unthreatening. They talked mainly about the new art school building and Mr Rivers said, 'You admire it, I can see, but that's not the same as liking it. Don't worry, I won't quote you. I'm just interested.'

'Of course I like it. It's brilliant. It has everything a student could possibly need. It's a work of pure genius.'

'Not exactly cosy, though.'

'Oh, well, if it's *cosiness* you want . . .' she said scornfully.

But his quizzical eyes were her undoing. Her lips twitched, and she blushed and, aware of it, blushed even more. 'It isn't fair. Really, I don't know what you expect me to say!'

'I wasn't sure whether loyalty or truth would prevail. But never mind. Perhaps it would be safer if we talked about something where there's no danger of them clashing? Can I interest you in a cucumber sandwich?'

'Thank you.'

There was still a hint of amusement in his eyes as he went on, 'I've sometimes thought how strange it must have been for you to acquire a brother out of the blue, as you did. Are you used to it by now?'

A sensible New Woman would have said, 'Yes,' and left it at that. But Tassie, after hesitating for a moment, suddenly found herself desperately anxious to persuade Mr Rivers that Max really was wonderful and truly worthy of Mr Rivers's and everybody else's admiration. Launching out with the declaration that Max was someone you *never* got used to, because he was so clever and unpredictable and such fun, she concluded breathlessly some time later – carefully omitting any mention of Mozart in between – 'and the bandmaster said, "As a matter of fact, Your Majesty, it wasn't a lament. It was 'Come where the booze is cheaper'." Don't you think that's a lovely story?'

Mr Rivers said, 'Very droll.'

Two or three weeks later, he invited her to Miss Cranston's again, and again she went because she wanted to, although it was against her better judgement. This time he began by asking her what use she proposed making of her artist's training.

'I'm best at applied art, not pure art, so I'll go into the commercial field.'

'Isn't that difficult for a lady?'

'The most difficult thing,' she told him sweetly, 'is persuading gentlemen that a lady knows what she is doing. Fra Newbery sends us out occasionally to gain business experience, and I may tell you it is the most frustrating thing having to creep around looking like a frump for fear of scaring the clients off.'

'A *frump*?'

She didn't dare acknowledge the compliment. 'But there's a trick to it, I've discovered. You have to look as plain as possible to begin with; you don't want to frighten the horses. And you have to stay plain – in fact, you have to stay almost invisible and inaudible as well – until the client realises that you're artistically competent and personally harmless. After that, very slowly, you can begin to look and act more normally until, in the end, you can do something gentlemen *can't* do.'

'Yes?'

'You can flutter your eyelashes to reinforce your arguments. It's called getting the best of both worlds.'

'That's immoral.'

'Mmmm. And very satisfying.'

He smiled his rather austere smile, eyebrows fractionally raised, one corner of his mouth curling. Tassie wished he didn't make her feel so gauche. 'What you are saying is, you're as good an artist as most men. Why should you have to work five times as hard to prove it?'

'Do you have an answer to that?'

'No. What does your brother have to say about it?'

Max wouldn't have recognised Tassie's sprightly tale of the encouragement and support he had given her once he had known she was serious about her ambitions, especially the bit where she allowed her imagination to run away with her and invented a particularly touching scene where Max had taken down the Millais from his bedroom wall to make space for his sister's sketches.

Tassie was never at ease with Mr Rivers and she knew perfectly well why. She was all too aware of becoming more self-consciously vivacious by the minute whenever she was in his company and, afterwards, told herself that she was a fool; that she was making him think her shallow and feather-brained; that he would never invite her out again if she went on prattling like that.

But he did, and she couldn't understand it.

He didn't, surely, think her such a fool as not to notice his obsessive interest in Max? And if he accepted that she did notice, surely he didn't think her such a fool as to supply him with the answers to the careless half-questions that studded their conversations, questions whose purpose she couldn't fathom but of which she was bound to be suspicious?

133

If his questions were honest and disinterested, why didn't he go straight to Max with them?

It was better that he shouldn't, of course, although Tassie suspected that he was unaware of just how much Max disliked him. When they had first met, he had made Max feel inferior, and it wasn't something Max would ever forgive.

But far more important was Tassie's certainty that it was *safer* for Mr Rivers to question her rather than Max himself. Max, nowadays, seemed almost to have forgotten the truth of his upbringing, which meant that it would be all too easy for him to make a fatal slip if he were asked about something that didn't quite fit into the Black House fiction. Tassie herself never forgot. Always at the back of her mind, when she was with Francis Rivers, was an awareness of the secret that, revealed, could destroy her mother, who had conceived her son in sin and then abandoned him. It made conversation horribly difficult.

Each time they met, Tassie told herself she shouldn't see Francis Rivers again. But she couldn't bear not to.

6

'Well, if you don't want him, I'll have him,' said Bess Baird through a mouthful of pins. 'Looks *and* class. And that sort of rumpled air, as if he needs looking after. I'd like to give him a right good cuddle. Must be my motherly instincts coming out. Turn round a bit.'

Tassie craned to see how Bess was getting on and, turning as instructed, replied with feeling, 'Well, if you want to cuddle Mr Rivers, please do. But don't blame me if he gives you a basilisk stare and turns you into a pillar of salt – or whatever a basilisk does. Anyway, I can't think of anyone one who wants or needs looking after less than he does. Oh, *do* hurry up! The rehearsal's at three and you know Fra. He'll throw a fit if his Queen with the White Lily turns up as a queen with no lily and a half-pinned hem. Where on earth can Norah have got to?'

One of the recurring torments of attending the Glasgow School of Art was the masques mounted by the Headmaster for the ostensible purpose of displaying the work of students taking the costume design class. In actual fact, everyone knew it was because he fancied himself as a theatrical producer. Under his perfectionist and highly temperamental direction, rehearsals could last for six hours at a stretch, and performers had been known to faint away for want of a cup of tea. The subject this time was 'The Kings and Queens of Scotland', and Tassie had been cast as Mary Stewart, not in deference to her acting abilities but because she happened to have the right colour of hair.

Bess said, 'Anyway, *why* don't you want him?'

'I didn't say I didn't want him. I just said it's all very well for you and Norah and the others to swoon over him; you don't have to put up with his idea of conversation.'

'Och, away, lassie. I could spend all day listening to him. He's got as good a mind as anyone I've ever met.'

'Yes, well, he ought to. His father was a professor – which, I may say, is the *only* personal thing I've discovered about him! Anyway, that's not what I meant. He's taken me out to tea four times now, but he's not interested in me at all.'

'Well, why d'you accept his invitations, then?' enquired Bess.

Loftily ignoring what she recognised as deliberate provocation, Tassie went on, 'I don't think he's interested in anything except his beastly newspaper. All he wants to talk about is my brother and his early life and whether he's going to take the company to the stock market soon, and things like that. I suppose he's hoping for a scoop. You know the kind of thing. "Max

McKenzie Smith's sister reveals plan to evade Dingley Tariff . . ." Brrrrrr.' She shuddered extravagantly.

'Dearie me!' Bess replenished her pins. 'I hope not. It sounds a bit shady. And what's the Dingley Tariff when it's at home?'

'I'm not very sure. But there you are, you see! Max says it's all perfectly legal and above board, but "shady" is just what people *would* think.'

The door burst open on a breathless Norah. 'Oh, there you are!' she said. 'I've been looking everywhere for you. There's your lily, Tassie. Be careful, because I ran out of thread and finished up having to paint the stamens and they're still wet. Though I must say, it beats me why Fra should want to have Mary, Queen of Scots, represented by a lily, when it's a symbol of chastity, purity and innocence.'

Tassie accepted the lily with relief. 'Ignorant Sassenach! It's a reference to Mary's marriage to the French Dauphin. The *fleur de lis*, remember? Anyway, I don't remember your precious Good Queen Bess being conspicuous for her chastity, purity and innocence.'

A cool, lazy voice from behind said, 'Just what I like to hear. Amity between nations.'

Francis Rivers.

Tassie didn't need to look. He would be leaning negligently against the doorpost, hands in pockets, dark hair ruffled, grey eyes sceptical, air indefinably rakish and manner all too definably touch-me-not. He was so abominably single-minded that he probably didn't even realise what effect he had on the susceptible female heart.

Not very politely, she said, 'What are you doing here?'

'I was invited.'

'Not by me. And certainly not to watch me dress!'

'True. On the other hand, one doesn't expect to find the museum doing duty as a lady's boudoir.'

Bess chuckled. 'That's my fault. When you're my size and get down on your knees in a crowded changing room you're a danger to traffic. How do you think she looks? Everything handmade on the premises.'

'Very fetching. I like the pendant especially.'

'Isn't that typical!' exclaimed Tassie in exasperation and with complete disregard for propriety. 'You would notice, wouldn't you! Well, as it happens, I have no talent for metalwork and my teacher refused to allow what he called my "travesty of a jewel" to leave the studio. So this is my own, and it's genuine sixteenth century. A family heirloom.' She felt no compulsion to add that her doting father had bought it at auction a dozen years before from the family whose heirloom it had been.

Pouring oil on troubled waters, Norah asked, 'Who did invite you? Fra, I suppose? You're awfully good to us, you know, giving the school so much publicity and taking such a personal interest. I didn't think editors stooped so low as to be their own reporters.'

'They don't. And from October on, I will have to give up stooping. I'm going into competition with the *Glasgow Herald* by turning the *Enterprise* into a daily instead of a weekly, so I shall be working from early afternoon until the small hours, and at my desk all the time.'

'Gosh, that'll curtail your social life.'

'It will indeed. I'm told you disperse for the summer holidays next week, but perhaps when you come back for the autumn term, I might invite you ladies to a farewell tea at Miss Cranston's?'

'Tea at Miss Cranston's?' said Tassie dulcetly. 'How utterly thrilling!'

Abigail Rivers removed her hat, swept an armful of papers aside, and seated herself, silver-haired, upright and domineering, on the sofa.

'Men!' she said. 'I don't imagine you have given a thought to the harm it might do Lucia, this new come-out of yours. As I understand the workings of news-papers, in the future you will be out every single night until the small hours.'

'You exaggerate. I will have Saturday nights free. In any case, I *have* given a thought to how it will affect Lucia and have made suitable arrangements. And I should remind you,' replied her irritated son, 'that this is my living room, not yours. Those papers were in order.'

'You amaze me. You inherited your untidiness from your father, I suppose. Perhaps you will be good enough to tell me what arrangements you have made?'

'They are perfectly satisfactory and I will not be cross-examined about them. Have you heard from Jonny yet?'

Miraculously, she allowed herself to be diverted. Her eyes glittering sardonically, she said, 'I had a letter on Tuesday which confirms me in my belief that he is a changeling. After being besieged in Mafeking for two hundred and sixteen days, all he can write about is the inspiring leadership of Colonel Baden-Powell and the benefit of daily prayer. He does admit to having had a touch of enteric fever, but I am not to worry, if you please.'

'As if you would.' Francis smiled wryly. He supposed that his mother must worry about her children occasionally, though she had never shown any sign of it, even when they were small. He, David and Jonny had been despatched in succession to boarding school and the care of a matron who was paid to do any worrying that might be necessary. It hadn't done them any harm. What it had done was make relations with their mother curiously impersonal. Only recently had Francis become aware of how little they knew about her.

'I'm glad he's all right.' Then, with a change of tone, he went on, 'And I have some news for you, too.'

'Yes?'

'Perhaps you ought to have something to fortify you against the shock. Tea, coffee, wine, sherry?'

'*Francis!*'

'If you insist. I have found out something you wanted to know. The date of Max McKenzie Smith's birth. Or the approximate date.'

Despite everything, he had thought her curiosity no more than a passing whim, and was taken aback to see that the breath had been arrested in her throat.

It was a moment before she spoke. 'Indeed. Then perhaps you should, after all, tell that Mistress Thompson of yours to bring in some wine. Preferably something cool from the cellar. How I dislike this heat! I cannot remember a hotter summer.'

8

She toyed neither with the long rope of her pearls, her ivory-headed cane, nor even her wine glass while Francis reported.

'I found out by putting two and two together from things his sister has let drop on various occasions. A nice girl, but rather young and ingenuous for her age. It seems Max hates being cold and attributes it to his being a January child. And you may remember my telling you that Max himself said his parents had moved from the Highlands to St Andrews soon after their son's supposed death, which suggested a date it would be possible to work back from. It wasn't easy to check, because you don't arrive in a place one day and set up a jute business the next. But my efforts have been rewarded, and I can now reveal to you that Mr Maximilian McKenzie Smith was born in January 1867. Which makes him thirty-three years old at the present time.'

Frowning slightly, he saw that the date meant something to her and that it was not something pleasant.

Her eyes came back into cold, grey focus. 'Yes,' she said, as if she were confirming her own thoughts. 'It means that he must have been conceived in April '66. And *that* means that Joss Smith made a harlot of my brother's wife. She must have been carrying the child for something like three months when Simon killed himself.'

It was a moment before Francis succeeded in taking it in. Mystified, he repeated, 'Killed himself? But I thought he was drowned in a sailing accident.'

'Suicide is not something one advertises.'

Abigail's twin, Simon, had died years before Francis was born, but he couldn't prevent a frisson at the thought of a despair so deep that it could lead a man to take his own life, a man only a year or two older than Francis himself was now. 'But why? Why should he have killed himself? Did he have some incurable illness?' It was a common, understandable reason for suicide.

Abigail's lips tightened. 'Yes. Hopelessness. Thanks to Josiah Smith, Lindsay Mills was on the verge of collapse and Simon was unable to face it. Or so I have always tried to believe. But now I wonder whether that was the only reason.'

His thoughts still lagging behind, Francis went off at a tangent. 'No, it won't do. There must be something wrong, somewhere. I wasn't aware that Joss had anything to do with the crisis at Lindsay Mills, but the idea of Grace Smith as a woman who would betray her husband with the man who had ruined him is simply not tenable. She's . . .'

Abigail snapped, 'Fiddle-de-dee! You have no need to tell me what she is, or is not. We were sisters-in-law, after all, though I was some years older than she was. She had a good heart, I'm prepared to admit, but not an atom of backbone. In all likelihood, she gave in to Josiah because she hadn't the strength of mind to withstand him. He, of course, was completely ruthless about getting what he wanted.'

'I wouldn't have thought he wanted an illegitimate son,' Francis said. It was a passing remark, lightly spoken, but it brought a disturbing response.

'No,' his mother said. 'That is what concerns me. It must have been very convenient for him that Grace should have become free to remarry between the time of the child's conception and its birth. In such a case, the question of illegitimacy would not arise. I have no idea, of course, of the actual date of their marriage. I was so ill that summer that it was months before anyone saw fit to tell me that Grace had retired with little Selina to Dunaird after the news came of Simon's death.'

'Dunaird? Selina?'

'Grace's family home in Wester Ross. Selina was her daughter and Simon's. My niece and your cousin.'

She held out her glass to be replenished, the only indication of the turmoil behind the imperious façade.

'No,' Francis said again, sitting down and running harassed fingers through his hair. 'What you are saying is that Joss deliberately allowed Simon to find out about the liaison, perhaps even about the child? And that it was the last straw? It's as good as saying that Joss murdered him. It won't do. Apart from anything else, he couldn't have relied on it having the desired effect.'

'It would be a gamble, with no real risk to Josiah. The only loser would be Simon.' Suddenly, Abigail sounded exhausted. 'Francis, I have to know.'

He moved to the sofa and sat beside her, the remnants of his once ordered papers fluttering to the floor. Then, for the first time in his memory, he took her hand comfortingly in his. 'Why? Why pursue an old tragedy? It was all so long ago. Can't you let it rest?'

Sighing, she said, 'An old tragedy to you, perhaps. But long months of heartbreak for me, more and deeper heartbreak than you can imagine. If I knew the full truth, perhaps I might be able embark, even now, on the process of forgetting. Try what you can find out for me, Francis. There is no one else to do it.'

As he helped his mother to her feet, he was reminded, and not only by the uncharacteristic weariness of her tone, that she was sixty-five years old and life had not been gentle with her.

So he said, 'I'll try, but I promise nothing. Will you see Lucia before you go?'

Abigail hesitated. 'I had intended to, but the time has disappeared too quickly. I have to preside over a meeting of the women's suffrage association in half an hour. So, not tonight. Next week, perhaps. Give her my love.'

9

Short of employing Pinkerton's to go off to Nantucket Sound and investigate the circumstances surrounding a thirty-four-year-old 'accident' at sea – and Francis didn't think either they or his bank balance would take kindly to the notion – no means occurred to him of finding out if Simon had known of his wife's infidelity before he killed himself.

Sherlock Holmes, he reflected, would glance through some dusty old family papers, question a few ancient retainers, resort briefly to his pipe or violin, and hey presto! But Francis had no such resources. There was only Grace Smith. And even if she were as foolish as Abigail maintained, he didn't think she would be foolish enough to tell him the answer to his question, unless by mistake.

In any case, the only route to Grace Smith was through her daughter. He found the thought dis-tasteful.

He would have to consider the situation carefully and decide his priorities. In the meantime, nothing would be lost if he continued with the plan he already had in mind. There were rumours that Max intended to take McKenzie Smith Flooring to the market in the near future, and Max's reputation was now such that the flotation was assured of success. The time, Francis thought, was right for an extended profile in the *Enterprise*. A human profile, because Francis had set his sights on a new kind of readership; intelligent, ordinary people who seldom read newspapers because they found them too polemical. Such people wanted some-thing fresh and new, and Francis was going to provide it.

It meant that, in the case of the McKenzie Smith profile, he would have to head for the Highlands and find a few witnesses to tell him about Max's early life. Neighbours, school friends, teachers, ministers of the kirk . . .

Duty coincided with desire. He owed himself a holiday before the relaunch and he couldn't remember a time when the Highlands hadn't cast their spell over him.

His father, that quiet, lovable man, had always said that late May and early September (before the equinoctial gales) were the best times, not only because the weather was more likely to be fresh and sunny than at any other time of year but because those two months effectively bracketed the midge season, making it possible to walk the hills and fish the lochs without being eaten alive.

As soon as his sons were old enough, John Rivers had begun taking them to Wester Ross for an annual week of glorious freedom, though only Francis had really enjoyed it, David – a year younger – being a natural worrier with no talent for freedom, and Jonny – two years younger again – a natural dreamer who had to be prodded into doing anything at all. Which was, no doubt, why the army suited him so well.

It had been Francis alone, therefore, who at fourteen had accompanied his father on a more protracted retracing of Boswell and Johnson's tour of the Western Isles. They hadn't completed the course, or expected to, because a professor's time was limited even in vacation, though it had been one of Professor Rivers's standing jokes that the 'leisured class' so beloved of politicians and journalists consisted, in bustling Glasgow, of precisely thirty-one members – the professors at the university.

During those weeks Francis had come to know his father better than ever before and had also found his own vocation. Sufficiently John Rivers's son to have developed an early love of literature, he had still felt no inclination towards the academic life. But listening to his father's leisured meditations during those few weeks had led him to think about the *uses* of literacy, to become fascinated by the challenge of communicating with the millions of people to whom parliament, his father said, would soon be forced to grant free elementary education.

It hadn't taken Francis long, after the experience of Cambridge and a couple of years of the *Textile Trades Journal*, to recognise that he didn't, after all, have the common touch, wasn't cut out to communicate with those whose education didn't go beyond the elementary; but by then he had been hooked.

There were few things, now, that gave him more pleasure than translating impenetrable parliamentary jargon into something literate and lucid, something that encouraged understanding instead of obscuring it. The languages of politics, business, science and medicine, he believed, were specifically designed to ensure that ordinary people never discovered what their betters were getting up to.

The weekly *Enterprise* had been a testing ground. The daily would be the challenge, and Francis was filled with excitement at the prospect. If it was successful . . . Firmly, he suppressed the other plans, the other hopes that crowded into his mind.

One thing at a time. In September, he would snatch a few days in the Highlands.

10

Tassie had spent four restless weeks with her mother at Dunaird Lodge before Grace, shaking her head in amused resignation, said, 'You're as bad as Max. My dear, I know you are anxious to get on with your life. If you want to go, I shall understand.'

'Oh, mother, would you mind? It's just that I have this painting to finish for the school exhibition, and I'm working on something that might – just might! – be good enough to enter for Munich next year. If only I could have a week or two's peace and quiet in the studio, before classes begin again . . .'

And so she had gone.

It was a lovely, fresh, breezy blue day when Grace decided to ride over to the coast, and as she rode she found herself marvelling at how strange her children were to her. Not Selina, who despite her sometimes abrasive self-confidence was by nature conventional, a round peg in the very particular round hole of St Andrews' society. Her father, Simon, had been like that, though without the self-confidence. All the confidence in Simon Lindsay's family had gone to his twin sister, Abigail. Remembering what an alarming young woman Abigail Graham had been, Grace wondered briefly what had become of her.

But Max and Tassie both had a vigour and a spirit of enterprise that came from Joss. Grace could see a little of herself in Tassie sometimes, but nothing at all in Max, who was as hard and dedicated as Joss had ever been. More so, perhaps, because his ambitions were higher and, to help him realise them, he had a personal charm that Joss had never possessed, a charm that he used both as weapon and defence. Grace knew that she herself had not penetrated his armour by so much as a fraction of an inch.

There was another difference between Joss and Max. Joss had always thought of the business he had set up and nurtured as something complete in itself, but Max had more than once referred to it, casually, as only a stepping stone. To what, Grace had no idea. She worried occasionally over his meteoric rise in the world of business, although she told herself it was only because she was old-fashioned. Even in St Andrews, one could not help but be aware that in the last few years the world had begun to change, as if, although the queen herself lingered on, the Diamond Jubilee of 1897 had marked the end of the Victorian era. Perhaps, now, it was a time for meteors.

It was reassuring that Tassie at least kept her feet on the ground even if her head was, privately, in the clouds.

Grace was still smiling to herself, as she so often did when she thought of her pretty, vivid, unaffected daughter, when the pony rounded a curve of the beach and she saw that there was someone sitting on the big, lichened rock, gazing out to sea.

It was no one she knew; certainly no one local. At this

time of year everyone was too busy reaping barley, and gathering bracken, and carting peats.

He leaped to his feet as she approached, clearly a gentleman despite his careless attire, and clearly embarrassed. In the last thirty years or so, tourists had begun to venture to the Highlands in increasing numbers, but Dunaird was so far off the beaten track that it had remained virtually untouched.

It was only as she bade the gentleman a slightly puzzled, 'Good day', that Grace realised she did know him, after all.

But even as she said hesitantly, 'Mr Rivers, is it?' she found herself frowning, remembering how at their previous meeting she had been fleetingly reminded of Selina's father. And now, again, she was reminded, perhaps because she had been thinking of Simon a few moments before. Simon – whom she had loved, romantically and sentimentally, when she had been of an age for romance and sentiment.

Her brow clearing, she said, 'I apologise for staring, Mr Rivers. For a moment, you reminded me of someone. But what a coincidence!'

'It is I who should apologise. I must be . . . Am I . . . I think I am trespassing. But everything is so beautiful, I was unable to resist.'

Apparently, he knew that Dunaird was hers, which surprised her. Tranquilly, she said, 'The foreshore belongs not to me but to the Crown, so I can hardly send you packing.'

And then she remembered that Tassie had met him once or twice in Glasgow, which might explain it. 'Did my daughter talk to you about Dunaird?'

After a moment, he nodded, and she went on, 'Then no doubt you know that she is fond of it, though in only small doses. As a matter of fact, she has just abandoned me to return to art school and her painting.'

The young man had still not wholly regained his

composure and, if the truth were told, Grace was curious. 'My daughter maintains that nothing ever happens in the Highlands, which is perfectly true and leads me to suppose that you cannot be here in your capacity as a journalist. Do you have family associations in the area, or are you on holiday?'

II

It was a new experience for Francis to wish he had never been born.

'I've been on a walking tour down the coast,' he said, knowing how bald it sounded but not daring to amplify. He could hardly say that he had spent several hardworking days in Ullapool, or that Dunaird House was his last port of call in an odyssey that had been nothing but frustration from start to finish.

He had gone to the little fishing port looking first for Max's foster mother, on the off chance that she might still be alive; her actual death had been only a presumption on the basis of Max's story. He hadn't found her alive, which was reasonable enough, but neither had he found any trace of a death certificate, or of anyone who had known her. And that wasn't reasonable. Argyll Street, Pultney Street, Market Street, Custom House Street – conscientiously he had quartered the little town with its decaying huts and houses and its overpowering smell of herring, asking, asking, asking. He had been offered three Jeannie McKenzies, but all of too recent a vintage.

The only alternative line of approach had been through Robbie, Jeannie's drowned son. But Francis had drawn blank there, too. In neither town nor kirk records was there any trace of Robbie – birth, baptism, short life or tragic death. The minister of the 1860s was long gone, and the other people Francis questioned about a small child's drowning more than thirty years before had replied only with soft, apologetic negatives.

Parish records in isolated areas were seldom reliable, but to find nothing at all . . . He had begun to feel as if he were chasing creatures of the mist.

It was possible that something had escaped him, of course. The parish clerk of the time had had a remarkably illegible hand, and everyone in the district seemed to be called McKenzie, a goodly proportion of them Robert or Jean. But Francis had been as thorough as he knew how.

The local gossip of Dunaird had been his last hope, until he discovered that there was nothing there but a house, and that house a ruin, long abandoned. But it was a beautiful day and a beautiful place, and he had settled himself in the sun to review the results of his investigation. That they had been entirely negative told its own tale.

Someone had been lying, and that someone had been Max McKenzie Smith.

He had just reached this unamused, though not altogether unexpected conclusion when Grace Smith had ridden into view.

Seeing her again, he was confirmed in his impression of gentleness and probity – which was a queer word to spring to mind, but a precise one. He couldn't imagine her lying and yet, when Max had told his less than truthful story half a dozen years before, she had concurred in it by her very silence.

Was it possible that she hadn't known he was lying?

Highland hospitality had its laws. Mistress Smith, after a momentary hesitation, said, 'When we are at Dunaird, we stay at the Lodge. I am afraid it is six miles away, but we could offer you refreshment if . . .'

Grateful that it wasn't just around the corner, Francis said, 'Unfortunately, this is my last day and I ought to be setting off back to Gairloch to collect my belongings. It has been a great pleasure to meet you again, even so briefly.'

'You must be very full of energy, to walk so far twice in a morning!'

He smiled. 'Sometimes I cheat. My pony is tethered behind that outcrop of rock over there.'

He should have said, 'Please give my compliments to your son.' Instead, he tried and failed to think of some way of saying, 'Please don't tell your son I was here.'

Even people who were irreproachably honest tended to dislike journalists rummaging around in the debris of their past.

12

'As I walk along the Bois Boolong, with an independent air, You can hear the girls declare – "He must be a millionaire" . . . .' warbled the phonograph.

Max, as usual, joined in. ' "You-ou-ou can hear them sigh and wish to die, You can see them wink the other eye, At the – *man* who – broke the – *bank* at Monte Ca-a-a-arlo".'

Crossing the room, he began fiddling with the winding mechanism and Tassie wailed, 'Oh, Max, don't put it on *again*! Anyway, I never heard anything so ridiculous as having a phonograph in an office. Sir Leoday will be here soon and it will give him a very peculiar idea of you.'

'Well, we can't have that, can we?' Abandoning the phonograph, Max took his sister round the waist and whirled her from one end of the office to the other. 'Not when we're going to market.'

He was brimming with high spirits and Tassie, who had no idea what was afoot, couldn't resist laughing back at him. 'Are we? To spend lots of lovely money?'

'To *make* it, sister dear. Ah, I can hear our visitor arriving. Now, remember, young Ginger, just keep quiet and don't ask silly questions. Good God, it sounds as if he's brought the family with him! Oh, well, I've told mother to butter old Pelham up, and you'll just have to do the same for Freddy.'

'Oh, will I? And who,' she enquired provocatively, 'do you want Selina to be charming to?'

Max, treating her to a mock snarl, turned to greet the newcomers who, followed by Bruce Goudy and John Bell, were being ushered in by his secretary.

They all sat formally round the table, Max at its head and Grace, Tassie and Selina, the minor shareholders – the *very* minor shareholders – at its foot. On Max's left was Bruce Goudy, solid and serious, with greying brown hair and a heavy moustache; he didn't look at all the kind of gentleman, Tassie thought, to have fathered a brood of children numbering twelve at the last count. On his left was John Bell, unnaturally sober and sedate; no one could have guessed that his mouth, when he grinned, was as wide as the span of his eyes. Tassie twinkled at him, but he didn't respond, perhaps because on his other side was Mr Algernon Vale, Max's finger-waved 'financial adviser', who didn't appeal to Tassie any more now than he had done on her seventeenth birthday at the Carlton.

At least they were spared Mrs Merton.

Freddy Pelham sat on the opposite side of the table with his father and sister, having announced cheerfully, 'Not invited, but thought you wouldn't mind Genny and me coming along to keep the pater up to scratch. He's wavering a bit.'

Surreptitiously watching Genevieve, Tassie found it hard to believe that she would be of much help in keeping her father up to scratch, since she appeared to be so shy as to be incapable of meeting anyone's eyes without blushing and dropping her own, which were of a pure, baby blue. She had a fair, pink-cheeked prettiness and her innocent lips seemed always to be slightly open, revealing a hint of pearly white teeth. Tassie guessed her to be not more than seventeen, though it was hard to tell in view of the massed hair, the huge hat with its flowers and aigrettes, and the too fashionable afternoon dress, all pink silk and cream lace.

No question but that Sir Leoday was a widower. No mother would have allowed a seventeen-year-old daughter out in such an extravagant rig. Which was, moreover, completely unsuitable for a visit to a jute factory.

Genevieve couldn't have known, of course, that the route to Max's office was by way of the factory floor. Tassie's father had designed it that way so that he himself was always a presence to the hands, someone who came and went, frequently and not always predictably. Tassie supposed it must have worked the other way, too, reminding him that, whatever the issues under consideration in the rarefied atmosphere of his office, everything still depended on his workers.

Workers like Aggie, Doris and Queenie, whom Tassie had come to know a little. They earned ten shillings a week, and Genevieve had just walked through the weaving shed with the equivalent of three months of their combined wages on her back.

13

Sighing, Tassie turned her attention to Max's exposition of his plans for the company. It was time, he said, for expansion, and if the firm were to take full advantage of its opportunities – which were great – it needed a substantial injection of capital.

Tassie understood that. Times without number, she had heard Max say how necessary it was to spend in order to earn.

When Max began talking figures, she wasn't quite so sure of her ground. 'I propose, therefore, to turn the existing firm of McKenzie Smith into a holding company, which will take over a quarter of the stock of

McKenzie Flooring. McKenzie Flooring will be floated with an ordinary share capital of £1,000,000 and a 4% preference share capital of £335,000. Since I am advised that the offer cannot be anything but a success, I have concluded, after discussions with bankers and brokers, that the most satisfactory – that is to say, profitable – method will be to make an issue by tender. The offer will be of 800,000 ten-shilling shares at a minimum of twenty-five shillings per share. Are there any questions?'

No one said a word. The financial experts had already had their say and the non-experts preferred not to display their ignorance.

All except Tassie. She said, 'A *minimum* of twenty-five shillings? Does that mean people might pay more?'

'It does.'

'A lot more?'

'Possibly.'

'And that would give us even more capital?'

'Yes.'

'But what happens about our existing shares? There are thirty-four in all and mother and Selina and I each have one of them. If the company is floated, does that mean we have none, or more, or what?'

With an irritation that only Tassie recognised, Max said, 'Some other time, Tassie. It's not relevant at the moment and, besides, this is hardly the occasion for an explanation of how the stock market works. Now, to proceed . . .'

She had learned not to argue when Max said, 'No,' but it was frustrating because she was virtually sure that everyone present, with the exception of the three accountants, would have been very grateful indeed to have had the stock market explained to them. Though not, perhaps, Genevieve, who struck Tassie as a fledgling manhunter whose technique would consist largely of winsome little smiles from under her lashes

153

and frequent, admiring exclamations of, 'You are so clever, and I'm so dreadfully stupid!'

Max was saying, 'To help make a company's prospectus attractive to shareholders, it is customary to name the persons who have agreed to sit on the board, and the more distinguished such persons are, the better. That is why Sir Leoday Pelham is here today. I hope he will be persuaded to do us the honour of joining us. No one could lend the company greater distinction.'

Sir Leoday didn't look in the least distinguished. In fact, he looked very much as his son Freddy would look thirty years on – stout, unhealthily pallid, rather poached around the eyes, a man of no great intellect but a good deal of kindliness.

He turned red and said, 'Harrumph. Er . . .'

Appointing himself interpreter, Freddy explained, 'He's flattered but not sure it's quite the thing to do. I've told him it's all right. Plenty of peers doing it these days. The fees aren't to be sneezed at, and you wouldn't expect him to *do* anything, would you?'

'No, certainly not. Though I would have to ask him to attend board meetings once in a while.'

'You could manage that, couldn't you, pater?'

'Spose so. Wouldn't like to be the only fellow who's doing this kind of thing, though.'

'I've told you. It's all right. Max, give him a few names!'

Max smiled. 'I suppose the most distinguished that springs to mind is the Marquess of Dufferin and Ava. He's on the board of Whitaker Wright's London and Globe Corporation. Then there's . . .'

'Dufferin and Ava?' said Sir Leoday. 'The fellow who was governor-general of Canada?'

'That's the one.'

'And viceroy of India?'

'Yes.'

'Annexed Burma, or some such thing?'

154

'Yes.'

'Oh, well!' Sir Leoday pursed his lips thoughtfully. 'Oh, well, if it's good enough for him, it's good enough for me. And – ummm – director's fees, you said?'

'I'm sure we can agree a satisfactory emolument.'

14

After they had gone, Tassie said, 'Max, are you serious about this? Having Sir Leoday on the board, I mean? He's a dear old boy, but he doesn't know anything, does he? He won't even understand what you're talking about at board meetings.'

'So much the better,' said Max, blowing a satisfied smoke ring. 'Titles cut a lot of ice in this world, and if you have to have amateurs in business, it's best to have stupid ones who do what they're told. I don't want anyone interfering with the way I run my companies.'

After a moment, he went on meditatively, 'Sweet little thing, that girl of his, though. Don't you think?'

Speechlessly, Tassie stared at him. There were a number of things she could have said, none of them tactful. Especially the bit about Mrs Merton mincing Genevieve up and having her on toast for supper.

CHAPTER TWO

I

'Hengler's circus?' Mr Rivers suggested. 'Or there's a dance at the University Union.'

Tassie looked downcast. 'You mean *not* tea at Miss Cranston's?' And then, 'Will they be doing the Cakewalk?'

'Indubitably. And it's Herr Wilhelm Iff and his band,' Mr Rivers added temptingly. 'Nothing but the best.'

'Will they let us in? You're not a Glasgow graduate, are you?'

'No, but my father was professor here and we have an arrangement.'

She hesitated. The circus would be safer. Mr Rivers could scarcely pump her about Max against the competition of clowns and jugglers and Indians scooshing around in canoes, whereas at a dance there were a lot of pauses, a lot of sitting out. Though there would be compensations . . .

For months she had been dying to feel his arms around her.

Inspired, she suggested, 'Can Norah and Hugo come, too? You haven't met Hugo. He's Norah's brother and he's training to be a barrister. He's only here for a few days and we're at our wits' end because he's staying with us and expects to be kept entertained. He's that kind of person.'

'He sounds the ideal companion,' Mr Rivers

said amiably. 'Perhaps we should go to the circus after all.'

'No. Anyway, foursomes at a dance are more fun than twosomes.'

'Thank you. That puts me in my place, doesn't it? But all right, if you insist.'

'A lady,' she pointed out, 'shouldn't have to insist.'

He laughed, something he rarely did, and Tassie's heart performed a dizzying pirouette. In the years since their very first meeting, during which her looks had improved and her acquaintance widened, she had become sensitive to men's reactions to her and had been finding it extraordinarily frustrating that the only man who really interested her should be as pleasant to her, and as personally remote from her, as if she were still an overweight thirteen-year-old.

She wanted to go to the dance, but didn't dare without Norah and Hugo. Going unchaperoned to such an affair with *any* gentleman would give Max a perfectly legitimate reason for complaint. Going with Francis Rivers . . . Even without knowing about Mr Rivers's visit to Dunaird – her mother and she having tacitly agreed that there was no need to mention it – Max had been furious to discover that Tassie had been seeing something of Mr Rivers and had tried to forbid her to see him again.

There was nothing unusual about Max trying to dictate to her because, like most men, he subscribed to the belief that – simply because he was a man – he was a superior being, which meant his word was law. But while she was prepared to submit to Max in a good many things, Tassie had no hesitation about digging in her heels where Francis Rivers was concerned. She would choose her own friends, she told Max firmly, and if he were worried about Mr Rivers's occupation, she was perfectly capable of conducting a conversation with that gentleman without letting any cats out of the bag.

She hadn't mentioned that, once or twice, it had been a close call.

2

Francis was not, in general, a traditionalist, but although he appreciated that 'Rational' dress was convenient to the wearer and even approved it as a statement of female independence, it offended against his sense of what was beautiful.

On the evening of the dance, therefore, he was pleased to see that, although Norah St John was clad in what appeared to be a sack tied round the middle, Tassie had let the side down badly by turning out in a silvery grey tulip skirt which admirably outlined her slim waist and shapely hips. With it there was a matching short-sleeved jacket over a blouse of lettuce green chiffon, whose long full sleeves belled out gracefully from elbow to wrist and whose colour subtly enhanced her eyes.

She looked delectable, and he said so.

Hugo appeared to be of the same opinion.

Hugo also appeared to be under the misapprehension that he and Tassie made a pair. Proprietorially, he helped her on with her coat. Proprietorially, he took her by the elbow and guided her downstairs to the street. Proprietorially, he enquired whether she was warm enough, since there was a nasty, damp wind.

'It's not far,' she said. 'Please don't fuss. I'm fine, Hugo, really I am.'

It didn't stop him from hanging protectively over her.

Norah, walking behind with Francis, muttered sepulchrally, 'He's smitten.'

'So I see. Does it always take him this way?'

'I don't know and I don't care,' said the young man's sister frankly. 'I don't see much of him, thank the Lord. What worries me is, if it lasts, he's likely to be up and down between London and Glasgow like a yo-yo – every time he has a night off from dining in chambers, I suppose. And he's a pest to have around the house.'

He was a pest to have at the dance, too. Glasgow undergraduates were a relaxed and democratic breed, and Hugo St John didn't fit at all. He knew it, though he did his best to convey that it wasn't him but the others who were out of step.

A tall, slender young man who carried himself so erectly that it appeared as if his spine must run straight up into his skull, he had large and unblinking brown eyes, hair much darker than his sister's, but an accent that was equally cut-glass. Unfortunately, he spoke rather too fast and gobbled his words, which made him difficult to follow, and when he laughed his voice descended the better part of an octave.

Briefly intrigued, Francis realised that never before had he encountered anyone whose laugh sounded as if it had been lifted directly off the printed page. Which Hugo's did. It was a quite unequivocal 'Ha, ha, ha!' and Francis, remembering a dog of his acquaintance who gave the impression of barking because that was what dogs were supposed to do, found himself wondering whether Hugo had read in a book that 'Ha, ha, ha!' was the way people were supposed to laugh.

Hugo was undoubtedly the kind of person who would always do what he saw as the correct thing, which included maintaining his own high standards however low the company in which he found himself. Maliciously making his own small contribution to the lowness of the company in the Union, Francis eased the collar of his shirt, ran his fingers through his hair, lounged to his feet and opened his mouth to ask Tassie to dance.

Hugo was before him, bowing ceremoniously over her hand and formally requesting the pleasure.

Francis had to ask Norah instead, which was something of a penance since she had little sense of rhythm and, in any case, was less interested in dancing than in bringing Francis up to date on the progress of the suffrage movement. He was still in thrall to what Mrs Fawcett had said in London last week when the next dance came and he had to watch Tassie being whisked away by an enterprising stranger. Then, returning from a foray in search of tea for Norah, he discovered that Hugo had forestalled him again. After that, Tassie said she would love a cup of tea, too.

When Francis returned, she was saying, 'I don't think I ever told you, Norah, but that detestable friend of Max's, Mrs Merton, once said to me, why should a clever woman struggle for the vote, when all it offers is the privilege of being reduced to a single voice among millions?'

'Millions of *women*, though!'

'Yes, that's what I said, too, and she just laughed and told me to put my money on feminine wiles.'

'What nonsense! I mean, there's the principle involved . . .'

Enough was enough. Rising to his feet again, Francis said autocratically, 'Drink up your tea, Miss Smith. This is my dance, and so is the next one, and the one after that.'

3

It was an Eduard Strauss waltz, played in slow and sentimental time, which encouraged some joker to slip round the room turning the lights down low. 'Dae a proper job and pit them oot, Jimmy,' pleaded a hopeful voice from somewhere at the back.

'Goodness,' said Miss Smith weakly.

Francis smiled. It was the first word she had uttered since they stood up together and was to be the last for some time. She was very light on her feet and a pleasure to dance with, but Francis sensed that she was feeling shy, and she kept her eyes fixed on his tie throughout. With a mental shrug, he settled his arm more comfortably round her waist – a nice waist, as pliable as it was slim – and gave his mind to his leading article for Monday's paper.

Thirteen days earlier, Whitaker Wright's London & Globe Finance Corporation had held its annual general meeting, under the chairmanship of the Marquess of Dufferin and Ava, and had approved its usual prosperous-looking set of accounts. Yesterday, it had rocked the City to its foundations by going into liquidation. Which meant that thousands of small shareholders were going to lose not only an important part of their income but most of their savings as well. There had been no warning, no hint of trouble.

Somebody had been fiddling the books. Francis's leader was going to be on the urgent need for regulatory legislation in the field of company accounting.

Suddenly and with clarity, his partner's voice said, 'You're looking very severe,' and it was borne in on him that her earlier shyness had been superseded by an entirely different emotion. She was young and female and pretty, and he had been ignoring her. She was cross about it.

He thought at first that it was only amusement that tingled through his veins. But then, as with a chuckle he gathered her closer to him and prepared to pay her the attention she required and deserved, he discovered that there was something more to it than amusement. Something that went beyond warmth and a mild liking. Something that involved an entirely unexpected physical attraction.

During this last year, she had got right under his skin, and he had been too preoccupied to notice.

He should have taken her back to their table, should have left Hugo to partner her, should have confined himself for the rest of the evening to polite conversation and not so much as the touch of hand on hand. Flesh on flesh. Should, in future – for his own private and compelling reasons – shun her company like the plague.

Instead, he kept her at the edge of the floor until the next dance began, and once more, when the break came. And a fourth time. And a fifth.

But then the lamps were turned up again, the harsh yellow-green gaslight softened by drifting scarves of cigarette smoke. Herr Iff's eye was on the clock – it was against the local laws for Saturday night festivities to overflow into the Sabbath – when he announced that the next dance, the last but one, would by popular request be the Cakewalk.

To prance, high-stepping and semi-detached, round the floor was quite out of tune with Francis's mood and, he supposed, with his partner's.

Breaking their long, aware silence, he asked in an impersonal tone, 'Are you going home to St Andrews for the New Year?'

'Yes. On Monday.'

He left it to Hugo to dance the last waltz with her.

4

Next day the rain was lashing down and there were gales shrieking around Hillhead Street. Every now and then came the crash of a chimneypot landing on the pavement and the sharper, shattering sounds of slates flying from the roofs. The windows rattled in their frames and draughts howled under the doors and the fires roared in the grates and leapt up the flues so that, for safety's sake, it was necessary to smother the flames with pailfuls of coal dust.

Woefully, her fingers numb with cold, Tassie tried to

do her packing, her mind possessed by the notion that there was some symbolism in it all. Warmth inside chilled by the draughts of rejection. The hasty flames banked down by the dross of self-doubt.

She had been sure as they danced – blissfully, ecstatically, frighteningly sure – that Francis Rivers had been as aware of her as she was of him. But then a curtain had come down between them and he had reverted to his everyday self, a pleasant, lightly sardonic near-stranger with a disconcerting quality of remoteness. Never in her life had she been so abruptly dashed from the heights to the depths.

It was just as well. She didn't want to be in love with him, and not only because she was afraid – although she was – but because, however determinedly she might stand up to Max when he tried to dictate to her, it was unthinkable that she should betray him in such a way. Being attracted to Francis Rivers, imagining his touch, had been one thing. Loving him was quite another.

Yet the imp inside her would not be silenced. She couldn't believe that the current which had flowed between them had flowed only in her imagination; she *wouldn't* believe that, for him, it might have been real but brief, no more than a passing attraction.

Inexperienced in love she might be, but a number of impressionable young gentlemen had declared their admiration for her over the course of the last three years and she had observed with interest, her own heart untouched, their erratic progress through the various stages of infatuation. She had thought of it as something rather charming. Like the gleam on a sea-washed pebble, it came with the tide and went with the wind, transient by its very nature and without depth.

All her instincts told her that the attraction that had flared between herself and Francis Rivers wasn't like that. But her brain said – you can't know. You haven't any idea what goes on inside that handsome, aloof head of his. You know almost nothing about him. Forget him. Or if you can't, wait and see what happens.

Wait and see. The most dismal and defeatist of all supposedly good advice. She didn't know whether she could manage that, either.

5

It said in the *Enterprise* next morning that the whole country had been swept by gales and flooding, and that at least fifty people had died.

Tassie's journey to St Andrews took three times as long as it should have done because of rubble on the roads and fallen trees on the railway line. She later discovered that her mother, who never used the telephone herself – not only because she considered it beyond her competence but because she suspected it of being dangerous as well – had prevailed upon Max to telephone Hillhead Street and advise Tassie not to try and make the journey. Unfortunately, the storm had added so much to the normal crackle of static on the line that, despite Max's considerable lung power, Tassie had been unable to make out even who was speaking, far less what he was saying.

It was eleven o'clock at night when she finally arrived, cold and tired, but in better spirits than when she had set out, because she was there to see the New Year in with her mother and Max. It was the first time since 1896 that Max had spent New Year at Graceholm.

Being Max, he had, of course, provided champagne for the occasion, and in quantity. Nothing offended him more than stinginess.

'A jeroboam,' he announced, displaying it for their inspection. 'Holds the equivalent of four bottles. One bottle each for the three of us and one for the servants.'

Grace exclaimed, 'Max!' but Tassie said with weary cheerfulness, 'It's all right, mother. If we don't drink it all, we can bath in it. Wasn't there some lady in Paris who used to do that to entertain her gentleman friends? She had a bathtub on the dining table and . . .'

'You mean Cora Pearl,' Max said sternly. 'She was no lady and I'm shocked that you know about her.'

'Oh, we artists know about all sorts of things.'

There was more reason for champagne than the New Year. The flotation of McKenzie Flooring had been a rousing success and bidding for the shares had been frantic. They had gone to double the offered minimum.

'But that's not all,' Max said.

He was so pleased with himself that he was almost sending off sparks, and Tassie, laughing, responded as she knew he intended. 'Tell us!'

'In a minute.'

Then all the bells rang out, and he flung one arm round Tassie's shoulders and one round their mother's. 'Do you remember what I said that evening when we had our first anniversary party?'

Some day, soon, the newspapers are going to be calling me 'the millionaire raised in a Black House in the Highlands.'

Tassie gasped, 'You don't mean it!'

'I do. This new year of 1901 dawns not on Max McKenzie Smith, proprietary partner of a Dundee jute company, but on Max McKenzie Smith, millionaire! I said then and I'll say it again now, there's *nothing* I can't do!'

6

A few neighbours, first-footing, dropped in for whisky and black bun. Even Selina and Dudley subdued their dislike of Max sufficiently to drive down from Seamount with Monty and Basil, now eighteen and sixteen respectively and working hard at being languid and grown up. Monty was better at it than Basil, having been an affected brat since the day he was born. When

Dudley said, 'By the by, Max, about those Japanese cotton shares you advised me to buy after the Galveston hurricane last September . . .' Monty intervened with, 'Really, papa! I'm sure Max doesn't want to be bothered with your beastly little investments on an occasion like this.' He wasn't so much patronising his father, Tassie thought, as trying to ingratiate himself with Max.

Dudley huffed and puffed a bit, but Max looked at the boy consideringly and said after a moment, 'There is no such thing as a "beastly" little investment if you happen to be the company that's being invested in. The first rule of business is, never turn down money when it's offered.'

'Is that how you became a millionaire?'

'Partly. The other part was pure genius.' It was said with Max's most disarming smile, and everyone smiled back at him except Selina, who gave an audible sniff.

Tassie, more than half asleep and having lunched, dined and supped on nothing more than a slice of black bun and rather too much champagne, felt as if she were floating, disembodied, somewhere up towards the ceiling, observing the scene with unnatural clarity but in no way involved. Dreamily, she perceived that, although Max was passing his mention of genius off as a joke, it wasn't a joke at all. How queer, she thought.

The next thing she knew was that everyone was leaving and her mother was shaking her reproachfully and saying, 'Darling, how *could* you fall asleep like that!'

7

'A breath of air, that's what we need!' Max declared with revolting vigour the following afternoon. 'Blow the cobwebs away.'

Tassie, resisting the temptation to clutch her aching brow, murmured, 'If you absolutely *must* trot out one cliché after another, do you think you could do it more quietly, please?'

It was no use. He was well into the Plain Man incarnation he had been assiduously cultivating over the last year or two. 'What's wrong with a good clitch? Useful things, clitches. They say what they mean and everyone understands them without even having to think. The essence of communication, in fact.'

'Stop it!'

He grinned. 'All right. But come on, let's take a walk along the West Sands. Now that everything has worked out the way I hoped, we have some planning to do.'

'*We?*'

This time, Tassie did clutch her aching brow. In general, the only pronoun given the free run of Max's conversation was 'I'. She said, '*We* have to plan? What are you talking about?'

'Get your coat.'

8

The sky was flat and grey, and the sea the colour of lead with great white horses chasing one another in from the horizon. The tall, spiky marram grasses binding the dunes were whipping in the wind as Max and Tassie fought through to the midpoint of the wide, mile-and-a-half stretch of ochre sands, staggering as the full, gusting power of the wind hit them. Except for one or two hardy souls walking their dogs far away at the town end, the beach was empty even of footprints.

Tassie shrieked, 'I don't know how you think we're going to talk here.'

'Let's go further up towards the estuary, then we'll have the wind at our backs when we turn. It'll make it easier.'

Max detested being cold. He disliked the wind. He never took exercise. Tassie couldn't think why he should have suggested walking the West Sands on a day like this.

By the time they turned, her ears and nose felt as if they were about to drop off, even though she had tied her hat on with a scarf and wound the ends round as much of her face as she wasn't immediately in need of. Pulling a layer down from her mouth for a moment, she screamed, 'What did you want to talk about?'

'Plans!' Max shouted back. 'Business plans. The flotation has given me money for expansion, but I need more than that if I'm going to make a real impact on the market. I want McKenzie Flooring to be the world leader, and that means everything has to be right – price, quality and design.'

'I didn't hear. Price and what?'

'Quality and design.'

She had no premonition of what was coming. 'Why aren't we talking about this at home in comfort, in front of the fire? It's not as if we're a couple of Russian anarchists plotting to blow someone up and not wanting to be overheard!'

He ignored the question. 'So I want you back at the works.'

She frowned in puzzlement. 'But I can't. Not now. I still have at least another two terms at school.'

'Not if I don't pay your fees.' His smile was full of warmth and friendliness, although his nose was red with the cold.

He didn't mean it, of course. After almost three hardworking, enchanted years of learning, of identifying the boundaries of her talent, of beginning to feel independent and looking forward to being in control of her own life. Of falling in love.

'You can't.'

'I can.'

Her brain didn't seem to be working properly. After a moment, she said, 'No! I'll pay my own fees, if I have to.'

'What with?'

Not with her pin money, certainly.

'The flotation . . .' she began, then, since it was apparent that he couldn't hear her, swallowed hard and raised her voice to a shout. 'If *you* made a lot of money from the flotation it must have been through your shares in the original business. So my one poor little share must have made some kind of profit, too.' The question of her – and her mother's and Selina's – shares had been overlooked in all the excitement of Max becoming a millionaire.

He was shaking his head. 'It was McKenzie Flooring that was floated, a company I created. You had no stake in it.'

'But . . .'

'You still have your share in the holding company, but it won't earn much until the flooring subsidiary begins making worthwhile profits.'

She thought she was weeping, but couldn't be sure because of the cold and the wind and the drizzling rain. 'How *could* you? How *could* you!'

'Don't blame me, my pet.' Even at the pitch of his voice he contrived to sound warm, reasonable, sympathetic. 'I simply took my advisers' advice.'

She didn't believe him. Max gave orders; he didn't take advice. And it hadn't been the shares she had been talking about, anyway.

'So you do see,' he went on, 'why it's very much to your advantage to do all you can to make the flooring company a success? The better your linoleum designs, the sooner it will happen. And really, when you come down to it, isn't that what you want – a purpose for your art?'

She flung round at him but, absurdly, answered as if

they were having a rational conversation, as if what he had just said had some relevance to the pain inside her. 'Art! Floor coverings haven't counted as art since Roman times!'

He didn't know what she was talking about. Coaxingly, he went on, 'I want to start advertising, too. So you can draw pictures of interiors for me. The stylish, fashionable kind! I know you can do it.'

She needed to think and she couldn't think with the wind howling, tearing, battering at her. Was this why he had brought her here? Here, where reasoned thought and reasoned argument were impossible. Knowing him, she knew that, having gone through the process of telling her, he would consider everything settled; that she would be at a hopeless disadvantage when she reopened the subject later and more calmly.

If she could ever be calm again. Desperately, she cried, 'I won't leave art school. I won't!'

He put a consoling, brotherly arm round her shoulders and she threw it off violently.

'No, no, and *no*!'

Then she turned and ran, labouring over the wet sand and through the marram grass to where the brougham was waiting.

But when she told Robertson to drive home – this minute! – he said, 'I canny do that, Miss Tassie. It'd be as much as my job's worth. We'll huv to wait for the master.'

9

The master. Whose word was law.

In the night that followed, Tassie went over and over everything in her mind, running the gamut of misery and incomprehension.

Why was he doing it? Hadn't he realised how much it would hurt her? Hadn't he seen how much it mattered?

Surely he should know better than to dismiss the violence of her reaction as no more than a weak-minded feminine tantrum.

She thought back to the idyllic weeks and months after he had first come into her life, when, despite the difference in their ages and worldly knowledge, an instinctive and deeply rewarding companionship had grown up between them. She had worshipped him, and she still did, although her worship now was more adult and perhaps more critical.

Her mind warily circling the events of the past, she found herself thinking that, in a queer way, Francis Rivers had been responsible for the companionship that had grown up between herself and her new brother. In the course of interviewing Max, he had punctured the bubble of his self-assurance and made him aware of his deficiencies, while at the same time – Max being Max – fuelling his overriding determination to succeed. For some reason, the interview had also fuelled Francis Rivers's mystifying – and dangerous – curiosity. Tassie suddenly saw them as a pair of fighting cocks, two unusual, attractive and dynamic men aware of being different from ordinary men, each of them hating the knowledge that the other, too, was different.

For a moment, she allowed reason to give way to emotion. Why was she doomed to love both of them? *Could* she love both of them? It was a question that she couldn't bring herself to confront.

It was a long time, now, since she and Max had gone blackberrying or walked in the ruins. As he had become increasingly successful, he had been away from home more and more, rarely feeling any need to tell his mother or sister where his business trips took him, or why, unless it was somewhere unusual or exciting. A few weeks ago, he had been to Switzerland and then Germany. Tassie remembered how passionately she had envied him his visits abroad in the early years of the business. She still did.

It was inevitable, she supposed, that some of their closeness should have been lost during the years. That was why he didn't fully understand how much her studies mattered to her.

Once before she had fretted wakefully through a night like this. The night of her seventeenth birthday, when he had refused to countenance the idea of her going to art school at all. Later, he had relented, when she proved the strength of her desire, although she still suspected that there had been an element of diamond cut diamond about the whole thing, that he had been paying her back for trying to trap him into revealing that he didn't recognise the music of Mozart when he heard it.

This time there could be no such teasing justification. This time he had nothing to pay her back for.

Except seeing Francis Rivers when he had forbidden it.

No. It had been a childish game, and they had grown out of it long ago.

All she had to do was tell Max how she felt, seriously and sensibly.

10

She tried, next morning, but it mattered so urgently to her that she didn't wait to choose the right moment, launching in when Max was absorbed in the news-paper reports of the Whitaker Wright scandal, which didn't seem to shock him at all. He was even amused by Mr Wright's incompetence, and the fact that Lord Dufferin's reputation seemed likely to be ruined simply because he had been trusting enough to believe in Mr Wright and his balance sheets moved him only to a mild irritation over the prospect of having to talk

Sir Leoday Pelham out of yet another attack of indecisiveness.

He was as resistant to her rational arguments of this morning as to her emotional ones of yesterday. 'My mind is made up,' he said, 'and I don't know why you're making such a fuss about it. I need you at the factory, and I need you now. I only ever promised you one year at art school in the first place.'

'Yes, I know,' she said, 'and I see your point of view. But why won't you see mine? Won't you even try and imagine how you would feel if you were denied any say in your own future?'

'I'm a man. The situation is entirely different. Now, for God's sake, go away and let me get on with my reading.'

Her mother, despairingly resorted to, said, 'My darling, I'm sure Max knows what is best. And you're so clever at your drawing! Will a few more months' lessons make very much difference? I know you want to fly high but – am I being selfish? – it would be lovely to have you at home again.'

Tassie allowed the subject to drop. She couldn't very well explain that she had grown away from the little world of Graceholm; was in danger of growing away even from her mother.

Teeth gritted, she sat herself down with pencil and notebook and began adding up figures.

11

By the second week in January, everyone who was anyone in trade or journalism had heard that 'the Black House millionaire' – or 'Black House Max' as he had been nicknamed by the Grub Street brigade – planned to make McKenzie Flooring a household name all over the world.

Everyone wanted to interview him about his plans, including Francis.

This time, however, there was no question of tea at home with the great Max. This time Max was too busy to give individual interviews. This time he would make himself available for questions from representatives of the major newspapers at his London office in Silver Street on January 18th at 2 pm precisely.

The Glasgow *Enterprise* was not a major newspaper. However, Mr McKenzie Smith's assistant was pleased to inform Mr Rivers that Mr McKenzie Smith had agreed to make an exception in Mr Rivers's case and he would be receiving an invitation in due course.

Mr Rivers, repressing a natural desire to tell the young man what Max could do with his invitation, presented himself at Silver Street on the due date and seated himself in the last of the half dozen rows of chairs that had been set out in the boardroom.

It was an impressive room, handsomely panelled, richly curtained, floored not with linoleum but with a rather nice Axminster, and well furnished with books and portraits. Drily, Francis supposed that new businesses these days must be able to buy portraits by the yard, as they did books. Whose walls, he wondered, had the rakish gentleman in the 1820s cravat once adorned, and whose the High Victorian paterfamilias with the Old Testament beard? Strange that they hadn't yet been joined by an image of Max himself.

On the stroke of two, Max walked into the room and sat down facing his audience. He had brought neither files nor notes with him, which suggested not only complete mastery of his business affairs but an unusual openness and honesty of approach. Most of the journalists present, to whom files and balance sheets meant things for chairmen to shuffle through when they needed time to think, warmed to him immediately.

'An hour should do it, I imagine, gentlemen,' Max said, laying his watch on the table before him.

'Now, who's going to start us off? How about the Thunderer?'

It was a tactful acknowledgement of protocol, although *The Times*, the power of its voice diminishing with its circulation figures, was easily out-shouted nowadays by the brash young *Mail* and the infant *Express*. Its industry correspondent, however, smiled a small, wintry smile and wondered by what precise means McKenzie Flooring proposed to corner the world market.

It was a large question.

'Price, quality and design,' Max replied succinctly, and waited while everyone wrote it down. 'That is to say, my prices will be competitive, my quality the best, and my design right up to the minute. I expect to sell not only in the domestic market, but also to banks, shops, theatres, hospitals, railway companies, passenger liners . . .'

As a statement of intent, it sounded good. Statements of intent usually did. It was putting them into effect that was the problem.

The man from the *Daily Telegraph* chipped in. 'That's fine for the home market, sir, but how do you propose to overcome the problem of French, German and American tariff barriers? Won't they force your export prices up to uncompetitive levels?'

'Good question,' Max said. 'And I have a good answer. I'm going to leap over the barriers.' There was a murmur of interest as he went on. 'I have already bought a small factory in France, near Paris. I'm negotiating for another near Stuttgart in Germany. And I have agents looking for a suitable site in America, about ten acres, probably somewhere in New Jersey.'

This time there was a louder buzz of conversation, because it was an ambitious programme for such a very young company. Only Francis knew enough about the jute industry to ask awkward questions. 'Next door to your major competitors, Nairns, in every case. Any reason for that?'

At his first word he was aware of a change in Max, a vigilance, a controlled resistance. Since he didn't recall ever having criticised Max in print or been other than courteous to him in person, he supposed he had Tassie to thank for that. She must have reported back on his interest. Or perhaps her mother had mentioned his visit to Dunaird.

'Coincidence,' Max said curtly. 'Though of course we have the same needs in the way of labour, water, access to railheads and so on.' And that was that, it seemed. 'Yes, Mr Johnson? You're the *Daily News*, right?'

'Aye. Yer expansion plans'll give plenty of jobs to furriners, but whit are they gaun to dae for the kettle-bilers o' Dundee?'

Max glanced round. 'Everyone know what a kettle-biler is? No? Well, in the jute industry, most of the workers are women and there's high unemployment among the men. They're left at home to boil the kettles for tea. But that's going to change. Because the answer to your question, Mr Johnson, is yes. Linoleum manufacture is men's work, so there will be plenty of jobs for the kettle-bilers, too.'

Francis listened and watched. Max's charm was functioning at full power and everyone was responding to it.

The *Daily Mail* even became waggish. 'Your foreign companies will all have to be separately incorporated, won't they, sir? Which means you're setting up a complex operation. Will you be taking lessons from Whitaker Wright?'

There was a general laugh, and Max said, 'That would be difficult, since he seems to have fled the country. But I've taken careful note of the fact that the Crown isn't prosecuting him because there's no law against publishing a false balance sheet. You can never tell when that kind of knowledge may come in useful!'

This sally was greeted with an appreciative roar and Max had to raise his voice as, grinning broadly, he added, 'Though I can assure you I've no intention of putting it to the test in the case of McKenzie Flooring!'

After that it was all about Max the man, the boy from the Highlands and how he had made good. Max was wonderfully fluent about the Black House and the influence of his foster mother on his early development; about the little town where everyone knew everyone else; about the kindly minister and good neighbours and the tragedy of his foster brother Robbie's death. In his audience, scarcely a wither remained unwrung.

Francis, who no longer believed a word of it, left the meeting with a deep sense of unease. Until now, his interest in Max had been essentially personal, a product of Abigail's obsession with the sins of Josiah and Grace Smith. But no more. Because a man who was so dishonest about himself would have little hesitation about being dishonest on other levels, too, and Max's plans for McKenzie Flooring offered plenty of scope.

For a company to succeed, it needed strong leadership and the ability to grasp opportunities and make strategic decisions. But if it was led by one dominating individual with unfettered powers of decision, an individual prepared to deceive his board, to railroad the company along lines of his own choosing, many people could be damaged in the process.

Francis was going to have to think very carefully about how the *Enterprise* should handle future episodes in the McKenzie Smith saga, because Max was becoming so popular with the press that an open vendetta would serve no good purpose. Rather the opposite.

In the meantime, he found himself devoid of ideas for putting Tassie on her guard.

One could scarcely say to the girl with whom one had

no intention of becoming involved, 'Though I don't have any firm proof of it, my instincts tell me that the brother you worship is a liar and a cheat, a danger to everyone who deals with him. Don't trust him.'

Pure melodrama! Moodily, Francis tried to shrug it off. But he couldn't.

CHAPTER THREE

I

Queen Victoria was dead.

'One can scarcely imagine the world without her,' Grace mused. 'I suppose she must have been on the throne since before most of her subjects were born. She seemed quite old to me even when I was a child, though she can't have been, of course. So she has gone at last. Well, well.'

Max said, 'And high time, too. We'll see some changes now. Perhaps we might even have some fun. There'll be a lot less kowtowing to people who've nothing but ancestors to recommend them. From now on, money and achievement will be the pedigrees that matter.'

Tassie felt a little tickle at the back of her neck. He couldn't possibly, she thought – could he? – have set his sights on a title? It would be just like him, and with his extraordinary talent for success he would probably manage it.

'Well, I wish you'd tell me when the mourning's going to end and the fun begin,' she said crossly. 'I mean, how soon will it be all right to banish loathèd melancholy and welcome in this wonderful new era with quips and cranks and wanton wiles, nods and becks and wreathèd smiles . . . Yes, well, what I'm saying is, how can I do linoleum designs or lay out next month's *Studio* advertisement if I've no idea whether everyone's going to want their floors covered with embossed funeral urns or *trompe l'oeil* five-pound notes?'

Another man might have said, 'Tromp what?' but not Max. 'I'm glad to hear you're giving your mind to the subject.'

'Off and on,' replied his sister frostily.

2

She had been forced to compromise over her rebellion. During two weeks of marching – with determination and steadily decreasing optimism – into every single one of Glasgow's numerous art dealers' shops, she had succeeded in selling only four of her watercolours. Wylie and Lochhead had bought a design for a poker-work candle sconce in unblushing imitation of the Liberty style, complete with Biblical motto – 'Thy light has come' – and thought they might be able to use her on their room displays at the forthcoming International Exhibition. She had also persuaded John Brown's shipyard, who had just laid the hull of a luxury passenger liner, to commission her – when the time came – to design the stained glass windows in the saloon.

And that was all.

Norah had said, 'Portraits? You're awfully good at catching a likeness.'

'Not in oils. And the people who want their portraits painted are mainly stout gentlemen in black broadcloth and gold watch chains. They don't want a likeness; they want to look like pillars of respectability, and who ever heard of a pillar of respectability in watercolour? Anyway, with two hundred portrait painters working in Glasgow already, I don't fancy the competition.'

Meticulously applying clay slip to a large aspidistra pot, Norah had offered, 'If you're worried about the rent – well, I'll be paying the landlord whether you're here or not, so your share isn't a vital factor. I can manage, really I can.'

Tassie hugged her. 'What a good friend you are! But I can't take advantage of you like that.'

So she had reached a reluctant agreement with Max. For her linoleum designing, he was to set up a workroom at the factory, where she would have access to technical advice; he would also convert one of the spare bedrooms at Graceholm into a studio where she could do her advertising layouts in peace and quiet. She was to devote Fridays, Saturdays, Sundays and Mondays to working for McKenzie Flooring. Tuesdays, Wednesdays and Thursdays she could spend at art school, meeting her own fees and living expenses out of her infinitesimal independent earnings and the scarcely less infinitesimal salary Max had finally consented to pay her.

He refused, as a matter of principle, to call it a salary. It was, he pointed out, her family duty to do as he asked, without thought of gain. However, he would increase her allowance.

She didn't know how long she was going to be able to keep it up, working seven days a week and rushing back and forwards from St Andrews to Glasgow to Dundee, but at least it was a start. She closed her mind to the thought that she had committed all her Saturdays for the forseeable future to Dundee and St Andrews.

Saturdays were the only free days Francis Rivers had, and he had them in Glasgow. Not that it mattered. She hadn't heard a word from him since the dance.

3

It was a crisp, sunny Friday in April and Tassie was working on an advertisement for *The Builder* when her concentration was shattered by an alarming scrunching noise in Graceholm's drive, accompanied by an hysterical pop! pop! pop! and a long, nerve-scraping squeal that suggested, at worst, someone in mortal agony, at best, something badly in need of oiling.

Even before she reached the window, she had guessed what it was. And, indeed, there was Max, perched next to a uniformed chauffeur on the front bench of a motorcar, beaming like a child with a new toy.

Max McKenzie Smith, pioneer automobilist.

'An MMC,' he boasted, 'built at Coventry but assembled by John Love at Kirkcaldy. It'll do eight miles an hour.'

'Goodness! Almost as fast as a horse!' Tassie, although she hadn't quite forgiven him, couldn't withstand his brimming good humour. She beamed back. 'Is it comfortable?'

'A damn' sight more comfortable than a horse, anyway!' Max had never learned to ride and it was clear to his sister that, from now on, horses would be consigned in his conversation to the same archaic limbo as Bach and Botticelli, while the motorcar would be up there in front with 'Lily of Laguna' and Draffen and Jarvie's shop in the Nethergate as one of the most influential weapons in the cultural armoury of modern man.

She giggled. 'If you'll forgive me for asking, where were you thinking of going in it? Unless you can drive on water, of course. It'll take five hours to get to Dundee by road compared with half an hour on the train!'

'Yes, I'll have to start stirring Dundee Corporation up about building a road bridge across the Tay. But in the meantime, young Ginger, I am not a fool. Tomorrow morning, I am taking you and mother for a ride with me. A long one. I have something to show you.'

With misgiving, Tassie asked, 'Who's driving?'

4

The chauffeur, Shields, was driving, and what Max had to show them was a huge and palatial mansion in the Border country.

'It's called Kirklaws,' he said.

They were standing on a nearby hilltop looking down on it, Tassie wondering whether Max was hoping to sell the housekeeper some new flooring for the servants' quarters, and Grace thinking that, if her son happened to know the owner, a cup of tea might be a possibility. She felt as if she had swallowed as much dust in the last few hours as in the whole of her previous life. It had really been quite fortunate – although it had annoyed Max – that Shields had found it necessary to stop at frequent intervals to feed the machine with water or petrol, or remove the bonnet and fiddle with wires or blow down something called the carburettor. At least she and Tassie had been able to lift their veils for a moment and breathe something resembling fresh air.

Max went on, 'I've just bought it.'

There was a momentary silence before his mother and sister turned their eyes away from him again, back to the turrets and battlements, the little leaded cupolas, the acres of flower gardens and parkland and trees, the marvellous site overlooking the broad, swift-flowing waters of the Tweed. There were even some fallow deer grazing on the river bank. It might have been lifted straight out of some book of *Picturesque Views of Noblemen's and Gentlemen's Seats*.

Tassie, recovering first, found that there was only one thought in her head. Apart from senior employees like Bruce Goudy and John Bell, no one who slaved at the mills or factory, including herself, earned more than fifteen shillings a week.

Kirklaws must have cost Max tens of thousands of pounds.

'How much?' she asked with hard-held restraint.

She didn't expect a proper answer, and he didn't give her one. 'Don't ask such vulgar questions. Anyway, not as much as you might think. It belonged to a Galashiels woollen manufacturer who used to send seventy-five per cent of his production to America and now, thanks to the McKinley Tariff – not to mention a failure to keep up with modern tastes – sends only five per cent. He can't afford Kirklaws any more.'

'How dreadful,' Grace exclaimed. 'Poor man. Where will he live? What about his family?'

Her son exploded into laughter. 'Mother, you're priceless! I have no idea!'

5

Ten minutes later, as Max ushered them across the threshold into an interior replete with marble pillars and tapestried walls, Queen Anne chairs and Boulle marquetry, Tassie remembered him crossing a very different threshold seven years before, almost to the day.

'From urban villa to stately home in seven years,' she said. 'Where do you plan to move to next? Buckingham Palace?'

He was too pleased with himself to be other than amused. 'A little less sarcasm and a little more sisterly pride wouldn't come amiss. In any case, you don't yet know . . .'

Their mother's gentle voice interrupted him. Doubtfully surveying a Gobelins tapestry populated by leering Cupids, under-dressed nymphs and excitable-looking white stallions, she said, 'But, my dear, you can't mean to live here? Apart from anything else, it's ridiculously large just for one person, and you would need the most enormous staff.'

'True, but you don't know what I'm going to do

with the place, do you? If young Ginger would make up her mind about whether she's going to hurl that piece of crockery at me, we could go through to the breakfast room. I told the caretaker's wife to make us some tea.'

Replacing the Meissen figurine, with care, on its brass-galleried table, Tassie said, 'You haven't bought the contents as well as the house, have you?'

'Of course. Saves time, trouble and expense. Anyway, to have everything shiny new would be like sticking up a noticeboard saying "*nouveau riche*". And there was one thing about the furnishings I couldn't resist.' He grinned. 'You haven't noticed it yet but I'll give you a clue. The place was originally built and furnished in the 1700s. For a lord.'

Frowning, Tassie began looking at the details rather than the whole, but it was several minutes – during which Max stood patiently waiting – before she saw that, unobtrusively worked into lantern brackets, footstools, chairbacks, table inlays and almost every other surface where such a thing might reasonably, or unreasonably, be accommodated, was an armorial crest surmounting a single initial.

The initial – of course – was an 'M'.

'Oh, bad luck,' she said tartly. 'If it had been an "S" for Smith you could have pretended the peerage was yours.'

He moved, then, and, taking her unwilling hands in his, looked down into her eyes with the warm, quizzical smile she so rarely saw nowadays, saying, 'Tassie! Tassie! When are you going to stop being angry with me?'

The years dropped away and she was thirteen years old again, immature, inexperienced, all too anxious to be disarmed by the adored new brother who was so much more worldly-wise than she. The colour rose in her cheeks and she heard herself saying gauchely, 'I'm sorry. I'm not angry. I was being selfish and I've no right to criticise. It was just that . . .'

She had given in and it was enough for Max. His smile broadening, he didn't even wait until she had finished but strolled off to the breakfast room to look out at his trees and green acres, his river and his hills; to revel in his new rôle of country landowner.

Tassie, angrier with herself than with him, followed, and sat down at table, and stared into the cup of tea her mother had poured for her, and said no more.

Grace, after a questioning glance at her daughter, turned and addressed Max's broad and admirably tailored back. 'Well, my dear, tell us about these plans of yours.'

6

'I can see you think I've been extravagant, but there's method in it. Certainly, I intend to live here, and you'll both live here, too, of course. No, don't interrupt, Tassie. You and mother can have the west wing, and I'll have the east. The central block will be partly, though not entirely, McKenzie Smith's new headquarters. I intend to move the senior administrative staff down here – there's plenty of space in the attics for them to sleep – and . . .'

Grace said, 'But, my dear, should you tear them up by the roots like that? Think of their wives and children. Think of poor little Mistress Goudy. She would be quite lost in the country.'

'*Mistress* Goudy? You don't suppose I mean to fill the place with wives and brats? God forbid! If the men want their families with them, they can find somewhere to live in Selkirk or Melrose. Otherwise, they can take the train back to Dundee after work on Saturdays.'

Tassie opened her mouth and, closing it again, told

herself that Max knew how to run a business. She didn't.

'The main thing,' he went on, 'is to have a head-quarters that looks rich and imposing. Money begets money, and looking rich inspires trust. The more money I'm seen to spend, the more successful people will believe I am. There's an extension to that, too. Even though Kirklaws will be the business heart of McKenzie Smith Holdings, it will still be primarily a grand country house in which, with the support of my mother and sister, I intend to do a lot of entertaining. There's a mystique about country houses and, in our new Edwardian world, I'll guarantee that more business will be done at country house weekends than in any office in the land. That's why I've bought Kirklaws, for the sake of the business.'

Tassie could see the force of his reasoning, but she sensed that the reasoning was only the gilt on the gingerbread. Max had bought Kirklaws because he wanted it, because it was the kind of house that said, 'Look at me! I'm rich. I'm successful!' She had never minded him showing off before; he was entitled to. But this was going too far.

'If you'd bought something a little less ostentatious,' she said in a carefully controlled voice, 'you might have been able to pay the hands a living wage.'

Max groaned. 'Not that hoary old chestnut, please! I pay them the standard wages for the industry. You don't seem to realise that, no matter what you pay the lumpenproletariat, they're *never* going to admit that it's a "living" wage. They'll always want more. Besides, the logical conclusion to your argument would be for my headquarters to get smaller, and smaller, and smaller, every time I agreed to give them a raise!'

'You know that's not what I meant. What I meant was that, if the firm can afford Kirklaws, it can afford to . . .'

'I know what you meant. But if I were soft-hearted enough to pay my workers more than the business can afford, the business would be ruined – and where would the workers be then? Why in hell's name are we having this conversation, anyway? I'm not buying Kirklaws with the kind of money you use for wages. It's a matter for financiers and banks and backers. Millionaire I may be, but only on paper.'

'Oh,' said Tassie, deflated. 'Well, why didn't you say so before?' Then, rapidly recovering herself, 'A *paper* millionaire? What a letdown! I've never been so deceived.'

He winked at her. 'Don't waste your time crossing swords with me, young Ginger. You'll never win. Now, come on. Enough's enough. Let's go for a stroll round the grounds.'

7

It was pleasant, although there was a damp chill in the air when the sun began to go down.

After a time, standing on the lawn under a spreading cedar that looked as if it had been planted specifically to cast its shade over a white damasked table laden with silver teapots and bone china cups, cucumber sandwiches, pound cake and cream-filled éclairs, Grace shivered and drew her fur collar more closely round her throat.

She said, 'Max, my dear, though I don't wish to disappoint you, I would prefer not to come and live here.'

'No? Why on earth not?' His brows sat like a thick ebony bar over eyes whose expression, in the fading light, was unreadable. 'If you're afraid of losing touch with your friends in St Andrews, there's no reason why you shouldn't invite them to come and stay now and then.'

'Thank you, my dear, but it isn't that. Being alone doesn't trouble me. But although Kirklaws is beautiful, for me it is too soft. It's not a landscape I could live in, although I will come and visit you, of course. I will soon be in my fifty-seventh year and the truth is that I don't want to leave Graceholm. Or not for anywhere other than the house where I was born. And since that is impossible, I shall stay where I am.'

It was rare for Grace to make a stand and, when she did, she always explained her feelings to others in the way that seemed least likely to hurt or offend. Which meant that the reasons she gave were not necessarily the only reasons. In the present case, she couldn't say that, at Graceholm, even with Max as its master and owner, she was able quietly and unobtrusively to exercise control not only over the house but what happened within its walls, whereas at Kirklaws it would be different. At Kirklaws, Max would be in control. If Grace had been sure of his love, she would not have minded.

Max didn't like being crossed. His face stiffened a little, and for a terrible moment, Tassie thought he was about to tell their mother that she couldn't stay where she was, that Graceholm was his and that he proposed selling it as soon as he found a buyer.

Instead, he shrugged and said, 'As you wish. I shall keep Graceholm, of course, for when I have to visit the works. But you must promise to come here when I need you. You know I always like to have you and Ginger to give me moral support.' Unexpectedly, his brilliant grin flashed out. 'To keep me on the right lines, just as you used to do in the early days.'

Tassie grimaced at him. 'You're impossible!'

But she couldn't help smiling to herself as she remembered the occasions on which she had saved him from some dreadful faux pas by self-sacrificingly making a worse one herself. It hadn't happened very often. He had been quick to learn. Nowadays, he no longer needed a mother and sister to lend him countenance, but it was nice to know that he remembered.

'Dunaird House,' he murmured. 'I wonder . . .' Then, brushing it aside, he went on, 'We're spending the night here, by the way. It's too far to go back. I've ordered supper for seven thirty and told the caretaker to make up rooms for us. One of the maids at Graceholm packed all the things she said you'd need – so don't blame me if she's forgotten something vital.'

Grace said, 'My dear, you think of everything!'

'I try.'

8

Max had always been exciting to live with because, when he was struck by an idea, he didn't give it protracted thought, didn't smother it in ifs and buts, and dismissed all potential problems as soluble provided the idea itself was worthwhile.

So, when he said later that evening, 'I have an idea about Dunaird House,' his mother and sister prepared themselves not for idle speculation but for something feasible, and more than feasible – something real and positive.

Having bathed in monogrammed tubs, changed into dust-free clothes, and supped from monogrammed trays before the monogrammed fireplace in one of Kirklaws' four gilded drawing rooms – not the one with the nymphs and stallions – they were sitting in the candlelight for which the house had been designed and which did much to soften its excesses. Every room was a clutter of furniture and ornaments, and there was scarcely a straight line in sight or a single colour of the rainbow missing from the décor. But it was comfortable beyond measure. Dreamily, Tassie pondered on what Mr Mackintosh would say about it all and decided that she didn't care. Purity of line and space might be dear to the heart of genius but they weren't exactly cosy.

Francis Rivers had said something like that once and she had tried to pretend she didn't agree. She brushed the thought aside.

Grace, stirring her coffee for longer than was strictly necessary, looked up. 'Yes?'

'What would you say to me having it rebuilt for you?'

It was so unexpected that, for a moment, the room became utterly still except for the crackling of the logs and the flutter of a flower petal falling. It was as if the world had stopped breathing.

Grace's lips parted and her eyes glowed green as a mermaid's in the soft, seductive light. 'What do you mean?'

'What I said. It's a ruin. You seem to love it, though God knows why. Do you want me to have it rebuilt for you? Not the whole house, perhaps, because you wouldn't want a great barn of a place, but the tower at least.'

Tassie thought, *Please God, he must mean it. He wouldn't say something like that if he didn't mean it*. But why? Max never did anything without a reason.

And then she knew he must be saying it out of love, because he himself had no interest in Dunaird at all. She looked from Max to her mother – seeing the same discovery in Grace's eye – and thought again, *Please God, let him mean it*.

It was impossible, she knew, for Max to understand Grace's feeling for Dunaird. She hadn't understood, herself, until that first visit seven years before. There was a lot she hadn't understood before then, when her understanding had been that of a child and St Andrews the only world she knew, and other things that she had only gradually come to understand since.

She knew now that although in temperament she would never resemble her mother, peaceful and accepting, perhaps she might have done if she had been born and brought up in a place where what couldn't be cured had to be endured, where the tenor of life was unrelentingly slow and any attempt to hurry it doomed from the start. Patience, she had learned, wasn't just a virtue in the Highlands; it was a necessity if you were going to stay sane.

She had learned something else, too, something far more important. Once or twice, in the uncomplicated days of her childhood, she had unhappily suspected her mother's gentle fatalism of arising from some weakness of character. But the ruins of Dunaird had taught her that something far deeper and more complex was involved, that it was the expression of a hardihood of spirit that drew its sustenance from the landscape, from the very air and the stones; the landscape that was not open to human challenge, that not only created but ruled, as autocratically as some primeval god. To fight was impossible. But yielding gave strength.

She knew now that her mother only truly lived during the few snatched, annual weeks in the Highlands, when she was free to ride over to the coast and sit by the ruins that were part of her, as she was of them. It wasn't the kind of passion a hurrying world was capable of recognising, but it was passion, for all that.

Now, her nerves quivering like violin strings, Tassie sat upright on the damasked cushions, willing Max to say more. To convince them both that he would, and could, do what he said. That the impossible had become possible.

'It would be the answer to all my dreams,' Grace murmured, smiling with a touch of sadness. 'But it would cost too much. I wouldn't ask it of you, especially after what you said about being rich only on paper.'

'Nonsense.' Max waved a dismissive hand. 'Don't worry your head about that. It can be arranged. Anything can be arranged, if you want it badly enough. We might need to transfer the ownership temporarily into my name, to simplify the financing, but when everything's finished, I'll make it over to you again. All you have to do is say yes.'

There were tears in Grace's eyes.

So softly that her voice was barely audible, she said, 'Then, yes. Yes.'

When she had gone, her eyes still shining, Tassie said with an attempt at lightness, 'Max, after that . . . I mean . . . Oh, heavens! All I can say is that you've compensated for every single one of your sins, past and present, and probably all sins to come, as well.'

Trying to laugh, she found that she was weeping. So she hugged him convulsively, and ran from the room.

9

'But the queer thing is,' she said to John Bell a few days later, 'that although I've made my peace with Max, and although he's being so wonderful, *really* wonderful, about Dunaird – he's even allowing me to do the preliminary drawings for it – I feel more and more uncomfortable.'

The two of them were up on the high gangway in the inlaid linoleum shed, looking down on the long line of perforated zinc trays and the slowly moving canvas beneath. Every tray was, in effect, a huge stencil and, as the canvas passed under each of them in succession, a different colour of linoleum grains was fed through so that, by the time the canvas reached the end of its run and was ready for pressing and fixing, the full design was laid out on it like a jigsaw puzzle built out of loose granules of cork and linseed oil compound. It was a system that had its limitations in the matter of fine detail, and Tassie, worried about the intricacy of one of her new designs, had asked Max's permission to have a test run.

She had waylaid John Bell for an opinion, although it was none of his business, and, as they scanned the moving canvas, had found herself confiding in him. They knew each other quite well by now and there was no one else to confide in, or no one who was closely acquainted with Max without being emotionally involved with him.

'That's looking a' right,' John said, peering at the skeletal silvery marbling that had just been laid down by Tray Three. 'So why are ye no' comfortable?'

Tassie inhaled deeply and then wished she hadn't. The smell of boiled linseed oil permeated the entire factory, warm and sweet and thick, so that it was like breathing vapourised honey. 'Part of it is that he's so unpredictable. But you know that as well as I do. I remember you telling me so, years ago; that day I came to you looking for a job. Sometimes I think he keeps us wondering just for his own entertainment.'

She broke off suddenly and pointed. 'There, look! That's what I was afraid of. The mid-grey vein up in the top left corner of Tray Five. It's too thin. The darker grey from Tray Six is overflowing onto it and breaking the line. See?'

'Aye. Well, that's no' too hard to mend, is it?'

'I suppose not. But oh, how I hate linoleum!' She sighed. 'The basic problem is that he controls all our lives. Not just here at the factory – that's to be expected – but at home and in every way. I feel sometimes that everything my mother and I do is in response to him or his actions. It's more insidious than just relying on him for our bread-and-butter and the roof over our heads. It's emotional dependence.'

John Bell shrugged. 'I'll admit I've got a few wee reservations about your brither, but ye can hardly blame him for that kind o' thing.'

'I don't. It's not his fault. I suppose it must always happen with strong personalities, but it makes me feel as if I have no will of my own, almost as if I'm not real. I've only been back at the factory for three months, but I don't think I can go on like this and I don't know how to get away.'

'Aye, well. Do I no' remember seeing somewhere that it's beneficial for an artist to starve in a garret?'

With asperity, she said, 'Possibly, if you're the kind of artist who's content to spread his bread with nothing but painty fingerprints. I, however, am just a competent draughtsman with a good deal of facility and an excellent eye for colour. Hunger would merely exacerbate my temper and do nothing for my art.'

He laughed, the corners of his mouth rising almost to his ear lobes, so that his chin looked like a garden trowel. He was an extraordinarily nice man, even if he no longer laughed as readily as once he had done. Tassie had hesitated about asking if there was anything wrong, and decided against it. His worries might be to do with his personal life rather than the factory, in which case she had no right to intrude.

So she said, 'Never mind. Will you explain all about holding companies and incorporations to me some day? I'd like to understand, and it's useless asking Max. All he does is confound me with explanations that leave me even more confused than I was before.'

John Bell's grin faded. 'Aye, well. Your brither and Goudy are the only ones who've got a' the details at their fingertips, so ye'll jist have to persevere wi' him. I'd better be getting back to my desk now. But if it helps, I like the look o' that pattern. A wee bit more work is all it needs.'

'I know,' Tassie said. 'Isn't it *boring*!'

It was midsummer when Tassie and Francis Rivers met again, a summer the like of which Glasgow had rarely known. No one could believe it as one brilliant, blue-skied day followed another throughout the whole, six-month course of the great International Exhibition.

Kelvingrove was packed to bursting point with visitors. Even Czar Nicholas came for a look, although Glasgow's citizens derived more pleasure from the continuing presence on the bandstand of Mr John Philip Sousa, a little, dark-bearded man in a braided uniform who had every foot in the park tapping to his rhythms, the big, deep-throated trumpets oompahing away with a gusto born of the knowledge that half their audience was saying to the other half, 'Nothing to beat a bit of Sousa in the park on a fine, sunny day, is there?'

Tassie, taking a break from her duties indoors, was sitting listening to the 'Washington Post' with her eyes firmly closed when a familiar voice from above enquired affably, 'Tired?'

She didn't gasp, or twitch – or not visibly. She didn't even open her eyes. 'Not in the sense you mean,' she said. 'It's just that there's a limit to how long I can stand the sight of all these architectural nightmares. What are you doing here?'

'Having a day off. And you?'

'Plunking school.'

'I beg your pardon?'

'Playing truant. I'm supposed to be in the Wylie and Lochhead Pavilion explaining to anyone who's interested how mother-of-pearl butterflies are inlaid into leaded glass and why Mr Taylor decided to stain the furniture purple and green. You're a stranger. How are you?'

'Overworked. And you?'

She opened her eyes then, on a gurgle of laughter. 'I, also.'

'Dear God, how alarmingly grammatical of you.' His own eyes crinkled responsively. 'Yes, I ran into Miss St John the other day and she told me what you were up to – in intervals of enthusing about Norwegian women's enfranchisement. How do you like the linoleum business?'

'I don't.'

'Oh. That's frank, at any rate.'

Her heart was still doing a war dance, but she gathered herself together. 'It's very successful, though. Half the floors in these horrible fake Spanish Renaissance halls are covered with the McKenzie product.'

'And what about the floors in our nice, new, equally horrible, fake North Italian Gothic art galleries? Or hasn't Max yet succeeded in persuading the Glasgow Corporation that linoleum is superior to marble?'

Mr Sousa's brass gave a final oompah and stopped, so that her voice rang out with unnatural clarity. 'I don't know why you always have to sneer at Max!'

'Was I sneering? I wasn't aware of it.'

Pinkly conscious of the glances being cast their way, Tassie dropped her voice. 'Well, you were.'

Suddenly, it had become more than a light-hearted exchange. Francis Rivers's face was thoughtful as he said, 'Shall we try and find a cup of tea?' Neither of them mentioned Miss Cranston's. Private jokes savoured too much of an intimacy that had never been real and was now very much out of place.

Silently, they made their way across the grass to one of the kiosks and found themselves a small, isolated table under a tree.

'Cream bun?' Francis asked, after the waitress had gone.

'No, thank you.'

'Tassie,' he said, and it was the first time he had ever addressed her as such. It had always been 'Miss Smith' or, mockingly, 'young lady'. She wasn't even aware of the silence that followed because, tentatively, disbelievingly, she was exploring the discovery that he must have come to think of her, in the privacy of his mind, as 'Tassie', just as she had come to think of him as 'Francis'. Though she doubted whether she would ever have the courage to call him 'Francis' outright.

He began again. 'Tassie, may I talk to you about Max for a moment?'

Brought back to earth, she subdued an undeniably pettish desire to snap, 'When did you ever talk about anyone else?' and instead replied firmly, 'Not if you're going to criticise.'

'Don't you ever criticise him yourself?'

'No, of course not. Well, yes, I do. But that's different. He's my brother.'

'So your criticisms aren't sincere?'

'I didn't mean that. I meant they're based on knowledge, not prejudice.'

'Which puts me in my place.' His long mouth curled a little at the corners. 'As it happens, I was not proposing to criticise. It's merely that I'm mystified about something and I thought you might be able to help me.'

Warning bells rang in her head. If it had been anyone other than Francis Rivers, she would have stopped the whole thing there and then by saying, 'I doubt it.' But, seeing him again after six long months, she didn't dare. If talking about Max was the price of his company, she would talk about Max. And perhaps she might persuade him to be less sceptical.

She wished he didn't disturb her so.

'Your brother is becoming an important man,' he said carefully, 'and I have been thinking for quite a while that I'd like to do an extended profile of him in the *Enterprise*. Not right away.' He grinned suddenly. 'I'm so busy with the news of the day that it might take years, because I won't do it until I can do it properly. What I have in mind, you see, isn't just the kind of padded-out career summary that passes as a "profile" in the business pages. He's beginning to be well known in the news pages, too, and that means that readers are – or soon will be – interested in him as a human being.'

Brightly, Tassie said, 'Oh, well, if you want to know what he wears to work, and what he has for supper, and what fun he is to be with . . .'

'I'll come to you. Yes.' His tone was dry.

The physical attraction he had felt six months before, the attraction that had kept him away from her until this afternoon, when their encounter had been wholly accidental, hadn't faded as he had assumed it would. What he really wanted to say to her was that the sun was rimming her hair with pure gold, that her eyes were exactly the colour of a northern sea, and that when she held her head just so all he wanted to do was take her in his arms and kiss her – rather seriously.

But it was impossible, so he turned his own eyes away, narrowing them against the light, and went on, 'What I had in mind was the story of his life, not just as he tells it but rounded out by interviews with other people. People who knew him when he was a child, for example. Now, I happened to be up in Wester Ross last September . . .'

Clutching at straws, Tassie interrupted, 'Yes, my mother said she'd found you at Dunaird. She thought it was coincidence.'

'But you didn't?' There was no way of asking whether either of them had mentioned it to Max.

'I wondered. Max is going to have the tower rebuilt, you know? For my mother, not for himself. I've done the preliminary drawings, but he's arranging everything else. In fact, he's made my mother and me swear not to go near the place until everything's finished. He says there's no magic in a transformation from ruin to castle if you've spent the intervening time standing around watching the plasterers and plumbers at work.'

'Let's hope it doesn't take too long, then.'

Her face lit up mischievously and Francis had to tell himself again, *It's impossible*. She said, 'Well, regardless of what Max decrees, I have every intention of paying a private visit now and then to keep an eye on things.'

'Very wise. But to revert to what I was saying, when I was in Ullapool I thought I might take the opportunity of looking for some background material, what we journalists call "colour" material. But I didn't find any.'

'Really?' Her voice was suddenly perfunctory. 'Then perhaps you should ask Max himself, instead of . . .'

'Snooping? But Max would have been too young to remember anything about little Robbie's death, for example. And I'm afraid that the tragic drowning of an innocent child is just the kind of thing to tug at readers' heart strings and bring a story to life.'

It was Tassie's turn to look away, to narrow her eyes against the sun, to see Norah over by the steps to the Arts and Crafts Pavilion and wish she would come and join them. And then wish that she wouldn't.

She couldn't say that Francis hadn't been able to find out anything about little Robbie because little Robbie had never existed. She couldn't say that Francis had failed to find the Black House in which Max had been brought up because there was no Black House to find. She couldn't say that, on the strength of Joss Smith's contributions towards his son's keep, Jeannie McKenzie had moved away from Ullapool altogether.

If she told Francis any of that, she would brand Max a liar. If he found out for himself, Max would still be branded a liar. If neither happened, Francis Rivers would go on being suspicious.

All things considered, it seemed the least of the evils. She said, 'Well, it's very odd that you didn't find anything. But it's thirty years ago now. People will have forgotten.'

'The Births, Marriages and Deaths registers shouldn't have forgotten.'

'You didn't waste time looking for Max's *marriage*, I hope!'

'Very witty. No, I didn't. And just to save you the trouble of pointing it out, I readily admit that almost everyone in the district is called McKenzie.'

'There must be a lot of Johns, too. You do know that Max's first name is John?'

He closed his eyes. Sousa was giving his all to the 'Stars and Stripes Forever'. After a moment, Francis said resignedly, 'No, I didn't know about the John.'

'Well, there you are, then!'

Norah said, 'Oh, *there* you are, Tassie! And Mr Rivers, too. How nice! Tassie, you're wanted back on the stand. There's someone who's desperate to know how the violet and green stains are applied. No, don't worry about Mr Rivers. I'll look after him.' She simpered outrageously at Francis. 'As a highly magnetic young lady, perhaps I might invite him to some interesting conversation in my very chic suite?'

Tassie, already on her feet, said accusingly, 'Norah! You've been reading the Personal columns again!'

And then an amused Francis Rivers replied, 'Thank you, but no. My – er – needs are already catered for.'

II

Quietly, Francis let himself into the house and made his way to the living room with the laudable intention of getting some work done. But ten minutes passed without his having done more than pick up a pencil and sit holding it, balanced by the middle, staring at it.

Then – as sometimes happened and sometimes didn't – he became aware of a murmuring of voices upstairs, followed by Lucia calling, 'Francis, is that you?'

After a second or two, 'Yes, my dear,' he called back. 'I'm coming.'

August 1901

CHAPTER FOUR

I

It arrived out of the blue, addressed personally and confidentially to Mr T. Smith, Advertisement Artist, McKenzie Flooring Ltd, Dundee, North Britain.

Mr Augustus B. Silvermann, the letter said, was deeply admiring of the artwork by Mr T. Smith which had recently featured in a number of advertisements for McKenzie Flooring, and took the liberty of wondering whether Mr Smith had ever considered extending his talents to a wider and possibly more lucrative field. It was Mr Silvermann's impression that Mr Smith was possessed of an adaptability of style that might be put to valuable use in the profession to which he himself had the honour to belong. He spoke, of course, of the advertising profession, with its correlative instrumentalities. As a citizen of the United States of America, it was Mr Silvermann's belief that interchanges between England and the United States in this new and upcoming science could be of inestimable value to both, and it was for this reason that he himself had come to London six months previously in order to set up an agency that would combine American knowhow with English taste and refinement . . .

And so it went on, for three typewritten pages.

'Goodness me!' Grace said. 'I feel quite breathless. And what in the world is a correlative instrumentality? Do you suppose all Americans talk like that?'

'I've no idea,' said Tassie, her head in the clouds. 'I've never met one.'

'Max has. He says every other peer of the realm nowadays has an American wife. It's the money, I suppose. Americans do seem to have a lot of it. Vanderbilts and Jeromes and Leiters, and people like that. Why don't you ask him?'

'No,' replied her daughter vehemently. 'And don't you dare mention it to him, either, mama. He probably wouldn't even let me answer the letter. And I can't go on like this, really I can't. I'm twenty years old, and whatever he says about family duty it's not fair that I should be at his beck and call all the time. I can manage to keep myself for one more term at art school, and then I have to make up my mind about what I should do. And one thing I am *not* going to do is devote the rest of my life to linoleum!'

'Oh, dear. Max will be upset.'

'I know. But *one* of us has to be upset, and I'm tired of it being me. Anyway, I don't see why he should have all the fun.'

Her mother said absently, 'Isn't it odd – I haven't heard him mention Mrs Merton recently. Have you?'

Tassie dissolved into a giggle. 'Unless that was a complete non sequitur, you should be ashamed of yourself. What an improper train of thought!'

'It was, wasn't it? But it's so unsettling, not knowing what the relationship is. I mean, having spent a whole evening in her company at your birthday party and then being fobbed off, ever since, with nothing but passing mentions! I know Max is *just* like your father, as close as an oyster when he feels like it, but I wonder if there's something else in Mrs Merton's case – if he's simply being tantalising, trying to keep us guessing?'

'Of course,' Tassie said cheerfully.

'Yes.' Grace sighed. '*My* fault, no doubt, for suggesting he might like to bring her to St Andrews on a visit. I suppose, at thirty-four, no gentleman likes to feel that his private life is being monitored by his mama, though I only — truly — wanted to be reassured that . . . that . . .'

'That she wasn't as awful as you thought?'

Grace looked unconvincingly reproachful. 'I'm sure she's a perfectly delightful person, when one gets to know her. Why are we talking about her, anyway? Oh, I remember. I was thinking that, if only Max were married — though *not*, perhaps, to Mrs Merton — he would be too preoccupied to fuss about what his sister was up to.'

'I hadn't thought of that. What a good idea! We must do something about it. But in the meantime, there's no harm in my writing to Mr Silvermann, is there?'

Grace, acknowledging the appeal in her daughter's eyes, shook her head resignedly. '*Is sona esan a sheasas air Torr-na-fiughair.*'

For her mother to relapse in Gaelic was almost unprecedented. 'What?'

'An ancient proverb, my love. "Happy the one who stands on the Hill of Expectation." You make me wish I were young again, with the world before me. When I was your age, the only world before a girl was marriage. How quickly things change.'

'Not quickly enough,' declared Tassie. 'You should hear Norah on the subject!'

Grace who, on her occasional visits to Glasgow, had heard Norah on that and allied subjects more times than she cared to remember, laughed. 'No, thank you. But it does make me wonder . . . Mr Silvermann thinks you're a gentleman. What if he doesn't favour the idea of employing a lady?'

'Then I'll just have to convert him, won't I!' said Tassie stoutly.

She knew absolutely nothing about how the advertising
profession functioned, with or without its correlative
instrumentalities, because her only role at McKenzie
Flooring had been to supply the designs, while at school
– although Fra Newbery liked his students to have a
working knowledge of typography and insisted on
them learning the mechanical processes by which art
was reproduced in books and high–class periodicals like
The Studio and *Ver Sacrum* – advertising illustration
didn't figure in the curriculum at all. Probably because
art scarcely figured in advertising, either. Most
advertisements were just words, and plenty of them;
when there was an illustration, it usually looked as if it
had been done by the office boy in his spare time. Tassie
remembered seeing somewhere that *The Times* didn't
permit illustrations in its advertising columns at all,
which suggested that, 'profession' or not, advertising
wasn't very respectable.

It sounded lovely.

It also sounded as if things might be different in
America. Otherwise a gentleman with such excellent
artistic taste as Mr Silvermann wouldn't be offering Mr
Smith a job.

It was even possible that Americans didn't mind
employing ladies. Tassie, having shared lodgings with
Norah for three years, could hardly avoid knowing
that, in at least four American states, they had actually
been given the vote.

3

London in August was quite unlike the London of any
other month. But 'quiet' and 'empty' were not the first
words that would have occurred to Tassie as her
hansom rattled away from the station in the direction of

Bayswater, where the St Johns had their town residence.

Norah had assured her that she would be a most welcome guest; the St John parents, with their younger progeny and most of the servants, were in the country, so that Norah and Hugo had the house to themselves. Hugo was immersed in legal precedents and Norah herself slaving away at a bookbinding that Fra Newbery thought might (just) be good enough to enter in next year's Turin Exhibition – though if there were any gold medals going, Norah was prepared to bet that it would be Jessie King who carried them off.

Tassie's sole previous visit to London had been in the company of her mother and Max, for the famous birthday supper at the Carlton, and it was only now, when she was on her own, that she felt the full force of its overwhelming size, its busyness, its raucousness. But, sniffing the summer smells of wood paving, flowers, fresh paint and horse droppings; listening to the organ grinders, the street vendors' cries, the clatter of hooves on cobbles; seeing the people thronging the pavements and the carriages thronging the streets – broughams, landaus, drags, victorias, cane-sided sociables, and score upon score of elegant hansoms like her own, their drivers wearing top hats and red buttonholes, their horses impeccably groomed – she thought, *yes*.

London would solve all her problems.

4

Although it was barely six weeks since she and Norah had seen each other, they could always find plenty to talk about, even when they had to make concessions to the presence of Hugo. It wasn't, in fact, such a penance as usual. Over supper, Tassie discovered that he was much less of a trial on his home ground than he had been on his visits to Glasgow, as if being host rather than guest was enough to bring out the best in him. He was a good host, too, assured, attentive, completely in control. If it hadn't been for his habit of fixing soulful eyes upon her when he thought she wasn't looking, she would have found herself quite liking him.

Later, when she had retired to her room and was plaiting her hair for the night, Norah tapped on her door to ask if she had everything she needed.

'Sorry it's all a bit disreputable,' Norah said, waving a hand round the comfortable but decidedly old-fashioned room. 'Ma and I have been fighting over styles and colour schemes for the last three years, with the result that nothing's been done at all. I say, a slumber suit! How daring of you!'

'Yes, isn't it?' Tassie had designed and made it herself in palest green lawn trimmed with goffered frills at neck, wrist and ankle. 'It's lovely to sleep in. I'm so tired of getting tangled up in long flannel nighties, aren't you?'

Norah laughed. 'When you've a figure like mine, flannel nighties have much to recommend them. At least I don't have to avert my eyes every time I catch sight of myself in the mirror.'

Then, almost without a pause, she went on, 'Why are you so anxious to come and work in London? Don't think I want to put you off, but from the heights of my five years' seniority I feel entitled to point out that there's a difference between coming because you want to come, and coming because you want to run away from somewhere else. It's an awfully big step and, in your own mind, at least, you have to know why you're doing it.'

Norah could be uncomfortably perceptive at times. '*Might* be coming,' Tassie said automatically. 'It depends on Mr Silvermann.'

Thumping herself down on the rug before the

fireplace – screened off for the summer with a huge vase full of dusty pink ostrich feathers and dried grasses – Norah said, 'Don't quibble. It's Francis Rivers, I take it? That remark of his at the Exhibition?' Norah had been annoyed with herself, afterwards, for not taking the opportunity to ask him outright what he had meant by it. As it was, guesswork was all she had to go on. But he didn't strike her as a married man. 'What if he does have a lady friend?' she said. 'Why not do something about it? Why not set your cap at him! After all, faint heart never won fair gentleman.'

Tassie's answering smile didn't carry conviction. 'Yes. Well, I'm not such an advanced thinker as you. I was brought up with the word "ladylike" always ringing in my ears, and ladies do not chase gentlemen. They certainly don't ask them what they mean when they say, "My needs are catered for". That would be dreadfully fast.' Dolefully, she added, 'In fact, I'm not sure I'm really a New Woman at all.'

'You're a feeble-minded romantic, that's what you are! Letting yourself fall in love! No backbone.' Norah broke off on a snort of mirth. 'Oh Lord, I can just hear myself. There used to be a mistress at my school who talked like that.'

'Thank you,' Tassie said. 'I see that I'm on the losing side whatever I do. I'm a disgrace to New Womanhood for falling in love in the first place, *and* a disgrace for not doing anything about it in the second place. No, I've made up my mind. If I don't see him again, at least there's a possibility that I might forget him.'

'But *why* forget him? Why not fight for him?'

'How can I? Even on the most mundane level, I can scarcely throw myself in his arms. We only meet in the most public places and, anyway, I've only seen him once in the last eight months . . .' It came out as something of a wail, then, observing the speculative look in Norah's eyes, Tassie added hurriedly, 'No.

Don't you dare try and arrange some "accidental" private meeting. I *won't* chase him, and that's all there is to it. If he isn't interested enough to come to me, what's the purpose?'

'Rubbish,' Norah said. 'Men don't have any sense! Half the time they don't even know what they want until someone tells them.'

With exaggerated astonishment, Tassie stared at her. 'Really? Knowing Francis Rivers and knowing what I've told you about Max, you can say that?'

'Pooh, it's nothing but a façade,' replied Norah, who didn't believe in letting reality interfere with her prejudices.

'Anyway, what if I did throw myself at Francis's head and it turned out that he *did* know what he wanted – and it wasn't me!'

It seemed unlikely to Norah. Tassie was an exceedingly attractive girl, and an intelligent one. She also, Norah sometimes thought, had the sweetest, most open-hearted nature of anyone she had ever known. Now, seeing her perched on the bed, the bright auburn plait hanging down her back, her eyes darkened to emerald and filled, despite her attempt at lightness, with trouble, Norah reflected that, if Francis Rivers had walked into the room at that moment, everything would have been resolved. He couldn't have done anything else but take her in his arms.

Norah had never been in love herself and, for a passing moment, regretted her ignorance of its joys and sorrows. A touch irritably, she said, 'Well, at least you'd know where you were, wouldn't you?'

5

Mr Augustus B. Silvermann's secretary, a deceptively serious-looking young man who was going to make a fine copywriter some day, stuck his head round the office door and said, 'Your visitor's arrived, sir. The artist – er – Mr Smith.'

Gus didn't look up. 'Show him in.'

A moment later – restraining, with difficulty, a whistle of admiration – he was leaping to his feet and drawing the visitor's chair forward, exclaiming, 'Say, I wasn't expecting a lady!'

The lady, blushing slightly, sat down. 'I know. I thought perhaps you might not want to see me if you knew.'

His mind was already racing. In England, he had discovered, ladies were not employed in the vulgar arena of commerce except, though increasingly, as clerks and typewriters. Which meant that, if he employed her, he would be bucking the system. On the other hand, he figured a looker like this could sell any man anything, if she set her mind to it. She wasn't pretty in Mr Cadbury's chocolate box style; more like a young Mrs Patrick Campbell or Irene Vanbrugh. Soft red-gold hair, wide cheekbones, friendly mouth, and big, wide-set green eyes that, even in embarrassment, held a hint of humour. Good figure, too. And he just loved that faint Scotch accent.

He couldn't believe his luck.

'I have no predisposition against employing ladies,' he told her gallantly, omitting to mention that his staff was presently one hundred per cent male. Not until later was he to begin worrying about how to sanitise everyone's language so that it was fit for a lady's ears, and wondering where in tarnation he was going to find space to install a ladies' bathroom.

She said, 'Oh, I'm glad. But I thought that, just in case you had doubts, it might be better to meet face to face so that I could prove to you that I'm quite a businesslike and hardworking person. In other words, I don't spend all my time having the vapours and that kind of thing. And I've brought my portfolio with me, so that you can see I'm quite versatile.'

She bent to pick up her portfolio, affording Gus a view of a charming profile that, he thought lyrically, would beat the pants off a Greek coin any day. Leaping to his feet again, he said, 'Allow me!'

Her work was good. Much of what she had brought consisted of paintings of interiors, and they confirmed for him that she had a knack of matching the style of her draughtsmanship to that of her subjects; lightness and simplicity of line for modern interiors, elegance of detail for what Gus thought of as the Old Money kind.

Now and again, she would say, 'That one looks rather flat and dull, but it's because it was designed for the printing process rather than the living eye.' It wasn't something Gus needed to have explained to him, but he was impressed by the fact that she herself knew the difference. If she was already knowledgeable about reproduction techniques, they were off to a flying start.

The interiors were essentially works of information, and Gus was of the opinion that the artist's rôle there was soon going to be taken over by photography. But the story illustrations, poster roughs and costume designs that made up most of the rest of the portfolio weren't limited by the need to be representational and had an imaginative, lighthearted charm that was very appealing.

Closing the portfolio, he said, 'I guess you know what you're doing. Tell me something about yourself. Where did you study?'

'The Glasgow School of Art. And my brother owns McKenzie Flooring, so I've been doing linoleum and advertising designs for him.'

Gus, giving no indication that he was filing McKenzie Flooring away in his mind as a potential client for the agency, said, 'Glasgow? Now, that is a most interesting institution. Important, provocative and puzzling are the words I seem to recall hearing applied to it.'

Miss Smith twinkled delightfully at him. 'It puzzles a lot of people, especially the behind-the-times ones. I don't know about America, of course, but Glasgow was the first school of art, ever, to allow women to become full students. We're even allowed to draw live models.'

'No!'

'Yes! Draped, of course. And under chaperonage.'

'Miss Smith, you're a great girl! D'you want to come and work for me? I'll go get someone to make us an English cup of tea – though, boy! I wish I could find some drinkable coffee somewhere in this little island – while you take time to think about it. Okay?'

'Er, yes. Thank you.'

6

Tassie gave a weak internal 'Ooooh!' as the door closed behind the overpowering Mr Silvermann. So that was what Americans were like!

She didn't know what she had expected from his letters – someone either thin and bespectacled and pompous, or someone short and black-avised and pushy. Instead he was of middle height, neither thin nor fat – though he looked quite well fed – with curly brown hair and the innocent, dimpled face of a grown-up cherub. Tassie supposed he must be somewhere in his thirties. He positively vibrated with energy and she suspected that he might have rather a short fuse – a bit like Fra Newbery – but life within his orbit would never be dull. His courtesy struck her as a trifle oppressive, but she consoled herself with the thought that it was bound to wear off after a while.

Her mind already made up, she found herself behaving like a child in a toy designer's workshop.

Hopping to her feet for a swift inspection, she saw that Mr Silvermann's shelves were full of new-looking reference books, mainly of the kind devoted to lists of names and addresses but including an *Illustrierte Geschichte der Buchdruckerkunst*, *Napoleon en Images* and twelve quarto volumes of *British Portraits 1502–1833*.

A moment's consideration told her that these must be sources for ideas. 'If a dear one,' she improvised delightedly, 'had given Napoleon a pair of Merriweather's Fleecy Lined Gloves for Christmas, he would not have had to keep his hand tucked inside his coat all the time.' And, 'If someone had recommended Page Woodcock's Wind Pills to King Henry VIII, he would not have suffered from internal discomfort and a consequently nasty temper, and Anne Boleyn would not have lost her head.'

Smothering a chuckle, she turned to Mr Silvermann's display of tins and jars and boxes. Huntley and Palmers biscuits with a picture of an electric tramcar. Colman's Mustard, featuring Dr W.G. Grace striding out of the pavilion to bat. The Union Jack and Beecham's Pills jointly presiding over the digestion of the British Empire. And Omar Khayyam with his jug of wine, his book of verse and – as the 'thou' beside him in the wilderness – the very latest thing in phonographs.

7

She was still fizzing slightly when Mr Silvermann returned, greeting him with her sunniest smile and unwittingly causing havoc in the heart of the boy following with a tray containing a chipped brown earthenware teapot, saucerless cups, a silver tea strainer and a flowered china slop bowl.

'Thought about it?' Mr Silvermann asked as the boy set down the tray, a tin one painted with a picture of a Gallic-looking chef licking his fingers and declaring,

'Armour's Extract of Beef has that rich, meaty flavour.'

'Yes. I would very much like to come and work for you. But I still have one more term at art school, so I couldn't really come until after Christmas. And,' she took a deep, invisible breath, 'could we talk about salary, please?' She felt diffident about mentioning it, but she couldn't afford to let him think he could get away with paying her a pittance just because she was a female. 'I'm afraid I need a salary I can live on.'

'Don't you trouble your pretty little head about that!' he told her expansively. 'There is no problem that can't be fixed.'

He sounded just like Max.

'Now,' he went on, pouring half a pint of milk into her cup and topping it up with another half pint of pure tar, 'let me tell you what I have in mind for you.'

Advertising agencies, it seemed, dealt not only with newspaper advertising but everything from biscuit tins and cigarette cards to giveaway bookmarks, badges, blotters, and the eight tons of Quaker Oats hoarding erected on the White Cliffs of Dover the previous year.

'Letters to *The Times* about that,' Mr Silvermann said disapprovingly. 'A Chicago firm setting up shop on the heights that symbolise England's defences against the world. Bad policy. I would never recommend anything like that to my clients.'

'How do you find your clients?'

'Some of them come to me, and there will be more of those in time, as I get established. But, as of now, I go looking. And I want to put you in charge of department and furnishing stores.'

'But . . .'

'Not right away,' he assured her. 'When you're ready. In the States our stores are pretty enterprising, but here most of them reckon it's enough to take a seasonal half page thanking their patrons for past support and respectfully inviting them to come again and inspect the new range of calicos, bombazines, silks and taffetas. Though there are the slick ones, too, of course, the kind who plaster their windows with "Awful Sacrifice" placards. Not a thing that isn't going cheap because of bankruptcy, merger, flood, shipwreck or fire. I swear to you, they even singe the goods specially.'

'They don't!'

'They do!' He grinned back at her. 'But the day sure is coming when the stores are gonna have to advertise and sell the way Marshall Field, Macy and Wanamaker do. And when that day comes, I intend to be in on it. Yes, sir! Lady customers today have a lot more say in disbursing the family income than they used to, and the stores must learn to take their tastes into account. I reckon they need a lady like you to teach them. Does that idea appeal to you, Miss Smith?'

Tassie said thoughtfully, 'I don't know how Marshall Field and the others go about it, of course, but – well – yes, Mr Silvermann, it would be fun to try!'

'Great!' said Mr Silvermann. 'I'll pay you a percentage on every new account you bring in, as well as your salary as artist, of course. So, how about you start on the day after New Year's? Which I guess must be,' he glanced at a wall calendar advertising Richmond Gem American cigarettes, 'Thursday. January second. Okay?'

'O-*kay*,' said Tassie.

8

He escorted her down to the street door, and since to hesitate would have been to ruin her impersonation of a young lady in charge of her own destiny, she walked off briskly down Chancery Lane with an air of complete assurance and no idea where she was going. Except to find a decent tea shop where she could sit down and think.

Norah had warned her that London was a foreign country when it came to tea shops. It was either Fuller's, the home of expensive cakes and floors so clean that there was no need to hold up one's skirts, or an Aerated Bread Company shop, where there were no cloths on the tables, where every scone had to be ordered individually and the tea came with its milk already added, as at a Sunday school treat. The trusting Glasgow habit of setting out an array of dainties on the table and leaving it to the customers to tell the cashier what they had consumed was not one that had caught on in London.

Tassie didn't mind which kind of teashop it was. Finding herself in what turned out to be Fleet Street, she saw an ABC, walked gratefully in, and came face to face with Francis Rivers.

9

He was with an elderly lady, and they were just leaving.

Aware of the shock on her own face, Tassie saw it mirrored in Francis's. Saw too that the elderly lady with the ramrod spine had noticed. She had the kind of eyes that would always notice.

'What a coincidence,' Francis said. 'Are you on a visit?' But before Tassie could reply, the gimlet-eyed lady said, 'You may introduce us.'

So this was his mother, Tassie thought. He had once described her as something of a tartar and Tassie judged that the lady wouldn't object to the description. Certainly, she dressed up to it. White hair under a black hat with a wide, curved brim. A long sautoir of pearls and a severely cut dress in self-striped black silk. White gloves and ebony cane.

She and her son weren't unalike in looks, but Tassie sensed that Mistress Rivers's hauteur was an ingrained feature of her character whereas with Francis it was something he adopted from time to time for reasons of his own – though it wasn't any the less intimidating for that.

Tassie felt her own spine stiffening under the lady's regard, which was so intense as to be very nearly rude. And then Francis said, 'Mother, we must go or we'll be late.' And to Tassie, 'We have to visit my youngest brother in hospital. He's just back from South Africa, complete with war wounds.'

'Oh, dear.'

'Nothing serious. But my mother has been sitting here patiently waiting – or fairly patiently – while I looked at an office I'm thinking of renting nearby as a London base for the newspaper. It took longer than I expected, which is why we must hurry.'

'Yes, of course. I hope you find your brother on the way to recovery.'

'Thank you.'

And then they were gone.

10

She had to walk all the way up Chancery Lane again to rejoin the Tuppenny Tube, which took her to the Bank in a waft of sulphur and a welter of emotions so absorbing that she almost missed her station. Then she had to fight her way through endless City lanes, crowded with drays and waggons, shouting porters and overhanging pulleys, in search of the building she was looking for.

Seeing another ABC, she was aware of a craven desire to dive through its improbably ancient, lath-and-plaster portals in search of another cup of tea to restore her courage, because she had made up her mind that she must break the news to Max now, today, about her decision to go and work for Mr Silvermann.

She didn't want to.

Entering through the half-glazed doors with the brass plate saying, 'McKenzie Smith Holdings', she saw, on her left, a high, wooden, brass-railed partition behind which sat a side-whiskered gentleman who looked as if he might be the cashier. Opposite him was an area boxed in with five-foot partitions glassed to the roof, which was presumably the preserve of some equally important functionary. In between, two alert young gentlemen, unmistakably bagmen, were sitting bolt upright on what seemed to be the visitors' bench, while everywhere else were ranges of tall, stand-up desks, high leather stools, and doors, doors, doors. Far away in a corner were three washbasins, a safe, and a desk marked 'Office Boys'.

Tassie hesitated as various doors opened and closed, admitting or emitting a variety of subdued-looking gentleman clerks and assured-looking lady clerks. Max liked his aides to scurry about; in Dundee, too, his office was always a hive of activity. But at last a smart young woman came towards her, and she was able to say who she was, and there was a rather lengthy interval before the woman returned to usher her through one of the doors into Max's spacious private office.

There was another visitor already there.

Mrs Merton.

Her beautiful, calculating eyes scanning Tassie's deliberately plain outfit, she said, 'My dear Tassie, how delightful to see you – and how very businesslike you look!'

Tassie couldn't remember ever having been tempted to scratch anyone's eyes out before, but her voice could not have been more honeyed as she said, 'Thank you. Are you on your way to a garden party?'

Broderie anglaise and Valenciennes lace, and *very* expensive.

Mrs Merton, gesturing lazily, was all too obviously on the verge of murmuring, 'This old thing?' when

Max interrupted with one of his deep, infectious chuckles.

'Now, now, ladies! What are you doing in London, Tassie?'

'Well, I had to come for . . .'

Not Mr Silvermann yet, she thought; not with Naomi Merton sitting there looking amused and patronising.

'For the Arts and Crafts Exhibition. And I had to see somebody at the South Kensington Museum about the National Art Competitions. And . . .'

'Dull stuff,' Max interrupted cheerfully. 'Never mind, I'm glad you're here, because I've something to tell you.'

He exchanged a glance with Mrs Merton before he went on. 'You can be the first to congratulate me.'

Long familiar with Max's taste for the dramatic, Tassie felt no special need to hold her breath.

Until he said, 'I'm getting married.'

11

Her horoscope for that week had said Wednesday would be a day full of incident. She had always regarded astrology as something of a joke, but now she began to wonder.

If Naomi Merton hadn't been there, she would have thrown her arms round Max's neck and exclaimed, 'How wonderful! Tell me everything!' As it was, all she managed was a faint, 'Oh!'

'Don't let excitement carry you away,' Max said a little huffily. 'You could try and sound a bit more pleased about it. However . . . The alterations at Kirklaws should be finished by the end of September, so the wedding will be there, at the end of October.'

'Will it? Yes. How thrilling.' Tassie succeeded in recovering herself. 'And of *course* I'm pleased for you!

It's just that you've never given us the faintest hint. You still haven't even told me who the bride is! Do I know her?'

Max, his buoyancy restored, said, 'Know her? Yes, of course.'

It couldn't be, it mustn't be, Naomi Merton. But if it wasn't, why was she sitting there looking so self-satisfied, all sweeping dark lashes and amber lips? They had been pink last time, Tassie remembered, which meant that they *must* be artificially tinted.

'It's little Genny,' Max said. 'Genevieve Pelham. You remember? Sir Leoday's girl. Freddy's sister.'

'*Genevieve?*'

She was eighteen at most, and Max was thirty-four.

'You're thinking she's too young for me, are you?' Tassie couldn't believe it. Max looking embarrassed? 'Well, perhaps. But she's so shy and sweet and I feel I want to protect her. She's not one of these fast New Women who think they know everything.'

Clearly, it hadn't occurred to him that there were two New Women in the room with him at that very moment. Mrs Merton, who had made her own way in the world – and successfully, if the clothes on her back and the rings on her fingers were any guide. And his sister, who was going to do the same if it killed her.

Meditatively, even sentimentally, he went on. 'She thinks I'm wonderful. Worships me. And she'll soon grow into her position as my wife. Coming from a titled family, she's got a good grounding in how things should be done. She won't cause me a moment's worry or trouble. She's a dear little thing.'

As a statement of undying passion, Tassie didn't think much of it, but she supposed that the daughters of the aristocracy were brought up to look at marriage as a business arrangement, not to expect love but to be grateful for liking and a measure of affection. And although Tassie hadn't thought about it before, it was almost impossible to imagine Max himself falling in love. He wasn't the kind of person to give hostages to fortune. To give away part of himself.

Francis Rivers wasn't, either. *Damn* him.

Producing her best and most sisterly smile, she said, 'Well, I'm delighted.' It was true, despite her reservations. 'Mother will be, too.'

'And so, indeed,' said Mrs Merton's voice melodiously, 'will be the newspapers. The handsome hero of commerce and his pretty young princess – what more could they ask? A fairytale romance, my dear Max.'

Max smiled. 'Yes,' he said.

October 1901

CHAPTER FIVE

I

Even Francis, who was not easily impressed, found himself whistling over the guest list for the Smith-Pelham wedding.

It would have been stretching the truth to say that everyone who was anyone would be there. Their Majesties were notable absentees, and so was the prime minister, Lord Salisbury. The Marlborough Set was poorly represented, and there was no one at all from the arts. So it wasn't quite 'the wedding of the year'.

But there were lesser lords and ladies galore; a sprinkling of maharajas and foreign grand dukes; assorted politicians – though not quite so indiscriminately assorted as to include Keir Hardie or David Lloyd George – several mercantile men-about-town including Tommy Lipton and a brace of Sassoons; and a contingent of financiers whose names were less well known than Rothschild's or Cassel's, but who still exerted a good deal of monetary muscle.

It wasn't difficult to tell who were Smith guests and who Pelham, but even if a good many of them had accepted only out of plain, vulgar curiosity, it was quite a feat to have enticed them all away from London to Scotland at a time of year when a high proportion of them had just made the trip in the opposite direction; most of them were of the breed who spent August and

September decimating the population of Scotland's deer forests and grouse moors.

Max was really pushing the boat out. There was to be a huge house party at Kirklaws starting on the day before the wedding and ending on the day after, with a grand costume ball as its climax. The host and his bride, it was announced, would thereafter depart on a three months' honeymoon tour of Europe.

The press were to be there in droves, but only a select few, mainly editors of the nationals, had received a personal invitation to the wedding ceremony. Francis was not one of them. He was, however, one of the slightly less select few who had received an invitation to the ball.

He wondered why.

2

In a well-established country house with an experienced staff, everything would have been running on oiled wheels despite the imminent invasion of five hundred guests, more than fifty of whom were to be accommodated in the house itself. None of the frenetic belowstairs bustle would have been permitted to impinge on the comfort of the family above stairs. Unfortunately, Kirklaws was not well-established and its staff had barely had time to become acquainted either with the house or one another.

As a result, on the morning after she and her mother arrived, Tassie was waylaid on her way down to breakfast by a housekeeper enraged by the butler's interference in her arrangements. Listening, more than a little taken aback, to a torrent of complaint, Tassie found herself weakly agreeing that yes, it was intolerable, and yes, she herself would speak to Mr Waterlow, and yes, it was indeed undesirable that the maids should be exposed to the temptations of spirituous liquor. On the other hand, *someone* had to distribute the brandy decanters to the gentlemen's bedrooms and perhaps the footmen were too busy to do it, what with having to trim and fill the oil lamps, clean the knives, polish the wine glasses and all that kind of thing.

Leaving the housekeeper still muttering about it not being what she was accustomed to, Tassie beat a harassed retreat to the breakfast room, where she found her mother placidly addressing some cold ptarmigan.

'Sit down and have your breakfast, my love,' Grace said. 'Tea and toast may be all very well in the city, but I learned in my youth that it is the purest folly to begin a country house day on anything less than three courses.'

Tassie, rejecting the porridge, helped herself to an omelette and some devilled kidneys from the row of silver dishes on their spirit burners and hesitated between the two teapots, one with a yellow ribbon round its handle to signify China, and one with a red, which meant Indian. Then, remembering Mr Silvermann, she decided it was her duty to begin adapting to American ways and poured herself some coffee.

'I've never seen such disorganisation,' she said, sitting down. 'We can't possibly be ready in time for the wedding, can we?'

Her mother was untroubled. 'It's probably just that the servants aren't accustomed to working together. I will see them myself after breakfast and we'll soon have things set to rights. It only needs a guiding hand.'

It was something Tassie always forgot, that her mother's upbringing had been so unlike her own. But Dunaird and its shooting lodge had once played host to many guests and Grace, as the daughter of the house, must have grown up absorbing the knowledge of what had to be done and how. Tassie also knew from direct experience that she had the most extraordinary knack of managing servants. Perhaps it was because she treated them as people.

'Where's Max?' Tassie asked, perseveringly sipping her coffee, which tasted like brown dishwater.

'In the smoking room, having a disagreement with Dudley. Selina and the boys are there, too.'

'Oh, dear. Is it serious?'

'Dudley seemed to think so, although he becomes so incoherent when he loses his temper that all I could discover was that he was accusing Max of ruining him. Such nonsense. As if Max would.'

Dudley and Selina, invited to Kirklaws for the wedding, had arrived late the previous evening, four days before time and quite without warning, and it had been obvious to both Grace and Tassie that Max had been anticipating trouble. At the sight of their carriage, he had groaned, 'Damnation! It's been a long enough day without Dudley!' and, with a grin and a wink, had departed for his room, tossing an instruction to a footman to tell the new arrivals that their host had already retired for the night.

Tassie chuckled. 'Do you remember the last time Max and Dudley had a disagreement?'

The day when Max's true identity had been revealed.

Grace, buttering a scone, said, 'Pass the honey, my dear. Yes, I remember. And I remember that it was Dudley who finished up on the floor. But I'm sure it won't come to that.'

3

It didn't, but only because Monty and Bazz were there to restrain their father as Max turned to stalk out of the smoking room, saying he had better things to do than listen to Dudley's ravings.

If, said Max, Dudley had sunk all his money in Japanese cotton following rumours that last year's Galveston hurricane would result in a shortage of the American staple, he should have recognised the risk he was running. It was Dudley's bad luck that the shortage hadn't materialised and the artificially inflated price of the Japanese product had dropped back to its normal level.

'But it was you who advised me to buy!' Dudley yelled.

'Rubbish. You must have misunderstood something I said.' Max buttoned up his coat, amusedly eyeing the large, frustrated figure in the smoking room doorway, a son hanging on each arm. Accepting his hat and gloves from a footman, he went on, 'I am driving in to Selkirk now to arrange additional transport for my guests, and I hope you will have come to your senses by the time I return.'

'Don't worry, Max,' said Monty in his affected drawl. 'We'll see to that.'

Max studied him coolly for a moment and then departed to attend to more important matters than the financial ruin of his brother-in-law.

4

'Max *told* him to buy!' Selina said. 'And now we've lost everything.'

She was sitting at the dressing table in her room, on the verge of tears, though not the kind of tears that normally accompanied one of her tantrums. They weren't tears of self-pity, either. Selina was frightened.

Helplessly, Tassie said, 'It can't be as bad as that.'

'It can. I told Dudley not to trust Max, but he wouldn't listen. He detests him, but he knows how good he is at making money. So when Max advised him to buy the cotton, he sank every penny we possessed into it. Dear *God*! I don't even know whether we can afford to keep the school open. What are we to do!'

It was hard to feel compassion for Dudley, or even for Selina, who always lived on the edge of her nerves, so taken up with the urgencies of everyday life that she never troubled her head about other people's feelings, didn't even try to enter into them. Although she demanded sympathy for her own troubles, she never had any to offer. Even her love for her sons struck a hollow note, as if it were a concession to the proprieties rather than a reflection of genuine warmth.

People who could only see one side of a question were impossible to reason with, but Tassie tried. Taking care not to make it sound like a criticism and unaware that she was repeating Max's own words, she said, 'Dudley must have misunderstood something Max said.'

'No.' The tears overflowed. 'Max did it deliberately. He hates us both and he wanted to teach us a lesson.'

Sighing, Tassie bit back a recommendation not to be silly. That wasn't the way to handle Selina. She wasn't sure that being soothing was the way, either, but she tried it.

'You don't mean that,' she said, putting a comforting arm round her sister's shoulders. 'You're tired out after that long drive yesterday, and being tired always makes things look worse than they are. Dudley simply misunderstood what Max said, and plunged more heavily than was wise.' She smiled coaxingly. 'I mean, if you think about it, you must admit that if Max *had* wanted to ruin you he's clever enough to have found a less hit-or-miss way of doing it.'

Selina flung to her feet so sharply that Tassie was thrown off balance and found herself half sitting on the stool her sister had vacated while Selina, her face an unbecoming scarlet and the tears pouring down her cheeks, stood over her shrieking, 'Don't patronise me! Max, Max, *Max*! Wonderful brother Max! Well, I *did* mean what I said. Max *does* hate Dudley and me. Max hates *anyone* who crosses him!'

This time, Tassie did exclaim, 'Don't be silly. You're hysterical!'

'No, I'm not. You don't hear the Dundee and St Andrews gossip any more, do you, because you're never there except at the factory. Well, let me tell you that Jack Morrison's gone out of business. Remember him? He was the one who opposed Max being elected to the Harbour Board. And John Guthrie. Max wanted to join the Masonic Lodge, and John Guthrie put a stop to it and, you know, it's a queer thing, but his yard hasn't had a single naval order since that day. And . . .'

'Coincidence!' Tassie tried to keep her voice calm. 'Envious gossip! Selina, it's nonsense. Apart from anything else, you can't possibly believe Max has the Admiralty in his pocket!'

'A word here, a word there. Max would do *anything*.'

Tassie's patience snapped. 'No, really. I can't listen to this any more. Goodness knows, you've never done anything to make Max like you but he certainly doesn't hate you. If there's any hating being done, you're the one who's doing it.' Suddenly, she was almost as overwrought as Selina. 'You've always loathed poor Max for no reason at all – just for existing! I don't understand you!'

'*Poor* Max?'

There was a long, vibrating pause, and when Selina spoke again, it was in a very different tone, low and unnaturally level. She didn't look at Tassie and what she said was muffled by the spread fingers half covering her mouth, but there was no mistaking the disastrous words.

'Yes, I loathe "poor Max", but not just for existing,' she said. 'Poor Max. Poor *brother* Max. The first day we met, he raped me.'

5

Like ice water, the words ran through Tassie's veins.

After a moment, she tugged her long, knitted jacket

more closely around her, and cleared her throat, and said, 'No.'

'Yes.'

There was no easy way out. No possibility of saying, 'You misunderstood', or 'You were imagining things'.

Either Selina was telling the truth, or she was lying.

With a dragging reluctance, Tassie forced herself to look at her sister's face, and knew that she wasn't lying. She said, 'Sit down, for goodness' sake. Shall I go and make you a cup of tea? The servants are busy.'

Selina shook her head and there was such a depth of misery in her eyes that Tassie suddenly held out her hands. 'Oh, Selina. My dear, don't!'

For the first time in Tassie's memory, Selina responded to her. Collapsing to her knees, she buried her head in Tassie's lap and, the words pouring out in a torrent, moaned, 'I've never told anyone. I couldn't. It was so awful. I have nightmares about it still. I don't think I'll ever feel clean again.'

Tassie had no personal experience of sex, nothing beyond chaste kisses, and no one had told her the facts of life, though she knew her mother would, on the night before her wedding. If she ever married. But she would have had to be very obtuse not to reach her own conclusions. She had visited the farm at Dunaird many times and, although there were always fig leaves and draperies and chaperones in the sculpture class, they never quite succeeded in obscuring the basic facts of human anatomy.

For Selina's sake, she knew she had to say, 'Tell me what happened,' but it was a struggle, because she didn't want to hear. A few bald words, however dreadful, might be buried or forgotten, in time. But expanded, made graphic, fed to the imagination, they would remain trapped there forever.

'It was at Graceholm that first day. You and mother were expected from Dunaird, but not until the late afternoon, so I went early, because the lawyers seemed to be doing nothing about the Will and I thought I could try and persuade our so-called cousin to be reasonable. I'm good at persuading people, when I want to be.

'I thought that, if I asked him nicely, he might do something for the boys or, at the very least, give Graceholm back to mother.'

She sat up suddenly, sniffing and rummaging in her pocket for a handkerchief. 'I shouldn't be telling you this. It's not proper. You're not a married lady.'

Tassie said, 'It's too late for that, Selina.' She could guess that her sister didn't want to live it again; that having uttered the word 'rape' she thought she had said enough. But it was Max they were talking about, and if Max were to be condemned it was necessary that all the evidence should be laid out. There must be no doubt.

'Go on,' she said.

'He was quite nice at first, as if he was ready to be persuaded. And then I went upstairs for something – I can't even remember what it was.' Her eyes brimmed over again. 'He followed me, and he was smiling, and he said he was a red-blooded man and he knew an invitation when he saw one. And then he pulled me to him and I couldn't scream because of the servants, and he told me to stop pretending. That I wanted it, really. His hands were all over me and I thought I would die.'

Tassie thought, *Selina, Selina!* She had been flirting with him. She hadn't realised that what might be a perfectly safe, even rewarding, game when played with respectable gentlemen in a respectable little town, wasn't safe at all with an outsider who wasn't familiar with genteel society. Who wasn't used to ladies. Who didn't know the rules.

But there was no society in the world – was there? – where it was permissible for a man to bed his sister.

Gulping hard against the nausea rising inside her, she said, 'Yes?'

'I felt like a whore. And then he told me to make myself respectable because you and mother would be arriving soon. And I *couldn't* tell you. I had to pretend that nothing had happened.'

Awkwardly, Tassie said, 'I can imagine. It was awful. Dreadful. But . . . He's a man, and he's not immune to women.' Her fingers pressing tight against the pulses that thundered in her temples, she tried to think. There must be sense in it all somewhere. Max had his failings, of course. At the beginning, he hadn't been very expert in the courtesies . . .

What did the etiquette books have to say about rape?

She tried again. There were two points at issue. There was the rape itself. And there was the relationship.

Selina, innocently or not, had led Max on. How far had she led him?

His hands were all over me.

'Was it only his hands?'

'Only? You wouldn't say "only" if you knew what it was like. It was horrible. He did *everything* with them. He was in a hurry because you and mama were coming, and he didn't want to disarrange his clothes. He didn't care about mine . . .'

Her voice trailed off in a wail of wretchedness, and Tassie thought, 'So, he didn't rape her. He *didn't*.' But her heart refused to lighten, because it was only a matter of degree. Whatever the weapon, the sin was no less. Not with a sister.

And then she remembered.

The relief was almost inconceivable. Shakily, the world began to come to rights. 'But he didn't know you were his sister! He thought you were only a distant cousin.'

Selina, standing by the window, turned. 'Does that make it better? Do you even believe it? I believed it, too, at first. But next day – do you remember? – it was very clear that he had always suspected Joss of being his father. And he didn't know, then, that Joss was only my stepfather.'

Tassie remembered, but she fought against it. 'No. He *must* have known. The lawyers must have told him.' Otherwise, the whole thing was unthinkable. 'But I understand now why you fainted when it turned out that you and Max and I were all children of the same mother.'

Selina said with a sudden, cold detachment, 'Well, I'm glad you understand that, at least. Perhaps now you will also understand that I have never been able to look at him since without revulsion, and he knows it. That's why all this has happened.

'If you cross Max, he will always pay you out in the end.'

7

For the rest of that interminable day, Tassie followed at her mother's heels as Grace calmly advised on the selection of wine glasses, the floral arrangements, the seating plans, and the allocation of duties at the wedding breakfast. And all the time her mind was racing, trying to make acceptable sense of Selina's story.

Painfully reviewing it again and again, she proceeded from the desperate desire to believe that it *couldn't* be as bad as it seemed to the certainty that it *wasn't* as bad as it seemed. Limited though her experience was, she knew enough about the world to know that, if a woman appeared to be leading a man on, she had only herself to blame if he didn't believe her when, too late, she said no. There was no reason on earth why Max should be different from other men in that respect.

Fighting down her disappointment that Max wasn't, in fact, different, Tassie told herself that all men had strong physical desires. There had been no Mrs Merton to accommodate Max's in those first days. It was silly to feel let down.

And although Max might have suspected himself to be Joss's illegitimate son, he must certainly have known that Selina wasn't Joss's daughter. Max always took the greatest care to be informed of any relevant facts before he embarked on a new enterprise.

In fairness to Selina, Tassie closed her eyes and concentrated on trying to remember whether he had looked shocked, as well as astonished, at the discovery of his true parentage, but although she had an excellent visual memory it didn't help. She hadn't known him long enough, then, to be able to read his expressions.

It was a storm in a teacup.

Selina had just been a pretty girl, a distant relation, who had flirted with Max and tempted him into kissing and caressing her more ardently than she was accustomed to. It had probably come as a shock to her, after all the years of being married to Dudley, whose lovemaking, Tassie guessed, was probably as dull as he was. That was why Selina had made such a fuss about it, exaggerating as she exaggerated about so many things. Rape, indeed!

'Tassie,' her mother said amusedly, 'have you gone to sleep? Because, if not, I think you could very usefully begin writing out the place cards.'

8

Max came into the writing room while Tassie was at work and her heart pounded like a steam hammer as she made the herculean effort to behave normally. She felt

234

dreadful, awful, terrible, so suffused with guilt about having believed Selina's slanders that she was in danger of rushing to him and hugging him and showering him with apologies. Which wouldn't have done at all, because then Max would be justifiably angry with Selina for having talked about the episode and there would be no hope of a truce, ever. She would just have to make up to him in her own way, by being extra specially nice and considerate to him. He did, after all, have a great deal on his mind.

With deceptive interest, she smiled and asked, 'Transport all arranged?'

'Yes. Three motorcars to meet every train. Two for the guests and the third to follow in case of breakdown. Mother has everything in hand here, I gather?'

'It would be immortal chaos without her.' She took a breath. 'By the way, Dudley and Selina won't be staying for the wedding after all, though the boys will. But – I don't want to interfere – isn't there something you could do to help Dudley? His loss on the Japanese cotton has been very serious. Selina's distracted with worry.'

Max grimaced at her. 'What do you expect me to say? "Here you are, Dudley. Here's a few hundred pounds to make good your losses"? He's a grown man, Tassie, and if he chooses to throw his money away, that's his affair.'

'Yes, but . . . He seems to think you advised him to. And it must be dreadfully frustrating to know he's ruined while you're lavishing a fortune on Kirklaws and the wedding! The contents of this room alone would probably be enough to cover his losses.'

'*Dear* Ginger! What a lunatic little optimist you are. A sweet and lovable one, though. But I've told you before. There's a difference between cash and credit. And I'm not going to my bankers to say, "Lend me some money to pay off my idiot half-brother-in-law's debts".'

She sighed. 'I suppose not.'

'What I will do, however, is give young Monty a job. I need a personal assistant, a righthand man, someone trustworthy. He's family, even if his parents aren't my greatest admirers, and he has style. Clever, do you think? You know him better than I do.'

Tassie hesitated, remembering Dunaird Lodge and Monty aged eleven, twirling under the waterfall, tricking his mother into thinking he and Bazz were at death's door so that they didn't have to go crawling round in the heather any more. He had been a cunning boy even then, and Tassie had no reason to suppose that he had changed. It didn't seem worth telling Max about the Dunaird episode. He'd probably laugh and take it as a recommendation.

'He's clever enough, I suppose,' she said.

'I don't remember what age he is.'

'Nineteen next month.'

'Is that all? I've always thought he was older. Never mind. He'll do.'

'What if he doesn't want to work for you?'

Max grinned. 'My pet, he's been angling for it for the last two years.'

9

It was a storybook wedding, as Naomi Merton had predicted, and the less fastidious newspapers had the time of their lives with Black House Max and his fairy princess.

Tassie, suffering from nervous reaction and night-mares that ran counter to all her comforting daytime reasoning, was short-tempered and critical throughout, annoying most of the participants at one stage or other by expressing her dislike of the fussy Victorianism of it all and reducing the bride to such a state that she trembled at the very sight of her sister-in-law-to-be.

For Grace to reprove any of her children was a rare event, but on the morning of the ceremony she said, 'Tassie, I cannot imagine what is the matter with you. That poor child has no mother, no one to support her but us. Do, please, make an effort, if only for Max's sake.'

'Well, she has to learn to stand up for herself, and she'll have to grow up, too. Those coy little ingénue smiles from under her lashes will very soon lose their charm for Max, and if he ever hears her chattering with that bubble-headed friend of hers, Clara, he'll think he's strayed into the nursery. I'm barely three years older than she is, but I can tell you, the pair of them make me feel like an octogenarian.'

'She's young and has very little experience of the world. Give her time.'

'Mother, Max is the one who has to give her time, not me!'

'I'm sure he will. He's very fond of her.'

Tassie sighed. 'Heigh ho! I suppose we ought to go and help her finish dressing. That terrible outfit! Satin and lace and panniers and ruffles, not to mention the family diamonds. She's carrying such a weight of finery that I can't imagine how she's going to stagger up the aisle.'

'It was her mother's wedding dress,' Grace said, 'and I think it's charming that she should want to wear it. And while diamonds are heavy, it pleases her father that she should show them off. I will, however, concede that your bridesmaid's dress isn't quite what I would have chosen . . .'

'Ha!' Tassie glanced down at the dress in question, which was of ivory satin, ruched to within an inch of its life, and girdled and trimmed with blush pink. 'If I thought Genny had a brain in her head, I would say she had chosen it with the express purpose of making her bridesmaids look their worst so that she would be sure of outshining them.'

Grace said, 'Her taste is perhaps a little uneducated, but it is her wedding, after all. Promise me you'll try to be kinder to the child, my dear? She must have someone to depend on.'

'Oh, very well,' Tassie replied ungraciously.

Not even to her mother could she say that she pitied and was irritated by Genny in equal measure. How hurt would the girl be when – if – her husband began to take his pleasures elsewhere?

Naomi Merton was coming to the wedding.

What a mess it all was.

10

Costume balls were immensely fashionable. Francis had never been able to decide whether it was because the rich took a childish pleasure in dressing up, or because such events gave them an unparalleled opportunity to display just how rich they were. The extravagance of Henry VIII's Field of Cloth of Gold could have been as nothing compared with the two most famous balls of recent years, at Warwick Castle and Devonshire House, Piccadilly, where, between them, the Countess Daisy as Marie Antoinette (at the first) and the Duchess Louise as Zenobia, Queen of Palmyra (at the second) had worn enough gold embroidery, ermine and ancestral jewels to fund the entire British Empire.

As he was driven up the long avenue to the house, lined by torch-bearing flunkies with powdered hair and pale blue liveries, Francis wondered how the Kirklaws ball would match up. It looked and sounded dazzling enough, the huge house lit from end to end, the marquee ablaze with Chinese lanterns, music and laughter ringing through the crisp October air. Max had the luck of the devil. It might have been pouring.

As it was, Francis was feeling a touch chilly in the outrageous raiment which was all the theatrical costumiers had been able to offer him; or all that fitted, anyway. The theme of the ball was 'Tudor Glories' and Francis, clad in pleated ruff, peascod doublet, shoulder cape, minimally short puffed trunk hose, and fitted stockings that revealed everything from the top of his thighs to the tip of his toes, was supposed to be Hilliard's 'Portrait of a Young Man'.

As he might have expected, Max was strikingly got up in gold and velvet – Henry VIII with Anne Boleyn at his side. Historically, it wasn't the happiest conceit, even if the bride was wearing an unequivocally modern pearl choker whose six huge, creamy strands looked as if they would be perfectly capable of deflecting the headsman's axe. The groom's wedding gift? Francis wondered. Pearls were rarer and more expensive than diamonds, and Max, of course, trading with India, was in a position to get them wholesale.

Having queued to pay his brief respects to the happy couple, Francis scanned the ballroom, glittering in the light of the electric chandeliers, its great crowd of occupants as brilliant and colourful as birds of paradise. Expensive birds of paradise, even the more soberly clad of them.

Taking his time about it, Francis counted three Cardinal Wolseys, two Thomas Mores, a small Armada of Francis Drakes – one humorist among them bearing over his shoulder a kitbag marked 'Bowls' – a solitary Erasmus, countless Shakespeares, no Calvins or Luthers or Bloody Marys, but four Glorianas and six Mary, Queen of Scots, of whom Tassie was easily the best looking.

Skirting the orchestra and the ferns, he made his way over to her.

11

She had known he was coming, had indeed been fortifying herself against it with Moët et Chandon, despite Max's ruling that, at £3 a dozen, it was an FHB item. In Tassie's view, even if the Family did Hold Back, it wasn't going to do much to reduce the final bill. Although she knew that this kind of affair was a normal feature of life in the circles where Max had begun moving, privately she thought it indecent to spend so much money on such an affair. She couldn't help thinking of the women at the mill – big, bouncing Aggie; thin, starved Doris; Jean with her terrible cough and a seventh baby on the way. With what Max was spending on this one evening, they could have lived in comfort for the rest of their lives.

Similar, if less disinterested thoughts appeared to be in the mind of the lanky Edward VI lounging beside her like a spectre at the feast.

'You'd think Max could have spared a few hundred from all this to save Dad's bacon, wouldn't you? It isn't right.'

'But, Bazz, it was your father's own fault,' she said for the dozenth time. 'And you know Max doesn't have any patience with people who do stupid things.'

'It was Max who advised him.'

'Let's not go into that again. Max says not.'

'Monty and I don't believe him. And we're going to get our own back, just you wait and see.'

'I have no patience with you,' Tassie said with asperity. 'Revenge is the most unproductive motive there is, and melodrama is no way to stave off bankruptcy. Why don't you try doing something useful instead? Such as earning your living.'

And then she saw Francis Rivers coming towards her, and her heart began playing its usual tricks. For once, however, she didn't have to make a deliberate choice as to which mask to wear to hide her love-sickness.

Her eyes dilating with laughter, she exclaimed, 'Goodness, what long legs you have, grandmama! I've never seen anything so improper in my life!'

'You've seen Michelangelo's "David", haven't you?'

'Only in pictures. Anyway, he's a *statue*!'

'That makes a difference, does it?' Francis asked equably.

It did.

The amusement still on her face, she became aware that something extraordinary was happening to the rest of her, something melting and magical, something she didn't understand. There was an ache at the base of her spine, an emptiness as if the marrow had drained out of her bones and the blood from her veins. The life force that powered all thought and movement seemed to have turned traitor, so that her brain didn't work and neither did her limbs. Briefly, within Miss Tassie Smith there existed nothing but a wild and wonderful anarchy of physical sensation.

It didn't show, except in a slight widening of her eyes, but such was the chemistry between them that Francis couldn't help but sense something, something that brought his own body leaping to life.

It was a problem he hadn't foreseen when he'd donned the appallingly abbreviated trunk hose. All other feeling subordinated to a sudden hilarity, 'Christ!' he thought, trying and failing to keep a straight face. 'And not even a codpiece to shelter me!'

Fortunately or unfortunately, the distracted Tassie had noticed nothing untoward – the trunk hose being, in fact, longer than they felt – and promptly misinterpreted his amusement. With a tinkling laugh, she said, 'You seem to find my naïvety entertaining. That being so, perhaps I should introduce you to some of Max's more sophisticated guests.'

She had already turned and was sweeping, in a very stately way, across the floor when he stopped her with an iron hand on her arm.

'What a touchy young woman you are,' he said, his voice almost as hard as his grip. 'I wasn't laughing at you, as it happens.'

'Let go of me. People are looking.'

'People be damned. Dance with me.'

'I can't. My dance card is full.'

He took it from her. There were five empty spaces on it.

She said, 'I can't commit myself to every dance. Genevieve and my mother need me to help with the hostess's duties.'

He wrote his own name in all five spaces.

Tassie had kept one of the waltzes free, just in case he should ask her, but, 'No!' she exclaimed. 'What will people say?' To dance with the same gentleman more than once at such an affair was enough to raise eyebrows; more than twice was tantamount to a declaration.

'People be damned,' said Francis Rivers for the second time.

12

The previous December he had danced with her and afterwards ignored her. In the summer he had dropped a remark about his romantic – his physical – needs already being catered for. And now, when Tassie was full of champagne and harassment over the wedding itself and the emotional crisis preceding it, he was demanding an improper five dances and she knew it was because she had been curt to him, and he was doing it to teach her a lesson. Tit for tat, just like Max.

She could have wept.

Not until years later was she to understand that, in

those two brief, quarrelsome minutes, their relationship had taken a greater stride forward than in the whole of the previous two years.

Fate had it that their first dance should be The Dashing White Sergeant, a savage romp which only native Scots were prepared to essay while the English guests stood on the sidelines, laughing and pointing like children at the zoo. It was a dance that, so great was the expenditure of energy involved, ruled out any possibility of sustaining even a conversation, far less a quarrel.

It was also a dance that hadn't been designed for cap and ruff and half a ton of blue velvet, or indeed for the crystal jewel that bounced at Tassie's waist as if it had taken on a life of its own. Terrified of the chain breaking, she had to free her hand every few seconds to steady it.

Afterwards, he said breathlessly, 'It is a lovely thing, isn't it? I remember thinking so at the masque last year, and it looks magnificent against that particular shade of blue. May I see?'

Slipping the chain over her head, she handed it to him.

It was a pendant, a teardrop about two inches tall and almost as wide, carved out of rock crystal, framed in a delicate mesh of gold, and polished first by the *cristallier*'s burnishing tool and then by four hundred years of caressing fingers until it was almost as smooth as glass. The slight natural irregularities in its surface enhanced its beauty, so that it had the same unique, fluid richness as a baroque pearl.

'Is it a reliquary?' Francis asked.

'No, but it does open.' Taking it from him, she slid the tiny catch in the gold mesh to reveal, in the heart of the tear drop, a tiny but perfect sculpture of the Virgin Mary with the infant Jesus and an angel. The figures were enamelled in white and gold, red and ultramarine,

243

the bright colours mellowed by the patina of the centuries since they had left the craftsman's workshop.

It was the only thing of value Tassie possessed. Her father had bought it for her when she was a child, because it had appealed to him and was reputed to have belonged to Mary Stuart herself, most perverse and tragic of queens. 'A Catholic trinket,' he had said morosely, already regretting it even as he gave it to her in its big, velvet-lined box. 'I don't know when you'll ever be able to wear it.'

It was true that it was unwearable with modern dress, but Tassie was passionately attached to it, thinking of it as her own private talisman. When she needed to, she took it out of its drawer, and held it, and was calmed.

'It's so fragile, I'm surprised you dare wear it,' Francis said, returning it to her.

'It's very precious to me, and I don't, usually. This is only the second time in my life. Max hadn't even seen it before tonight though I doubt if he'd have noticed except that Mrs Merton asked about it.'

'Mrs Merton?'

'Over there, talking to Freddy Pelham. I'm not sure whether she's meant to be Catharine of Aragon or Catharine Parr.' The first and the last of Henry VIII's wives. Neither was exactly diplomatic but perhaps Mrs Merton, being foreign, didn't know any better. Max certainly didn't. It was a miracle that he'd even heard of Anne Boleyn.

She said, 'Naomi Merton. She knows a lot about jewellery and she wants to borrow it to have it valued. Max says it ought to be insured.'

'He's right.'

'Goodness!' she exclaimed brightly. 'Can he possibly have said something to earn your approval? Now you must excuse me. I've promised the next dance to Sir Leoday.'

'By the looks of things, you'll have to prise him away

from your mother by force. Is your sister here, by the way? I've never met her.'

Selina, Grace Smith's daughter by Simon Lindsay. Francis's full cousin. It had occurred to him that it would be interesting to meet her though without, of course, mentioning the relationship.

'No, she couldn't come,' Tassie said, and there was an undercurrent of something Francis was unable to identify.

So he resigned himself to making the acquaintance of the stylish Mrs Merton. He had a feeling that her name was familiar, but couldn't think why.

13

Three of Tassie's dances with Francis had come and gone. Supper had come and gone. And now they were dancing for the fourth time, and it was a waltz, which brought them physically closer than the other dances had done. But they were silent, because words would have said either too little or too much.

Max's interruption wasn't welcome. 'Rivers, my dear fellow, you'll forgive me if I borrow my sister from you? She's needed.' His manner was polite but his tone was cursory.

Following him out of the ballroom, Tassie sighed, anticipating some world-shattering crisis such as Genny having lost an earring or torn the hem of her dress. And then she reproved herself. Genny had done very well during these last two, trying days. It had been, at the very least, inconsiderate of Max to expect her to preside over a fashionable ball on the evening after her wedding night, but he had consulted no one about his plans until it was too late to alter them. The trouble was that he had no idea what a strain his love of display placed on other people. But if Genny suddenly felt in need of moral support, it was no more than her due.

'Close the door,' Max said as Tassie followed him into the study, which had been locked against guests. Genny wasn't there and Tassie looked at her brother questioningly.

'I cannot imagine,' he said without preliminary, 'what you think you're up to. You have done nothing but dance with that damned fellow Rivers all evening, and I won't tolerate it! I won't have my sister making an exhibition of herself. Do you understand?'

If he had taken a milder tone, she might have responded differently. As it was, with all her emotions in disarray, she flared, 'I'll make an exhibition of myself if I want to. Though if mama hasn't seen fit to complain about it, I don't see why you should.'

'Mother's far too tolerant. In any case, I'm the one your bad behaviour reflects on.'

It took an immense effort of will not to say something catastrophic about people in glass houses, because he wouldn't have let it pass. She knew him too well and, whether in the end she explained or whether she didn't, it would cause irremediable damage to their relationship. She didn't want that. Anyway, it had all been a storm in a teacup. Max might not be quite as perfect as she had always naïvely thought, but he was her brother and she loved him.

It didn't mean that she had to let him bully her. 'Then you'll just have to issue one of your famous statements to the newspapers. Or perhaps you could put one of those advertisements in the Personal columns disclaiming responsibility for my wicked deeds.'

At any other time, he would have grinned at her and told her she was being pert. As it was, he threw down the pen he had been fidgeting with and snapped, 'I mean it, Tassie.'

'I *know* what you mean, and it's not what you said. What you mean is that you detest Francis Rivers! If I'd been dancing with Freddy Pelham you wouldn't have uttered a word of complaint.'

Astonishingly, his face lightened. 'I see,' he said, as if all had been revealed. 'You're just doing it to pay me out.'

'What? I don't understand.'

He took three steps towards her, put his hands on her shoulders and spoke softly, understandingly. 'My poor little Ginger. That's why you've been so fretful all week, isn't it? What a blinkered idiot I am not to have seen it. We've always been so close and now you think Genny's come between us. You think she's stolen my love from you. But that's not so, my dear. No one could ever do that.'

Tassie stared at him. He didn't appear to be drunk. Torn between exasperation and a powerful desire to giggle, she said, 'Max, I know you mean well but I've never heard anything so nonsensical in my life! Besides, if it's jealousy we're talking about, I would have expected Naomi Merton to be the jealous one.'

She had intended it as a mild joke, but it wasn't a clever thing to say. The limits of Max's sense of humour were very clearly defined, and deriding Mr Max McKenzie Smith, even if only by implication, was strictly off limits for everyone nowadays, even sisters.

Regretting the words almost before they were out, Tassie thought she saw puzzlement in his eyes. But then the shutters came down and he moved back from her to stand, legs astride, hand on hip, looking in his slashed, jewelled crimson doublet and wide-shouldered overgown every bit as autocratic as the Holbein portrait from which his costume had been copied. He was handsomer than Henry, of course, but his expression was just as forbidding.

'And what,' he enquired shortly, 'was that supposed to mean?'

247

'Nothing. I'm sorry. In any case, it's none of my business . . .'

'That is *very* true.'

'What I was trying to say in a roundabout way was, you *will* remember that Genny doesn't yet know much about the ways of the world?' His expression didn't change, but Tassie struggled on. 'You will be kind to her, won't you? She's young and she's dependent and she's bound to make demands on you.'

'Not too many, I hope.'

Tassie still didn't know how much in love with his bride Max was. But he did have a great capacity for love. If ever she doubted it, she only had to remember his promise to Grace about Dunaird, the promise that had revitalised her own love for him and subtly changed Grace's attitude, too, as if for the first time she had perceived something that had been lacking before.

'Oh, don't worry,' he went on after a moment. 'I'll be a model husband. But do bear in mind that, although she thinks I'm wonderful, she's also marrying me for what I can give her.'

'Whereas the fact that *she* comes from a titled family and has a great many blue-blooded friends and acquaintances didn't influence *you* in the least!'

From the ballroom they could hear the skirling and hooching that betokened an Eightsome Reel.

Max said, 'What an unpleasantly cynical way of looking at the matter. Now who, I wonder, put that idea into your head?'

'As it happens, I thought of it all by myself. I don't need Francis Rivers to put ideas into my head, if that's what you think.' Or not ideas of that kind. 'For goodness' sake, Max, it's years and years since that day when – probably quite unintentionally – he showed up your ignorance of the jute business. No one could possibly call you ignorant now, so why persist with this silly feud?'

'Because I don't trust him. He's too damned superior, as if he doesn't believe a word I say about anything, and there's a barb in everything he writes about me. I believe it would give him great pleasure to destroy me. Well, he won't. I can promise you that.'

She shook her head despairingly. 'You make it sound as if he's persecuting you. But he's just interested. That's all. You're a very interesting person.'

She had said the right thing, though not of intent.

Miraculously, his mood altered again. 'I am, amn't I! Remember that day when I first turned up on Graceholm's doorstep? I've come a long way since then, haven't I?'

His face was as full of excitement and mischief as a little boy's and suddenly she felt a huge rush of warmth. There had been occasions in the last two or three years when they seemed to have lost each other, but now, all at once, they were together again, tied by blood, tied by love, gleefully allied against the world of respectability, the stuffy people, the spoilsports. The smile on Max's face was the smile she remembered from his first months at Graceholm, those magical months of companionship and discovery.

Her voice unsteady, she said, 'You've come a long way.'

14

There wasn't anything more that needed to be put into words.

She loved Max, and she was in love with Francis Rivers. But Max had priority.

He might hurt her, he might disappoint her, he might do things that, in someone else, she would have condemned. None of it mattered. He was Max, her brother. Choice didn't enter into it.

They went back to the ballroom, and she stood up for

her last dance with the man to whom she had no commitment except for a passion that might be – *must* be – transient.

15

He whirled her out into the spangled darkness and away across the frost-crunching grass down to the river bank. Despite the soft silver splendour of the moon, every star in the firmament was sparkling independently in the crisp night sky and the air was like a tonic after the overheated, scented warmth indoors. Sweetly, faintly, the strains of 'Florodora' floated down from the house towards them.

They stood for a moment, his arm round her waist, and then he turned her to him and for the first time kissed her.

It seemed the natural thing to do.

He thought – insofar as he thought at all – how extraordinary it was that she should be at once so innocent and so arousing. But there was no danger in kissing her here, with the house so close and a scattering of other unseen couples, like themselves, seeking a moment's private respite from the ballroom.

He deceived himself into thinking he could kiss her lightly, satisfyingly, without urgency, so that it would be pleasurable for them both, but only that. He knew she was attracted to him, as he was to her, and he didn't want to risk her heart being damaged.

She sighed as he settled her in his arms, but made no other sound.

16

She had dreamed and this was her dream come true, the kiss, the embrace, the tenderness and something more.

Absorbed, responsive, filled with enchantment, she stood in the circle of his arms and received his kiss and wanted only that it should last forever. All life, all existence, all desire were in it, and behind the darkness of her closed eyes there was consciousness of nothing in the world but the rightness of it.

It was a long, long kiss, deep as the sea, motionless as the rocks, infinite as the heavens. She was locked in it, lost in it.

But it was she who put an end to it, not Francis, although it was the movement of his long-fingered, flexible hands drawing her more closely to him that sent a quiver through her and brought her back to the frosty, moonlit earth. To the here and now with its burden of duties and loyalties. To the decisions that had already been made and were not to be abandoned for the selfish indulgence of a love that must pass.

Despite what she had once thought, she couldn't love Francis Rivers and go on lying to him, even from the best of motives. And if she didn't lie, Max and her mother would pay the price.

'It's cold,' she said. 'Shall we go back in?'

They were halfway across the lawn to the house when she went on, her voice ruthlessly controlled, 'By the way, I think this may be the last time we shall meet. For some reason, Max very much dislikes our – friendship – and I have a duty to him.'

If she had been looking at Francis, which she was taking care to avoid doing, she would have seen his jaw muscles tighten.

Without pausing, she added, 'And also, although I haven't yet broken the news to Max, I am leaving McKenzie Smith and going to work in London at the beginning of next year. So perhaps we should say goodbye now.' She gave him a swift smile, and wasn't aware how tremulous it was. 'I have enjoyed our acquaintance. Thank you.'

It was, of course, the answer to everything, but Francis felt only anger.

Max. Always Max.

PART THREE

1902 —
1903

January–April 1902

CHAPTER ONE

1

The blast of air from the tunnel was sulphurous, the station platform gritty and grimy, the roar of the tube train an offence against the eardrums, but it would have taken more than that to dim Tassie's spirits as she set off for the offices of G.S. Advertising on the first working day of the year 1902.

The guard gave a toot on his whistle, dropped his flag, and she was swept off towards her new life, waving a metaphorical goodbye to a situation that had become intolerable, to a truly abysmal year of physical and emotional stress during which there hadn't seemed to be a single day when she wasn't worrying about one thing or another – about where her own future lay, about Max and Kirklaws, Max and Selina, Max and Genny.

And about her feelings for Francis Rivers and her need to deny them.

It was all over now. It had to be.

2

By the end of the afternoon, heading back towards Marble Arch again, she knew that she hadn't made a mistake.

The last tremors of doubt gone, she smiled to herself as she began sorting out her impressions, knowing that, although Norah would be perfectly happy to hear the events of the day tumble out helter-skelter, Hugo would be lost unless every little fact was neatly documented and presented as a logical extension to every other little fact. Instinct and imagination weren't Hugo's forte.

It had been Norah's idea – of course – that Tassie should take up residence with them in the family's London house, with the result that, the St John parents being no more proof against their strong-minded daughter than Tassie was, she now had a comfortable eyrie, half bedroom and half sitting room, on the third floor of the house on the Bayswater Road.

There had been no awkwardness about the financial side of things because, although Norah's parents would have been aristocratically offended by any suggestion that the guest who had been foisted on them should pay for her keep, Norah herself – knowing Tassie – had announced that she proposed setting up as a landlady and intended to rook Tassie for a fair rent, since Tassie was earning and she wasn't. Tassie suspected that Norah was asking very much less than 'a fair rent' for the centre of London, but she hadn't yet worked out what, if anything, she could do about it. And, if she were to be honest, it would be a relief not to have to live on too tight a budget.

Money was something she had been trying not to dwell on, in case her new job turned out to be a mistake.

Somehow or other, she had never found an opportunity to break it to Max that, when he returned from his honeymoon, he would find his sister gone, and she had no idea how he would react – except that it wouldn't be favourably. She had done her best for him in the weeks before she left St Andrews, finding a student to take over the linoleum designing, one who admitted to being so short of the ready that even a starvation wage wouldn't come amiss. She had also succeeded in persuading Bruce Goudy to consider putting McKenzie Flooring's advertising into the hands of a professional agency, because it was really too much for one artist to handle.

He'd said, with his dry, quirky smile, 'Ye're maybe right, but . . .'

'But my brother is contrary by nature, and I needn't expect him to give the account to Mr Silvermann. It's all right. I know that!'

She also knew that she couldn't expect Max to go on paying her allowance once he learned of her defection. It meant, as she had told Mr Silvermann at the start, that her salary would be all she had to live on, because her share in McKenzie Smith Holdings was still paying no more than a few pounds a year. Max had told her this was because the parent company's profits were all being put to reserve against future acquisitions – which sounded all right, except that he hadn't told her how much the profits amounted to. For the time being, she had given up trying to understand how the company structure worked, had given up even thinking about it.

She had resolved to give up thinking about Max, too; to stop feeling like a moth perpetually fluttering round his flame; to break free and take responsibility for her own life.

He had marked her twenty-first birthday the previous month with a bouquet of hothouse roses delivered four days late and a note postmarked from Monte Carlo promising something more interesting when he was home again. Even the note hadn't been in his own hand, though for that Tassie forgave him. His spelling was still atrocious and he always dictated his letters. It wasn't only his bride he had taken on the honeymoon but a whole retinue of secretaries and accountants.

Wondering whether the 'something more interesting' would ever materialise, Tassie sighed. When Max was there, in the flesh, he could always disarm her, make her feel that he was the most important person in the world, sometimes more important even than her mother. But when he wasn't there, the faint, the very faint dissatisfaction that had begun to mark their relationship on the evening of her seventeenth birthday returned to tarnish, each time a little more, the surface of a devotion that, deep down, was as strong as it had ever been. Perhaps it was inevitable, a result of Max growing more successful – and of Tassie herself growing up.

3

'Well?' demanded Norah.

'I think I'm going to like it. In fact, I *know* I'm going to like it.'

'Speak! And for heaven's sake, speak before Hugo gets home and starts cross-examining you. I hope you remembered to check that the ventilation's adequate and to measure the square footage and make a note of any dangerous machinery that ought to be subject to the Factory and Workshop Act?'

'Of course.'

'And you can reel off advertising rates and commissions and typographical restrictions for all the leading newspapers?'

'Of course.'

'You won't mention dangerous chemicals, though, will you? He just needs to see a bottle of benzene in my studio and he's off about user liability and fire insurance claims and goodness knows what all.'

Tassie laughed. 'I won't mention them. And perhaps I ought to steer clear of whether there should be a code of ethics for advertisers?'

'Oh, you needn't worry about that,' Norah assured her blithely. 'Whoever heard of a lawyer caring about ethics? Now, tell me about the other people on the staff.'

'Yes. Well, they're all gentlemen, as you know . . .'

'Gentlemen, or men? You're not in St Andrews now.'

It was true that, in St Andrews, all men were gentlemen unless they were either in trade – in which case they were 'grocers' or 'bank clerks' or 'tailors' – or members of the labouring classes, when they were 'road menders' or 'handloom weavers' or 'kettle-bilers'. It was an odd convention, and Tassie supposed it must date back to the stuffier years of Queen Victoria's reign, when ladies never met anyone socially who *wasn't* a gentleman.

'*Men,*' she said firmly. 'And they're all English, except for Mr Silvermann, of course, though they seem to have picked up some of his turns of speech. If you hear me saying, "Yep!" you'll know who I caught it from. He's the most amazing man, brimful of what he calls "get-up-and-go".'

'Does he have a sense of humour?'

'Yes! He's also the one who has all the bright ideas. His second in command is known as the copy chief. He writes the advertisements. Then there's the space buyer, who buys the advertising space and fights with the newspapers over whether we're allowed to use illustrations or not. And there's the layout-and-production man, who fits the copy and illustrations, if any, into the space the space buyer has bought . . . Are you following me? There's also the account manager, who acts as a kind of buffer state between client and agency. Keeping the clients sweet is *very* important, I should tell you. And last and, at the moment, least – except for the office boys – there's the studio designer. Me.'

'Are they nice people?'

'I don't know yet. I don't think they're very keen on

having a female cluttering the place up. It means they'll have to mind what they say.'

Norah snorted. 'Well, you can always drop them a hint that, after three years mixing with male art students, you're immune to bad language.'

'Ummm. I foresee problems with Mr Fothergill – that's the layout man – who'll need to be convinced that I know about the technical side of illustration and printing. And I'm bound to tread on the toes of Mr Binns, the account manager, whatever I do. Mr Silvermann wants me to concentrate on ideas for the furnishing stores *and* to sell the ideas to them *and* carry the ideas through. He says retail businesses are the only ones who have something new to sell not just every year, but every month and every week, and if I can establish a direct relationship with them – me, not Mr Binns – I ought to be able to persuade them to take ever more, bigger and better adverts.'

'In other words, he's giving you your own little empire?'

'Only if I show I can do it. But Mr Binns seems to resent the whole idea. It's a very queer feeling to know that someone dislikes you before they've even met you. I'm going to have to be very, very charming to him.'

'What's he like?'

'Dark, smart, smooth, cold eyes. About forty, I should think.'

'Well, you can't join the big, harsh competitive world of business and expect everyone to go on liking you the way they've done in the past. Your Mr Binns probably doesn't even see you as Tassie Smith. He sees you as a danger to him, and charm alone isn't going to rectify that.'

'I don't know,' Tassie objected. 'Look where Max's charm has got him!'

Norah regarded her sardonically. 'I said charm *alone*. From what you've told me about Max' – which had been a good deal, none of it calculated to persuade Norah that Max was even remotely worthy of his sister's adoration – 'I'd guess that he has plenty of other strings to his bow.'

'Yes. Plenty,' Tassie said gloomily. And then, 'Oh, here's Hugo. Just the man I need. Hugo, Mr Silvermann wants permission to put a giant pair of Shillibeer's Patent Eyeglasses on the statue of Blind Justice over the Law Courts. Have you any idea who would be the right person to bribe?'

4

Although only its owner and his bankers were privy to the fact, the Glasgow *Enterprise*, now three years old and doing well, had been set up primarily to test the waters of what Francis saw as the journalism of the future.

It would soon be time for the next stage, a London-based national edition. In preparation, Francis had begun establishing contacts with stringers all over Europe who could supply him with news items and background information. The Reuters service was invaluable, but its news was available to anyone who was prepared to subscribe. Francis wanted exclusives. He also wanted people of his own on whom he could rely to follow up stories that weren't yet, but might well turn out to be, newsworthy.

From what he knew of Mr Max McKenzie Smith, a honeymoon tour of Europe was unlikely to consist entirely of strolling down the Champs Elysées, admiring the pictures in the Uffizi, or shopping in the Unter den Linden. So he had told his stringers that if they happened to learn of any intriguing or unusual activity on the part of a gentleman whose progress would, no doubt, be well publicised, Francis would be interested to hear about it.

By the middle of January, he had been able to collate a list of the financiers in Paris, Rome, Madrid, Berlin and Vienna, with whom Max had had private talks. They were all impeccably respectable.

But just before the end of the month, in the last days of Max's honeymoon, Francis's stringer in Switzerland reported a curious deviation, all the more curious for taking place at a time of year when the weather was at its least hospitable. Leaving both wife and entourage at Brenner's Park in Baden-Baden, Mr McKenzie Smith had set off alone for Zurich, where he had visited two banks and the Companies Registration Office. He had then proceeded to Vaduz, the capital of Liechtenstein where, accompanied now by a young Englishman whose name the stringer had been unable to discover, he had also visited two banks and the Companies Registration Office.

In case it suggested anything to Herr Rivers, said the stringer, the young gentleman concerned had been of medium height, slight build, elegant style, with light brown, waving hair worn somewhat longer than was customary, blue eyes and a full mouth. His manner for one so young was unusually *hochmütig* – the stringer wondered whether 'disdainful' might be the correct English rendering?

Next day, Mr McKenzie Smith had returned to Baden-Baden while the young gentleman had boarded the express for the north.

The stringer said apologetically that he had no contacts in the Companies offices and, of course, Swiss and Liechtenstein banks were notorious for refusing to disclose information about their customers. He had made one or two enquiries but had abandoned them because some of the people he had questioned had been unduly curious about the reason for his interest. He feared that he had failed sufficiently to disguise this and hoped that it would not redound to the discredit of Herr Rivers.

However, there could be no doubt that Mr McKenzie Smith had been engaged on registering one or more new companies. The absence of secretaries and accountants – though one did not, of course, know the rôle of the *hochmütig* young gentleman – suggested that he preferred to keep these transactions private.

What in hell, Francis wondered, was Max up to?

5

By the end of her first month, Tassie's life in London had settled into a routine. Monday morning until Saturday noon were dominated by working on advertisements at the office and thinking about them at home. Mildly surprised, she recognised that, although during her time at art school she had thought about work a good deal, she had never been totally absorbed in it. Ideas in the context of art, she supposed, were self-limiting, whereas in the context of advertising they appeared to be limitless. It was like being drawn into an enormous firework display, with ideas sparking off from one another in all directions.

Mr Silvermann – popularly known as G.S. – said with deep satisfaction that she was 'a natural' and that if anyone was about to convince William Whiteley, founder of London's first department store, to break his lifelong rule of never advertising in the newspapers, it would be Miss Smith.

'I'll try,' she'd said. 'But could I practise on someone easier first?'

As a result, in intervals between painting pictures of ladies on bicycles (for The Safety Velocipede Company) and ladies playing golf (for the Sporting Corset Company), she was working on a speculative campaign for Waring's, who claimed to have in their showrooms the widest conceivable collection of furniture in the widest conceivable variety of styles, both ancient and modern (though not as modern as Mr Charles Rennie Mackintosh). Usually, Waring's just listed them – Elizabethan, Jacobean, French Renaissance, Flemish Renaissance, Louis XIV, Louis XV, Louis XVI, Empire, Sheraton, Chippendale and Adam – as if anyone knowledgeable enough to shop at Waring's was knowledgeable enough to tell one from the other.

'It won't do,' Tassie told Mr Silvermann firmly. 'Most people don't think about historical periods in terms of things you sit on or eat your dinner off. They think of kings and queens and generals and poets. What Waring's need to consider is giving their advertising a human context. Businessmen who think of themselves as modern Napoleons – as I'm told most of them do – may not know what "Empire style" means, but they'd feel an instant kinship if Napoleon himself were in the picture . . .'

'How's about Josephine?' G.S. interjected hopefully.

His studio designer ignored this frivolity. 'And Louis XIV needs to be the Sun King instead of just a name and number. Long curled wigs and embroidered coats, dainty panelling, mirrors, chandeliers – all very glossy and extravagant, so that it positively shouts, "I've got money!" '

'Ye-e-ep,' G.S. conceded. 'As a Democrat, I don't approve, but as an advertising agent I do. But how's about Jacobean? I am not an authority on the history of England . . .'

Not for the first time, Tassie wondered how to tell him that there were separate places called England, Scotland, and Wales, and a joint place called Great Britain, and it was time Mr Silvermann learned not to use 'England' to represent all four.

'But it is my impression,' he went on, 'that King James I is not a monarch universally admired in your country.'

'He was Scots and he wasn't as bad as all that. But never mind, because Shakespeare was still alive in his day, so we could use him instead. Anne Hathaway's cottage and that kind of thing.'

'You're a great girl!' exclaimed Gus Silvermann, and then blushed with embarrassment. 'Gee, I'm sorry.'

He really was a most endearing man. 'I *like* being "a great girl",' she assured him.

London's winter weather – cold, pearly, grey – imposed limitations on outdoor activity, although there was still plenty to do at weekends. On Saturday afternoons Tassie and Norah went shopping, in company with half the population of south-east England. Tassie was kept in a bubble of amusement by the discovery that it was a London habit for ladies to carry their lists not in their pockets or purses but pinned to some convenient part of their apparel, and was constantly being diverted from her search for ribbons or buttons by an irresistible urge – which Norah said was extremely childish – to try to read them. From some of the finer specimens, it was possible to deduce the whole background to the list-writer's life. 'Baby's food warmer, Tom's cricket bat, beetle trap for kitchen, registry office to interview new cook, Mudie's Library (Ethel recommends Miss Lyall's *In Spite of All*), something neat in the blouse line for Mamie . . .'

On Sundays, unless it was raining hard, they went for a walk or bicycle ride round Hyde Park, mistily beautiful even in January, listening to preachers, lecturers and cranks at the Reformers' Tree, watching the fashionable Church Parade, admiring the horsemanship in Rotten Row.

In the evenings, zealously escorted by Hugo, they went out to dine and be entertained, sometimes at the theatre, once at a Temperance Hall where moving pictures were being shown. The main feature was a newsreel of the funeral, four months earlier, of the assassinated President McKinley and Hugo said that moving pictures would never, of course, be able to compete with newspapers, but it was interesting none-theless.

On another occasion, he took them to the New Lyric Club – the only one of his clubs to admit ladies – for dinner at eight, followed by a concert of vocalists, reciters and mimics in the pretty little cream and gold theatre, followed in turn by a tour of the latticed Egyptian Room, the Bamboo Room and the Cabin Room – which was just like being on board an ocean liner – and concluding with supper in the Ladies' Drawing Room.

Norah, who had been exposed to the New Lyric before, murmured to Tassie on the way home, 'Respectability, respectability! How would you feel about dressing up as a man and gatecrashing the Savage or the Eccentrics?'

6

Early in February, Tassie's mother wrote to say that, in view of the smallpox epidemic, she hoped Tassie was avoiding public places.

She said also that Dudley had succeeded in staving off bankruptcy, but that Monty – ungrateful boy! – had had a shockingly public row with his parents which had culminated in his shaking the dust of Seamount from his feet forever. He had been working for Max for the last month or so.

Max and Genevieve were home from their honey-moon, and Max had settled Genny in at Kirklaws – she was in the family way *already*, and wasn't that delight-ful? – and was now at the factory catching up with what had been going on during his absence.

When he had heard of Tassie's desertion, all he had said was 'Indeed?'

7

A few weeks later, Tassie was leaning over Mr Fothergill's desk, saying, 'If you were to move the illustration down and to the right, you could fit the lettering in above it,' when she heard firm, heavy footsteps in the corridor outside.

Since the office consisted of one large, communal room – only G.S. having the luxury of a cubbyhole to himself – everyone else heard them, too, and all eyes were therefore on the door when it opened to admit an expensive-looking, handsome, dark personage in a top hat and fur-collared greatcoat who halted immediately inside and surveyed the offices of G.S. Advertising as if he owned them. Henry Irving himself couldn't have made a more lordly entrance.

Tassie, successfully containing her pleasure at seeing Max again, thought seethingly, wasn't it just like him! She hadn't heard a murmur from him since he had returned from his honeymoon and now here he was, casually dropping in as if it were the most natural thing in the world for a gentleman to pay a social call on his sister during working hours. It wasn't as if he knew no better. Any employee of McKenzie Smith who received visitors at work would have been sacked on the spot.

Pink with embarrassment, she strolled across to him and murmured, 'Max, it's lovely to see you but this is not a good time. Can we arrange to meet later?'

'Nonsense,' said Max robustly, making no attempt to keep his voice down. 'I want to see the kind of company my sister prefers to her proper place at home with me.' He scanned the room again. 'Mmmmhhh.'

'And what does that mean?'

Behind her, Tassie heard Mr Pearson, the space buyer, murmur to someone, 'I say! Isn't that Black House Max?' She was annoyed, because it was a relationship she had taken care to keep quiet from everyone except G.S.

'Introduce us,' Max said. 'Explain to me what everyone does.'

'No. I've work to do. We all have work to do.'

'Nonsense,' Max said again. He had a very carrying voice, and Tassie thought, *Please, Mr Silvermann, don't be tempted to come out to discover what's going on, because then Max will have you at a disadvantage, too.*

'Be a good girl, Tassie.' This time Max's tone didn't brook argument.

She was relieved that, as they made the rounds, he asked perfectly well-informed questions. Not that she would have expected anything else, although he could be thoroughly obtuse when he felt inclined. In the end, she had no choice but to knock on Mr Silvermann's door. His voice said, 'Come.'

Dear Mr Silvermann! He looked up from behind his desk, innocently surprised at the entry of a visitor who didn't have an appointment. He didn't jump to his feet or ask Max to sit, but waited patiently while Tassie stumbled through an explanation. When at last he rose, having successfully established that there was only one boss on the premises of G.S. Advertising, he was able to be courteously considerate when Max announced, 'I've come to take my sister out to tea.'

'Well,' he said, 'I guess that a brother getting back from his honeymoon isn't the kind of thing that's liable to turn into a regular habit. Off you go, Miss Smith. You can come in early tomorrow to catch up.'

Tassie – no lover of the dawn – went to take off her smock and fetch her hat and coat, muttering darkly.

8

Max's new Daimler York Phaeton – six brake-horse-power, he said, and the first motorcar of its type to be fitted with pneumatic tyres – was waiting to take them to the Cecil Hotel, a kind of Venetian palazzo on the Thames, next door to the Savoy and considered by connoisseurs to command one of the finest views in any of the world's great capitals.

As they settled themselves at a table among the potted palms, Tassie cast a glance round the quiet, luxurious acres of marble, glass and inches-thick carpet, sniffed the scent of flowers in the air, and said artlessly, 'It's nicer than the ABC. So, how are you? I've heard the wonderful news about the baby. You must be delighted.'

'Yes. It's time I had a son.'

'A daughter wouldn't do? Is Genny all right?'

'She's eighteen, she's healthy, and she comes from good breeding stock. If it weren't for these damn' doctors, she'd be fine.'

'Doctors?'

'You know what they're like. Most of their income comes from pampering perfectly hale and hearty females into invalidism. Child-bearing is a woman's natural function, but all I hear is, "The doctor says I have to be careful. He says I've been rushing about more than is good for me." What Genny needs is something to take her mind off her woes. So I've given up my chambers in Duke Place and signed a lease on one of the new houses in Audley Street. I've told her she may have a say in *some* of the decorating – bedrooms and drawing rooms, but that's all. You'll see, it'll be all lampshades like frilly petticoats and lace dripping from the curtains.'

Then, smiling indulgently, he dropped his bombshell.

'I thought you could do the rest of the house. I trust your taste, and anyway, if you're coming to live with us, you ought to have some say in the matter.'

A mere half hour in Max's company and he was trying to shape her life again.

'Coming to live with you?' she gasped. 'Of all the . . . No, I'm not.'

'Of course you are. Genny needs a companion when I'm away, and you promised you'd be a sister to her.'

'Not to that extent,' Tassie said, recovering her breath. 'I'm sorry, but I have my own life to lead and . . .'

Coaxingly, Max said, 'Come on, Tassie! You can't go on working for that shoddy little business. You may not think so, but I did understand your motives. However, you've made your declaration of independence and had your fling, and you can now return to a genteel, ladylike existence with a clear conscience.'

'What do you mean "return"?' demanded his sister astringently. 'As I recall, my previous "genteel" existence was a thoroughly unrewarding round of designing linoleum in a filthy factory and doing your advertising illustrations for a wage Silas Marner would have turned up his nose at. No, thank you.'

'Perhaps I didn't phrase it very well. Ah ha! Chocolate éclairs. Tassie?'

'No, thank you. I don't want to spoil my palate for the ABC's scones.'

'All right. Now, just listen, because I've something in mind that's a lot more amusing than linoleum. Genny and I spent four weeks on the Riviera, and I've had a great idea. Guess what I've decided?'

Since Max's great ideas rarely, if ever, turned out to be to Tassie's advantage, she merely said, 'What? Though if it involves me, don't bother to tell me. I'm not interested.'

'You should be. I promised you something special for your twenty-first birthday and that something special is a one-third share in a new venture.'

Forbearing to remark that she hoped it would turn out to be more profitable than her share in McKenzie Smith Holdings, she eyed him warily and, feeling like the straight man in some comedy double act at the Tivoli, fed him the question he was obviously waiting for. 'And what new venture might that be?'

'I'm opening a gambling casino in Mayfair.'

10

'A *what*?' Her eyes dilating, she thought, 'Oooh, how wicked! Oooh, what fun!'

Max could see it, of course. He grinned. 'That surprised you, didn't it!'

'But you don't even like cards.'

'No, but I like money. Genny and I spent almost every night in the casinos at Nice and Monte Carlo, and I reckon their profits must be phenomenal. Especially at roulette. It's not all cards, you know.'

Gathering her brain together, Tassie said, 'But that kind of gambling's illegal here, isn't it?'

'Not in the case of a private club, a gathering of friends. There's no law against playing bridge for pennies at home, is there?'

'I suppose not.'

'It will be members only, and I want it to be the kind of classy place that members won't hesitate to bring their ladies to.' He grinned again. 'Honestly, Ginger, you'd have laughed to see Genny at Monte Carlo! She thought vingt-et-un was such sport that she frittered all her pin money away in less than an hour and then accused me of being horrible when I wouldn't give her any more. Oh, yes, I definitely mean members to bring their ladies!'

When Max was excited by an idea, his enthusiasm was infectious. Against her better judgement, Tassie found herself saying thoughtfully, 'Would it work in London, though? The Riviera must have a constantly shifting population, and when people are on holiday they *expect* to spend. Will they be prepared to throw money away on their home ground?'

'A good point.' Max's tone was the one he always used when he hadn't thought of something himself but was about to sound as if he had. 'But you don't join a gambling club unless you're a gambler, and it's the essence of gambling to throw good money after bad. What's more, I'm going to make the place so fashionable that no one who's anyone will be able to stay away.'

Now and again, Tassie remembered that she was a dutiful daughter of the Church of Scotland. Taking a firm line with the cheerfulness bubbling up inside her, she said, 'It doesn't sound very *moral* to encourage people to waste their money.'

'My pet, what's business – what's advertising, come to that! – but a way of encouraging people to transfer money from their pockets into your own? There's nothing immoral about it!' He laughed and it was a joyful sound. 'It's one of the laws of the jungle. And gambling's exciting, I can tell you. I don't think I've had such fun for years as I did at Monte Carlo.'

'Did you win?'

'A bit at roulette, not much.'

They had wandered from the point at issue. 'Well, thank you very much indeed for my share in it all,' Tassie said. 'It's a *lovely* present. There's only one tiny thing. What do you expect me to do in exchange?'

'Nothing,' Max said, injured. 'I told you, it's a twenty-first birthday gift from your loving brother.'

'But . . .'

'Ah, well, if you put it that way. I mean, if you *want* to do something in return . . . The thing is, I think the place should be like a private house – rich, elegant, gracious – which means it needs a woman's touch. If you wanted to take a hand in finding suitable premises and decorating them and so on, I wouldn't object.'

'That sounds more like it. And while we're on the subject, perhaps you'd like to define that "and so on"? It doesn't, for instance, include drumming up members?'

'No, Freddy Pelham will do that,' Max replied blandly. He had such a talent for ignoring sarcasm that Tassie sometimes thought he didn't even recognise it for what it was. Most of the people he dealt with probably hadn't the courage to be sarcastic with him. 'And young Monty,' he went on, 'will supervise the management when I can spare him from other things. That boy is being very useful to me already.'

'I'm sure he is. It may be a silly question, but does he know anything about managing casinos? Or anything else, for that matter?'

'He'll learn,' Max said comfortably. 'If he doesn't, he'll be out on his ear.'

'You've made that clear to him, have you?'

'Of course.' He pursed his lips. 'It's pity I can't hope to open in time for the coronation. Three months ought to be long enough to get the premises ready, but I'm not sure Freddy can bring in enough members by then.'

'Not *sure*? That doesn't sound like my omnipotent brother.'

'Well, I'm in good company. Rumour has it that the hereditary Earl Marshal of England, no less, admits to being "not *sure*" of the coronation ceremonial because the last one was so long ago that no one can remember what happened at it.'

And then his face softened into the warm, intimate, humorous smile that Tassie found so hard to resist. 'Come on, Ginger. Do it for me. It'll be great.'

Miraculously, she succeeded in resisting. She wasn't going to be drawn back into the mesh of Max's plans. Her declaration of independence hadn't been just a

273

gesture, as he thought, but more, much more than that. She still loved him, would still defend him to the death, but her life now was her own and she wouldn't allow him to control it.

'No, Max, I'm sorry,' she said. 'It's a gorgeous idea, but I'm not prepared to leave my job, not even for you, and I don't have much spare time. If you find someone else to handle the designing and decorating, I'll give you an opinion, if you like. But no more than that.'

After a long, considering silence, he said, 'Don't try and cut yourself off from me, little sister. Because you won't succeed.'

CHAPTER TWO

I

There were flowers, flags, illuminations and triumphal arches everywhere. Royal visitors flocked to London from the Continent, troops from the colonies, and ordinary people from every corner of the British Isles. The country hadn't seen a coronation for sixty-four years.

But then they all had to turn round and go home again because, on the day of the final rehearsal at Westminster Abbey, the new king underwent an emergency operation for appendicitis and the coronation was postponed indefinitely.

The house in the Bayswater Road, which had been full to bursting point with St John parents and progeny ranging from two years of age up to a self-conscious sixteen, emptied again abruptly, to the unfilial relief of the eldest St John daughter who regarded large families, even her own, as no more than a means by which men kept women in subjection.

Fortunately, not everything had to be cancelled, and one of the celebrations that went ahead once it became known that the king would pull through was a dinner for the poor of London, at which almost half a million people were to sit down and eat at the royal expense while fifteen hundred entertainers, including Dan Leno, Little Tich, Vesta Tilley and Marie Lloyd, moved from one to another of the seven hundred venues, giving their services free.

Thousands of His Majesty's more prosperous subjects also volunteered to give their services free, including the barristers at the Inns of Court who declared themselves ready to roll up their starched white sleeves and take charge of the potatoes – something over a ton of them – for guests at their local venues.

Hugo, who had never seen a potato before except in a serving dish, insisted on being briefed in advance, and it took Norah, Tassie and the cook the better part of two hours to initiate him into the intricacies of their preparation.

'No, Hugo,' Norah said exasperatedly at one stage, 'a potato is not like an orange. There is no law that says you have to start at the stalk end. In fact, there isn't a stalk end, so you can stop looking for one. Start peeling wherever you want to. It really isn't difficult.'

A few moments later, 'Sakes alive!' exclaimed the cook, awed. 'If yez peels them as thick as that, there won't be enough left to give a man a dacent mouthful.'

Tempted, Tassie added her mite. 'And that means you'll have to peel even more of them, to make up.'

'Dash it all!' said a harassed Hugo.

He peeled the next potato so thinly that it took him fifteen minutes.

Norah said, 'This is insanity! Why on earth don't they just scrub the beastly things and boil them in their skins. Hugo, are you sure you've got it right?'

Her brother, struggling with an embedded eye, frowned. 'They only said *washing*, as it happens, but one never knows. I shouldn't like to find myself in the position of being asked to peel one and not knowing how. It wouldn't be the thing at all.'

With Norah showing signs of impending apoplexy, Tassie thought how like Hugo it was to waste their time in anticipation of a minor contretemps that anyone else would simply have laughed off. Somewhere, deep down, she supposed there must be a real Hugo, but in general he was more like an artificial creation, the product of what other people thought of him.

Norah was as unlike Hugo as Tassie herself was unlike Max. Families were queer things.

2

A few days after the dinner, during which time Hugo had applied more lanolin to his toilworn hands than most scullery maids did in a lifetime, he suggested to Tassie that they go out on their bicycles for a spin. Five miles would take them deep into the countryside, to sleepy old villages clustering, as they had done for centuries, round church and forge and inn.

The English countryside wasn't Tassie's natural habitat. Like her mother, she found it too bland and soft. But the prospect of exercise was alluring and it was a lovely evening. Norah, claiming that her feet hadn't yet recovered from serving dinner to three hundred people, declined an invitation to accompany them. Tassie could hardly be said to need a chaperone when she was with Hugo.

The roads were clear except for huge and fragrant haywains, an occasional herd of cows being driven home for the milking, and outside every cottage gate a squawking of suicidally inclined hens. The motorcar was still a rare intruder into this rural peace – Hugo, unlike Max, didn't think the motorcar would ever catch on – so that there were no petrol fumes to pollute an air scented by green fields, woods and hedgerows. Even the fine, white dust that in spells of drought sprayed the hedges shoulder high had been grounded by a brief afternoon shower.

They talked very little, skimming along almost without effort, coasting down hills, tinkling their bells on village corners and once or twice dodging some old gentleman who stepped out straight into the road as if their bicycles were no more than a mirage.

When it was almost time to turn back, they found an inn of antique charm set beside a village green with trees and a duckpond. The host, who looked as if he might have been there since Mr Jorrocks's day, served them with genial small talk, delicious ginger beer from a cold stone bottle for Tassie, and a fine old ale straight from the cellar for Hugo.

All in all, it had been a most satisfactory evening until they were halfway home and Hugo suggested stopping for a moment. They could find a gate to lean on and listen to the owls in the twilight and the swifts shrilling overhead.

Since Tassie had no particular fault to find with this except that she was hungry, which she politely refrained from mentioning, they propped their bicycles in the ditch and wandered away from the road in search – Hugo being an entirely literal person – of a gate suitable for leaning on.

Dutifully, Tassie said, 'Isn't it peaceful!'

'Yes.'

After a few minutes, she ventured, 'And so quiet. You wouldn't think London was just over the hill.'

'No.'

Hugo wasn't relaxed, but he never was, so Tassie didn't give the matter a second thought. After a further few minutes, she began to be bored. 'Should we go? I'm beginning to think I would like my supper.'

And then there was a flurry of movement beside her, and Hugo was down on one knee with her right hand in his, and he was looking up at her, his eyes large and doggy in the fading light. And he was saying, 'Oh, Tassie! Dearest Tassie! I had intended to wait until I was fully established at the Bar before I declared myself, but my feelings will not be repressed. You must allow me to tell you how ardently I admire and love you . . .'

Now, where had she heard that before? Torn between amusement, astonishment and exasperation,

Tassie withstood the temptation to reply as promptly and unequivocally to Hugo as Elizabeth Bennet had done to Mr Darcy.

The trouble was that Hugo almost certainly didn't realise that his words were anyone's but his own. He must have been made to read Jane Austen at school, Tassie supposed.

'Urrr . . .' she said.

But Hugo was not to be silenced.

'I have very little to offer you at this moment, but my prospects are excellent. I have already established a reputation as a sound man, someone who has no truck with unorthodoxy and holds the letter of the law as sacrosanct. And, of course, some day I will inherit my father's title, though not for many years, I hope. In the meantime, I believe I will soon be able to offer you the domestic felicity which, despite your brave attempts to disguise it, is what your heart truly desires.'

No one had ever addressed Tassie in such rolling periods before. Thinking, 'Dickens?' and ignoring, for the time being, the small matter of what her heart truly desired, she said, 'Yes, but Hugo . . .'

'Oh, Tassie, will you promise yourself to me? Since you are of age, I believe I need not apply to your brother for his permission, but if you wish me to do so . . .'

'*Hugo!*' she exclaimed. 'Don't you dare go near Max!'

And then, since it had sounded altogether too minatory – not to mention ungrateful and unromantic – she moderated her tone and, resorting to the formula which had served her on three occasions during her student days, went on, 'This is so unexpected. I don't know what to say.'

'Say yes!' he beseeched, spoiling the effect by shifting slightly, as if he were kneeling on a stone.

A few weeks earlier, Tassie had gone with Norah to see Madame Bernhardt in *La Dame aux Camélias* and, remembering the dry sobs and heartbroken despair of that lady's farewell to Armand, now found herself regretting the limitations of being so disgustingly young and healthy. But she could think of no good reason for declaring the love between herself and Hugo to be doomed, so she was forced to fall back on murmurings about being honoured, and holding Hugo in the greatest esteem, but regretting that her heart was not engaged.

She didn't want to hurt him, and perhaps her rejection didn't sound, to a young man who lacked insight into the minds of others, quite as decisive as she would have liked. Because he wasn't in the least cast down. He had probably read somewhere that a modest and wellbred young lady always rejected a suitor at the first time of asking.

He said, 'You are right to hesitate, when I cannot yet offer you the comforts to which you are accustomed. But although you may not love me now, I will wait, knowing that, when I ask you again, you will give me a different answer.'

Tassie couldn't very well say outright that she thought it highly unlikely. So she compromised with, 'Perhaps,' and then, 'Do get up, Hugo. You'll have grass stains all over your trousers.'

3

During the remainder of their ride home, she thought only of Francis Rivers.

Her days were so full now that, when she went to bed at night, she no longer drifted off to sleep thinking of him. She didn't even dream about him, didn't relive those moments of searing physical delight that had possessed her at the wedding ball, didn't feel the firm touch of his hand in the small of her back as they danced, or the long, warm eloquence of his kiss.

The bad times were in the mornings when, waking,

she lay quietly, gathering herself together for the day in the knowledge that this would be just one more day, in a lifetime of days stretching before her, when she would not see him.

If Hugo had tried to kiss her, she couldn't have borne it.

4

Norah was in her studio when they reached home, stitching away at a surplice that, designed according to the most advanced precepts of the Glasgow School of Art, seemed likely to give the vicar of Prebend's Caundle a seizure when Sir Halbert and Lady St John ceremonially presented it to him.

'Pleasant ride?' she asked.

'Yes, thank you,' said Tassie.

'Yes,' said Hugo, whose vocabulary didn't include the words 'thank you'.

'You had a visitor when you were out, Tassie,' Norah reported, a gleam in her eye that made Tassie look at her suspiciously.

'Who?'

'You'll never guess! The famous Mrs Merton. And I must say, I would *love* to know something about that lady's background. You don't become as consequential as that without putting in some pretty hard work on it.'

Intrigued, Tassie said, 'Do you think so? I've always thought she must have been born that way. I mean, it's impossible to imagine her as a child making mud pies! What did she want?'

Norah anchored her needle in the satin and pointed to a small package on the drawing table. 'She brought back your pendant. She's sorry it's been so long and she still doesn't have a valuation for it, because it seems valuers rely on comparisons and nothing similar has come on the market for aeons. I said that sounded hopeful – rarity value, and so on – but she just smiled and told me, "Not necessarily." Connoisseurs today, apparently, draw a line between art with a moral message and art that is merely religious. They fall over each other bidding for the first, but have very little interest in the second.'

'You mean they'd rather have Alma-Tadema than Michelangelo? But that's ridiculous.'

'Yes. It makes you see why Fra Newbery always told us never to judge art by its market price, doesn't it? Anyway, your exotic friend says the valuers have made some sketches and taken notes and will go on asking. It seems the insurance companies don't accept valuations conjured out of thin air.'

Hugo said, 'You can't expect them to. If you consider . . .'

And he was off. Having been briefed the previous year to appear in Huddersfield for a small insurance company – in the matter of a claim amounting to £4.3s.7d – he knew everything there was to know about insurance. To give him credit, he was capable of being every bit as fluent on subjects about which he knew nothing at all.

As Tassie went upstairs to take off her hat, Norah called after her, 'Supper's ready, so don't be long. Oh, and by the way, Mrs Merton said the pendant needed cleaning, so she's had it done for you. No charge.'

What had come over the lady, Tassie wondered, that she should be indulging in good deeds?

5

Later, preparing for bed, she unwrapped the package and opened the velvet-lined box, relieved to have the jewel back again, taking it out and fingering it, her own private talisman, longing for its reassurance.

But her fingers recoiled from it and her heart, too,

was disturbed. She had come to know the feel of it so well over the years, but something was different now. Wrong. Studying it under the lamp, she saw that in the course of cleaning it had lost the lovely patina the centuries had given it, so that the subtle smokiness of the crystal had become clear as glass and the enamelling, once rich and muted, was almost gaudy. It looked, now, as it must have done when it first left the craftsman's workshop four hundred years before, a bright new ornament for some Renaissance beauty's neck.

After a time, with depression and a curious distaste, she returned it to its case and put the case in a drawer. Why had she ever let it out of her possession? She supposed people whose homes had been burgled must feel like this, must have this same sense of desecration, of distress over something deeply private and personal having been contaminated by the touch of strangers.

She shivered.

6

Max and Genevieve's new house in Audley Street had been finished four weeks before the baby was due, and Max had moved in immediately.

Though determined to wet the baby's head with champagne as soon as it was born, he had pointed out that he was much too busy with the casino to waste time loafing about Kirklaws with Genny, waiting for her confinement. *Ergo*, he had said – a word he had picked up somewhere and was currently working to death – Genny must arrange to be confined in London. 'All the best doctors', he had written temptingly.

Accordingly, escorted by her mother-in-law and a bevy of servants, a complaining Genny had travelled down to London from Kirklaws in the very last stages of her pregnancy.

Even Grace found it difficult to defend Max. Escaping from Audley Street at the earliest opportunity for a cosy supper with Tassie and Norah, she crossed the threshold of the house in the Bayswater Road saying, 'Don't on any account mention Max's lack of consideration for Genny or I shall leave again at once.'

Hugging her convulsively, Tassie exclaimed, 'How heavenly it is to see you. You look amazingly well. Was it a terrible journey? What's the house like? Does it have lingerie lampshades? Is it livable in?'

'Professionally decorated and quite without soul. I shall have to do something about making it more homely, because Max doesn't notice and Genny has only one thought in her head. In fact, you would imagine no young woman had ever had a baby before.'

Tassie, laughing, said, 'What's this – criticising? You? Genny *must* have been giving you a difficult time!'

'Don't! Norah, my dear, what a pleasure to see you again.'

No one could have guessed that Grace entered the St John residence with a certain unease, having spent the previous six months concerned less about the office in which her daughter was working than the house in which she was living. It had sounded just a little Bohemian, with no mature adult to keep an eye on three high-spirited young people. Grace didn't for a moment doubt their virtue and knew that an arrangement which would have been shockingly unconventional in St Andrews was probably perfectly commonplace in London, but she was in need of reassurance. Tassie's letters, bubbling over with enthusiasm for her work, customarily ended with, 'Goodness, look at the time! Must stop now. Am very comfortable at the St John house and Norah sends her love.' There was no intention of misleading. It was just that it never occurred to children to tell their parents what their parents really wanted to know.

Grace hoped that Mr Hugo St John, whom she had not met, would put in an appearance at some stage of the evening. She would feel more comfortable if she were able to judge him for herself.

When Grace had related as much of the St Andrews gossip as she felt Norah could decently be expected to listen to – omitting, of course, Dudley and Selina's repeated and slanderous assaults on Max's good name – Tassie said, 'With all this excitement over Genny and Audley Street and the casino, I keep forgetting to ask Max how things are going at Dunaird. Have you heard? Has the rebuilding begun?'

'Not yet. Max has had such a busy eighteen months that one could hardly have expected it.' Then, recognising that her daughter was on the verge of saying something impolite about Max's priorities and because she herself was, truthfully, just a little disappointed, she went on without pausing, 'But he has found an architect who has been up to Dunaird and taken measurements and done drawings. The difficulty is that he is working on other commissions at the moment and cannot leave London for any extended period. Max says that, since Dunaird is so isolated, he will have to live "on site" – is that the expression? – while the work is being done. So he must arrange to have the months between April and September completely free. Apparently that is always difficult for a busy architect.'

'Who is he?' Norah asked.

'A Mr Delafond.'

Norah and Tassie exchanged raised eyebrows. 'He could be one of those frightful chaps who specialise in restoration work,' Norah suggested, and Tassie chuckled.

'The kind we were never allowed to know about!'

Grace, scenting impropriety, asked anxiously, 'Why not?'

'Don't worry, mother.' Tassie patted her hand. 'At

school we were taught that restoring old buildings was equivalent to turning them into fakes. The correct thing to do was tear them down and start again, preferably with a lovely new design by . . .'

She waved an imaginary baton at Norah and, in perfect harmony, they warbled, 'Mr Charles Rennie Mackintosh!'

Grace felt a rush of warmth for the pair of them, so young and cheerful and uncomplicated, so different from the complaining Genny – poor child – and from disingenuous Max, whose mind Grace was still unable to penetrate. It was strange, when she thought about it, because she had always been able to read his father without difficulty.

Smiling, she said, 'I imagine he must be "a frightful restoration chap". Although Max claims to be The Modern Man in everything else, he is blessedly un-modern in his architectural tastes.'

To her surprise, she discovered in the course of the girls' chatter that Norah and Max had never met, though on reflection she thought that perhaps it wasn't so surprising after all. Max had been possessive of Tassie since the very beginning, when he had relied on her to instruct him in all the things he didn't know. It had been charming, then, but perhaps a little less charming later, when he found it impossible to free Tassie from his thrall and accept that she might have a life of her own and friends of her own. Certainly, Max would have made no effort to become acquainted with Norah.

And perhaps Tassie herself had kept them apart, knowing that they wouldn't get on. Max would unfailingly have said something about women's suffrage or women workers to set Norah's hackles up.

Norah would have invited it, of course.

Indeed, at this very moment, sitting over coffee in the drawing-room, she was demanding of Grace, 'Did you

see that news item about Glasgow magistrates insisting
that all the city's barmaids had to be sacked in the interests
of "good order, morality and propriety"? They claimed
that the respectable life of a barmaid was only three years!
The appeal court overturned the ruling but really, what
can you do with people like that? And it isn't as if it's only
Glasgow. Last year, a woman surgeon in Macclesfield
had to resign because her men colleagues refused to work
with her. And in the State of New York they've
introduced a bill to prohibit flirting in public, and the
Prussian government has forbidden women – not men,
mind you! – to form political associations, and . . .'

'Norah!' Tassie intervened tunefully.

'Oh, all right. But your mother ought to know about
such things. *All* women ought to know about such
things.'

Just then, they heard the jangling of the front door
bell.

'That'll be Hugo,' Norah said.

7

It wasn't Hugo. It was an American gentleman with
curly brown hair, engaging dimples, a rangy figure,
and an artist's portfolio. Finding himself in the presence
of no less than three ladies, he added to his other
attributes a faint blush of embarrassment and some
voluble apologies.

Being Gus Silvermann, however, he showed no
inclination to beat a retreat saying, 'It can wait till
tomorrow'. Business was business, after all.

Waiting only for the introductions to be completed,
'We have a problem, Miss Smith,' he said. 'Dodge and
Draycott. One of their dratted new chair designs – if
you'll pardon my language, ma'am – hasn't come in to
the warehouse, and they refuse to okay the advert as it
stands.'

'But the artwork has to go to the blockmaker first thing in the morning or we'll miss the deadline!'

'Just so.' He produced a scrap of pencilled paper from the portfolio. 'They want that one shown instead. Can you do it?'

Norah said, 'Use my studio, Tassie. Would you like some coffee, Mr Silvermann? I'll go and see to it.'

As she followed Tassie and the portfolio out of the room, Tassie murmured to her, 'Tell cook to make it strong enough to dance on.'

8

Half an hour later, Tassie returned to the drawing room, saying as she entered, 'I think this ought to do.' But no one noticed her.

Hugo was seated beside her mother, looking like a cross between an obedient foxhound and a cleancut young English gentleman and submitting courteously to a stiff *viva voce* on his past life, present condition and future prospects. Norah was noticeably tidier than half an hour before – even her fine, flyaway hair, which always began to come down within minutes of being pinned up, looked very nearly respectable – and was listening raptly to G.S., who was well launched into the arcana of the coffee bean, its multifarious varieties, geographical preferences, cultivation requirements, rules for roasting and grinding, and methods of making.

Mother, suitor, friend, employer – all cosily settled in, getting to know one another, forming opinions.

Ruefully surveying them, Tassie was struck by the thought that it wasn't humanly possible to live a life entirely of one's own. Or not without keeping every person one loved or liked – or disliked – in a separate compartment.

That was something she could not do.

Max could.

She wasn't sure about Francis.

9

On the following Saturday, in order to free Grace to go shopping for some home comforts for Audley Street – 'Don't forget the antimacassars!' – Tassie volunteered to accompany Genny on a drive round Hyde Park.

The penny chairs, from Hyde Park Corner to the Albert Gate, were thronged with smartly dressed ladies and gentlemen and prim little girls and boys, while the truly fashionable people, their offspring despatched to Kensington Gardens in the care of Nanny, drove round the magic Ring, revelling in seeing and being seen.

Three times round the park was the formula. On the first circuit, Genny was full of vivacious chatter, admiring handsome turnouts and laughing at extravagant hats.

By halfway round the second circuit, she was yearning after the elegant dresses she couldn't wear because of the baby and envying all those ladies whose husbands had the time and inclination to accompany them.

'Max hates horses,' she said disconsolately.

'I know.'

'And I adore them. I had the dearest little pony when I was a child.'

'The baby can have one, too, when it's old enough.'

'I don't know whether Max would allow . . .'

'Genny, you must stand up to him!'

Genny sighed deeply. 'It's all very well for you. You know how to talk to him. He thinks I'm featherbrained. He never talks to me properly, not the way he does to That Woman.'

Tassie didn't have to ask who she meant.

'She came to dine that evening mother-in-law was

visiting you, and I had to sit at my own table –
absolutely *ignored* – while she and Max discussed
politics and business and all sorts of other boring things.
I was *humiliated*.'

'You shouldn't let it worry you. They've known
each other for years. I felt exactly the same the first time
I met her. I hadn't a notion what the pair of them were
talking about. Max probably didn't realise that you
were feeling left out. You should have said.'

'How could I? That Woman would just have looked
at me with her horrid, condescending smile and made
me feel six inches high.'

Something, Tassie thought, was going to have to be
done about Naomi Merton. It really was most unfair of
Max. 'Ask mama to have a word with Max, then. He'll
listen to her.'

'Oh, I wouldn't dare! She's so fond of him and so
serene, herself, that she wouldn't understand. She
would think I was just letting it all get out of proportion
because I'm so nervous about the baby.'

She twirled her parasol petulantly and then, seeing an
unknown gentleman eyeing her with admiration – her
advanced state of pregnancy being concealed by the
sides of the carriage and a whole haberdasher's worth of
scarves and shawls – smiled shyly back at him from
under her lashes.

'If it weren't for the baby I could be having such fun,
even without Max. I never have any fun at all. I didn't
even have my comeout last year with everything being
cancelled because of the queen's death. And I missed
Ascot last month because I was banished to Kirklaws
and Max said he wouldn't have taken me anyway
because it wouldn't have been decent with the baby
showing so much. I'm just *miserable*.'

She sniffled.

'Well, if today is a specimen of your normal conversation,' Tassie said, trying not to sound unkind, 'I'm

not surprised that Max prefers talking to Mrs Merton. He's a clever man, and you can't expect him to put up with such vapourings. You really must pull yourself together, Genny!'

'I suppose so. I'll try, once the baby arrives. But just now I feel too awful and I don't get any sympathy at all. It isn't fair.'

Tassie persevered. 'And when the baby does arrive, don't for heaven's sake turn into one of those mothers who can't think or talk about anything else. Max won't thank you for spending all your time goo-gooing about what an "adorable little bunny" it is.'

She might as well have saved her breath.

'No.' Genny, wearing victimhood as another person might have worn sainthood, eyed some bunting that had been left strung from the trees to bridge the gap between coronation days. 'I wish I weren't going to miss all the fun of the coronation, too. Max wants us to give a huge party and he was horridly cross when I said I wouldn't be well enough. But mother-in-law took my side, so he gave in.'

Tassie, aware of an increasingly urgent desire to scream and drum her heels on the floor of carriage, saw with relief that they were approaching the Stanhope Gate exit from the park, so, encouragingly, she said, 'I know you're not well and feeling depressed, but you must try and look at things more optimistically. If the baby arrives when it's supposed to, you'll have two whole weeks to recover before Coronation Day. You'll be able to go to all the parties you want to.'

'But I've nothing to wear.'

Through clenched teeth, Tassie said, 'Max will be so proud of you that he'll pay for as many beautiful new dresses as you could possibly want.'

'Mmmm.' Genny was thoughtful for a moment, her blue eyes lowered. 'I really don't know why he married me. If all he wanted was sons, I'd have expected him to marry someone cleverer than me. I think he just wanted to have a Sir as a father-in-law.'

'Don't be silly.' Tassie's reaction was automatic and she regretted it at once, as she found herself wondering whether Genny was, after all, quite as brainless as she seemed.

10

Edward Maximilian McKenzie Smith was born with obliging promptitude on the 26th July 1902. He was named, of course, after the king.

Mother and son were both well.

Max was almost as effervescent as the champagne he poured liberally for everyone who crossed the threshold, right down to the knife grinder who, his street cries eliciting no response, stepped uninvited into the kitchen in case they hadn't heard him and was found by Grace, two hours later, curled up in a corner, snoring blissfully.

Fortunately, the shops were still open when the baby arrived and Max was able to drive round to Hennell's, where they had put two diamond tiaras aside in anticipation of the happy event, one a light and lacy confection like woven ribbons, the other – unmistakably the more expensive – a wreath of stars.

'It's a boy,' Max announced.

The manager congratulated him with great sincerity and, without another word, returned the cheaper tiara to its cabinet and wrapped the expensive one for Mr McKenzie Smith to take home as a reward for the mother of his son.

11

The coronation, this time, took place as scheduled and the king stood the strain very well. It was the

Archbishop of Canterbury who was overcome by dizziness as he was placing the crown on the royal head, and had to be helped from the scene.

Tassie, who had spent a goodly part of the preceding months incorporating likenesses of the imperial couple into advertisements for everything from custard powder and dentifrice paste to metal polish and lamp oil, was relieved when it was over and said so to Norah as they turned away from watching the procession, a disappointing and rather badly managed affair marked by such long gaps that thousands of people had gone home early, thinking it was over.

'I'd guess His Majesty must be relieved, too,' remarked Norah. 'Someone gave me a "Spratt's Patent Dog Cakes" bookmark the other day illustrated with H.M. in full regalia, crown and all. I must admit, he did look a bit like a Labrador.'

Tassie giggled. 'Poor man. It must have been a very tiring day for him, especially after being so ill. And I suppose he has to face a Coronation Banquet and Ball tonight, too, just like the rest of us.'

'Well, at least he has his own fancy dress outfit, what with all that ermine and velvet and stuff. I tried to persuade Hugo that the only dressing up *he* needed to do for the Walters's affair was to put on his barrister's gown and that silly wig and gaiters and pass himself off as Judge Jeffreys of the Bloody Assize. But he wouldn't have it. He said the theme was "Royal Romance" and romantic he was determined to be.'

'Oh, dear.'

Norah grinned. 'Yes, my girl, you'd better beware. He's going as Bruce and the Spider.'

'Ugh! What a funny idea of "romantic"!'

'Try, try, try again . . .' murmured Norah.

12

Norah was dressed as Queen Anne, because she said Queen Anne had been no sylph, either, and the country cousin who was making up the four arrived as King Arthur, fortunately *sans* armour, though he said they had a very nice suit of it at home.

Tassie, who had had quite enough of Mary, Queen of Scots and was, besides, disinclined to wear her jewel, had scanned the roster of royal inamoratas and decided on Nell Gwyn as being not only more fun than Madame de Pompadour but much less expensive to dress.

'Oh, very fetching,' exclaimed Norah when she appeared in her outrageously low décolletage and panniered skirt. 'You're sure that neckline will hold up? Stitchery was never your strong point.'

Hugo, unaccustomed to seeing quite so much of the lady he intended to marry, goggled as, ignoring the slur on her stitchery – which was entirely justified – Tassie flirted her skirts seductively and said, 'Shall we go?'

It was a very smart occasion – a banquet for a hundred people and a ball for five hundred – and the generous scale of it, said Norah, wasn't unconnected with the fact that the host and hostess, Gloucestershire neighbours of the St Johns, had five plain but good-natured daughters to get off their hands. Sir Walter, she added, was something important in the City and Hugo was looking forward to receiving some profitable briefs from that direction. 'Nothing like a bit of neighbourly nepotism to help a young man get established.'

Since there were a good many such affairs being held across London that evening, which meant that the most sought-after members of Society were hotfooting it from one great house to another to spend a bare half hour in each, there was a constant coming and going. Snatching a glance out of the tall windows as Hugo whirled her past, Tassie was amused to see that, with one exception, the queue of conveyances outside consisted entirely of covered horsedrawn carriages. No lady wanted her coiffure windblown or her costume covered with dust, which were among the inescapable hazards of travelling in a motorcar.

The one exception, her quick glimpse told her, was a Daimler like Max's.

It was Max's. Some few minutes later, Henry VIII entered the ballroom with, on his arm, not Anne Boleyn but Mary, Queen of Scots – a Mary clad in an uncanonically pale blue velvet that matched her eyes, a traditional, heart-shaped headdress on her untraditional blonde hair, and her pearly teeth showing prettily through slightly parted pink lips.

Round her neck she was wearing Tassie's jewel.

13

The jewel she had left in her drawer at home . . .

'Hugo, will you put that stupid spider in your pocket. It's tickling the back of my neck. And you haven't met my brother. Come and I'll introduce you.'

By the time they had woven their way through the crowds, Max and Genny were deep in conversation with someone, but Max winked cheerfully at Tassie as if there was nothing wrong at all.

People with flaming hair were reputed to have tempers to match, but Tassie's temper had always been equable. Until now, when she discovered what rage was. How dared her high-handed brother borrow her jewel without permission! *How* had he borrowed it without permission?

Even so, when Max and his wife turned towards her, remarking that they hadn't expected to see her here, she was able to control herself sufficiently to make the introductions. She even said, her voice shaking only a very little, how pretty Genny was looking, and that she

295

hoped she had completely recovered from the baby's birth.

Genny said she still felt awfully delicate but it was lovely to go to parties again.

Finally, baldly, Tassie said, 'My jewel.'

Max's eyes didn't flicker. 'Your jewel? No. Only a trinket, my dear. With fancy dress balls all the rage, Naomi Merton had the notion of having a copy made for Genny. A charming thought, in my view.'

It sounded possible, even plausible.

After a moment, Tassie said tightly, 'She should have asked. *You* should have asked.'

Max shrugged. 'If you're annoyed, I'm sorry, though I don't know why you should be. Genny, that's Masterson over there. Come along, I want to have a word with him. We'll see you later, Tassie.'

But even as he spoke, Tassie was saying, 'May I see?' and taking the jewel into her own, unsteady hand.

The crystal was faintly smoky and rubbed, not clear as glass. And the enamelling was not as bright as if it had come straight from the craftsman's workshop. It was soft and mellow, rich with the patina of centuries.

Tassie, her eyes stark, looked up at Max and knew he must be able to read the fury and the pain in them.

But the faint smile on his face didn't falter.

Surrounded by half the fashionable world, she couldn't cry out that her brother was a cheap, common thief.

14

Hugo took her home early, Norah saying she might as well come, too. One ball was very much like another, and King Arthur wouldn't mind being left to his own devices, would he? King Arthur, his eye on a pretty little Cinderella who was there with her parents, said he didn't mind at all.

Norah knew when not to ask questions, even if she found it difficult sometimes. She had always felt towards Tassie like a mother hen with a peculiarly trusting and unworldly chick. All she said, however, when they reached home, was, 'There's something badly wrong. Can I help?'

But Tassie shook her head, and went to her room and took out her pendant and looked at it. Unnecessarily.

It was the worst night of her life, worse than the night after Max had told her she must leave art school, worse than the night after Selina's revelations, worse even than the night of the wedding ball, when she had decided never to see Francis Rivers again.

15

At eight the next morning, on her way to work, she called at Audley Street, but Mr McKenzie Smith had already left. At seven in the evening, on her way home, she called again. Mr McKenzie Smith had not yet returned, and Madam was dressing for dinner. At ten, she went back. Mr and Mrs McKenzie Smith were out at a party.

She left a note, but Max didn't answer it.

Five days passed before she caught him at lunchtime in his office, with the phonograph grinding out, 'In the good old summer time'.

He said, 'My dear girl, you're not still fussing about that trinket? Really, I'm not in the mood for discussing it. I have more important things on my mind.'

The edge of her anger had dulled, as he must have known it would, but the misery remained. And the incomprehension.

'More important things than my feelings? I suppose so. I suppose that when you're the Great Max, ordinary human considerations come very low on your list of priorities.'

With an exaggerated sigh, he sat back in his chair. 'You disappoint me, Tassie. Emotional blackmail isn't worthy of you.'

'In that case, let's leave emotion out of it. Let's forget that you're my brother and that I love you. Let's forget that I thought you loved me, too. Let's just talk about the jewel. I gave it to you to give to Mrs Merton for an insurance valuation. A few weeks ago, she brought it back, saying she had had it cleaned. I thought that was why it seemed different. But now I know that what she gave me was only a fake, and that Genevieve has the real jewel.

'I thought at first that I wanted an explanation from you, but I don't any more. I don't care. Just give me back my pendant and let's forget the whole affair.'

She had spoken with deliberation and a weary contempt; which brought a frown to Max's brow. No one spoke to Max McKenzie Smith with contempt.

The phonograph wheezed into silence.

'*Your* pendant?' he said, the dark bar of his eyebrows rising. 'My dear girl, it's a family jewel. It should have come to me with the rest of the estate.' His voice was dismissive, as if he were ending a board meeting that had gone on too long.

She tried to hold his gaze, but his eyes were already returning to the papers on his desk.

'Max! Look at me! That isn't true. It was a personal gift from my father. The jewel is mine, and you stole it from me.'

Then, suddenly, he was grinning at her and saying, 'Well, it was worth a try! And it's your own fault for refusing to help me with the casino.'

'What?'

'It was a joke, young Ginger. Diamond cut diamond, remember? I had to teach you a lesson!' He was looking amused and coaxing and pleased with himself all at once.

Her heart fluttering and her voice uneven, she said, 'You mean all this has been – a punishment?'

'That's putting it too high. It was only meant to be a rap over the knuckles.' His smile was that of a guilty small boy caught in the orchard and pretending he had every right to be there.

'For God's sake, sit down, will you!' he said. 'It was a mistake, to begin with. What happened was that the pendant and the copy were in similar boxes and Naomi dropped one of them in at the Bayswater Road on her way to dine with us in Audley Street. It was only when Genny opened hers that Naomi realised she'd left you the wrong box. She was going to change them but I said not to. I said you probably wouldn't even notice. I thought I'd tease you about it and make you feel thoroughly embarrassed when I finally gave you the right one and explained what had happened.'

Mischief. Nothing but mischief.

'Mind you,' he went on, 'I take it a bit hard, you accusing me of stealing it. Such a thought should never have entered your head. I'm Max, your brother, remember?'

It was true. Why *should* it have entered her head, so immediately and so convincingly?

After a moment, she said, 'It's an explanation, but not a justification.'

Then she rose and, taking the false jewel from her purse, tossed it down on his desk. 'I'll drop in at Audley Street tomorrow and collect the real one.'

'No. I'll send one of the servants round with it.' His eyes narrowed. 'Don't be such a spoilsport, Tassie! It was just a bit of fun.'

But she turned and left without another word.

16

She had always known that Max loved stimulus, loved making things happen and keeping people on the hop, that he took a positive pleasure in seeing how much he could get away with. It was one of the reasons why he was so successful in business.

She had tried not to be hurt on the occasions when he had played the same tricks on her. It was just Max being Max. It was the kind of person he was.

Did all men, she wondered, carry something of the schoolboy with them through life? An echo of the destructiveness of adolescence, when it was a sign of being grownup and devil-may-care to send cricket balls through people's windows, or pull the wings off butterflies, or throw cats in the water and watch them drown. There was nothing else to explain the blind spots in an otherwise mature and intelligent adult, the dulled imagination, the habit of equating sensitivity with weakness, the inability to sympathise with emotions he didn't share.

Were all men like that? Tassie didn't know. After eight years she was only just beginning to understand Max. How could she tell what Hugo, or Gus Silvermann – or Francis Rivers – was really like inside?

Max had no conception of the enormity of what he had done. And that meant she must forgive him, although she didn't think she could forget.

17

Mr Silvermann's voice said, 'Miss Smith!' and she had to turn her attention to the poster for the Automobile Club's reliability trials on the 1st September. The run was to be from the Crystal Palace to Folkestone and back, and G.S. wanted some extra specially striking lettering for the headline. 'Automobiles – as reliable as the railways!'

Betrayed into something approaching a laugh, Tassie murmured, 'The triumph of optimism over experience!' and Mr Silvermann grinned at her.

'You'll find out,' he said, 'because it is my intention to enter my De Dion. A small, refined streamer along the side – which you will letter for me – will say "G.S. Advertising" and, since all autos are expected to carry a full complement of passengers, you will also accompany me. Mr Fothergill can come, too, as I understand him to be familiar with the mysteries of the internal combustion engine. And perhaps,' he hesitated briefly, 'your friend Miss St John might be willing to make a fourth?'

'I'm sure she'd be delighted.'

Afterwards, sorting through her lettering pens, she wondered whether Max was entering the Daimler and then, frowning slightly, realised that there was still something about his explanation that nagged at her mind, something small, specific and wrong, but she couldn't think what it was.

It probably wasn't important.

CHAPTER THREE

I

The woman in the bed shrieked and shrieked, crying out in words that had no form to them, burying her face in the pillows and turning again instantly, as though blindness were more fearful than sight, tearing at the lace coverlet, staring, opening her mouth to shriek again.

It would have been hard for a stranger to tell what age she was, because though she was slight as a girl, though her skin was unlined and her hair invisible under a cap, her eyebrows were grey.

Hurrying through the door and across the room, Francis put his arms round her. 'Lucia, Lucia, my love,' he said. 'It's all right. She won't harm you.'

Then, with Lucia clinging desperately to him, shaken with dry sobs, he turned to his mother and said, 'Can I not leave you alone with her for five minutes?'

Abigail sat rigid in her chair at the foot of the bed, her face as blanched as her pearls. 'I did not even speak. Why do I terrify her so?'

Francis didn't answer. It was a question that had been asked and answered too many times before.

2

When Lucia was sufficiently calm to be left in the care of Mistress Gunter, her nurse, Francis and his mother went downstairs to where Jonny was waiting for them, a twenty-six-year-old army lieutenant in full regimentals who could face up to the Boers without a qualm, but not to Lucia.

He said anxiously, 'Is she all right? I heard her screaming. I didn't know whether I should come up.'

His mother and brother stared at him for a moment, handsomely, insolently alike. And then the tension faded and their mouths twitched in amusement.

Abigail said, 'A noble impulse, my dear, but we wouldn't ask it of you. Francis, perhaps your housekeeper would make us some tea. David and I have been closeted with one of our suppliers and I have had nothing since midday.'

'Jonny?'

'Yes. For me too, please.'

When the tea had been brought, Abigail said, 'Save for Lucia's room, I have rarely seen a more comfortless, uninviting house. What is the purpose in employing a housekeeper, if not to give the place at least an appearance of being civilised?'

'She keeps it clean. She is forbidden to tidy up because, when she does, I can never find anything. And since I don't entertain, I see no need for soft lighting, comfortable armchairs, lace curtains and aspidistras.'

'Monastic, that's the word,' said Jonny, quietly triumphant. But although his brother rewarded him with an admiring glance, his mother ignored him.

'Perhaps, then, you should mend your ways and take the trouble to do some entertaining. It might make you some friends. You appear to be in need of them.'

From the depths of her old-fashioned black velvet reticule she produced a newspaper cutting and tossed it over to Francis. 'Have you seen that?'

He glanced at it. 'No. Today's?'

She nodded.

Francis had first become aware of the gossip some

weeks before, when fellow journalists had taken to remarking, 'Hear the *Enterprise* isn't doing too well, old chap? Bad luck.'

It was untrue, and he had said so firmly and frequently. But he had not succeeded in scotching the rumours, which had continued to gain currency until now paragraphs were appearing in the national press. There was one thing you could always be sure of in the newspaper business – dog would eat dog, and with gusto.

Francis's first thought had been that it was a spoiling operation, a way of undermining his new national newspaper before it had even been born. But the more he considered it, the less likely this seemed. No one but he and his backers knew of the project; not his present staff, not even his mother and brothers. It was to no one's advantage to talk out of turn and for someone to have found out by accident was equally unlikely. The offices he had rented in Fleet Street were small and suitable only as the London base for a provincial newspaper. It would have taken prior knowledge to start someone asking about the premises next door, currently occupied by a long established law firm whose lease was due to fall in at the end of 1903, just when Francis was ready to take it over.

His eyes skimming the cutting, he saw that the tone was one that had become spitefully familiar by now, the argument even more hollow than usual. There was some windy dialectic about the social duties of the Fourth Estate, what people wanted of their newspapers, and how only a lifetime in journalism could supply it. Although editors were willing – nay, proud – to fill their pages with contributions on politics and science, medicine and literature by the most knowledgeable and distinguished men of the age, they were not themselves, could not be, and indeed should not be, experts in any particular field.

Therein lay the seeds of the professional editor's greatness. With an instinct for balance nurtured over many years of experience, he strove to provide his readers with the material which would enable them, under his own impartial guidance, to distinguish truth from equivocation in the conflicting pronouncements of the great.

'The editor of this journal,' quoth the piece of newsprint in Francis's hand, 'takes pride in declaring that he not only edits for the common man. He *is* the common man . . .'

Queasily, Francis wondered what on earth had possessed him to want to be a journalist in the first place.

'. . . and this,' continued the cutting, winding up to its peroration, 'is why even the greatest of editors would scorn to have academic initials appended to their names. This is why, when some pretentious young sprig from a university comes among us, we watch his progress with tolerance and wait to see him make mistakes, as he inevitably does.

'Two years ago, a Glasgow weekly newspaper called the *Enterprise* – a dashing title, you will agree – was launched as a daily by an owner with letters after his name (Cambridge BA, no less), an owner who declared his intention of creating a new kind of newspaper for a new kind of reader. We old hands, we fear, had heard it all before. As was to be expected, the result has been a fiasco.

'We understand the newspaper is on the brink of failing. There is a moral here, as there is a moral in every tale of the sort. It is that clever young men should stick to their Latin and Greek. The world of today, the world where events of great pith and moment are taking place, the world not of the Classical dead but of living people – such a world is not for them.'

Abigail said, 'I have rarely read such unmitigated twaddle. What have you done to offend?'

'Nothing. Or nothing that I know of.'

'Then why is there such a strong note of personal animosity?'

'I have no idea.'

'I take it there is no truth in the rumours?'

He shook his head.

'Then we need not concern ourselves.'

It wasn't quite a question, but Francis felt impelled to say, 'As it happens, I have certain plans afoot that might be damaged by such talk.'

'Then make a public denial.'

He smiled. 'That might work in the cotton business. In journalism it would merely increase speculation. No, if this is an attack on me, personally, as it appears to be, the solution may be for me to remove myself from the target area for a while.'

The idea must already have been at the back of his mind, he later realised, or it wouldn't have sprung so suddenly to the forefront, fully formed. He needed time away from everything and everyone, and if he didn't go soon he would have no other opportunity in the forseeable future.

It had been a particularly busy year, not only because he had been engrossed in planning but because, with one political drama following on the heels of another, he had been working a seven-day week most of the time. He couldn't remember when he had last had a Saturday off. His staff had always complained about him being a singleminded bastard, but until the last few months they hadn't known the meaning of the words.

What he would do was take a few days' break in Wester Ross first – just to reassure himself that his new deputy could be trusted to handle the *Enterprise* in his absence – and then hie himself off to foreign parts in search of change and stimulus; in search, too, of reliable stringers in the further flung corners of the globe. The *Enterprise* already felt the lack of them, and they'd be essential when he went national.

Aloud, he said, 'I'm considering going abroad. On business, but it will give the gossip here time to die down.'

'What about Lucia?' his mother demanded instantly.

The inevitable question. The question that followed him everywhere, like the black dog at his heels.

'I'm not sure yet. She might not miss me. There are times, now, when she doesn't even recognise me. I'll consult with Mistress Gunter.' And then, 'When do you have to report back to barracks, Jonny?'

'Next Tuesday.'

'Let's travel down together a couple of days before. I've some things to do in London.'

'Spiffing.' Jonny's fine, romantic features lit up. 'That would give me a chance to watch the start of the A.C. trials on Monday. One of our fellows has entered a Peugeot, though I think it's dashed unpatriotic of him to have bought a Froggie machine. Why don't you come, too?'

'I'll think about it.'

4

Max returned the pendant, though not until a week had passed. He didn't send a servant, but turned up himself, unannounced, at the house in the Bayswater Road early one evening when Norah was in her studio, Hugo still slaving – as he was prone to describe it – in chambers, and Tassie sitting brooding in the drawing room over an idle pencil and notebook.

She had never known Max apologetic before.

He sat, leaning forward with hands clasped and

elbows on knees, and asked her to forgive him. He hadn't realised, until the scene in his office, how deeply she felt about something that had seemed to him no more than a pretty toy.

'You know me,' he said earnestly. 'I'm not a great one for sitting at a desk, meditating. What excites me is the idea that suddenly flashes to life. That kind of idea – instinct, or whatever you like to call it – is something that's always worked for me, and I suppose I've fallen into the habit of thinking that all my ideas are good ones. And they are, mostly!' His smile flashed out briefly. 'But I'm truly sorry to have upset you, little sister. The thought of this coming between us has been giving me sleepless nights.'

His eyes were looking full into hers and, even if she had wanted to disbelieve him, she couldn't have done. More, almost, than anything in the world, she wanted to be persuaded. A little moistly, she smiled back.

'I should apologise, too, for jumping to the wrong conclusions.'

'That's true,' he replied provocatively. 'But I can see how it happened.'

The trouble was that Max hadn't the slightest doubt that he could repair the bonds that had been broken. For him, it was as easy as charming the birds from the trees, and his conviction was infectious. But Tassie knew that, this time, it wouldn't outlast his presence. This time, trifling though the cause might seem in comparison with his earlier sins – his tyranny over her art schooling, his violation of Selina – the damage was irrevocable. Before, when he had repaired the bonds, they had been very nearly as good as new. This time, the repair would always be visible, an eternal reminder, a weak point forever. Tassie recognised it but Max, being Max, didn't.

He turned the conversation. 'I've never been here before. It's a handsome house in its old-fashioned way. Am I allowed to meet your friends?'

So Norah was summoned down and, somehow, neither she nor Max said anything to upset the other during the remaining fifteen minutes of his visit.

As he left, he remembered something. 'By the way, Tassie, I've entered the Daimler in the Automobile Club trials next week. The chauffeur will be driving, of course, but would you like to join Genny and me as a passenger?'

'That would have been lovely, but Norah and I are going with Mr Silvermann.'

Max shrugged. 'Oh, well, I'll just have to take Monty. I'll see you there.'

5

Two flat caps, two boaters and a bowler hat had managed to cram themselves into the Clément, the first vehicle to catch Francis's eye as he and Jonny arrived at the Crystal Palace gathering point. On closer inspection, one of the flat caps turned out to be Dr W.G. Grace, the cricketer.

Thoughtfully, Francis strolled over to a vehicle with a large notice on the bonnet saying 'Judges' and was in the midst of noting down the names of several other newsworthy participants when Jonny, who had gone off to find his friends, anxiously rejoined him.

'I say, Francis,' he murmured, 'Jack Silbert and Beppo Barnard haven't turned up and the other fellows are desperate. The rules say they have to have a full load of passengers, and that means four in the case of the Peugeot. Would you like to take a chance? They can let us have goggles and gauntlets and things.'

Francis, who had a number of other things to do, was opening his mouth to say, 'No,' when his informant among the judges concluded, 'And Mr Max McKenzie Smith in a Daimler York Phaeton. There he is, just arriving.'

Through the throng of small boys who were always to be found in the vicinity of an internal combustion engine, Francis saw Mr Max McKenzie Smith, with his wife and an unknown young gentleman, making their way from a horsedrawn hansom towards where a Daimler stood waiting, its leather coated and gaitered chauffeur completing the lengthy fillings and greasings and wiring checks that preceded any run of more than a few miles. This run was to Folkestone and back, 139 miles in all, and every inch of space that wasn't taken up by the passengers would be crammed with spare parts, tools, drums of oil and two-gallon tins of petrol.

Searching his memory for the likely identity of the fourth member of the party, Francis unexpectedly came up with his Swiss stringer and Max's *hochmütig* fellow visitor to the Companies office in Liechtenstein. Light brown waving hair – slightly too long – full lips, blue eyes, good style . . .

He said to the judge, 'Do you have a list of the passengers' names?' but the judge shook his head. And even as Francis wondered whether an introduction might be forthcoming if he made his way over to wish Max and his party bon voyage, the Daimler was trundling gently off towards the starting area.

Abruptly, he made up his mind. 'Yes, Jonny, I'll come,' he said. 'Why not?'

6

Tassie and Norah, on the instructions of Mr Silvermann, were dressed to resemble Egyptian mummies in coats and hats, boots, gauntlets, mufflers and thick veils. Until they set out, they had thought themselves overdressed; always, before, the vehicles in which they had travelled had been lonely pioneers of what Max called Progress (with a capital P), sharing the road only with horses and pedestrians. But they very soon discovered that the dust kicked up from loose road surfaces by sixty-three heavy and touring-class automobiles was enough to blind drivers and passengers, block engines, smother goggles and dangerously obscure the curves and bends in the highway.

Before they had gone a dozen miles, they were seeing the evidence of it, passing a Sunbeam with its nose up the bank and, further on, an Argyll with a farm horse harnessed to it, towing it out of the ditch. Soon after, there was an Albion on its side, its passengers putting their united efforts into levering it right way up again.

'Dog,' yelled the driver to the De Dion as it passed. 'Still on the loose!'

Dogs were maddened by the sound of automobiles and often hurled themselves under the wheels, though when drivers swerved to avoid them it wasn't so much because they loved animals as because an immolated dog could do a good deal of damage to the machinery.

Through his mask, 'Can you see it?' G.S. shouted to his passengers.

'Can't see *anything*,' Norah shrieked back cheerfully.

'Sorry. Can't do much about that right now. Only way would be to get ahead of the field, and with a twenty-mile speed limit and most everybody keeping up to it, it's not a proposition.'

'This thing can go faster than twenty, surely?'

Taking one hand from the wheel, G.S. made a gesture that might have signified assent or simply a need to waggle his wrist. Driving could be a painful occupation, with every bump in the road transmitting a shock through the linkages to the steering wheel.

Choosing the interpretation she preferred, Norah leaned forward. 'Tassie and I could keep a lookout for the police and the Judges' vehicle, if you wanted to try and accelerate a bit and get ahead. I mean, if we can't see *them* for the dust, it's a fair assumption that they can't see *us*!'

The driver's shoulders shook with laughter and Tassie beamed invisibly at Norah as she was awarded the accolade of being a great girl.

But Mr Silvermann wasn't prepared to overtake. 'I'm playing safe. Let them all fall by the wayside is what I say, so long as we keep going.'

7

In the Peugeot, Jonny's friend Billy was complaining, 'We're getting through petrol at the devil of a rate. Must get some more. Where's the next town? Jake, I told you we should have reconnoitred the route in advance to note the hardware stores and likely-looking chemists! Ha-ha!' He tooted triumphantly on the bulb horn as they passed a stranded Wolseley.

Because of the late inspanning of Jonny and Francis, the Peugeot was well back in the procession, and Francis was suffering mild frustration over having lost touch with the McKenzie Smith Daimler. But there was nothing to be done about it. They might see the Daimler in a ditch – he hoped – or catch up at Folkestone, or suffer some disaster themselves. In which case, he would camp by the roadside until the Daimler appeared on the homeward journey. It had been carrying only three passengers. Perhaps he might cadge a ride in the rumble seat.

That would be ideal.

8

They didn't reach Folkestone. Five punctures later, on the edge of one of the villages north of Maidstone, the Peugeot had an argument with an Arrol Johnston and damaged the differential. The Arrol Johnston went tooling on its way, no more than dented, but it took two hours and the ingenious use of much hemp, wire and string to repair the Peugeot.

By that time they couldn't go on and spend the night at Folkestone, because Jonny, Billy and Jake were on duty next day. Bowing to the decree of fate, therefore, they unpacked the picnic basket and settled themselves well back from the verge to watch their fellow enthusiasts go honking past, engines smoking and exhausts unhealthily popping, drivers and passengers so covered with fine white dust that they looked, as Francis remarked to his unliterary and uncomprehending companions, like ghosts from an enchanter fleeing.

To his own surprise, released from goggles, mouth mask and gauntlets – and despite being covered with grease and grazes from the differential – he was enjoying himself very much indeed. It was like having restored to him the years of youthful irresponsibility that, for what had seemed good reason at the time, he had allowed to pass him by.

During the last few months, he had written editorials on the Boer peace treaty, the king's illness, the resignation of Salisbury and accession of Balfour, the collapse of the campanile of St Mark's, Venice, the case of Sir Redvers Buller, the coronation, the visit of the Shah of Persia . . . Sitting on the grass thinking about nothing-in-particular was a rare and pleasurable sensation.

Propped on one elbow with a glass of vintage champagne in his hand, he watched, with deep delight, the approach of a homeward bound De Dion.

Behind the driver sat two ladies, muffled beyond recognition. The third passenger seat was, however, empty because its occupant was sitting crosslegged on the bonnet, a long-spouted jug in his hand and all his attention focused on the uncapped radiator into which he was pouring a thin, steady stream of clear water. An equally thin and steady stream of not-so-clear water was emerging from the underside of the motor, leaving a trail in the dust as mute witness to his labours.

Jonny, who never hesitated to state the obvious, remarked, 'Oh, dear. Leaking radiator. Poor fellow.'

And thirty miles still to go, back to the Crystal Palace. Francis threw back his head and laughed as he hadn't laughed for years.

There was a blazon along the side of the De Dion, saying 'G.S. Advertising'.

It meant nothing to Francis.

9

Mr Silvermann, craning round Mr Fothergill in an attempt to see where he was steering, yelled, 'Are you okay?'

'Yes.' It sounded faintly surly.

Norah exclaimed, 'Tassie! That was Francis Rivers sitting at the side of the road, wasn't it?'

Engaged on adjusting her veil, Tassie said, 'Was it? I didn't see.'

10

Not far behind, chugging along the last stretch out of the village, was a Daimler.

They needed a dog, Francis thought. Or a horse. A small boy would be even better. With the Daimler conscientiously observing the eight-mile-an-hour speed limit for built-up areas, no one was going to be damaged.

Unhurriedly, he rose and began to stroll across the road to a stream that ran along the opposite ditch. 'Toss me one of those empty bottles, Jonny,' he shouted back. 'I'll fill it in case the Peugeot decides to have radiator trouble on the way home, too.'

Jonny threw it, but unaccountably Francis missed

314

the catch and the bottle fell and shattered on the road.

The Daimler was already slowing down as Francis began brushing up the shards of glass with the side of his foot, but it was too late.

Puncture.

The Daimler rocked, hit a bump in the road, and rocked again sluggishly, as if wondering whether or not to overturn. The three young officers leapt to prevent it.

Then, solicitously, they helped the passengers down onto terra firma.

By some amazing stroke of luck, neither Max nor his passengers had seen how the glass came to be on the road. All they had seen was Francis helpfully trying to sweep it up. It didn't mean that Max wasn't suspicious.

Lifting his goggles, he said, 'Well, well. Mr Rivers, is it not? It appears we owe you our thanks.'

The *hochmütig* young man said, 'How tedious.'

The chauffeur had certainly seen but, like all good chauffeurs, said nothing.

Pretty little Mrs McKenzie Smith also said nothing, being too much occupied in smiling from under her lashes at the extraordinarily handsome young man who, having helped her down from the motor, continued to hold her hand as if it were made of porcelain.

'Christ!' Francis thought. Aloud, he said, 'Jonny, come and give us some help pushing the motor to the side of the road.' The military rallied round nobly, while Max and the young man stood and watched. Genevieve, recognising Francis from the wedding ball, flirted her eyelashes at him, too, but not for long. Clearly, she didn't think him a patch on Jonny.

'Salmon sandwich?' offered Billy hospitably when the weary-looking chauffeur had set to work with his repair kit. Then, unwittingly, he played into Francis's hands. 'Perhaps we should introduce ourselves.'

The young man, it transpired, was one Monty Fitzalan. 'My nephew,' said Max, 'and business assistant.'

Which meant that he could only be the son of Selina, Francis's cousin. Even if Francis had wanted to claim the relationship, by then it was much too late.

It didn't occur to Max or Monty to ask if their rescuers were also having trouble with their vehicle and if there was anything they could do to help. They merely lounged against the bank, smoking and saying little, until their chauffeur had completed his repair.

When Max handed his wife up into the Daimler again, she turned to give Jonny another of her shy little smiles and thank him, most charmingly, for having saved her from a horrid accident.

And then they were trundling off into the distance.

II

Two days later, with some trepidation because she knew that most employers regarded holidays as just that – holi*days* – Tassie approached G.S. to ask if she might have a week off. No, there was no family crisis and she knew it was unbusinesslike of her, but she thought perhaps she was tired because her brain wasn't working as it should.

Gus had noticed, though 'tired' wasn't the word he would have chosen. Tiredness, in his experience, was something that built up gradually, whereas he could put an exact date to the beginning of Miss Smith's loss of creative vigour. Something had happened to worry her around the time of the coronation and she hadn't been herself since. If a short vacation would be enough to fix it, he was more than ready to cooperate.

'Sure,' he said. 'The sooner the better, because we're about to be swamped by the Christmas campaigns. You'll have to clear the Sansom, Colley and Dodge adverts before you go, but you should manage that by the end of this week. Don't forget to leave me a note of anything else outstanding. Get some fresh air and some peace and quiet, young lady! That's what you need.'

It was true, Tassie thought as she thanked him, aware suddenly of how her needs had changed. Once, peace and quiet had given her the fidgets, but, once, there had been peace and a cheerful kind of quiet in her mind. Not now.

Though she and Max were on perfectly amicable terms again, the affair of the pendant had left a residue in her spirits of something that wasn't quite depression, more an absence of vitality. She had thought her natural resilience would return of its own accord. And then she had caught a brief glimpse of Francis Rivers on the Folkestone road, happy as a sandboy, and it had forced her to stop trying to pretend that everything was all right. Because it wasn't.

She had to make peace with herself, and there was only one place she could think of where it might be possible.

That evening, she called in at Audley Street, where her mother was still installed, supervising the nurse who was supervising the nurserymaid whose duty it was to supervise baby Edward. Max and Genny were out at a party.

'Of course, my dear,' Grace said. 'Though it's a very long way for just a few days. I'll telephone Graceholm tonight – you'll notice I have learned to say that without a quiver? I have become really quite expert at telling the operators which number I want and insisting on having it! Anyway, if I telephone tonight, Murdo and Mary will have time to reach Dunaird before you do and can give everything a good airing. No, why should they mind? They have been living a life of perfect idleness for these last weeks, with no one to look after.'

As Tassie left, her mother said, 'I hope you have

remembered to thank Mr Silvermann nicely for allow-ing you to take a holiday? Such a gentlemanly man, in spite of being an American! It was a pleasure to meet him, the evening I came to supper. Remember me kindly to him, will you?'

Walking up towards Marble Arch, Tassie found herself smiling at the memory of that evening, with Norah trying to pretend that she wasn't smitten by G.S. and Hugo arriving home, late and tired from a day in court, to have her mother, intent on discovering what kind of young man he was, put him through his catechism.

That was it! She stopped dead in the middle of the pavement. That was what had been worrying her about Max's explanation of the confusion over the pendants.

He had said, *The pendant and the copy were in similar boxes and Naomi dropped one of them in at the Bayswater Road on her way to dine with us in Audley Street.*

But Genny had said, *She came to dine that evening when mother-in-law was visiting you.*

The two statements didn't fit. Naomi Merton had dropped the pendant in at the Baywater Road two evenings before Grace had come to visit. She had dropped it in on the evening when Tassie had been out with Hugo, being proposed to.

It didn't matter, Tassie told herself, crossing at Marble Arch almost under the wheels of an incensed motor omnibus. A slip of memory on Max's part, or a misunderstanding of what Naomi Merton had said.

She was so taken up by this minor mystery that it wasn't until she reached Dunaird four days later that she remembered she hadn't warned her mother not to tell Max about her visit. He'd made them both promise not to go near the place until the rebuilding of the tower was finished. Oh, well. He could only be cross.

She knew work hadn't begun yet, but there ought to be some sign of the preparations, which would be interesting.

The tower still stood, untouched, unchanged, immune to the weather and the passing years, looking as if this was how it had been since the beginning of time and how it was meant to be.

Tassie sat on the beach gazing frowningly up at it, mentally superimposing on it the drawing she had done with such care under her mother's guidance. But frown as she might, call up as she might all the resources of her imagination, she couldn't breathe life into what she saw. Obstinately, all that her mind's eye would acknowledge were a drawing – and a shell.

Wryly, she thought what ecstasy the place would have aroused among people of taste in the eighteenth century, connoisseurs of the picturesque, worshippers of dramatic effect, romantics for whom a goodlooking ruin sublimely demonstrated the triumph of time over human endeavour.

Which was all very well for them. They didn't have a mother who wanted to live in it.

It had a peculiarly irritating air of self-sufficiency, she thought as it stared imperviously back at her, as if human beings were irrelevant, unworthy of its atten-tion. It gave no hint of having noticed even a single visitor since Tassie had seen it last, although her mother had been there – and Francis Rivers – and the architect.

Sermons in stones there might be, but not stories. Stones didn't tell stories; they only confirmed the stories one already knew. Hugo had said, once, that when he visited Rome he had sensed the roar of lions and the screams of dying Christian slaves in the amphitheatre. He had been most displeased when Norah, unimpressed, had asked, 'Would you have sensed them if you hadn't already known?'

Tassie didn't expect the stones of Dunaird tower to have a story to tell, but she badly needed them to confirm one for her. Two days at the Lodge had loosened the worst knots in her nerves, but all the good work would be undone if the stones didn't confirm that Max's architect had, indeed, been here. Max was all too good at staving off inconvenient questions by making authoritative pronouncements that were impossible to check.

Sometimes it didn't matter.

Sometimes it mattered more than anything else in the world.

13

Francis, revelling in the warm September sun and the soft salt breeze, swung cheerfully along the road to Gairloch, counting his blessings, chief among which was four days – to date – of perfect weather during which he had succeeded in forgetting all about the Smith family – with the sole and subversive exception of Tassie, who had taken up residence in the most private corner of his heart. It was a year, all but a few weeks, since he had last seen her, and nothing had changed. It was still impossible.

Shaking off the thought, he turned his mind to the prospect of tea and scones in the little whitewashed village with its long line of shops, hotels and dwellings strung out along the shore. In general, Highlanders were not very sophisticated cooks, but their tea and scones were nectar and ambrosia. He smiled to himself.

But his healthy hunger was not to be satisfied. As he entered the village, he saw someone he recognised, someone who was propping a bicycle against the kerb and making for the little shop that sold newspapers and tobacco and sweeties.

Francis, his journalistic instincts now on full alert, hurried round the corner to the McLeod croft and said, 'Do me a favour, Donnie? Lend me one of your ponies for a few hours.'

When the young man mounted his bicycle a few minutes later and set out along the road that led south and west out of the village, Francis gave him a long start and then followed. But the road was empty and Francis soon began to feel uncomfortably exposed, expecting at every bend to find the cyclist lurking round the corner, waiting for him.

After about five miles, he had little doubt as to the young man's destination. There was nowhere else he could be going but to Dunaird Lodge, and no reason why he should not be going there. He was Grace Smith's grandson, after all, and had every right.

Coming to a junction, Francis decided to abandon the pursuit. Instead, he turned his pony's head to the right, along the track that led directly to the coast and the ruined tower of Dunaird. There had been something, he remembered, about Max promising to rebuild the place, but it wasn't curiosity that drew him this time, as it had drawn him once before. Even his research into Max's past had been put on temporary suspension and he had long given up hope of trying to find out, as Abigail wanted him to, how much her brother had known before he died.

It was the tower itself which drew him. He didn't know why, but the attraction was compelling.

14

Tassie didn't know what she had expected to find as proof of the architect's visit, though he must have taken measurements, might have brought surveying equipment, had certainly sat down somewhere to rest, to look, to sketch.

But the sun was declining, and still she had found nothing at all. No chalk marks on the walls, no new scratches from nailed boots, no spiked hole in the ground that might have supported an Abney level, no pencil shavings or cigar butts swept by the wind into the corners of the second floor to join the dust and feathers, the dead leaves and the detritus of house martins' nests that had accumulated over the years. Nor, trapped among the rocky outcrops on the edge of the cliff, were there any weatherworn scraps of paper bearing figures or drawings.

Perhaps the architect had been an unnaturally tidy gentleman. Perhaps the wind and the rain had destroyed the signs of his visit.

Perhaps he had never been there at all.

Why, why, why?

Promising to rebuild the tower was the kindest and most loving thing Max had ever done, something shining in whose light even the sins of the last two years could be, had to be, forgiven.

It wasn't possible that it had been a promise without substance.

She would have one more look before the setting of the sun forestalled her. There was a full moon tonight, so she didn't have to worry about the long ride back to the Lodge.

15

To the mind of a rational man, second sight and telepathy were, at best, expressions of the romantic imagination, at worst, mere confidence tricks. But a rational man was not the same as a wise man, and Francis's knowledge of the Highlands had made him aware that there was nothing imaginary about second sight, however fallible it might sometimes be. He knew also, from his mother, that telepathy could and did exist; she and her twin, she said, had experienced it often, though not reliably. It was, she thought, something that happened only when both minds were deliberately open and receptive. Or when one of them was deeply troubled.

There were tears pouring down Tassie's cheeks when Francis, having tethered the pony to a tree, walked silently across the turf and found her sitting on the sunwarmed grass at the foot of the tower.

The far hills had shaded to grey and violet and indigo, the sea was like worn silver, and the rose-gold sun hung low over the horizon under a sky that was still pale and blue as aquamarine, touched faintly with saffron. Somewhere a chaffinch was singing, and a pair of oystercatchers were skimming along the water's edge, black and white and scarlet, strong-winged and silent.

She looked up, startled, and her green eyes widened, catching lights of gold and silver from the sun and the sea. Her hair was coming down and there was a smudge on her nose. But the happiness in her face had been there, despite the tears, before she saw him.

It wasn't for him.

If he had taken her in his arms, then, before she had time to speak, many things might have been different. But in those few calamitous seconds he was too busily engaged in fighting the last battle with himself and, anyway, on a more prosaic level, she had her fists clasped tightly to her chest, like armour against him. Telepathy might have brought him there, but he found himself thinking with bitterness that it had not been at her command.

Smiling tearfully, brilliantly, as if they had never been apart, or as if their separation had been of no importance to her, she said, 'It's all right. Look!' and held out her hands.

Whatever it was that was all right, it had nothing to do with Francis.

Polite as a stranger, he dropped down beside her. 'What is it?'

'A plumb line. Surveyors use it. I found it buried in

the rubbish in a corner of the ground floor. He must have dropped it and not been able to find it. And there were some chalk marks after all, though I hadn't seen them before because of the angle of the light. So he really was here, after all. Max's architect, I mean.'

Max. Always Max.

Who mattered more to her than anyone else in the world.

17

She recoiled from the sudden blaze in his eyes, and the harsh tightening of his mouth, recognising only the rage, not the jealousy that caused it.

He tore the plumb line from her hand and tossed it away, without looking. Then he gripped her arms and shook her roughly and, his voice almost unrecognisable, grated, 'You stupid little fool! Damn your precious Max! Don't you know he isn't to be trusted an inch? Don't you know he's a charlatan, a fraud, a liar? Can't you see beyond the success and the charm, beyond the fact that he's your brother? *Won't* you see beyond them?'

For half a dozen seconds his eyes stared into hers, thunder-grey into shocked, lucent green, and then his hands moved, and he pulled her into his arms and kissed her with no hint of gentleness, stifling her startled cry.

She had thought, for a fleeting, magical moment, that heaven was in her grasp. Filled with relief at the discovery that what Max had said was true, tearful from the reaction, lulled by the beauty of the evening, she had looked up to see the one man in the world she wanted to see, whom she had not dreamed of seeing.

A year before, she had chosen to try and stop loving him, but she had learned since then what a mockery that choice had been. Other things had changed, too.

His face had been in shadow, but she had held out

her hands to him so that he might share what she felt.

And then everything had gone wrong.

She struggled against him at first, against the embrace that locked his body to hers but, soon, her head swimming from his kisses, her very skin quivering from tension and fear and the desire for it to be right and the knowledge that it was wrong, her resistance collapsed, gave way to a despairing passivity. Nothing mattered except that she loved him, had dreamed of him loving her, making love to her properly – improperly – completely. But not like this.

And then, as he pulled her even more closely to him, imprisoning her in his arms, one hand sliding imperatively down the whole length of her back, he touched a nerve somewhere at the base of her spine and she quivered convulsively – body, heart and mind – and then she was dissolving, drowning, consumed by sensations she had experienced, briefly, once before, but experienced now a hundred – a thousand – times more compellingly.

As she gasped aloud, she felt the change in his body, too, the hard independent movement against her. Taking his lips from hers he forced her down onto the grass and, grey eyes locked again with green, propped himself on one elbow and with careless care began tearing her shirtwaist open and thrusting the shift aside.

Then his hand was gliding from throat to breasts to waist, smoothing itself over the youthful silky skin, stroking her, sliding down to her hips and forward over the curve of her stomach, and all the time she could feel him throbbing against her so that every feeling was banished but a searing, beautiful agony and the premonition of an ecstasy more intense than she could ever have imagined.

She was lost. She was lost. And wanted to be.

18

Then, brutally, the world stopped.

Sensible only of the wild, unmerciful tide surging through her, she failed at first to understand the cessation of his movements, the tension in him as he brought the formidable power of his will into play, the meaning of the lingering, tormenting withdrawal of his hand and the delayed, light touch of his lips again on hers. It wasn't a kiss this time, and the anger had gone.

Shivering, she lay under the silver moon that had wandered into the veiled dark sky, deprived of she didn't know what, denied the revelation of it.

It was hard to speak, but she succeeded in the end. 'Why did you stop?'

'Conscience. Consideration. Because I don't approve of rape. Because you wanted me to.'

Pride and hurt, fear and guilt conspired to smother the voice inside her, crying, 'No! I wanted you to go on, go on.'

The blood was still tearing through her veins, but the pounding of her heart was slowing, like some piece of machinery that came only reluctantly to a halt after it had been switched off. 'Because you're a gentleman?'

'Whatever that may be. Perhaps.'

'Don't make light of what's happened.'

He shrugged, not looking at her, running his fingers through his hair, pushing back the dark lock that strayed, always, over his forehead.

Helplessly, she said, 'I love you.'

A shadow flitted across his face, like a night bird passing. 'Not enough,' he said.

How dared he! A weak and weary anger coursed through her. 'What right have you to say that? How can you possibly know?' He didn't answer.

Instead, after a long silence, he said flatly, 'It's impossible.'

She knew why. *My needs are already catered for*. A wife? A mistress? How could she love him so much when she knew so little about him?

'Why is it impossible?' she heard her own voice say, and had to stop herself from following it with a cry of, 'No, don't answer.' Because she didn't, after all, want to know. She didn't want to know in case it was true and it was, indeed, impossible. She wanted to have some hope left.

He said, 'I can't explain. You must believe me or not, as you choose.'

She should have insisted, she should have fought for him, and would have done if he had been a different person, someone of her own age, someone to whom she felt equal, someone she understood. But Francis Rivers wasn't the kind of man you felt equal to. She had been a little afraid of him ever since she had known him; afraid of his cool, amused detachment, his impregnable self-sufficiency, his courteous air of 'touch me not'. She had tried, without success, to imagine him falling in love with anyone. It had been the stupidest of dreams to think that he might have fallen in love with her.

It didn't lessen the hurt.

'Perhaps I should apologise for wasting your time?' she said with the shamelessness of despair. 'If I had been a whore, you would at least have been able to see your lovemaking through, would have had a fuller return for your efforts. But I know, of course, that any interest you have ever shown in me has been only an extension of your interest in Max.'

The hard line of his jaw tightened, but she couldn't see his eyes.

'On which subject,' she went on, 'I cannot imagine how you dare speak to me of him as you have done. I don't know why you dislike him so. Envy, perhaps? In any case, nothing of what you say is true. Nothing. And you must know it. If you had any proof, any kind

327

of confirmation, I imagine it would have found its way into your loathsome newspaper long ago.'

She still had to defend Max, no matter what had come between them, because in defending him against intrusion into the background of his life, she was defending her mother. She had come to believe that Max's popular reputation was now so great that he would only gain if the truth about his early life became known. It would be Grace who suffered, for abandoning him.

Francis Rivers turned to face her. 'No, I haven't any proof that would stand up in a court of law, and I would scorn to do as Max has done and spread baseless rumours about someone I distrust.'

'What?'

'He's been trying to ruin the *Enterprise*,' Francis said dismissively. 'But that's by the way. Because – listen to me, Tassie! – I will find proof. Your brother is a man without principle, and I don't want you to be hurt by him. I don't want thousands of others to be hurt by him, either. And they will be, if he goes on as he is doing.'

Tassie couldn't mistake his sincerity, wrong-headed though she knew it to be. She rose to her feet. Her legs felt unstable, and she had to stop and shake out her skirts to give herself time.

Then, 'Why *should* I believe you?' she said, and went to search for the plumb line.

19

He held her pony while she mounted, taking care not to touch her.

Casually, he said, 'I caught a glimpse of your cousin Monty in Gairloch. I take it he's staying with you at the Lodge?'

'No. You must have been mistaken. He's in Dundee, I think.'

Momentarily, he raised his eyebrows, then released the reins and said, 'Goodbye.' No more.

Afterwards, she could remember nothing of the long ride home.

20

Monty strolled into the hall as she entered, a glass in his hand, a suave smile on his face which vanished as she snapped, 'What are you doing here?'

'What an ecstatic welcome! Just passing. An errand for Max to do with sails for the Ullapool fishing fleet, such as it is. But, Auntie dear, I am shocked to find you returning so late and alone. An assignation?'

If she hadn't been pale already, all colour would have left her face. As it was, she said, 'We can do without the sarcasm. As it happens, I have been visiting the tower. I would have preferred Max not to know, but since you are here I suppose I can give up hope of that. So perhaps you will take this back with you.'

From her pocket, she withdrew the plumb line. 'I found it on the floor of the tower. Max's architect must have dropped it.'

Pleasedly, Monty said, 'And you found it. What a clever girl you are. But, now you're back, perhaps we can have supper?'

CHAPTER FOUR

I

Three months later, Max's casino was declared open by a stout duchess with a foreign accent, her eyes sparkling far more brightly than all the serried ranks of her diamond necklaces, brooches, bracelets, earrings and hair ornaments, which were badly in need of cleaning.

'Quite a coup, what?' murmured Freddy Pelham in Tassie's ear. 'I had to bribe her, of course, but she's promised to look in at least twice a week for the next two months. Genny's cross as crabs. She wanted to do the opening herself but I said, no, can't have that. We need someone top-o'-the-trees, the kind of female who *makes* fashion.'

'Not in the dress sense, I hope. She looks like a Christmas cracker. It has always been my view,' added Tassie austerely, 'that diamonds are vulgar.'

'Oh, I dunno. Dashed useful for distracting the eye from wrinkles and double chins. It's all very well for you. With a face and figure like yours, no need to wear every bauble you possess. Gilding the lily, what?'

Tassie, uncomfortably laced into a cream chiffon hourglass dress with a deep neckline and no more ornament than a trimming of silk tea roses, smiled her thanks for the compliment and forbore to remark that 'every bauble she possessed' added up to no more than the pearl earrings, a twenty-first birthday gift from her mother, which she was wearing, and the Marian pendant, which she wasn't.

Glancing at Norah and Grace, Freddy said, 'Now, shall I take you ladies on a conducted tour?'

Grace, genuinely interested, said, 'How kind,' at the same time wondering what alternative way of passing the time there might be for three females who were there without a gentleman to escort them.

Tassie and Norah had firmly vetoed any idea of bringing Hugo who, as Tassie had pointed out, would be most unlikely to fall for the story that this was just Max having a few friends in for some private gambling, while Gus Silvermann, tentatively approached, had regretted that he had another engagement. Though perhaps he might join them later on in the evening, if that was okay? *Very* okay, Tassie had assured him.

Freddy, dismissing the ground floor and top floors as of no interest since they had been decorated exactly as if the house were the private residence it purported to be – a private residence registered in the name of, and already occupied by one Mr Monty Fitzalan – led his little party downstairs from the hall to a foyer which, in turn, gave onto a balcony overlooking the room which had been set aside for dancing. The dance floor was surrounded by damasked supper tables, gilt chairs and potted palms, while outside was a Mediterranean-looking, white walled courtyard decked with more potted palms and a spotlit fountain, gently playing. The palms, although Freddy didn't mention it, concealed a fire escape from the casino upstairs, an escape that Monty had had installed less as a provision against fire than against the intrusion of inquisitive officialdom. Not that he anticipated any problem. A good many *douceurs* had been dispensed in the appropriate quarters.

A fifteen-piece orchestra was already giving of its best. 'Good old Heinrich!' Freddy said. 'Spiffing chap, knows everybody. It just needs someone to come in

331

who's really *someone*, and bingo! Next thing, he's playing their favourite tune. And that's the great Marco talking to Lord Rowley. Max bribed him away from Dillon's to take charge of the supper rooms. Amazing how people will follow a *maître d'hôtel* from one place to another. If he were a chef, you could understand it. Seen all you want to see? Casino next, then.'

2

Following him upstairs, they were met on the first floor landing by two respectable-looking but unusually large and muscular gentlemen who smiled on them benignly. With an air of authority that sat oddly on his chubby countenance, Freddy said, 'Mrs Grace Smith, Miss Tassie Smith, Miss Norah St John. And you know me.'

When the gentlemen had checked their lists, Freddy produced a coin from his pocket and gave it to Grace. 'Flip it. Heads you win.'

A mystified Grace, whose long gloves were skin tight and who had no idea how to flip a coin anyway, did her best, which wasn't very good. Down on his knees under a marble and gilt console table, one of the large gentlemen asked, 'Heads or tails, madam?'

'Goodness. Heads?'

'Yes.'

Freddy, grinning, said, 'It's a notion of Max's. Just a bit of fun. The right call lets you have your first bet free.' The second large gentleman having presented Grace with a gilt disc embossed – of course – with Max's monogram, he went on, 'That's your entitlement token. You can keep it afterwards as a souvenir.'

Norah and Tassie both made the right call, too, which Tassie found slightly surprising. Freddy winked at her.

Then the double doors were opened for them and

Norah whistled in a most unladylike way. 'Gosh! Talk about glitter!'

'Another of Max's ideas,' Freddy said. 'We don't take any stakes except in gold. No counters, no plaques. Ain't a more beautiful sight in the world than a roulette table covered with piles of golden sovereigns. Look at it! Don't it make you feel there's real riches to be won?'

Grace glanced worriedly at him. She knew from Genny that he loved gambling and thought that having the free run of a casino must be dreadfully bad for him. Max said he was thirty years old and, if he wanted to throw money away, it was his own affair, but Grace knew that the Pelham family fortune was too slender to allow Freddy to lose with impunity.

High ceilings, marble, mirrors, chandeliers, brightly painted and baize-covered tables, roulette, chemin-de-fer, baccarat, vingt-et-un, trente-et-quarante. And already the room was full of people, some playing, some watching.

'Vingt-et-un,' Freddy said. 'That's the thing if you want some fun.'

So they stood and watched, Freddy explaining as the dealer, in answer to the players' signals, dealt to them or passed them by, pushed sovereigns over to them or raked them away. After ten minutes, Tassie said, 'Right!' with the air of one rolling up her sleeves, and slipped into an empty seat.

It was indeed fun, especially with Freddy whispering in her ear. When she had a total of eighteen before her he murmured, 'Stick.' The dealer dispensed a face card, a seven, another face card and a nine to other players, and then it was a five to the bank, an ace to the bank . . .

'Ace: that makes six.'

And a ten.

'Ten: that makes sixteen.'

And another ten.

'Ten: twenty-six. Too many.'

There was a deep sigh from round the table. Ten gleaming gold sovereigns were pushed over to Tassie.

A very young and rather overdressed girl standing behind Tassie squealed, 'Oh, Bobby, can I play now?' but Tassie's neighbour, a stout gentleman with a spade beard and a passing resemblance to the king, ignored her.

Freddy said, 'Put five of them back on, Tassie,' and she did. A few minutes later she had lost them. She put the other five on, and won. And lost them again. This time she only put three on. And lost again.

Norah said in her most cut-glass, county accent, 'I think I shall go and lose my token at the roulette wheel. It seems a quicker and easier way of going about it.'

Tassie and Freddy, engrossed in the next deal, didn't hear her. Even more clearly, Norah said, 'I think all my gambling instincts must be used up by the hazards of everyday life. Freddy, will you take us down to supper?'

But they had to wait until Tassie had lost her remaining two sovereigns.

3

On its way downstairs, the little party was augmented by two personable and willowy young gentlemen, friends of Freddy's, with whom Tassie was flirting outrageously when Max and Genny joined them soon after for a private glass of champagne.

Max was glowing with satisfaction. 'From what Monty tells me, everyone's having a roaring good time. If they pass the word along, we'll be as full as we can hold from now on.'

'*If!*' Tassie echoed in a very sprightly way.

Max beamed at her. 'I've taken steps to ensure it. Now, if you'll excuse us, Genny and I have to go up to the casino to make our grand entry and give a formal welcome to our guests.'

Tassie was having her hand ardently kissed by one of the young gentlemen. 'We'll follow you in a minute,' she cooed. 'But lend me some money, Max, will you? I've used up my token and Norah and mother are being spoilsports and won't let me have theirs.'

'Too bad,' Max said, and gave Genny his arm.

Tassie thereupon smiled wistfully at each of her swains in turn, who, being perfect gentlemen, said as one, 'You must allow *me*, dear Miss Smith.'

4

Half an hour later, Gus Silvermann arrived to find a deserted Grace and Norah still seated at the supper table, unobtrusively worrying. Norah, although – or perhaps because – Tassie had told her little about the Dunaird visit beyond the fact that she had happened to 'run into' Francis Rivers, was better able than Grace to guess at what was causing Tassie to behave in a way that was entirely uncharacteristic and could only be described as 'fast'. Norah sometimes thought that it would give her great personal pleasure to wring the necks of both Mr Francis Rivers and Mr Max McKenzie Smith. Then, at least, Tassie would be enabled to live her own life.

Scarcely had Gus raised his glass to his lips when they heard a huge roar followed by a wild cheering from the first floor and, being only human, sauntered upstairs with a careful lack of haste, to find out what had happened.

Lady Burns, it seemed, had won six times in a row at roulette and broken the bank.

Grace said, 'Oh, dear, how dreadful! Does that mean the casino has lost all its money?'

But there was a grin all over Max's face as he returned pretty little Lady Burns's ecstatic hug and then signalled to Monty and the croupier who began, respectively, tolling a funeral bell and unrolling a bolt of black crêpe over the roulette table. Then, to more cheers, a liveried servant bearing a large, red plush, gold-fringed wallet departed from the room like a guardsman at the trot.

'Gone to roust out some more cash,' said Gus Silvermann knowledgeably. 'I wonder how much of a float the table carries?'

Freddy's voice, faintly slurred by envy and too much champagne, said, '£4,000. Spiffing, isn't it? Couldn't have been won by a more popular lady, either. Place'll be a wild success after this. Shouldn't be surprised if we have His Majesty here before long. In one of his incognitos, of course.'

Tassie, appearing from amid the crowd, drew him aside. Her eyes limpid with innocence, she murmured, 'Freddy, when Max said he had taken steps to ensure that everyone would soon be talking about the casino, was this what he meant?'

'Now, now. Mustn't ask. Lips sealed and all that sort of thing.'

She pulled him into the window recess. 'Go on, tell me how he fixed it! I won't breathe a word. I promise.'

'Better not. Only needs the wheel to be tilted a little, that's all. Just a hearse breath' – he tried again – '*hair's breadth*. The croupier controls it with a spring thing sunk in the table under the baize. Even 'sperienced gamblers don't notice as long as it happens jus' now and then.'

'That's immoral!'

With his chubby features and thinning hair, Freddy looked like a harassed baby.

'Prob'ly never use it again after t'night,' he assured her, and then, realising that she was teasing him, went on, 'Anyway, only immoral if we used it to make people lose their money 'stead of winning, but Max would never do that. He don't need to, anyway. Bank always comes off best in the end. Oh, look. Here's Genny.'

Genny was bright-eyed and flushed in a blue dress that, as usual, matched her eyes even if, in this case, the satin was so lavishly embroidered with mother-of-pearl sequins and diamanté that scarcely a vestige of the colour was visible.

'Tassie,' she said breathlessly, 'the pins holding my tiara are slipping. *Do* come to the boudoir and help me fix them!'

Although the tiara looked perfectly well anchored to Tassie, she obligingly went with her sister-in-law to the empty, oppressively pink cloakroom and said, 'If you sit down, I'll be able to manage better.'

But Genny wasn't in the mood for sitting down. Genny was in the mood for stalking up and down the room liked a furious kitten. 'There's nothing the matter with the tiara,' she exclaimed. 'But I have to tell somebody. I only found out this afternoon. You won't *believe* it, Tassie, but I'm going to have another baby. Already! With Edward not even four months old!' She gave an enraged, grumbling sound in her throat. 'It's all Max's fault . . .'

Well, that was something to be grateful for. Not that Tassie doubted Genny's virtue, but there seemed to be a good deal of infidelity going around in fashionable circles these days. Tassie sat down on a pink velvet stool.

'. . . but when I ask him not to, all he does is say I owe it to him. It isn't *fair*! I was just beginning to have fun and now I won't be able to, or not for long. I'm so *cross*, I can't tell you!'

'It does seem a bit soon,' Tassie agreed. 'Are you sure?'

'I thought it was just that everything was taking a while to get back to normal after Edward's birth. But the doctor says there's no doubt, and I can't bear it!

I've been having such a lovely time these last few weeks.'

Tassie knew, and not only from Grace, that Max and Genny had been leading an extremely full social life. And as soon as Genny had begun being seen about, the newspapers had been reminded of the splash they'd made with last year's fairytale romance, with the result that Genny was now appearing in their columns almost as often as Max; in the case of the society picture pages, rather more often. And a very pretty picture she made. It had given her a new assurance, perhaps too much, because she was beginning to show all the symptoms of being spoilt. Next thing, she'd be appearing in picture-postcard series of 'Society Beauties'.

'I can't bear it,' she wailed again, 'having to stop going to races and parties and balls. Max doesn't like dancing but I love it and there are always dozens of young gentlemen dying to partner me.'

'Handsome ones, I hope?' Tassie asked a little drily.

Genny pouted. 'They're all right. But, oh, Tassie, I didn't tell you. On that stupid motorcar rally we met the handsomest young man I have ever, ever seen. He was an army officer and he saved me from being hurt when we had a puncture. He was *beautiful*, and so kind and considerate.' Deeply, she sighed. 'But I don't expect I'll ever see him again.'

'Perhaps it's just as well.'

'I suppose so.' Rather belatedly, she added, 'I wouldn't want to, of course. I mean, I love my husband.'

'Good.' It sounded rather acerbic, so Tassie went on brightly, 'Well, if you have any surplus of handsome young gentlemen, don't hesitate to let me know, will you?'

It gave Genny's thoughts a new direction, if one that was not entirely welcome. 'Goodness, yes. You're twenty-two next week, and no husband in sight. Not

338

even an admirer. How awful for you. Is there really no one or are you being naughty and secretive and is there someone you haven't told us about?'

Airily, Tassie said, 'I have, of course, had a very flattering offer from Hugo St John, but I don't think we should suit. I shall continue looking around, of course, but I am not sure that I would actually like to be married. It's such a waste of an education. I think I shall remain a spinster and devote myself to good works.'

'Oh, Tassie, you're so droll sometimes!' Genny gave a trill of laughter. 'You're making fun!'

Tassie smiled, her own lightly uttered words echoing ominously in her head, and said, 'Shall we go back to the tables?'

6

Francis, leaning on the rail as the ship nosed out from between the low, swampy banks and interminable jungles of the Hugli, eyed the ornamental villas, grassy lawns and luxuriant flowerbeds of Garden Reach with relief as well as interest. Four weeks of living in close proximity to his fellow passengers – the majority of them Indian Civil Servants returning to duty with their ladies and, in all too many cases, their husband–hunting daughters – had taught him, if he had needed to be taught, the pleasures of being alone.

The river was crowded with shipping as they reached Calcutta's landing place in front of the Maidan, a handsome stone esplanade flanked on the landward side with elaborate white mansions bowered in trees. Francis had been told that, in the cool of the morning and evening, the Maidan fulfilled the rôle of an Indian Hyde Park, where everyone went to see and be seen, where European and Bengali fashionables aired their dignity in dress uniforms and military decorations on the one hand, in silks and velvets, cummerbunds and gold chains on the other.

How many of them, he wondered, would be travelling to Delhi in the next two weeks, to show off their finery at the great Durbar being held to celebrate, close on five months late, the coronation of King Edward VII, Fidei Defensor and India Imperator. The viceroy, Lord Curzon, was said to be spending a fortune on displaying the fullest splendour of the British Crown to the inhabitants of the country that had been declared its brightest jewel.

Francis would be there himself to report on the spectacle for the *Enterprise*, but also because Kitchener of Khartoum had just come out as Commander-in-Chief-in-India and Francis anticipated an early and furious clash between the new C-in-C and the viceroy. It would be interesting to see how the two men, both autocrats of the deepest dye, comported themselves on such an occasion.

But before he left for Delhi, he had things to do in Calcutta. He wanted to find a reliable stringer in the capital of British India; he also wanted to make some enquiries about a certain jute mill on the Hugli and an up-country jute-buying agency, both of which had recently been acquired by Mr Max McKenzie Smith.

7

Norah and Hugo had gone down to Gloucestershire to spend Christmas with their parents, but Tassie had refused an invitation to accompany them.

She had also refused an invitation to stay at Audley Street.

'You don't want to rattle around in that tomb of a place all by yourself,' Max had said.

'Yes, I do.'

It was what she wanted most, to wander ghostlike

340

through the hollow silence of the empty rooms, nourishing her melancholy. For more than three months she had been bright and brittle, scarcely spending an evening at home, flirting with every eligible young man who came her way, and all it had done was plunge her deeper into dejection.

She wanted to be miserable in peace. Then she might get it out of her system.

But she couldn't avoid Christmas dinner at Max's, or the Boxing Day party. Max, Grace and Tassie herself, true to the Scots tradition, might set little store by Christmas, but Genny was determined on a proper English 'Yuletide', which meant that every visitor who crossed the threshold was precipitated not only into an Armageddon of warring smells – roast turkey, logs, fruit, candle wax, port wine, the Christmas fir and the Christmas pudding – but a decorator's nightmare of mistletoe, ivy, tinsel, streamers, witch balls, flags and Chinese lanterns.

If Tassie hadn't been laden with parcels, she would have turned tail and fled.

Mulligatawny soup. Oysters. Turkey with chestnut stuffing, sausages, forcemeat balls. A ham and a tongue. A blazing pudding crammed with silver three-penny bits. Mince pies, jellies, almond creams. Candied fruits, nuts, figs, dates, sweetmeats, preserved ginger, grapes and tangerines.

During the preceding weeks, Tassie had drawn so many tempting pictures of groaning boards (Jacobean, French Renaissance, Louis Quatorze, Empire, Sheraton, Chippendale . . .) that the very sight of the table was almost too much for her.

It was an awfully, awfully jolly dinner and Genevieve insisted that everyone wear paper hats. She, Max, Freddy and Sir Leoday all enjoyed themselves hugely, while Grace and Tassie succeeded in looking as if they did. Naomi Merton and Monty – no prizes, Tassie thought, for guessing who had invited *them* – behaved like a pair of tolerant adults at a children's party.

Baby Edward, brought down to see the tree and be presented with a gold-mounted coral teething stick from his papa and a silver rattle in the shape of Mr Punch from his mama, was very soon removed again, one of the maids following upstairs with a mountain of beautifully wrapped gifts, some of them from the Pelhams and Smiths but the majority from customers and suppliers of McKenzie Smith Holdings.

At seven o'clock, when the prospect of listening just once more to Max, Genny and Freddy joining the phonograph in 'Won't you come home, Bill Bailey?' became too much to bear, Tassie said, 'Genny, it was lovely. No, Max, I'd rather walk and no, Freddy, I don't need an escort. It's not far and I can carry my presents, thank you.'

Chocolates, various, from the Pelhams. From her mother, a Shamrock travelling clock illuminated by one of the new dry battery lights. From Monty, a chased silver visiting card case. From Naomi Merton, a set of turquoise-headed hatpins and matching buttons. And from Max and Genny, the most amazing 'Opera handbag' containing a purse and mirror, a wallet for the programme and another for handkerchiefs, and three special compartments fitted out with a powder puff, a fan, and a pair of opera glasses.

8

The fresh air and the quietness of the streets were a blessed relief and there was no need to hurry along, not on the edges of Mayfair where reassuring bobbies were everywhere to be seen. There was a faint mist, less than a fog, mantling the buildings and the park in mystery, diffusing the light from windows and street lamps, turning the moon and its aureole of clouds to pale yellow ochre against the purple-grey sky. London had its own magic and in this last year Tassie had come to love it in a way that she hadn't expected.

Dripping with parcels, she dawdled towards Marble Arch, trying to feel something of the Christmas spirit but failing sadly. Life was a mess, she thought, remembering with harsh and hurtful clarity the last time she had been alone under the moon – fourteen weeks and six days before – riding back to the Lodge from Dunaird tower, shivering from Francis Rivers's unconsummated embrace.

Shuffling her feet in a drift of dead leaves, giving them an occasional, moody kick – as if she were a badly behaved schoolboy rather than a New Woman who had reached the mature age of twenty-two just a fortnight before – she knew, as she had always known, that she was never going to find anyone else to love. The eligible young men with whom she had been flirting so busily in these last months had been no more than lay figures, images without substance, tempting-looking packages with nothing but emptiness inside.

She had been spoiled. Her standards were too high. Francis – and Max. Max – and Francis. Two vital, clever men; men with ambition, style, initiative, looks; men who made things happen. It wasn't that she believed they could do no wrong; any such illusions had long been shattered. It was something else. It was that, despite their faults, she knew she would never find any other man who came within miles of living up to them.

'It's impossible,' Francis had said with a flat finality that had been far more convincing than laboured explanation.

But *was* it impossible? The more Tassie thought about it, the more certain she was that it was a mistress, not a wife, she had to contend with. However hard she tried – and she had tried often and fearfully – she couldn't see him as already married. It wasn't simply a matter of careless neckties and untrimmed hair, although it would have taken a paragon of a wife to allow him to leave the house without first giving a corrective tweak to his tie and reminding him to go to the barber.

He just didn't have the air – the atmosphere – of a married man.

Not for the first time, Tassie told herself that nothing could be more preposterous than to think herself in love – and for life, no less – with a man about whom she knew almost nothing. He might, under the patrician façade, be somebody *thoroughly* undesirable, like Dr Jekyll and Mr Hyde, or Dorian Gray, or Jack the Ripper.

It didn't make the slightest difference.

The second worst thing she could think of was never seeing him again. The worst was never again feeling his lips or his body against hers.

With a sudden, healthy flush of anger, she thought, *damn* respectability and *damn* the conventions. She had been behaving as if she didn't have a mind of her own. Norah was right. If Francis Rivers had a mistress, what did it matter? She, Tassie Smith, would fight for her happiness, no matter what the world thought. Once, she had been convinced that she couldn't, shouldn't. Now, she knew that she herself would be his mistress, if she had to.

Mistresses ran in the family, after all. Her mother had been Joss Smith's mistress before she married him. And Max had Naomi Merton, even if she called him – in that amusedly continental way of hers – her *cavaliere servente*, as if it was a perfectly respectable thing to be.

Tassie didn't see why she should be left out.

Francis wouldn't come to her, so she must go to him. It meant that, somehow, she would have to arrange an 'accidental' meeting, which wouldn't be easy, with her in London and him in Glasgow.

It was time to stop behaving as if she had no say in the matter. She stepped out briskly, because there were plans to be made.

9

St Valentine's Day was on a Saturday and Norah received two Valentine cards, one from her smallest brother, Jamie, and the other anonymous, as such cards were supposed to be, but unmistakably American in design. It was decorated with a tasteful painting of violets and Norah, industriously hiding her surprise and pleasure, remarked that violets were supposed to be shrinking so it must have been delivered to the wrong address.

Tassie's haul was nine, none of them from the only person who interested her. She was easily able to recognise the handwriting on most, including Hugo's, although in his case she had no need even to try. It hadn't occurred to his great legal brain that his card might be identified by the simple fact of its turning up, unstamped and neatly centred on the mat, thirty minutes before the postman. She couldn't resist teasing him by setting it up against the marmalade dish at breakfast and speculating lengthily as to who might have sent it.

She was still feeling vaguely merry when she arrived at the office and Gus said, 'Time to plan the spring campaigns. I have to be out until noon, so I guess you and Mr Binns can borrow my office and give yourselves some space.' Being Gus and a gentleman – even if American – he saw no need to mention leaving the door open.

During Tassie's year and six weeks with G.S. Advertising, not one of the staff had put a foot out of line. After a while, they'd even stopped being overly careful with their language and by now were so reconciled to her presence that they treated her almost as if she were one of them, which she found very satisfactory.

Even so, she didn't like Mr Binns and Mr Binns didn't like her. She had shown far too much aptitude for getting on with clients and had even brought in four new ones – three furnishing stores and a Bond Street coiffeuse. Although he was formidably polite to her when other people were looking, his expression, when they weren't, hovered somewhere between a sneer and a leer. She knew perfectly well that he was trying to make her feel small, 'a mere female', but knowing it didn't make it easier to ignore.

She didn't want to be shut up with him in Gus's office, but when he closed the door behind them it seemed better to disregard it than make an issue of it.

It was all right for the first half hour, as they tossed ideas back and forth, some good, some not so good. But then Mr Binns was inspired to suggest that 'In spring, a young man's fancy lightly turns to thoughts of love' would make a rattling good slogan for Leetham's Self Raising Flour.

'With hero and heroine floating on a sponge cake cloud, you mean?' Tassie asked sweetly.

'Something like that, yes.'

'Mmmm, no. For one thing, it's insulting to imply that a young lady could, or should, try to entrap a man with her cakes. Or anything else.'

She had said it, she thought, quite reasonably, but Mr Binns apparently thought otherwise.

Looking as if he had found a cockroach in his custard, he said very much less smoothly than usual, 'And we mustn't upset the ladies, must we! It's not "modern" for them to make themselves attractive to a man. They still expect to be chased, though.'

Whereupon, he pounced.

Tassie was already halfway across the room, saying something on the lines of wasn't it warm in here and let's have the door open, when he laid hands on her. Even through her dress and petticoat she could feel the instant heat of them on her hips as he whirled her round and planted his mouth on hers.

It was disgusting. He clamped her body to his and she felt his tongue poking at her mouth, trying to open it as she struggled furiously to free herself. It wasn't the best moment to remember Selina saying that, when Max had forced himself on her, she couldn't scream 'because of the servants'. For the first time, she fully understood what Selina had meant. Because here was she herself, struggling against a man very much bigger and stronger than she was, and struggling in silence, with no thought of screaming — if she had been able to — because of the people in the outer office.

He was pushing hard against her, the whole weight of his body forcing her toward the desk, backwards and down, so that she was arched over it, the edge cutting into the base of her spine. And then one hand dropped and he was tugging her skirt upwards and the whole episode stopped being merely sickening and became something quite different.

Now that he was holding her to him one-handed, she thought she might be able to free her left arm, as long as she did it sharply and suddenly. But she had to decide first what use she intended to put it to. Scratching Mr Binns's eyes out, however appealing in theory, wasn't a practical proposition because her nails were too short.

Urgently, she tried to remember what was on the desktop and might be within her reach. There were scissors, she knew, and she would use them if she had to. But then she remembered the big double inkstand, could even feel a corner of it pressing into her shoulder.

She had never hit anyone over the head before, but she wasn't in the mood for worrying about the niceties. If she overdid it, that was just too bad.

As weapons went, nothing could have been better. Not only did the heavy block of onyx cause Mr Binns to reel, stagger, and clutch at his skull, moaning. It also decanted a quarter pint each of red and green ink over his head, his face, his shirt and his natty gent's suiting.

11

After a fraught minute during which Tassie succeeded in regaining her breath by way of a succession of sobs that hovered perilously between tears and laughter, she found her handkerchief and scrubbed furiously at her lips. Then, taking the small mirror from her purse, she tidied her hair before offering it wordlessly to Mr Binns.

He moaned again, mumbling, 'You bitch!' and this time she laughed outright.

Going to the door, she opened it, saying in clear and faintly amused tones, 'Well, if you *will* lay things out on the floor and then stretch up to the desk for a paper you can't reach, you must expect to bring everything down on your head.'

Afterwards, she went to see whether Gus had any samples of Beecham's Powders in his drawer. Not for Mr Binns's headache, but for her own.

12

Predictably, Norah asked, 'What did Gus say when he got back?'

'I didn't tell him. Binns had gone home by then and I'd tidied everything up. But really, men! You can't trust them. They don't have any sense.'

'Oh, I don't know. Some of them are all right.'

They were doing their Saturday afternoon shopping in Oxford Street and Tassie stopped dead in the middle of the pavement. 'That, coming from you! I remember you using almost exactly the same words to me a year or so ago. "Men don't have any sense", you said. "Half the time they don't even know what they want," you said. Talk about changing your tune!'

Norah grinned. 'I'm older and wiser now. Anyway, you've changed your tune, too. You didn't agree with me then. Those look like rather nice shoes in Peter Robinson's window. Let's cross over.'

'You've nineteen pairs of shoes already. You don't need any more.'

Expertly, they skipped across the road through a jam of steam buses, horsedrawn trams and hooting motorcars. 'Well, I agree with you now. Men have far too high an opinion of themselves. *All* men. And they have the impertinence to claim that women are more emotional and less logical than they are. They've no idea how women think or feel!'

Provocatively, Norah murmured, 'But they admit that we're more patient and morally more refined.'

'Ha! They should hear the women shifters and rovers in the mills at Dundee if they want to know about moral refinement. I've never heard such language! And you can hardly blame them, considering that they're completely at the mercy of men like my brother and Bruce Goudy. Their trade union isn't any use, either. All Max does is laugh – laugh! – when it asks for limitation on workers' hours or an end to piecework, and when the women textile workers petitioned parliament for the vote last year, you'd have thought it was the greatest joke ever.

'The truth is that he really hates his women workers, because he's used to people bowing down to him and the only people who don't bow down are the mill girls. They've no respect for him and when they get the bit between their teeth they don't hesitate to show it. You should hear them when there's a strike on! It's almost funny!'

Norah, whose interest in Max and his opinions was tepid, at best, peered. 'I like those grey *glacé* kid lace-ups with the matt silver buckles. Only nine and elevenpence. Let's go in.'

'Norah! I'm trying to tell you that you've won. I'm going to join the Women's Suffrage Society.'

'Good,' Norah said affably. 'I wonder how many other women have joined because they've been crossed in love.'

Seething, Tassie exclaimed, 'You haven't been listening. Being crossed in love has nothing whatever to do with it!'

'Hasn't it? I thought that bit about *all* men having too high an opinion of themselves might have had something to do with Francis Rivers.'

'Well, it hadn't!'

'All right. There's no need to get excited. I don't know if I told you, but there's to be a big rally of the suffrage societies in Glasgow at the beginning of May. I thought of going. It would be fun to see the girls at the school again, and I've a notion of trying to form a special artists' branch of the movement. Why don't you come?'

'Glasgow?' Tassie repeated in a voice that had suddenly become small and uncertain. 'I don't know. I'll have to think about it.'

13

It was pouring, which didn't surprise those who knew Glasgow but came as something of a disappointment to the hundreds of ladies who had ventured north from more reliable climes and didn't expect to be rained on in the merrie month of May. Under the assault of the rain

350

and three thousand pairs of feet, the grassy acres of Glasgow Green gave up the unequal struggle and subsided miserably into the mud.

'Royal weather,' Norah remarked from under the over-sized waterproof mob cap that covered her hat. The king and queen were due to begin a visit to Scotland the next day, which would – if only co-incidentally – have given the rally more news appeal, but the organisers knew that Sunday was the only day on which they could be sure of maximum attendance. The suffrage movement in England might be a middle class affair, but in Scotland's industrial belt working women played an important rôle. The kirk, as was to be expected, had thundered out against the rally as a desecration of the Sabbath, but most of the ladies present were of the opinion that, in such a good cause, the Lord would forgive.

Tassie, nervously scanning the crowd for representatives of the press – preferably tall, dark, handsome and carelessly dressed – said loudly, 'I can't even see the platform with all these umbrellas in the way.' Resignedly, the lady in front lowered hers and passed the message on, though not everyone was so obliging as to heed it.

The meeting fell quiet at last – the ladies of leisure, the merchants' wives, the harassed young mothers with babies in their arms and older children clinging to their skirts, the office clerks, the shop assistants and factory girls. On the fringes of the Green, the usual Sunday quota of Socialists and other advanced thinkers continued to harangue passers-by on the Nature and Existence of Chance and the eternally insoluble problem of the Chicken and the Egg.

Tassie, craning, said, 'Mother, can you see?'

'Not very well, dear, but it isn't important.'

It had been Grace's intention to go to St Andrews to interview replacements for Murdo and Mary, who were retiring, and then straight back to London for Genny's second confinement. But her choice of dates had been inopportune, enabling the girls to cajole her into changing her plans, and her route, so that she could accompany them to the rally. Her interest in the suffrage movement had never been great, but she had agreed to go because it occurred to her that, if she were better informed, the girls – Norah especially – wouldn't feel the need to lecture her about it, interminably, every time they met.

The introductory remarks of the invisible chairman were followed by a speech from a small, calm and kindly-looking lady, a Miss Clunas, who was a school-teacher and a member of the new Labour Party.

'Mr Gladstone,' cried Miss Clunas, 'always refused to countenance any extension of the franchise to women because he had too much respect for us "to trespass upon the delicacy, the purity, the refinement, the elevation" of our natures by involving us in the sordid machinery of political life. Rather should he' – her voice deepened dramatically – 'have *given* us the franchise, that we might bring our moral authority to bear on the task of transforming that machinery from something sordid into something fine.'

She sat down to wild applause.

After that came Miss Wilkie, also a schoolteacher.

'. . . and all too many among us are more conserva-tive than men, because of the narrowness and isolation of our lives, the subjection in which we have always been held, the punishment inflicted by society on all who step outside the prescribed sphere. It is not only men we must convert to our cause. It is women, too.'

More applause, though noticeably less enthusiastic.

Norah muttered, 'Criticising women doesn't go down nearly as well as criticising men. Ah, it's Miss Greig next. She won't make *that* mistake.'

'. . . the cosy world of cigar-and-brandy politics

. . . Men are afraid of us. They fear our influence, and especially our influence for good. They do not fear criminals, they do not fear drunkards, they do not fear lunatics. To all of those they grant the vote. But they fear women, and that is why women have no vote . . . We must fight. We must fight at home, we must fight at work. We must fight in the streets, if need be . . .'

If there had been a house, she would have brought it down.

'Goodness,' murmured Grace, 'what an alarming lady!'

The rain had gone off and the umbrellas had been furled by the time the chairman rose to declare the rally at an end.

It was only then that Tassie saw who the chairman was.

14

Francis Rivers's mother. Unforgettable, unmistakable.

Norah and Grace were already deep in discussion, Grace as usual wondering where they might find a nice cup of tea.

'Is it too much to hope that you can survive until we get back to the Lady Artists' Club?' Norah asked.

'Yes.'

Tassie made up her mind. 'Can you wait a moment? There's someone I want to talk to.'

As Mistress Rivers, in her magpie black and white, caught sight of Tassie approaching, her eyebrows rose fractionally, just as her son's always did when he was about to say something caustic. Tassie, uneasily relieved at the signs of recognition – which meant one barrier the less to be overcome – stood aside politely until two ladies from south of the Border had finished complimenting the chairman on the dignity of the meeting and the eloquence of the speakers.

Then, in case she had misread the signs, she said, smiling, 'We met once before. In Fleet Street. Your son Francis was with you. I just wanted to say how much I enjoyed the meeting.' Which wasn't what she wanted to say at all. 'I'm Tassie Smith, by the way.'

'I remember. My son told me about you.'

Tassie swallowed. 'He's well, I hope?'

'I imagine so. He is away at present on a tour of India and Australia.'

Tassie's 'How exciting,' sounded hollow in her own ears. There was little purpose, now, in pursuing the conversation, so she said, 'I mustn't keep you,' and turned away.

But Mistress Rivers's voice followed her. 'From what my son told me, I believe I may have been acquainted with your mother many years ago. You may remember me to her.'

Startled, Tassie said, 'My mother? But she's just over there. I'll bring her.'

She didn't see the sudden stillness in Mistress Rivers's face, or the hand raised briefly to stop her.

15

'Well, Grace?'

There was no sign, now, of hesitancy.

Mistress Rivers's name had meant nothing to Grace except in relation to the journalist whom Max so much disliked, and there had been nothing in the distant figure, face or voice during the rally to strike a chord of memory.

But, now, both the words and the tone in which they were uttered were more than enough to sweep away almost forty years of forgetting.

'*Abigail?* Abigail Graham?'

'You didn't recognise me? You, on the other hand, have changed very little. Though you are overweight. You should do something about it.'

'Only a few pounds,' Grace said automatically, almost apologetically. Abigail had put her on the defensive from the day they first met and, when Simon had died, it had been dread of his sister almost as much as obedience to Joss that had persuaded her to take flight to Dunaird, to cut off all contact with the Lindsay family, then and forever.

It had all been such a very long time ago. Abigail did not appear to have mellowed with the years but there was no reason, now, for Grace to feel cowed by her.

Even so, aware of an awkward silence, she instinctively found herself searching for a way to fill it and, since Tassie was looking bewildered, said, 'Mistress Rivers and I were sisters-in-law when I was married to Selina's father. She was Simon's twin. Her own husband was killed in a most unfortunate accident not long before Simon himself died and I had no idea that, like me, she later chose to remarry.'

Abigail snorted derisively. 'I, certainly, chose. But, knowing Josiah, I find it hard to believe you had any option in the matter.'

If it hadn't seemed, to Grace, a sting to be glossed over, she would not perhaps have added an apparently harmless remark to her daughter that precipitated a revelation which brought the world crashing round Tassie's ears.

16

'Mistress Rivers was acquainted with your father,' she explained, 'because he and Simon were originally partners in the cotton business in Glasgow.'

Tassie was opening her mouth to utter a polite, 'Oh?' when, explosively, Abigail Rivers echoed, 'Partners! Well, if a wolf and a lamb can be partners, I suppose they were.'

'That's most unjust, Abigail! You make Joss sound

like a monster.' His only guilt, to Grace's knowledge, had been in loving her when she was not free to be loved. And that was something Abigail did not know, and would never know.

'Fiddle-de-dee! He ruined Simon, coldly and deliberately, and you say he was not a monster?'

'Ruined *Simon*?' Grace repeated after a moment, dry-voiced. 'I'm sorry, but I don't understand.'

Abigail studied her for what seemed like an eternity and then laughed, without humour. 'I don't suppose you do. Simon wouldn't want to worry you, and Josiah wouldn't waste time talking to you about business. But while you, being you, no doubt assumed that the gentlemen knew what they were doing and did it in a gentlemanly way, I, being I, knew the first for a sweet-natured fool and the second for a scoundrel.'

There were hundreds of people still milling about, but none of them came near. It was as if the vibrations from the low-voiced little group had set up an invisible barricade against intruders.

Tassie said, 'Forgive me, Mistress Rivers. My father was a very astute businessman, but he certainly wasn't a scoundrel.'

'Astute? Perhaps. Though I can think of other words. If you're an intelligent girl, as my son tells me you are, you may be able to think of some too. It is obviously high time you knew what your father was really like.'

Grace said, 'Abigail, this is hardly the time or place for such a conversation and I have no intention of allowing you to blacken her father's name to my daughter. I really think we should . . .'

She might as well not have spoken. Abigail, her piercing grey eyes on Tassie, said, 'You've heard of the American Civil War forty years ago? Yes. Well, when the South was blockaded by the Yankees, exports of fine cotton dried up and all the cotton firms in Britain were in desperate straits, unable to keep the looms going or the mill hands employed. Josiah believed that the North would win and that the Southern plantations, deprived of slave labour, would never be fully productive again. He wanted to adapt Lindsay-Smith Mills' production to the coarser Indian staple. Simon, however, preferred to wait and see. My brother was not a decisive man; of the two of us, I was always the forceful one.'

Tassie opened her mouth, and closed it again as Abigail Rivers said sardonically, 'Yes. Your father *was* right. But having been outvoted, he did not allow the situation to rest. With the business tottering on the brink of extinction, he began buying every illicit ounce of Confederate cotton he could lay his hands on, principally from blockade runners and Yankee merchants who had come into possession of captured stocks. Very unsavoury people they were, too.

'Josiah's dealings might have been justified if he had been buying in order to save Lindsay-Smith. I might even have done the same myself. But he was buying – partly with the firm's money – in secret and on his own account, and reselling at a vast personal profit. In the end, he took his profit and broke up the partnership, leaving Simon with nothing in the world beyond the plant and a huge load of debt.'

Tassie, who had learned much about business ethics during her eighteen months with G.S. Advertising, thought that it had perhaps been rather sharp practice but not criminal, as Mistress Rivers was making it sound. It was natural, of course, that she should exaggerate, because she must have felt her twin brother's troubles very keenly.

Tassie was still busily making allowances when Mistress Rivers turned her cold eyes on Grace, and said with deliberation, 'Did Simon know before he died that Josiah had not only destroyed his business but stolen his wife, too?'

'*No!*'

It had been Grace's longest nightmare. Lies only bred more lies, but she had to defend herself, and Joss, and Max. Especially Max. 'That happened later.'

'Did it? I think you're lying. I think it was the last straw. I think that was why he killed himself.'

17

The rain had begun again, but none of them moved. Vaguely, Tassie hoped that Norah, who had diplomatically withdrawn from the scene, had found somewhere to shelter.

'Killed himself?' Grace's voice was no more than a whisper. 'Simon didn't kill himself. *It was an accident.*'

'No. I didn't allow it to be made public. One does not advertise a suicide in the family. Not when it is one's twin. Not when it is one's dearly loved brother.'

Tassie put an arm round her mother's shoulders. 'What a tragedy,' she said, 'but . . .'

Abigail Rivers shook her head impatiently. 'Don't be a nincompoop, child. You don't know what tragedy is. Grace, look at me!' Her voice was sharp. 'If Simon believed you to be a faithful wife to him, why did he make a new Will before he died, leaving what little he still possessed to me, nothing to you?'

Grace shook her head dazedly. 'I always supposed it was because you were newly widowed and dependent on him. You were expecting a child. You had nothing. I, at least, had Dunaird.'

Abigail's thin lips curved. 'During all the years when I was devoting my life to rebuilding Lindsays, single-handed, for my brother's sake, I might have believed you. Even when I heard that you had married Josiah, I might have believed you. But then my son, Francis, discovered the date of *your* son's birth.

'He was conceived when Simon was still alive. And

358

that means you betrayed my brother with the man who ruined him. If I believed in the power of curses, I would curse you by bell, book and candle. As it is, I will say only that neither I, nor any member of my family, will ever forgive you – or yours.'

18

Tassie at last remembered that she was carrying an umbrella.

Fumbling a little, she opened it and held it up over her mother and herself. Then, in a voice of which she was not ashamed, she said, 'It has all been most interesting, Mistress Rivers. But I think you will agree that there is little purpose in prolonging this discussion. Accusations, however ill-founded, are easy to make and hard to deny. In any case, stirring up the ashes of old tragedies is not a very rewarding occupation.'

'Let us by all means be civilised,' Abigail Rivers agreed, an odd little quirk at the corner of her mouth. It seemed she might have said more, but just then a young army officer materialised at her side bearing an umbrella large enough to shelter his entire regiment.

'Oh, there you are, mother! What a lot of people! I've been looking everywhere for you.'

'And it didn't occur to you that, as chairman, I might still be found near the daïs? No, of course not. Let me introduce you. Grace, Tassie, this is my youngest son, Jonny. And Jonny, my dear, these are Mistress Smith and Miss Smith. The mother and sister of the famous Max McKenzie Smith.'

The anxiety lifted from the young man's face and a light came to it. 'Really? I say, how ripping! I met Mr and Mrs McKenzie Smith at the automobile trials last autumn. I was able to help them when they had a puncture.'

Even through the dragging ache behind her temples,

Tassie remembered Genny's ecstatic description of her saviour. It seemed unlikely that there had been two such amazingly handsome young officers at the rally.

There was something about a uniform that did wonders for most men, but Lieutenant Jonny Rivers had absolutely no need of assistance. He had the same severity of feature as his mother and brother, but his colouring was warmer because of his outdoor life – perhaps also, Tassie remembered, because of his service in South Africa – while his expression was wide-eyed, loving and curiously innocent. The words might be soft, but the man, strangely, wasn't. Tassie thought that, if ever she had to paint the Archangel Michael, here was her model. He was *golden*.

And then all thought was suspended. Because he went on, 'The Arrol Johnston's parked by the side of Templeton's, mother. I'm afraid I'll have to hurry you if you want me to drive you over to Francis's place to see Lucia, because otherwise I'll miss my train.'

Lucia.

It was extraordinary how much damage could be accomplished in an encounter that had lasted for fifteen minutes at most.

May–September 1903

CHAPTER FIVE

I

Tassie, like Lieutenant Jonathan Rivers, had a train to catch if she was to be back at work in the morning, but all she could think of at first was the need to set her own troubles aside and stay with her mother to give her comfort, if that were possible.

She should have known better. Her mother had more strength than she.

They found Norah and went to the Central Hotel, and Grace asked to be left to herself for an hour or two. When she emerged from her room again, she was pale but completely in control. She would spend the night here, she said, and go on to St Andrews in the morning. Tassie was not to worry about her.

So Tassie caught her train after all, and alone, because Norah was staying over in Glasgow for a few days to see 'the girls'.

2

Hy-na-ma-noosh, hy-na-ma-noosh, hy-na-ma-noosh, hy-na-ma-noosh.

The rhythm that had always, before, hypnotised Tassie into a dreamless sleep, now beat on her brain like jungle drums, charged with menace, contaminating every thought with panic.

Revelation after revelation. Destruction, suicide

and a hatred that had not faded over almost forty years.

Tossing in her wayward bed, Tassie went over and over all that Abigail Rivers had said and implied, knowing her mother to be guiltless but unable, in the pitiless clarity of mind that so often came with darkness and solitude, to acquit her father, whom she had adored. She had always known him to be a hard, ambitious man who had loved his wife and daughter and no one else; it had been easy to forget that there were two sides to every story.

How much had Joss's love for Grace contributed to the tragedy of Simon Lindsay? Abigail Rivers said, everything. Grace said, nothing, but to Tassie her denial spoke more of persisting hope than any certainty of truth. Throughout their lives together, Joss had devoted himself to protecting his wife from anything that might cause her pain.

He hadn't always been a good judge. He had taken her baby son away from her.

But even then he had been acting, he must have thought, in her best interests as well as his own.

Round and round it went in Tassie's brain, relentlessly, endlessly, a turmoil that until the worst hour, the coldest hour, the hour before the dawn, allowed her to postpone the thoughts she couldn't bear to think. The thoughts of Francis.

The knowledge that what he felt for her was not love, but hate.

His anger on that evening at Dunaird eight months before had been an aspect of it. A furious rejection of the attraction that even he could not deny.

No. She stopped herself.

He was a rational man, not a creature of emotion. He wouldn't be ruled by a tragedy that had happened before he was born. Before Tassie was born. Her own instincts could not have been so deeply at fault.

But . . .

To grow up in his mother's implacable shadow, to be indoctrinated from birth with the belief that Joss Smith was an evil man, a destroyer . . . Like father, like child. Guilt passed down through the generations, every human being a product of nature and nurture. Even a rational man might be infected by that. Why, otherwise, was he so bent on destroying Max? Why, otherwise, had he never even hinted at their family connection?

Why, otherwise, had he gone to the trouble of seeking her out?

Desolately, Tassie reviewed their meetings, which hadn't been many, over the last three years, remembering his reserve, her own exasperated recognition of the fact that, however easy and pleasant he might be, there was always a distance between them. Even when he had been at his most relaxed and approachable, so that she too was relaxed, it had always been when Max was involved somewhere in the equation.

No, not always. For a brief moment, her mind flew back to the Christmas dance at the Union two years before, but it was too frail a sanctuary. Perhaps he had been simply piqued by Hugo's attentions to her. Or perhaps there had indeed been something relating to Max that she hadn't noticed at the time. She had been too busy falling in love.

It's impossible, he had said. And now she knew why.

A tragedy forever green.

And Lucia. Not a mistress, but a wife.

She had always recognised that she didn't know or understand Francis Rivers, but she had never imagined that her ignorance could be so profound.

At no stage of that interminable night did she weep. The pain went far beyond tears.

3

When she called in to see Max a few days later, he was in one of his exuberant moods, waltzing her twice round the office to the strains of 'Ida' before he would even allow her to speak.

'Did you read what Joe Chamberlain said? Thank God someone's come out at last against free trade. What British business needs is import tariffs and imperial preference. No more foreigners being given a free run of the market! There's a businessmen's petition being got up already and the Tariff League is to be launched next week with – guess who? – as one of its chief sponsors.'

In her new, misanthropic frame of mind, there was only one conclusion she could draw. 'I deduce that you expect to make a profit out of it?'

'Of course. That's what business and politics are all about. So, why are you here? At the office, I mean.'

'There's something I have to tell you and I think it would be better if we weren't interrupted, as we might be at Audley Street.'

'My, my!' He called to his secretary, 'No visitors and no interruptions until I tell you.' And then, raising an enquiring eyebrow, 'Well?'

She had never believed Francis's slanders but, aware that Max fell short of being an angel, neither had she ever been wholly sure that he was more sinned against than sinning. Now she was. A little hesitantly, she began, 'You've never liked Francis Rivers. And he has never liked you. I've found out why.'

As meticulously as she was able, she reported to him everything Abigail Rivers had said. It was hard at times, because Tassie still loved her father whereas Max had never known him. And although not once, even at the very beginning, had Max shown any resentment over his parents' abandonment of him, Tassie had always felt that, somewhere deep down, it must be there. He would have been inhuman, otherwise, and he was not that.

He didn't interrupt. Sometimes, he didn't seem even to be giving her his full attention. But his smile, when she had finished, was that of a satisfied shark.

Unexpectedly, he said, 'Good old Joss! That was a neat piece of work over the cotton. I'd have done exactly the same myself.'

'Would you?'

'Of course.'

Tassie felt very slightly better. In matters of business, she had no reason to question Max's judgement.

'And as for that patronising bastard, Rivers,' Max went on, 'I've always known he was after me, even if you, young Ginger, tried to persuade me he wasn't! When Genny and I were on our honeymoon, I took a quick trip to Zurich and heard afterwards that one of his contacts had been making enquiries about what I'd been doing there. He didn't find out, of course. But it was a bit of damned noseyparkering and I was annoyed. I wanted that particular venture kept quiet.'

Seeing the doubtful expression on Tassie's face, he grinned. 'Don't worry. Nothing you wouldn't approve of. Merely that, when you're trying to forestall a competitor, it's best not to advertise. I got my own back, though.'

Remembering, she said, 'You tried to ruin the *Enterprise*?'

'How do you know about that?'

She shook her head and, after a moment, he went on, 'Diamond cut diamond, my pet. I wonder . . . Perhaps, after these revelations from Madame Abigail, it would be wise to take further steps to protect myself. And mother, too.'

'How can you?'

She had thought, at first, that it would be better for

Max to remain in ignorance; if he knew about it all, he would probably start a war. But the war, in its own one-sided way, was already being waged, and he was entitled to know that he had to defend himself against an enemy driven by a motive far more compelling than mere personal dislike.

Now, watching him, knowing that he was brewing mischief, the bitter realisation struck her that she hadn't, in the telling, shifted the burden of knowledge from her own shoulders to his, or even halved it with him. Instead, she had doubled it. What damage would he do, unpredictable Max, given such an excuse?

'I wonder if Lindsay Mills is a private company?' he said thoughtfully. 'Perhaps I could mount a takeover. That would teach them a lesson they wouldn't forget.'

Abigail Rivers had spent a lifetime rebuilding what Joss Smith had so selfishly destroyed. Tassie said, 'No.'

'Why not?'

She couldn't explain, and Max certainly wouldn't understand, the uneasy balance of rights and wrongs that she had arrived at in her mind. So she said only, 'It would be descending to their level. You don't have to do anything, just be on your guard. And please don't tell me that attack is the best form of defence.

'I must get back to work now, but you have weeks, perhaps months, to think about it. Francis Rivers is away on a tour of India and Australia.'

It punctured the bubble of Max's good humour. His heavy eyebrows coming together in a bar across his forehead, he said, 'Is he, indeed?'

4

Winter though it was in the Nullarbor desert, it was still too warm for comfort at the surface workings outside Kalgoorlie when Francis eventually found the prospector he had been looking for, a man dressed in red shirt, dirty white trousers and slouched wideawake hat; a man so intent on shaking his tin basin with its load of soil and water that he barely glanced up at Francis's approach.

'Mr O'Donnell?' Francis asked.

'Who's asking?' The man had spent ten years and more, Francis knew, panning for gold, but his brogue was still as thick as on the day he had left Ireland. He was as poor now as he had been then. Not for him the prosperous life of Kalgoorlie with its hotels and taverns, its imposing public buildings and brave new reservoir fed by more than three hundred miles of pipeline from Perth. Not for him the deep, rich seams, the drives and crosscuts of the wealthiest gold mining area in the world.

Gold.

A substance inert and innately useless, hard to find and harder to keep. How, Francis had often wondered, had gold and jewels come to have such allure for mankind? Riches, once, had been measured in useful things like herds of cattle. Why, now, were they measured in metals and minerals?

At the Delhi Durbar six months earlier, gold had caparisoned the elephants, turbanned the princes, embroidered the ladies, the heralds, the trumpeters, the canopies and the carpets. The display had been blinding, the dust of the procession a grateful relief to the eye, shrouding the gold, the rubies, the emeralds and pearls in a topaz veil, mysterious, unearthly, magical.

'It's obscene,' Francis had said at one point, thinking of the beggars beyond the gates, and the District Officer beside him had shrugged. 'Perhaps it is. It's also India. Extremes, dear chap, extremes. You may think our honoured viceroy, up there on his elephant, is a representative of the British Crown, but he isn't and he knows it. He's an Indian ruler presiding over a display that, if it weren't for the electric lights in the camp and

367

all these kodaks pinging away around us, might have taken place at any time in the last two thousand years. It's a display they would have recognised in the days of Babur, in the days of the Guptas, in the days of Asoka. The beggars aren't envious. Some day it may be their *karma* – their destiny – too, to be dressed in gold and silks and jewels, and mounted on elephants.'

It had taken another three months in India before Francis had even begun to understand. Some day he would go back.

In the meantime, he said, 'My name is Rivers, Mr O'Donnell. I heard of you first in Coolgardie, and it has taken me six weeks to trace you here. I have some questions to ask you.'

'An' what makes ye think Oi'll be answering them?'

'If you're prepared to listen, I'll tell you.'

5

Night after night during the golden, early summer dusks of the Season, the West End of London was crammed with conveyances bearing white-necktied gentlemen and exquisitely coiffed ladies to dinner engagements designed to fortify them against evenings rarely less than six parties deep. Tassie, sufficiently familiar by now with the fashionable world to recognise some of the carriages, found herself speculating occasionally, as she walked from the Bayswater Road to Audley Street or Mount Street, as to where their occupants might be bound.

From the grandiose mansions of Belgravia to the leafy confines of St John's Wood there were red carpets laid out for them, doors standing open for them, perspiring kitchens waited to feed them. There were footmen to escort them upstairs and grooms on guard, downstairs, to chase from their sight the ragged Amelia Anns and Sarah Janes, the waifs from the slums with smaller waifs clutched by the hand, whose evening pastime was to stand outside the houses of the rich and watch the fine gentlemen and pretty ladies come and go.

It annoyed Max that the coming and going had ceased to include the casino.

After the launch in the previous December, everything had settled down nicely, though not quite as profitably as Max had anticipated. Not being one of the county set, he hadn't foreseen that, although its members might turn up in droves on Tuesdays, Wednesdays and Thursdays, it was their universal habit to decamp to the country from Fridays until Mondays. Then had come the Season. By the time it was half over, the energy of even the most dedicated socialites had begun to flag so that, after the sixth party, they were more inclined to go home to bed than drop in at Mount Street for a flutter at the tables.

And the Season was followed by high summer, when – as Max had again failed to foresee – the fashionable world once more decamped to the country, not just for the weekend but for a protracted period of recuperation. By late July, both London and the casino were dead as the proverbial dodo.

Tassie's overriding desire that summer, as it had been in the autumn of the year before, was never to be alone, never to have time to think. As a result, she had fallen into the habit of spending otherwise empty evenings at the casino, knowing that, if the worst came to the worst, at least there would be Freddy to talk to, and one or two of his friends, or even Monty as a last resort.

Max himself often dropped in, though never to gamble, and never with Genny, whose approaching confinement had, for the second year in succession, deprived her of the delights of the Season, so that she had become sulky and waspish, behaving as if the females of the family existed only to be moaned at.

Visits to Audley Street had become more of a penance than a pleasure and Tassie sometimes thought, guiltily, that if her mother hadn't been there she wouldn't have gone at all.

6

'Queer thing,' Freddy said one evening as he placed his lonely bet at the roulette table. 'I only seem to win when the place is empty. Never when it's full. Wonder what the odds are on that?'

'*Rien ne va plus.*' The croupier, impassive as always, set the wheel spinning.

Black. Evens.

Freddy sighed heavily and remarked, 'I said, "only". Not "always".'

The croupier closed the wheel down and went off for a break.

The room was empty except for three lethargic gentlemen playing vingt-et-un, a solitary soul engaged in a duel with the banker at the baccarat table, a couple of half-asleep waiters and Monty, standing by the closely curtained window, surveying his domain.

Dutifully, Tassie said, 'Bad luck, Freddy, though I wish more people would lose. I sometimes wonder what the point is in having a one-third share in this place when the profits are always having to be clawed back to keep the float afloat, so to speak.'

'Not as bad as that, surely? You ought to have turned quite a pretty little penny in the last eight months.'

'Well, I haven't.'

Monty strolled over, suave and smoothly tailored, looking as if managing a casino was what he had been born to. No one could have guessed that his only previous employment had been as acting, unpaid, deputy sports master at his father's school, or that he was not yet twenty-one years old.

'Why the heavy scowl, Freddy, old boy?'

Freddy wrinkled his button of a nose, causing two brief, horizontal lines to appear across the bridge, and making his features look as if they had been compressed by a pair of invisible hands into a small and exceedingly crowded compass in the centre of his face. He said, 'Don't understand why the casino isn't making a decent profit.'

Monty waved a languid hand round the empty crimson and gilt splendours and smiled, as if no more reply were needed.

But Freddy wasn't to be deflected. He had been frequenting casinos, not since before Monty was born – not quite – but for a good ten years longer than Max's young cub of a yes-man. Bluntly, he went on, 'Especially since I, for one, have been losing more than I should.'

'A common complaint.' This time, Monty's smile was unmistakably condescending, leading Tassie to reflect that a sock on his elegant proboscis would do her nephew nothing but good. It was too much to hope that Freddy would oblige.

'No,' Freddy replied, concentrating hard. 'I mean it. I know what I'm talking about.'

'You're not suggesting, I hope, that you're being cheated? You're a friend of the management, Freddy, old boy. Any cheating would be in your favour.'

'Maybe. Though I'd be the first to notice, I can tell you, if the croupier's sleeve brushed one of my bets from a losing to a winning square. Or vice versa. I grant you, I haven't seen that happen, either. But what *about* the croupiers? Not unheard of for them to line their pockets at the management's expense.'

Tassie, eyebrows rising, said, 'Really? How?'

'Patch of some sticky stuff just above the shirt cuff. Pick up a coin or two from the house winnings without anyone noticing. Adds up, that kind of thing.'

Monty sighed exaggeratedly. 'Max wasn't born yesterday, Freddy, and neither was I. All the croupiers are searched the moment they leave the room.'

Tassie, still innocent of the wicked ways of the world – or some of them – was mildly shocked at this lack of trust, but Freddy didn't blink an eye.

'Doesn't prevent them passing the money over to a confederate while they're still in the room, though, does it? What about the waiters?'

Monty sighed again.

Helpfully, Tassie suggested, 'Or the casino cat? Or even the mice?'

What she really wanted to do was scream. Instead, she asked, 'Have you heard from your mother recently, Monty? How is she?'

His expression didn't change. 'I have no idea. Much the same as always, I imagine. Since I came to work for Max, we have not been in touch. May I offer you some champagne?'

'I suppose so,' Tassie said.

7

And then everyone's boredom was alleviated by the entry of a cloud of cigar smoke, closely followed by Max. He was putting on weight, Tassie noted critically, though not too much – not yet. She had thought, on the day he had first entered her life, that his features didn't belong to a man who was born to be thin, and in fact the extra pounds helped to give him presence. They also exaggerated the air of bonhomie that, over the years, had become increasingly deceptive. However loyal she still was to him, Tassie knew that – as Gus would have put it – Max was no man's buddy.

He had probably been listening outside the door, too.

'What are you doing here?' she asked.

He beamed euphorically, several degrees less than

sober. 'I've come to see my favourite people. Come to tell you 'bout my invitation. Going to Cowes next month. Invited on the royal yacht. Tommy Lipton – sorry, *Sir* Tommy Lipton's taking me.'

A touch disparagingly, Freddy remarked, 'He's not a member of the Royal Yacht Club. The Club don't accept fellows who've made their money in trade.'

'Royal Yacht Club be damned. It's the royal yacht that matters. Going to meet the king. Great day for The Great Max.' He made it sound like a newspaper headline, which in due course it would probably become.

Over the last two years, Max had found himself elevated from 'Black House Max' to 'The Great Max' by a press that had fallen into the habit of soliciting his views on everything from the registration of private motorcars to Britain's falling birth rate and the slaughter of the Jews in Russia. Tassie was forever opening her newspaper to find Max quoted as representative of the man in the street or – in the latest catchphrase – 'the man in the Clapham omnibus', because he seemed to have a knack of voicing what a great many ordinary people were thinking, and voicing it in words that made it sound sensible and forthright instead of, as it all too often was, unblushingly jingoistic.

She said crossly, 'I wish they wouldn't call you "The Great Max". It makes you sound like a music hall turn.'

He beamed. 'That's what I am.'

'Anyway, Cowes Week's at the beginning of August.'

'Nail on the head. Clever little sister, my Ginger! At's to say, clever little Ginger, my sister!' He cocked an eyebrow. 'Something wrong there.'

'Yes, there certainly *is* something wrong!' She dropped her voice. 'Genny's due to be confined in the first week of August. You can't just go sauntering off to Cowes, king or no king.'

Pursing his lips, Max said, 'I dunno. Once a fellow's put a bun in the oven, isn't a lot more he can do till the bun's popped out, is there?'

'You don't have to be so vulgar about it! Genny will need you. You ought to be with her. You ought to be with her *now*, instead of here. It's not fair to leave her alone every evening. You know how she frets.'

'Yes,' said Max frankly. 'And damn' tedious it is listening to her.'

The vingt-et-un and baccarat players, the croupiers, the waiters, Freddy and Monty, had all abandoned their other concerns to give Max their full attention.

Tassie hissed, '*Max!*' but every member of his little audience might have had a direct line to the editor of the *Daily Express* for all he seemed to care.

'Yes, but 's true,' he went on, without lowering his voice. 'She never stops. Always complaining. Women's talk. Don' see why I should have to listen. She's got you and mother. Doesn't need me.'

Tassie lost her temper. Picking up a glass of flat champagne, she threw its contents in his face.

All Max did was shake his head slightly and blink.

Her voice still gratingly low, she said, 'You're her husband. You married her. You're responsible for her. Why should mother and I have to do all the running around? That's *your* duty. You're absolutely impossible!'

Removing the cigar from his mouth, Max surveyed it mournfully. 'Gone out,' he said. 'Pity. 'Swhat happens when people throw champagne at people.'

And then Tassie caught a gleam in his eye and realised that he wasn't drunk after all, or only a very little. He had been teasing her, and now, as if to say, 'It's all right, Ginger, truly it is!' his face relaxed into the conspiratorial, heart-stoppingly charming smile of old, the smile that unfailingly disarmed her.

She couldn't stop herself from responding, just a

little, from subduing her anger and allowing herself a reluctant twinkle.

It was enough.

She saw the imperceptible glaze of satisfaction come to his eyes, contaminating the smile, turning the warmth to a lie.

The anger she had denied flared to furious life again. He didn't care about her. He didn't care about Genny. He didn't care about anybody.

She couldn't trust her voice even to utter a 'Good night!' as she turned and almost ran from the room.

8

The new baby arrived on the second day of Cowes Week. Max came up to London to admire it on the third day, and went back on the fourth.

It was another boy and he was adorable. Although his elder brother had been stolid from the moment of his birth, little Frederick Maximilian McKenzie Smith clearly thought the world was a lovely place to be, and filled in the intervals when he wasn't placidly asleep by gurgling and chuckling at anyone and everyone who came within range of his newborn vision.

'Isn't he heavenly?' Genny said proudly. However much she hated being *enceinte*, she couldn't be faulted when it came to loving her babies. Grace said that, flighty though she might be in other ways, she was a wonderful mother and looked as if she would continue to be so. Perhaps it had something to do with having lost her own mother when she was young.

Tassie, holding the baby circumspectly and tickling him where he seemed to like being tickled, was assailed by a sudden sense of longing, the awakening of a maternal instinct she hadn't known she possessed.

It didn't leave her when she gave the baby back into his mother's arms, nor did it leave her during the

375

evening and night that followed, when wanting a baby of her own brought back all her misery and heartbreak. She hadn't dreamed it could be worse than before.

She had fought, and would go on fighting her passion for Francis Rivers, the despicable man who had trapped her into loving him, who had no feeling for her except perhaps a mild physical attraction muddied by an amused contempt. But, as in the very different case of her feeling for Max, she had learned that loving wasn't a matter of choice. Choice was something as shifting as the sands, love as inexorable as the sea.

She didn't know how to disentangle her feelings, didn't know whether this sudden, desperate longing for a child of her body was something complete in itself or merely an extension of her frustrated desire. It mattered, because all her instincts told her that children should be wanted for themselves, not as a remedy for loneliness of the heart.

Francis Rivers and fate between them had decreed that she could never be his lover, or his wife, could never bear his children.

She wasn't New Woman enough to conceive without affection and bear a child out of wedlock, a child to whom she could give all the warmth that was in her. She wasn't sure whether she could even bring herself to marry in friendship, as so many women did, for the sake of having children to love. Right or wrong? Wise or foolish?

She didn't know.

9

It was characteristic of London that it was nearly always noisy and smelly and dirty in a perfectly acceptable way. But sometimes, when the weather was hot, it wasn't so acceptable.

Tassie, struggling home from work a few days later,

found herself thinking that, where the traffic was concerned, the whole was greater – if that was the word – than the sum of its parts. Compared with two years before, when she had first made the city's acquaintance, there were hundreds more motorcars on the roads, but the noise and smells and dirt they generated, instead of maintaining some kind of separate automobiliar identity, fused with their horsy equivalents into a compound far more potent than either alone. She gave a violent sneeze, and thought that some fresh air would be nice.

Hugo thought the same. There was a cricket match at Hove, he said, and how did she feel about a day at the seaside?

She had always regarded cricket as like golf, more fun to play than to watch, but she hadn't seen or smelt the sea for almost a year – at Dunaird – and even the English Channel was better than nothing. Gus said she could have a day off, provided she came back with some beach sketches they could use in Swan and Edgar's bathing suit advertising next year.

It was a perfect day. The deck chairs round the cricket ground were full, there was a soft salt tang in the air, and Fry and Ranjitsinhji knocked up a century between them in the first hour.

Tassie, sketching peacefully with Bourne and Hollingsworth's cricket bats rather than Swan and Edgar's bathing suits in mind, glanced up to see Ranjitsinhji, with no more than a flick of the wrists, transform a thunderbolt into a shooting star and send it elegantly soaring from middle stump to fine leg boundary.

'Well, played, sir!' exclaimed Hugo and two or three hundred others, clapping decorously. 'Poetry in motion. Pure wizardry!'

And then it was C.B. Fry, handsome and absorbed, not so much playing the bowling as engaging it in philosophical discussion. It didn't stop him from hitting four boundaries in one over.

'Well, played, sir! Oh, well played!' Hugo turned to Tassie. 'Are you enjoying yourself? It's wonderful. Isn't it wonderful?'

'Yes, Hugo. It's wonderful.'

She couldn't help smiling. All too often, Hugo's enjoyment was a guarded thing, as if honest pleasure were undignified and unbefitting a barrister. He ate, worked, relaxed and presumably slept in a metaphorical wig and gown. But today he was like a small boy and she liked him very much better for it.

10

Perhaps it was because he sensed it that, hours later, when the moon was up and they were sitting on Brighton's stony beach for a last few minutes before catching their train, he said, 'You know why I suggested this particular day for our expedition, don't you?'

No explanation immediately sprang to Tassie's mind. 'No,' she said. 'Was there a reason?'

'Of course.' He took her hand in his. 'It's exactly a year since I asked you to marry me.'

It wasn't. If they were to be precise about it, she calculated rapidly, it must be nearer a year and four or five weeks. It had been after Hugo's initiation into the mysteries of potato preparation for the public dinner on 6th July, and before the birth of Genny's first son on the 26th. However, it seemed a pity to spoil his fun, so she said, 'My goodness, is it really?'

'Yes. And I said then . . .' His eyes were wide and unblinking, as they always were when he was privately unsure of himself, and she realised in sudden panic what was coming. It wasn't fair. It was all very well, at three o'clock in the morning, to go over, and over, and over,

378

the rights and wrongs of marrying in friendship for the sake of having children to love, but it wasn't three o'clock in the morning and at any moment the problem was going to cease to be hypothetical.

She wasn't ready, but she couldn't think how to stop him.

'I said then that, when I was better established at the Bar, I would ask you again. And, as you know, I have had several important briefs recently, and everything is looking very promising. So I am asking you again.'

She could feel her face stinging a little, as if her skin had caught the sun in spite of the straw hat with the artificial roses round its brim. It was impossible to sketch and hold up a sunshade at the same time.

'Are you sure?'

'What a question!' He looked slightly offended. 'I *never* say anything I am not sure about. You should know that by now. And I am sure that I want to marry you.'

'What I meant,' she said a little desperately, 'was are you sure you're ready for such a step? Marriage is such a tie, such a responsibility. It would be awful if it were to hinder your career.'

Releasing her hand, he lay back on the pebbles, propping himself on judicious elbows. 'I will concede that I am not free of concern on that score. But I know you have made the acquaintance of a good many eligible gentlemen in this last year and I would not like any of them to get in ahead of me merely because I was behindhand in reiterating my offer.'

'Oh, well, if that's all! Honestly, I can assure you I'm not thinking of marrying anyone else.'

'Has anyone else asked you?'

And that went too far. She fluttered her eyelashes and said, 'Really, Hugo. That is not the kind of question you should ask a lady.'

He didn't show any embarrassment. It hadn't

occurred to her before that barristers must be like poker players and croupiers and politicians, their faces trained to hide rather than reveal in case a display of feeling gave the game away. She had always thought that Hugo's face was just naturally expressionless.

'Perhaps not, but you must appreciate my uneasiness. I have no idea, for example, what goes on at that club of your brother's.'

He didn't mean to be offensive. It was just that he had no notion of tact. 'Are you suggesting that I'm not to be trusted?' she asked. 'Because, if so, then I think we should regard this conversation as at an end.'

He sat up sharply and reached for her hand again. 'No. No, of course not. It's just that you are too sweet and innocent for your own good. What if some dreadful rotter tried making up to you? You wouldn't see through him!'

With a faint gasp of hysteria, she said, 'Hugo, even if I were so innocent as not to be able to see through some dreadful rotter, I can assure you that Max would see through him for me. Or Freddy. Or Monty. Really, I'm very well protected.'

Enough was enough. Rising and brushing down her skirt, she said, 'We ought to go. We mustn't miss the train.'

Hugo rose, too.

She was surprised to feel his arms go round her. Harmlessly. Loosely. Non-committally. Always the barrister and the gentleman.

He said, 'You have not answered me.'

Tempted to reply, 'I've forgotten what the question was,' she resisted it. She shouldn't make fun of him. So she said firmly, 'Hugo, you know perfectly well that you don't want to get married for ages yet. I'm not sure I do, either. I'm touched that you're afraid of losing me, truly I am. But . . .'

She was still hesitating over how to finish, when he

said, 'I don't suppose – er – you would consider just being engaged to me, would you? We wouldn't need to talk about marriage until later on, when we are both more ready for it.'

The Channel waters lapped gently on the beach and from up on the brightly lit promenade came the sound of voices and laughter.

It was like being suspended between two worlds, offered a choice between them. But, as always, there was no choice, really, because there was a train to catch and no way to reach the station other than by the promenade. Life had to be lived.

Her back to the sea, Tassie said, 'All right.'

He kissed her then, on the cheek, but he didn't hold her hand on the train home because there were other people in the compartment.

II

'Yes, but . . .' Tassie said, for the third time in thirty seconds, and for the third time was ignored.

'. . . and though he's my brother and I'm fond of him, I know his failings too well. He's wrong for you, Tassie. You've never seen him sulking, have you?'

'No, but . . .'

'Or on his high horse?'

'No, but . . .'

'. . . or when he gets it into his head that someone has done him an injury?'

'No, but . . .'

'There you are, then. You've never known him other than besotted. Courtship's a queer thing. People are nicer than usual when they're in love and it's not just a matter of rose-tinted spectacles. I don't mean they set out deliberately to display their best qualities and hide their weaknesses – most people don't know what their own best qualities and weaknesses are, anyway. It's more as if niceness is a kind of unconscious love offering.

'I suppose what I'm really saying is that marrying someone you've never seen *out* of love is a dangerous gamble, because the state of "falling in love" doesn't last. Sooner or later midnight strikes and the coach turns into a pumpkin again. And lovers turn into their ordinary selves again.'

Tassie sat, her hands idle in her lap, and knew that Norah was right. It was ironical that, according to her definition, Francis Rivers would make an ideal husband. She had never known him in any state other than *out* of love.

After a moment, she said, 'You seem to have given a lot of thought to it.'

'I'm interested in how people tick.'

'Yes. Your argument doesn't leave much room for love at first sight, though, does it?'

'I suppose not. Though I don't know. Perhaps it does. Perhaps with some people the chemistry's so powerful that nothing else matters. But there's still a lot of learning to be done.'

'Have you finished?' Almost pleadingly, Tassie said, 'You're underrating me, you know. I do recognise some of Hugo's weaknesses, and I can guess at others. But – well – we've become quite good friends. I think we could live together quite amicably. Isn't that enough?'

Tartly, Norah asked, 'Enough for what?' but Tassie didn't answer.

She didn't guess that it had taken all Norah's willpower to refrain from asking the one, prying question she had wanted to ask for the last year, the only question that mattered. 'What about Francis Rivers?'

Gus Silvermann said, 'I guess you know that your brother happened by last evening?'

Tassie, whose umbrella had been blown inside out on her way back from Bourne and Hollingsworth's, removed her sodden hat and shook it vigorously. Mr Fothergill, unexpectedly showered on, exclaimed, 'Hey, mind my layout!'

'Sorry. Ugh, what a day! My brother?'

'Come in my office.'

Max, it seemed, had set up a new flooring company in New York, McKenzie Smith International, and, Gus being an American who knew the market, had decided to employ G.S. Advertising to publicise it.

'It's the first I've heard of it,' said an exasperated Tassie. 'Not just the advertising contract but McKenzie Smith International. Doesn't it sound grand? I sometimes wonder what my brother thinks he's up to. I've almost given up trying to keep track of all his enterprises. It's become so complicated that I don't even know which company's which, nowadays.'

Gus's dimples showed. They were remarkably expressive dimples and what they conveyed, on this occasion, was a friendly cynicism. 'That's business, Tassie. And whatever he's up to, he's pretty successful at it. He's a slick operator and I'm not about to complain at having a slice of the action.'

'Well, I am, if it means I have to start drawing *boring* linoleum again.'

Unconvincingly apologetic, Gus said, 'Yeah, well, that was part of the deal, I'm afraid. "My little sister", you know?'

'Oh, *no!*'

'Yep. He reckons you should make a quick trip to Dundee to see the designs they've prepared for the U.S. market . . .'

'Finest Olde Worlde Englishe, no doubt.'

'Got it in one. We Americans just love that kind of thing.' Gus paused reflectively. 'You say he has a lot of companies. Maybe you should try sorting out which is which. Help us avoid treading on people's corns. And if you could roust out copies of some of the other companies' advertisements? With big corporations it's good policy to maintain a unified house style.'

Tassie looked him straight in the eye. 'There's a flaw in that argument. If we're only doing – what's it called? – McKenzie Smith International's advertising, it doesn't make a pennyworth of difference which of the other companies is which. You're just being inquisitive, aren't you?'

Gus scratched the tip of his nose, a habit of his when he was trying to cover up embarrassment or confusion. 'We-e-ell . . .'

'It's all right,' she said. 'I'm beginning to feel inquisitive, too. It's about time I took an interest. I've been an unremunerated shareholder in the parent company for years and years, and it would be instructive to know just how many companies I'm not getting a dividend from. When do you want me to go?'

'Attagirl! How's about Friday?'

13

On the Thursday, south-east England suffered one of the worst storms in living memory. Several people were killed and the newspapers said there had been widespread damage.

Fortunately, the trains from London to the north weren't affected, and Tassie arrived at St Andrews more or less on time, to find the sun going down on what she was assured had been a braw, breezy day. And och, no, there hadn'y been mair nor a wee smirr o' rain.

It made her feel quite sentimental to be back at

Graceholm, even if only for a night or two, though it was sad not to find Mungo and Mary, who had been the mainstay of the household since before Tassie was born. The new butler and housekeeper, Boyd and Mrs Boyd – who wouldn't graduate to Christian names for a good five years yet – were a little stiff in manner but perfectly competent.

Strange, Tassie thought, that she had never had the house to herself before. All through the evening, she kept expecting to hear Grace's voice, or Max's. But Grace was still in Audley Street, overseeing Genny's recovery from her confinement, and Max, she heard next day, was at Kirklaws, presiding over a weekend conference involving, among others, Bruce Goudy, Monty Fitzalan and the oily Mr Algernon Vale.

'Aye,' said John Bell, 'He's still got those neat wee waves in his hair. It's well seen he never takes them out for an airing on the Firth o' Tay. That's a bonny ring.'

Tassie wasn't yet accustomed to being an engaged lady. She said, 'It's been in my fiancé's family for goodness knows how many years.'

It was a relief that Hugo hadn't insisted on going to Hennell's, especially since the family ring, a double band of diamonds with a band of pearls between, was one of the prettiest she had ever seen, early Victorian in date but still in the disciplined Georgian taste. She was taking the greatest care of it, not only because it was beautiful and valuable but because there was always the possibility that she might have to give it back some day. After four weeks of trying to imagine herself married to Hugo, of accepting his chaste occasional kisses with an appearance of pleasure, she was still no nearer certainty than she had been that evening at Brighton.

Shrugging the thought aside, she said, 'John, can you explain a few things to me? Why don't we go and have something to eat in one of the teashops? My treat.'

His mobile eyebrows shot up into the peak of his

hair. 'Don't come the New Wumman wi' me, young Tassie. Your treat, forsooth! I dunno what the world's coming to. It's an awfu' thing when ye want to take away a man's self-respect.'

'Oh, all right. If your self-respect insists on throwing its money about . . .'

14

It was another fine, breezy day by Dundee standards, which meant that, by the London standards to which Tassie had become accustomed, it wasn't actually pouring and there was a biting east wind.

She said, 'Brrrr! Scotch broth, please, and then I'll have steak-and-kidney pudding.' It was no wonder that people in the north were prone to stoutness, unless they were always on the go or played a daily eighteen holes on the Old Course – which was difficult for women, who had to tie their skirts round their ankles when it was windy and, even on calm days, needed a gentleman to pick up their balls so that they didn't have to bend down and display more of their nether limbs than was seemly.

Joining the women's suffrage movement had been a mistake, she sometimes thought. It had made her aware of far too many things she had never paid much attention to before.

'Continuing our conversation of three years ago,' she said, 'you told me to ask Max if I wanted to know about incorporations and things.'

He grinned. 'Aye. Did it do ye any good?'

'No, of course not. But if G.S. Advertising is to handle the McKenzie Smith International account, I really do need to know, at the very least, what its relationship is to the other companies. Gus Silvermann asked Max, and Max referred him to you.'

John Bell looked thoughtful. 'I wonder why? I'm

only the accountant. The figures go rolling past me, right enough, but only for sales and material purchases an' that kind o' thing. When it comes to shares and bank loans and setting up companies, that's Goudy's territory. I could tell you most of the share capitals, but it wudny help. A company's share capital's only a paper figure.'

'Then what was Max talking about?'

'Maybe he thought a skeleton outline was all ye needed.' But John Bell was frowning as if his words and his thoughts didn't quite match.

Carefully, Tassie said, 'Even a skeleton would be something.'

15

The soup arrived, steaming and savoury, thick as stew. 'Just whit the doctor ordered,' said John Bell and, picking up his spoon, applied himself to the task of blowing on it.

Tassie said, 'Yes. Now, let's start from the beginning. First, there was Josiah Smith and Company. Then, when Max took over, he changed the name to McKenzie Smith and Company. At that stage, the business consisted of three jute mills and one jute factory. Why don't you go on from there?'

'Aye.' John Bell tested the temperature with a genteel slurp. 'Next, yer brither set up McKenzie Flooring off his own bat. And then he turned the original McKenzie Smith into a holding company, which took over part of the assets of McKenzie Flooring. When he took McKenzie Flooring to the stock market it made him a millionaire.'

'It sounds simple when you put it like that. What exactly *is* a holding company anyway?'

'A company that holds the major share in another company.'

Tassie laughed. 'Ask a silly question . . . All right, when did everything start getting foggy?'

'Just after the flotation. That was when McKenzie Flooring began buying factories and raw material companies all over the place. India, France, Germany . . . Yer brither's been looking for a suitable site in America for three years and now he's found it, hence McKenzie Flooring International. Separate companies in every case, to avoid foreign tariffs.'

'And tax at home, too.'

John Bell, who had an unsuspected talent for talking and supping soup at the same time, finished his plate and said, 'By jings, that was good. And how do you know about tax avoidance?'

'Sir Leoday. He was in the casino one night after a board meeting and you know what an old stickler he is! He was mumbling about not being sure if all this was quite the thing; it seemed Max had said something about a subsidiary company being set up for the purpose of avoiding taxes.'

Pausing with her own spoon halfway to her mouth, she went on carefully, 'I'm not sure if I've got this right. Sir Leoday said that, if foreign earnings are retained by the subsidiary company instead of being credited to the parent company here at home, it isn't necessary to pay tax on them. *Is* that right?'

'Aye, it's right enough. And legal, too.'

Tassie frowned. 'But what happens to the earnings? Do all the directors of the holding company rush off abroad to spend them?'

'No. The subsidiary uses them to buy another subsidiary of its own.'

She thought about it. 'But that's ridiculous! It means there are increasing numbers of subsidiaries with the profits just going round in circles. Neither the business nor the shareholders here at home are gaining any benefit from them. Except by being able to say, "Look, aren't we big and important, with all these subsidiary companies all over the place!" '

'Aye, it wud look that way. But ours not to reason why.'

'Why not? It's like people saying, "Mustn't grumble", when they've every right to grumble. I'm sorry, I interrupted. Go on.'

'I've told you most of whit I know. As things stand now, there's two pillars of the business, first, McKenzie Smith, manufacturing company and holding company of McKenzie Flooring. And second, McKenzie Flooring, manufacturing company and holding company in its own right of the new American flooring company, McKenzie Smith International.'

'Which you think is also about to become a holding company in its own right?'

'Ye're learning. So there'll be three pillars, and if ye add all the subsidiaries, including some that don't seem to do very much except keep sets of books, ye'll see why those of us, like me, who aren't in the know, find ourselves getting a wee bit confused.'

The steak-and-kidney pudding was delicious but there was far too much of it. Tassie gave up, sighing. 'Max *is* awfully clever, isn't he? He really does know about business and money. I suppose he takes after papa.'

'He owes a lot to Goudy and Vale. They've the right, intricate kind o' mind. But – aye, yer brither's clever about money.'

Tassie had the uneasy feeling that John Bell had only refrained from adding, 'Too clever,' because he couldn't afford to lose his job and she was Max's sister and might let something slip.

He knew more than he was telling her, though he had also told her more than he knew. Just because she was female, young and goodlooking, he had made the usual masculine assumption that she wasn't capable of putting two and two together.

She sighed again. 'Oh, well. I'd better get back to the factory. I ought to go and ask after Jean's brood and have a gossip with Doris and Aggie.'

John Bell let out a roar of laughter. 'Ye're a brave lassie! Whenever I see yon pair coming, I duck into the nearest doorway till they've passed.'

She smiled, but only out of politeness.

Gradually, over the last two years, she had begun worrying about Max and the driving ambition that had him in its grip. On the rare – the very rare – occasions when the subject of business cropped up between them, he made it sound as if it was a game, like chess – though 'with more blood', as he had said once, long ago – with himself as the Queen, the most powerful piece on the board, feinting here, feinting there, gobbling up bishops, rooks, knights and pawns in all directions.

Perhaps it really had been a game once, but she didn't think it was, any more. She knew he would never do anything illegal, of course. But the implications of what John Bell had said hadn't reassured her in the least.

Had Max begun operating a little too closely to the boundaries of the law? He had always enjoyed taking risks for their own sake. He had always enjoyed seeing how much he could get away with.

Looking back, she realised that she could put a date to when his desire for wealth and success had tipped over into something else. Once he had become a millionaire, he had begun to act as if nothing could hold him and as if no one was *entitled* to hold him.

It was then, too, that he had set those who loved him on the long, hard road of learning that he was no longer altogether to be trusted.

PART FOUR

1903 —
1905

CHAPTER ONE

I

Lucia didn't recognise Francis when he arrived home, though it had nothing to do with his tanned skin or the vigour that had been so powerfully rekindled in him.

He hadn't realised how drained he had been by the stresses of the paper, Tassie, Max and Lucia herself, when he had left for India until, in Coromandel in February, the world had begun to look fresh and attractive again and he had found himself waking in the mornings not only glad, but exhilarated at being alive. By then, he had even been able to reflect, with self-derision, on the extraordinary fact that it had taken eight thousand miles' distance to enable him to see his problems in perspective.

From home he went to Lindsay Mills to see his mother who, to his mystification, greeted him not briskly, or with guarded pleasure or even qualified interest, but with something that in another woman might have been embarrassment.

He was already aware that Mistress Gunter had asked her not to visit Lucia again after a particularly disastrous occasion in May, but also knew that the deterioration in Lucia's condition had little, if anything to do with Abigail. Years ago, the doctor had warned him that it was bound to happen sooner or later, and that sooner would be a sign of the Lord's mercy. Francis had accustomed himself to the idea but his mother, for some reason, had not.

She said, 'You're back, are you? Was it a successful trip? It sounded from the reports of the Durbar as if that stiff-necked viceroy of ours was confusing himself with God.'

'He enjoyed himself. So did everyone else. And he's only stiff-necked because of an old spinal injury that forces him to wear a brace. How are you, mother?'

He bent and kissed her cheek, which was cool and dry. But the muscles of her jaw were taut.

Raising an eyebrow, he said, 'Yes?' and waited.

'I take it you went home before you came here? How is Lucia?'

'Frail. And absent. She didn't recognise me.'

'I suppose that woman Gunter told you I had upset her?'

'Yes.'

'I took her hand in mine. That was all.'

Francis said nothing.

'I know. It is something I would not normally do, but I was somewhat emotional at the time. And you may remove that look of exaggerated astonishment from your face. I had come straight from a rather trying encounter – with Grace Smith and her daughter, you may as well know – and I was remembering too much that would have been better forgotten. I had said things to Grace that I should not have said, told her things that in Christian charity I should have remained silent about.'

Francis, wondering what in hell's name his mother had said in front of Tassie, remarked, 'Christian charity, mother? You?'

'I am sixty-seven years old. Possibly my brain is becoming addled. You were right, by the way. The only sin of Josiah's that Grace knew about was his sin with her, and she has suffered enough for it. However, I don't wish you to think that I am trying to shuffle off responsibility for what happened with Lucia. As I say, I was distressed when I went to see her, and I suppose she may have sensed something of it. You cannot possibly blame me more than I blame myself.'

Francis said, 'As it happens, I don't blame you. I am not entirely lacking in perception, you know. In fact, I am more concerned about what you said to the Smiths. You never do things by halves.'

Confession was one thing, being interrogated by her son quite another. Abigail picked up her pen. 'I have a great deal of work on hand. Let us have supper one evening and you can tell me about your travels.'

'And in exchange you'll give me a verbatim account of what you said to Grace and Tassie? I suppose you made it sound like a full-scale family feud?'

'Certainly not.'

Abruptly, he laughed. 'My dear, you don't know what you started when you ordered me to find out about Max McKenzie Smith all those years ago! But we'll have to postpone our supper, because I'm off to Wester Ross tomorrow. I have some information that I want to follow up. And then I'm going straight to London. I, too, have a great deal to do.

'On 1st January 1904, the first edition of my new London newspaper will roll from the presses. Good-bye. Look after yourself.'

With a wave of his hand, he was off, leaving his mother, who was not easily astounded, with pen poised in her hand and her mouth very slightly open.

2

Francis had been a journalist long enough to know that the news on public holidays was a law unto itself. Editors ignored the serious in favour of the frivolous; politicians tried to slip their more scandalous deeds through when they thought no one was looking; and foreigners, lacking the Bank Holiday spirit, persevered with all the farflung revolutions and disasters that no one wanted to read about.

On the other hand, it was unthinkable to launch the national *Enterprise* on any other than the first day of the year. And not only the first day. The first hour and the first minute. Francis intended to have his paper on the streets before the echoes of 'Auld Lang Syne' had begun to die away and, to this end, had newsboys ready and strategically placed to supply the revellers outside St Paul's, in Trafalgar Square, and at the door of every hall in London where a Caledonian dance was to be held.

He had solved the news problem by devoting the front page entirely to pictures, pictures summarising the year gone by and hinting at the year to come – pictures, all of them, where past and future met. The king and President Roosevelt exchanging their first wireless message, the Wright brothers at Kitty Hawk, the inauguration of London's electric trams, Marie Curie winning the Nobel Prize, and one of Stanley Spencer's aerial photographs of the Pool of London, taken from a dirigible. It had been quite a year.

The real news – most of it foreign and bad, as he had anticipated – was inside. Japan had sent troops to Korea; there were unconfirmed reports of a tribal uprising in south-west Africa; and five employees had been arrested after the theatre fire in Chicago that had killed 587 people.

Watching the type being cast and proofed and the flongs moulded; watching the flongs, in turn, being remoulded in metal; watching the great rollers gearing up and the first printed sheets coming off the presses, he was too tense to be elated. But then everyone in the newsroom and the composing room and the works was brandishing glasses and cheering him, and he raised his own glass back at them and the relief and pleasure were too great to quantify.

Afterwards, he went out and compulsively walked

the wet New Year streets. One after another, the newsboys replied, '*Enterprise*, guv? Sorry, guv! Sold out. Waiting for the next edition!'

It was all right.

So far.

3

'Hugo's been retained as junior counsel and it's his first big case, and I wondered if . . .'

Gus Silvermann's dimples put in a resigned appearance. 'Yes?'

'I'd only want to go on the last day. It's the Whitaker Wright trial, and it'll probably be a long one, and I don't think I'd understand most of it, anyway.'

'Should the name mean something to me?'

'Yes, don't you remember the London and Globe Corporation collapse at the end of 1900?'

'No. It would be just before I arrived here.'

'Oh, well, it was a huge corporation and Mr Wright was one of the most important businessmen in the country. Then suddenly everything fell apart and it turned out that he had been juggling the accounts between his various companies. When one got into trouble, another made a loan to shore it up – that kind of thing. The money just went round and round.'

Uncomfortably reminded of saying almost exactly the same thing to John Bell a few months ago about the profits of Max's foreign subsidiaries, Tassie hesitated. But it wasn't the same thing at all.

She went on, 'He wasn't charged at the time because it isn't illegal to publish a false balance sheet, but a stockbroker whose clients had lost a lot of money entered a private prosecution under the Larceny Act. The only trouble was that Mr Wright had skipped the country and it's taken until now to trace and extradite him. Hugo says it ought to be an interesting case and

Norah and I thought we ought to go along and give him moral support. Only if you can spare me, though.'

Gus said, 'I'll do better than that. I'll come along, if I have no other appointments. I'd sure like to see British justice at work.'

For months he had been hoping to meet Miss St John again – by chance, because he was a careful man. Offered the opportunity, he wasn't about to pass it up.

4

The case began at the Law Courts on 11th January with Mr Rufus Isaacs, leading for the prosecution, advising the jury not to allow themselves to become confused by the intricacies of high finance but to concentrate on the simple, salient facts – which he went on to summarise in a speech that lasted five extremely long hours.

'I won't explain it all to you,' Hugo said that evening, 'because you wouldn't understand. But most of the profits shown in the balance sheets before the collapse were fraudulent. It was just one huge swindle, and it was possible only because Whitaker Wright was in personal charge with a staff mainly of clerks.'

Sweetly, Norah said, 'Tassie, let us pool our tiny little female brains. Do you think we dare ask Hugo how, if all these profits were ficticious, Mr Wright managed to buy himself a house in Park Lane and a country seat at Godalming and a yacht at Cowes and all the rest of it?'

'No-o-o.' Tassie shook her head. 'I mean, we don't want to embarrass him, do we? He might not know that it was probably all done with personal bank loans raised against the security of the businesses.'

'Gosh! How do you know that?'

Tassie smiled mischievously, but her smile died

when Hugo said, 'I would prefer that she did not know it. It is most unbecoming for a young lady to be cognisant of business practice.'

Contrary to what Tassie had hoped, being engaged had done nothing to endear Hugo to her. Sure of her now, he was becoming steadily more pompous and dictatorial and Norah, of course, didn't hesitate to raise an I-told-you-so eyebrow whenever it happened.

'It may well have been a matter of loans at the beginning,' he went on, 'but the subsidiaries were the key. Wright, as chairman of one foreign company, was regularly paid large sums by himself, as chairman of another foreign company. The companies were registered in countries where taxes are low or non-existent and Wright, I suppose, as a nominal "foreigner" here, would be able to buy houses and yachts without being liable to British tax. I don't know how the defence hopes to get round that sort of thing.'

'Oh, dear,' Tassie said. 'Don't you? Now, if you'll excuse me, I have to finish cutting the pattern for my spring suit.'

Norah had been right. She *couldn't* marry Hugo.

5

The case ended on the 26th and Mr Walton, for the defence, didn't succeed in getting round anything on Whitaker Wright's behalf, although he made a great deal of the Crown's refusal to prosecute, as if a private prosecution wasn't really serious.

While the jury was out and Hugo was explaining to Tassie how much he himself had contributed to the prosecution case – 'Merely because I didn't stand up and speak in court doesn't mean I did not have a good deal to say during consultations' – Gus drew Norah aside.

'I have been thinking, Miss St John,' he murmured, 'that you might be prepared to do me a favour.'

'Keeping an eye open for the police when you're speeding?'

He grinned. 'Since Tassie joined the firm, we've been getting a reputation for the quality of our illustrations, and I've more business coming in than she can handle on her own. She tries to kid me she isn't overworked, but she is.'

Norah nodded. 'That's true.'

'Now, I'm leery of taking on anyone extra, full time, as of this minute. But she sure could do with some help. How about it? On a basis of work-related fees or a monthly retainer, whichever you prefer.'

Norah didn't need to work, and didn't want to because she didn't like being tied. On the other hand, she did like Gus, quite a lot.

'I'm not as good as Tassie,' she said, equally low-voiced. 'She's an artist, a real one. The crafts are more in my line. And I don't have her feeling for traditional design.'

'Posters? Display cards, bills?'

'I could manage those. The only thing is, I'm committed to Mrs Pankhurst's new Women's Social and Political Union and I don't yet know how much time it's going to take up. We're going to be much more radical and active than the suffrage movement's been in the past.'

'I know. "Deeds not words". I guess I'm on your side there.' Suddenly, he raised his voice to a normal level. 'Why in tarnation are we whispering? We're in a court of law, not at the Mercy Seat. Say, here's the jury coming back. I wouldn't want to compete with Mrs Pankhurst, but . . . Well, why don't you think about it?'

6

But it was the Mercy Seat after all.

Mr Whitaker Wright, sentenced to seven years' penal servitude, stood chatting with his friends for a moment before being taken away to the cells.

As he chatted, and in full view of everyone – the cigar still in his hand, the regretful smile still on his face – he bit on a cyanide capsule. It turned out afterwards that he'd also had a loaded revolver in his pocket, just in case.

Tassie had nightmares that night, and the figure in them wasn't an elderly man with a Cheshire accent. It was Max.

The *Enterprise* wasn't the only paper, in a leader the next day, to demand a commission of enquiry into the need for stiffer regulation of company practice, particularly in relation to the publishing of accounts. Nor was it the only paper to demand that shareholders be given some measure of protection by an immediate investigation into the books of other complex webs of holding companies.

It was, however, the only paper to name names, and one of them was McKenzie Smith Holdings Ltd.

Tassie heard about it from Max.

In view of the publicity that had preceded and followed the new paper's launch, she could hardly have failed to know who owned and edited it, but she had never bought a copy of it or even sneaked a glance when Hugo brought one home. She also took the greatest care never to find herself in the vicinity of Fleet Street. She had no idea what she would say or do if she had the misfortune to run into Francis Rivers, who seemed to have no intention of allowing the feud to die.

When Tassie arrived at Kirklaws a few weeks later, the sun was peering tentatively out from between the clouds as if it weren't quite sure of its orientation; it hadn't seen Kirklaws, or any other part of the British Isles, for months.

A tweeded and knickerbockered Max greeted her on the doorstep, obviously in the best of good humours.

'Plenty of water in the river after all the rain,' he said, 'and the salmon are running well.'

'How nice.' She reached up to kiss his cheek. 'But Max dear, it's me. Remember? Your sister. I'm not here for the fishing. In fact, I don't know what I am here for. Perhaps I should warn you that Gus is charging you for my time and expenses.'

She hadn't been near Kirklaws since the wedding almost two-and-a-half years before, refusing invitations to house parties time after time, because of her work. But now the situation had changed. With G.S. Advertising handling the McKenzie Smith International account, Max was able to buy both her time and her presence.

She didn't like it, and neither did Gus who, to his private fury, had landed himself in a cleft stick by taking on the account. Briefly beguiled by Max's charm and aura of power, he had discovered all too soon that Max wasn't an ordinary client, that he was possessive – particularly of Tassie – and demanded services that an advertising agency didn't normally supply. Within weeks he had told Gus he expected him to act as a nominee, a front man, in buying a company whose true ownership Max preferred not to publicise. Gus had said no.

After that, Max had become more, rather than less demanding of Tassie's time.

The agency could have done without his business, of

course, and if Max hadn't been Max there would have been no problem. But he was too big, too well known, too popular with the press. If he and G.S. Advertising parted company, everyone in the trade would assume that Max had sacked the agency because it wasn't good enough. And that kind of smear was something Gus could not afford.

So, gritting his teeth, Gus had told Tassie, 'If your brother wants you at Kirklaws for this fishing weekend of his, you'd better go.'

9

Max tucked Tassie's arm in his, and said, 'Your visit can go in the accounts as "consultations". You know I've always liked having you and mother to give me moral support.'

He was grinning at her, and she responded as she nearly always did, even now. 'You need it, of course! Is mother here?'

'No, but Genny and the boys are, and I've a couple of dozen guests.'

'Anyone I know?'

'Shouldn't think so, except for old Pelham. There's Goudy, too, though he hardly qualifies as a guest. Let's go and have tea.'

The house had been cleverly divided, so that the offices didn't intrude on the living quarters. No one could have told that it was the nerve centre, the powerhouse of the McKenzie Smith corporation. Even so, there was a faint air of disuse everywhere, which was hardly surprising, since neither Max nor Genny had spent much more than occasional weeks and weekends in residence since their wedding.

None of the guests appeared to notice anything amiss, although most of them were the kind of people who wouldn't notice anything, anyway, beyond their own superiority and the size, somewhat magnified, of the salmon they had caught that day. Thanks to Max's swift social rise, they were all noticeably more distinguished than the wedding guests had been – full rather than courtesy peers, politicians of Cabinet rather than backbench rank, bankers who were household names in the kind of households that entrusted their financial affairs to private rather than joint stock banks. Only three of them had brought their wives.

10

Tea and egg sandwiches, scones and ginger biscuits, chocolate cake. Bridge in the gold drawing room. Change at half-past seven for dinner at half-past eight. Champagne all through dinner. The gentlemen left to their port at nine forty-five. More bridge in the music gallery at ten-fifteen. Devilled chicken, sandwiches and drinks at midnight while maids and valets poked up the fires in the bedrooms and switched on the pink silk reading lamps.

Tassie said, 'Max, are you going to have time to talk about the advertising campaign in the morning? Because, if not, I think I ought to go back to London. I've a lot to do.'

'Ginger, my pet, don't be such a damn' bore. You'll go when I say you can go.'

11

In the morning, at 8.30 a.m precisely, the passages filled up with sour-faced valets going to wake their masters with a brass can of shaving water in one hand and a brass tray of tea, toast and Marie biscuits in the other.

Half an hour later, the passages filled up again, this time with robed gentlemen slouching liverishly towards bathrooms redolent of Hammam Bouquet, lavender bags and Sanitas.

And half an hour after that, in stiff white collars, dark ties and tweeds, with eau-de-Cologne on their cheeks, Euchrisma on their hair and Regie cigarettes between their fingers, the gentlemen descended the red pile stairs to a breakfast of porridge, fishy things in sauce, omelettes and devilled kidneys, cold meats and game, scones, honey, marmalade and fruit.

By 10.30 a.m, most of them had gone fishing.

At midday, dressed in her big, fleece-lined, weather-all coat and the flat, cream cloth cap with the wide band and shiny black peak that so dashingly resembled a naval officer's, Tassie dumped her valise in a corner of the hall, told one of the servants she needed transport to the station, and set off to look for Max to tell him she was leaving, whether he liked it or not.

She walked straight into a crisis.

12

Max was in the library, lolling behind his desk, his wife standing on its other side, arms akimbo, addressing him at the pitch of her light, girlish voice.

'. . . I won't let you. I won't let you!' Her slender back was stiff as a poker in the admirably fitting dark blue gown. Under Grace's tutelage, her dress sense had improved enormously.

Sir Leoday was standing sideways to the window, hands in his trousers pockets, his nondescript face patchily red and his pale, watery blue eyes deeply embedded in the pouches that surrounded them. But it was Bruce Goudy who arrested Tassie's attention.

He was sitting in a winged chair, leaning forward a little, his hands hanging loosely between his knees, his normally healthy complexion reduced to a muddy pallor. A quiet man, with greying brown hair and a moustache like a blunted pyramid resting on his upper lip, he looked as if he were in a state of shock.

Everyone glanced up as she walked in and the sudden, motionless silence filled the air like glue.

'I see I'm interrupting something,' she said. 'I'm sorry. I just came to say, Max, that I'm leaving now. Perhaps you'd let me know next time you're in London and have time to discuss the . . .'

And then Genny was running to her and throwing herself tearfully in her arms. 'Tassie, you mustn't let him! Tell him it's wrong. He'll listen to you!'

Tassie patted her back with irritable sympathy. Much though she would have liked to, she couldn't very well avoid asking, 'What's the matter? What mustn't he do?'

Max was the only person in the room who seemed to be his normal self. And revelling in it. Amiably, he said, 'Take her away, Ginger, for God's sake. I never heard such a fuss.'

'What have you been saying to upset her?'

It was Genny who replied, the words pouring out, muffled in Tassie's shoulder and hard to follow. 'He's awful. He bullied my papa into joining his horrid board because he wanted a peer on it, but now he says he doesn't need him any more. It isn't fair.'

Tassie thought, 'Oh, dear!'

But Genny hadn't finished. 'And he only married me because papa has a title and the next thing is he'll be saying he doesn't need *me* any more, either. Well, I don't care.' Her voice rose hysterically. 'I've given him the sons he wanted and I'll never let him touch me again. I'll kill myself first! I will!'

Everyone stared at her except Bruce Goudy.

'What drivel,' said Max contemptuously. 'It's business, that's all. I've just told Pelham and Goudy that I'm dispensing with their services. Genny seems to take it personally.'

Tassie could understand that he should sack Sir Leoday, who wasn't very bright and had joined the board purely in the interests of Max's ambition and his own profit. But Bruce Goudy, kindly and trustworthy, who had given Smith's thirty years of loyal service; Bruce Goudy, on whom were dependent fluttery little Mistress Goudy and twelve small Goudies. What would they do?

'No, Max. You can't. It isn't right.'

'Balls,' he said crudely, and though Tassie didn't know the implications of the word, she couldn't mistake his meaning. 'Goudy's a frightened man and Pelham a useless one. Can't afford to employ people who aren't pulling their weight.'

Sir Leoday probably *was* useless. But Goudy – frightened? It was a queer word. And then she thought that for two thirds of his working life Mr Goudy had been accustomed to a straightforward, orderly existence in a business that had aspired to no more than local success. She could understand that he might find Max's headlong progress beyond him, might be frightened by it, as Max said. He might be nervous, too, at the thought of the formal audits that were being threatened as a result of the Whitaker Wright affair. Even the most conscientious people could be intimidated by official enquiries. But to sack him outright, when all Dundee would know of it? He would never find another job.

She said again, 'Max, you can't. If Mr Goudy isn't happy in his present position, why don't you find something else for him to do?'

But Max's eyes and voice were suddenly inimical. 'This is none of your business, Tassie.'

'I know it isn't. But I'm not criticising. I'm not trying to interfere.' All she could do was plead, because she didn't know any other way of persuading Max to show some humanity. Her father had given all his love and kindness to his family, and had none left over for others. Max was like him in that, as in other ways. How could she make him see that being humane wasn't a sign of weakness?

'It's just that you have so much more than Mr Goudy has, Max. How can you bring yourself to take everything away from him?'

'Easily,' Max said. 'You, if anyone, should know that what I have, I have had to fight for. These two don't have the stomach to fight. Now, will you take that silly wife of mine away and quieten her down before my guests get back from the fishing.'

13

There were only four mourners at Lucia's graveside as the bugle notes of 'The Last Post' pierced the soft, late summer air. Abigail had insisted on it – the lament, the melancholy lullaby.

'All is well, Safely rest. God is nigh.'

'If I were a Hindu,' she had said, 'I could believe that she would be reborn again, to a happier and more fortunate life. But perhaps our way is more realistic. If one thing is certain, there is no heaven on earth for anyone.'

Francis took her arm. 'It's over, mother. All over. Come away.'

David and Jonny followed them out of the cemetery, back to the automobile, and then to Abigail's house, where Lucia had spent her last unknowing months. The door to her room was locked, and would never be unlocked again in Abigail's lifetime.

Abigail said, 'There are no funeral baked meats. Let us drink a single glass of wine to the past and then go our ways. As Francis says, it's over.'

Surprisingly, it was Jonny who spoke for all three of her sons. 'But surely the past is never over?'

14

For almost three years Tassie had known freedom. However much Max had interfered in her life during that time, she had ceased to feel, as she had once felt, that everything she or her mother did was in some way a response to him or his actions, that he exercised an insidious control over them, that they were his emotional dependants. It had never been deliberate on his part, of course. It had been an accident of personalities – his strength, their mother's guilt and sense of loss, her own adolescent need to love and give.

But now it *was* deliberate. Now he was tightening the bonds again. And now he was harder to escape. She didn't recognise it at first, because it wasn't done openly except by way of the demands he made of G.S. Advertising, and those weren't much more than a nuisance.

He didn't even make a scene about her leaving Kirklaws after he had forbidden her. She had soothed Genny and consoled her a little, and then she had left.

A few months later, she had received a formal notification from Algernon Vale that, following a satisfactory trading year on the part of McKenzie Smith, she would in due course receive a cheque in the sum of three hundred pounds sterling. The payment, he pointed out, was being made *ex gratia* and not as of right or entitlement.

Not for the first time, she wondered about consulting a solicitor or an accountant over the whole, unsatisfactory business of her share in the parent company. But she knew enough to recognise that finding anyone equipped and prepared to contend with Max and his legal legions would be both difficult and expensive.

Even Hugo didn't understand why she should be reacting so ungratefully. She couldn't possibly imagine that her brother was cheating her? If she could not trust

Max, who in the world could she trust? Besides which, he was reputed to have one of the best business brains in the country and three hundred pounds was a great deal of money.

Hugo told her she was to spend half of the three hundred pounds on her bottom drawer and save the remainder for her trousseau.

So she went out and bought a motorcar.

She had come to detest the Underground and the sardine-packed buses, which were even smellier in a different way. But there was no other choice except a cab, which was expensive and, anyway, in May the cabbies had all gone on strike. Only now, when she unexpectedly found herself able to consider, seriously, the possibility of buying a motorcar, did she recognise how important her independence had become to her.

It was almost a fetish. She couldn't bear the thought of being beholden to anyone, not even her mother or Norah, who had never let her down, and certainly not Max, whom she still loved – with reservations – but was no longer sure she could trust, or Francis, whom she still loved but *knew* she could never trust. In his case, of course, the question was academic. In the privacy of her room, she wept a little about that, as she sometimes did, although by now it was almost two long years since she had seen him.

On Gus Silvermann's recommendation, she bought a Standard Model 7hp Oldsmobile.

'Low upkeep,' said the salesman. 'Trouble free operation. Light to handle, and ideal for a lady. Nothing to watch but the road. And all for – er – £150, which is reasonable. Really *very* reasonable.'

'Done,' Tassie said.

The salesman was surprised. Ladies daring enough to buy and drive a motorcar were very rare indeed and he had been expecting her to say, 'I'm only looking.'

'Oh, ripping, madam! We'll register it for you, and I

can let you have – let me see – number A 6000. Nice and easy to remember.'

'Goodness! Does that mean there are six thousand motorcars in London already?'

'Yes, madam. Something's going to have to be done about the traffic soon, or the city will grind to a halt. Now, have you a friend who can give you lessons, or would you like me to arrange them for you?'

'Would you do it, please?'

15

First the bribe and then the blackmail.

In other circumstances, it would have been a wonderful offer. Max was going to America on business that was partly to do with McKenzie Smith International and partly with some lands in the Dakota Territory belonging to the Dundee Prairie Land Company, in which McKenzie Smith had had a share-holding since Joss's day. In the 1880s the company had paid a twenty percent dividend but, since then, nothing. It was high time something was done, especially with Dundee having such an abysmal manu-facturing and trading year, and Max was going to do it.

'You're coming with me,' he told Tassie. 'Not to Dakota, but to New York. You can't handle McKenzie Smith International's advertising unless you know all about the American flooring market and domestic design at first hand.'

There was no, 'Will you?' There was no, 'If it's convenient.' There was no, 'If Silvermann can spare you.'

He wasn't giving her an option.

She said, 'No,' although she would have said, 'Yes,' with excitement and delight if he had broached the subject in any other way.

Gus, unfortunately, said, 'Yes.' Max wasn't giving

him an option, either. Tassie would accompany him to New York, he said with his most charming smile, or he would take his business away from G.S. Advertising.

They sailed in October on North German Lloyd's *Kaiser Wilhelm der Grosse*, claimed to be the largest, fastest and most luxurious liner on all the world's oceans.

Tassie had never in her life spent an entire week being waited on hand and foot, with nothing to do but amuse herself. Neither had she spent an entire week in her brother's uninterrupted company.

It didn't draw them closer. Even if Max had not, within hours, gathered a court of new and admiring acquaintances round him, he would not have confided in her, nor she in him. Max's thoughts were not for sharing; too long ago, the secrecy so necessary to his business dealings had overflowed into the personal compartments of his life. And Tassie's thoughts were not for sharing, either. She would not give weapons into her brother's hand.

But by the time they sailed into New York bay, Tassie gasping at the great copper statue on Liberty Island, at the shipping and the extraordinary city skyline, they had found a kind of companionship again, a sense of ease. She even felt able to say, laughingly, seeing the tall buildings, 'Do you suppose they took their model from Dunaird? How is the reconstruction getting on?'

He didn't turn the subject as he usually did, telling her to contain her impatience or reminding her that she had promised to leave everything to him. 'The rain last winter and spring held things up badly, and there was danger of a land slip, so that we had to shore up the foundations. But it's getting on. It's getting on.'

And then, with mock gravity, he went on to remind her that America was a foreign country, and to warn her that females of bad repute were banned under the immigration acts and that, just a few weeks before, a woman had been arrested for the crime of smoking on Fifth Avenue.

But despite the laughter, it was impossible to forget that she was not there by choice.

16

'Lady to see you, Mr Rivers.'

It wasn't unusual. Ladies were all too ready to supplicate newspaper editors, especially if they happened to have met them socially. Mostly, they wanted their pictures in the society columns, or didn't want their pictures in the gossip columns.

He said, 'Point her towards Mel Dewey.'

'I tried, but she wants you.'

It couldn't be the only lady he wanted to see, not after their last disastrous encounter in the shadow of Dunaird's tower. And most certainly not after Abigail had so helpfully entangled them both in her own, long-cherished feud; he knew, now, what she had said.

It couldn't be the lady he had almost given up trying to meet innocently and accidentally, at art exhibitions, theatres and concerts, the lady it now seemed he would have to entice to a private place and imprison, like some beautiful maiden in *Morte d'Arthur*. He was going to force her to listen to what he had to say, whether she liked it or not. After that, it was in the lap of the gods. But now, at least, he didn't have to think, always and always, 'It's impossible.'

He threw down his pencil. 'All right, Albert,' he said. 'Give it five minutes and then come and tell me I'm needed urgently in the composing room.'

17

Of all unlikely people, it was Genevieve McKenzie Smith.

She was looking very pretty and very helpless, although the bosomy fashions of the day didn't suit her slender figure and the large, feathered hat partially hid the lovely blue eyes under their fluttering lids. Francis wasn't accustomed to feeling protective – a relic of his mother's intrepid early influence, he had always assumed – but no red-blooded male could have resisted Genevieve's appeal.

Seated on the hard, dusty visitor's chair, she said, 'I don't know if you remember me? But you know my husband, Max McKenzie Smith. You were at our wedding. He's in America just now, on business.'

'I remember you very well,' Francis replied gallantly, as was expected of him. 'We met again at the automobile trials.'

'Yes. Your brother was awfully kind to me when Max's motor had that horrid puncture.'

What the devil did she want? Not Jonny's telephone number, Francis devoutly hoped.

She began to draw off her long, pale pink, wildly impractical kid gloves, more for the sake of occupation than for any other reason, he thought, and her attention was all on them as she went on, 'I don't know whether I should have come. I hope it isn't awful of me, but Monty said I should.'

Monty. Well, well.

Albert popped his head round the door. 'Wanted urgently in the composing room, Mr Rivers.'

'Go away,' said Mr Rivers.

Unsurprised, Albert went. With a stunner like that in his office, no editor could have said otherwise.

'It's my father.' Genevieve's words came out in a rush. 'He and Max had a disagreement, and my father isn't on Max's board any more and people seem to think it's because he wasn't a good board member or something. And it's upsetting him dreadfully because he only joined in the first place because Max insisted.'

'Yes?'

'And I thought – I mean – I know you're one of the people who don't think Max is marvellous – he's always complaining about you – and I wondered whether you might like to write something nice about my father, to put things right.'

Momentarily deprived of thought, Francis said, 'Er – what kind of something did you have in mind?'

'I don't know. I thought you would.'

Sir Leoday Pelham, a kindly old buffer with no more brains than you could shake a stick at . . .

If it hadn't been for that mention of Monty, which argued wheels within wheels, Francis would have found some soothing way of dismissing his delectable guest. But Monty, to the best of Francis's knowledge, was Max's most devoted henchman.

Genevieve said, 'If I gave a little party, you could meet my papa and see for yourself that he's *quite* above reproach!' Her cheeks were pink with earnestness and her eyes sparkled at him in the little slanted, upwards smile that no man was ever likely to forget, and whose trustfulness it would have been criminal to betray.

It occurred to Francis that Tassie might well be on the guest list for such an affair.

'All right,' he said, smiling, 'though I can't promise anything.' It was extraordinary how sweet and naïve Mrs Max still was, despite three years of marriage to her far from sweet and naïve husband.

And then she took a little gold-mounted notebook and matching pencil from her muff and said, 'Perhaps your brother might like to come, too? Will you give me his address? Then I can send him an invitation.'

When she had gone, Albert popped his head round

the door again with an urgent and perfectly genuine
message from the composing room and was taken
aback to find the boss laughing fit to bust.

18

Francis arranged for Mel Dewey to write a piece about
the unsung heroes of the business world, the gentlemen
of ancient lineage who lent their names and centuries of
inbred experience to the boards of modern industry.

Sir Leoday Pelham, who had recently retired from a
non-executive directorship of the McKenzie Smith
corporation, was a case in point. Like so many of his
fellows, he was largely unknown to the general public,
but in his veins ran the blood of men who had presided
over their ancestral acres and cared for the health and
happiness of their tenants over many generations,
imbuing their heirs with a selfless knowledge of human
needs and human values. This humanity was the
greatest gift of such men to companies which, having
risen swiftly to prominence, might otherwise have
lacked the compassion that came with time and
experience. Etcetera, etcetera.

There were pictures of the Pelham family seat, and
notes on one or two Pelham ancestors who had
achieved a small measure of fame thanks to tangential –
a polite word for 'illegitimate' – relationships with
royalty. Sir Leoday's daughter was, of course, well
known to the public as the charming society hostess,
Mrs Max McKenzie Smith.

'Ugh!' said Francis, when Dewey showed him the
article in proof. 'Take it away.'

'It's a perfectly tenable thesis,' his features editor
replied. 'You wouldn't find a soul in the House of Lords
to disagree with it.'

'That's a thought. Send 'em all a free copy and an
invitation to subscribe.'

19

Genevieve was delighted, not only with the article but with Francis.

Before he knew where he was, he had been enrolled as friend, occasional escort and regular confidant. Although he recognised, amusedly, that he was being manipulated by a young woman who was by no means as naïve as she appeared, he still wasn't proof against her fine natural talent for inspiring men's chivalrous instincts nor, indeed, her very real desperation. It wasn't long before he heard that her husband didn't understand her, thought her feather-brained, neglected her, left her to her own company for months on end; that she adored her children, was nervous of Monty Fitzalan – who spied on her – and hated Naomi Merton, who spied on her, too, especially when Max was away.

Francis had gone to a good deal of trouble over the last year to find out about Naomi Merton, but wasn't averse to finding out more.

That, and anxiety over Jonny – who had fallen so swiftly and madly in love with the seductive little Mrs Max that he wouldn't listen to reason – encouraged him to continue taking a far closer interest in the McKenzie Smith household than was wise.

20

London was the largest city in the world and New York only the second largest. That being so, Tassie had spent the better part of five months wondering why it seemed twice as big and ten times busier. It was said that the surface and elevated railroads carried more paying passengers in a year than all the other railroads of North and South America combined, and when she asked about the source of the perpetual underground roar she was told that subways were being built to carry even more of them.

It was a city of the mostest – the most brilliant street lighting in the world, the greatest number of legitimate theatres, the greatest amount of construction work going on, the newspapers with the largest circulation, in Luna Park the finest pleasure garden. Not to mention the steamiest steam heating and the largest hotel in the world, the Waldorf Astoria.

Max and Tassie were occupying two of its one thousand rooms. Tassie felt like a worker bee. In the streets she felt more like an ant. No one moved at a normal speed. Everybody hurried.

Nothing, however, could have been more languid than the atmosphere in the places where she spent so much time – the studios of interior designers like Willard Parker Little, and the houses they were employed to remodel.

Max had been right about one thing. American domestic design was in a class of its own. Tassie was more than a little depressed to find that rich Americans felt it necessary to live in a style of antique European grandeur. After the twentieth drawing room combining influences from the Ducal Palace at Mantua and the Palazzo Repeta in Venice, with overmantels in the style of Puvis de Chavannes and Beauvais tapestries as fire screens, she was beginning to suffer from visual indigestion. Linoleum, she told Max crisply, wouldn't stand a chance unless it imitated Tuscan tiles or terracotta *fiorentina*.

'For the rich, perhaps, but they don't want linoleum. They can afford the real thing. Our market is the middle classes.'

'Whose sole design ambition is to *emulate* the rich. Cheaply. And that means tile-patterned linoleum. I could have told you that after the first week. It's been great fun, but I want to go home. I'm wasting my time here.'

'Well, waste it! I'm paying. Anyway, I have to make one more trip to Belle Fourche, and we can't miss the presidential inauguration next week. You haven't seen Washington yet.'

'No, and I shouldn't think I'm likely to. All I'll see is millions more people!'

She was right. President Roosevelt rode in splendour from the White House to the Capitol and then reviewed the biggest parade ever held in Washington. Tassie and Max were invited to a party in the evening, and Tassie had no doubt that it would be more magnificent than any other party, ever. American parties always were.

If she had been in Washington, in New York, in America, as herself rather than as a shadow being trailed around by her brother, she would have loved it.

As it was, dressed for the party, she confronted her image in the glass with only modified rapture. She had had her hair professionally coiffed and was wearing a ball gown she had bought in New York, a heavy silk affair in a warm, creamy shade that flattered her complexion and, especially, her hair. Although her hair was one of her best features, there was no denying that it was a problem in relation to the light, clear colours of current fashion. It wasn't just that its shining red–gold ruled out the wearing of anything pink; she was coming more and more to feel that it made all colours look vulgar. Or vice versa. Green to match her eyes was too obvious, blue clashed with them, yellow was garish. Neutrals seemed to be the only answer.

The dress had a wide, shallow neck, an elegantly gored skirt and elbow length sleeves and had been grossly overtrimmed when she bought it. But line and colour had been the deciding factors, and after she had unpicked all the diamanté, spangles and lace and stitched her favourite trimming of creamy silk roses round the neck, she had converted it into something quite stylish.

She looked all right – she supposed.

21

There was a tap at the door and she called, 'Come,' which was the only form of the command that the chambermaids, mostly new immigrants, understood.

But it wasn't a chambermaid. It was Max. A Max who was cock-a-hoop, flushed, and very much less than sober.

She was standing partly in the shadows, half turned away from him as she fastened her second earring.

He strode straight across the room, swung her round, pulled her to him and kissed her full on the lips. Hard, harder, and harder still, his tongue beginning to probe. He was holding her against him very much too tightly, along the whole length of their bodies.

Her shocked disbelief lasted no more than a second. Because her hands had been raised to fasten the earring when his arms had gone round her waist, her own arms were free. With no trace of hesitation, she wound her fingers in his hair and pulled with all her might, at the same time stamping furiously on his foot with her slender evening heel, again and again.

It should have been enough to bring him to his senses. But it wasn't. His left hand moved up to immobilise her right, and his powerful muscles tightened cruelly so that she could scarcely move at all. Only her left hand remained, tugging at his hair, scratching with ineffectual, smoothly manicured nails at his cheek.

She felt panic rising, swelling in her throat. This time there was no heavy inkwell to hand. There were no scissors, no weapons at all. There were only soft lights and a big, inviting bed.

This was her brother.

Then his tongue forced her mouth open and lunged into it, deep, deeper, and deeper still until she thought she was going to choke.

She used the only weapons she had left. Her teeth.

22

With a howl, he fell back, hands over his mouth, the blood from his tongue pouring down his chin.

Tassie, shaking with emotional and physical revulsion, turned and ran to the bathroom, locked the door and was violently sick not once but several times.

It was almost half an hour before she was sufficiently in control of herself to go back into the bedroom. Max was still there, sitting on the edge of the bed, rocking back and forward. There was a scarlet handkerchief in his hands and another on the floor.

Thickly, he said, 'The bleeding's almost stopped.'

'The tongue heals quickly.'

He gave a queer sound that might have been a laugh. 'Thanks. Did you have to be so ferocious about it?'

She didn't think she would ever stop shaking. 'You didn't give me any choice. Why? *What were you thinking of?*'

'Wasn't thinking. Just heard the Dakota deal's gone through. Pleased with myself. Drinking. Didn' rec'gnise you in new dress, hair. Wanted a woman, s'all.'

He giggled. 'It's a laugh. Didn' rec'gnise my own sist'r, own little Ginger. My tongue hurts.'

It was ludicrous, it was obscene.

'Your shirt's covered with blood,' she said. 'Are you sober enough to find the way back to your room?'

He didn't resist when she pulled him to his feet and pushed him out of the door, not caring whether he found his room, or not. Then she went to the telephone and told the desk clerk to book a cabin for her on the first liner sailing from New York or Boston to London, Southampton, Liverpool, Le Havre, it didn't matter which. She would be leaving Washington first thing in the morning.

That done, she collapsed on the big, inviting bed and wept through most of the long, dark, Inauguration-noisy night.

CHAPTER TWO

I

Two weeks later, Tassie walked into the drawing room at Audley Street, unannounced and with impeccable timing, to discover Max's wife in Francis Rivers's arms.

That Francis looked uncomfortable and Genny was in floods of tears did nothing to ameliorate Tassie's mood, which the mystified St Johns and Gus Silvermann had already discovered to be polite but intractable. Palely, she had said that America had been very interesting and she had learned a great deal about its tastes in interior decoration, thank you. Full stop. Now, perhaps they could bring her up to date on what had been happening here?

Francis's eyes met hers over Genny's quivering shoulders, but told her nothing. Tassie's eyes, on the other hand, were sparkling like chips of washed green ice and Francis had no difficulty in deducing that she was in a thundering bad temper. Far from disturbing him, it filled him with relief.

Learning from Genny that she was in America, he had made some apparently casual enquiries that had taken him to the Bayswater Road and Norah St John, who had subjected him to a protracted and paralysingly candid lecture about gentlemen who played fast and loose with young women's susceptibilities, and took such a very long time about it, too. Who absented themselves for months – years! – at a time, without so much as a word. Who might as well be dead, for all that the said susceptible young women might know.

She had told him, in conclusion, that since Tassie was a very private person, she had no idea how Tassie now felt about him. If she were indifferent to Francis, as it would seem from her engagement to Norah's brother Hugo, it was Norah's view that Francis had no one to blame but himself. The remedy – if there was a remedy – was in his own hands.

It was the first Francis had heard about Hugo and it had worried him badly, causing him to spend a good deal of time reassuring himself that she had far more sense than actually to marry such a stuffed shirt.

Now, noting the look of strain that tightened the muscles at the corners of her generous mouth, made her cheekbones more pronounced, and her eyes – impossibly – larger, seeing how much she had grown up during the years that lay between them, he had little difficulty in conducting himself as the situation required. Without privacy, and time, they would never come together.

He said quietly, 'Genny, you have a visitor.'

She leapt away from him and turned, pure horror on her face.

'Oh! Tassie!' It was a wail of relief. 'I didn't know you were back! Oh, my Lord, Max isn't with you, is he?'

'No. Fortunately.'

It was necessary for Genny to utter a series of breathless little 'Ohs', a hand to her throat, before she recovered sufficiently to say, 'Thank heaven. He would have jumped to *quite* the wrong conclusions.' Then, noting Tassie's expression, she added tartly, 'And there's no need for you to do the same. You don't know Mr Rivers, do you?'

'Yes.'

'Oh, I suppose you met him at our wedding. It was only that I was so miserable just now, and Mr Rivers's shoulder just happened to be there. There wasn't anything at all improper!'

'You were missing Max, were you?'

'Yes. Yes, that was it. I've been so lonely.'

Tassie snorted – there was no other word for it – and said, 'I decided to come ahead. I would guess that you have another week before he follows and I would suggest that, in the meantime, you break yourself of the habit of weeping on other gentlemen's shoulders. Especially Mr Rivers's. Because I can tell you that all he's doing is using you in his war against Max. If you spend enough time in his arms, he thinks you'll end by pouring all your troubles out to him. I hope you won't, because he's not to be trusted. Not an inch.'

'Tassie, you're wrong!' Genny squeaked protestingly. 'You're wrong.'

Francis said nothing, hoping Genny wouldn't spoil it all by blurting out that it wasn't him but Jonny whom she loved more than anyone else on earth.

Tassie said, 'I'm not interested. If you want to wreck your marriage to Max, that's your affair, and it's probably too late, anyway. I imagine that Monty and Naomi Merton, between them, have all your sins written down in their little black books and are just dying to reveal them the minute Max gets back.'

'Oh, dear, do you think so?' Genny said weakly, dabbing at her eyes with a scrap of lawn and lace. 'Would you like a cup of tea?'

But Tassie had gone.

2

In one thing, at least, Tassie was soon proved right.

A week after Max returned in glory, his coup over the sale of the Dakota prairie lands making headlines, a furious Genny telephoned Tassie to say that he was banishing her to Kirklaws. Monty had spitefully told

him about Mr Rivers, about both Mr Riverses, in fact –
a parenthesis which caused Tassie to groan, silently,
remembering the other, the golden Mr Rivers – and had
told him far more than the circumstances warranted.

'Because, really,' Genny complained in a tone of
injured innocence, 'nothing in the least improper
happened.'

'Yes, you said so before.'

'Well, it's true. And it was Monty who started it by
sending me to see Francis in the first place. I don't know
what he thought he was up to. But Max says it's all part
of Francis's vendetta against him and that even someone
as stupid as I am should have guessed. Though I don't
know how I'm expected to guess there's a vendetta if no
one tells me.'

'No. How tiresome for you,' Tassie said.

What *had* Monty been up to? Distantly, Tassie
remembered Bazz saying something about the two
boys planning to get their own back on Max for ruining
their father, but that had been ages ago, long before
Monty had become Max's righthand man – an exacting
but in many ways cushioned job that even the devious
Monty wouldn't want to lose.

No, it was a silly notion.

She didn't care, anyway. She *really* wasn't interested,
not any more. Not in Monty or Max or Genny or
Francis Rivers.

3

But then, suddenly, she did become interested. So did
every other newspaper reader in the land.

It began with a small paragraph in the *Mail*. The
lovely young society hostess, Mrs Max McKenzie
Smith, had left London for Kirklaws.

The *Mirror* followed it up. The beautiful young
leader of society, Mrs Max McKenzie Smith, had left

London for her husband's Scottish estate. At very short notice, and right at the beginning of the Season, too.

Three more days and the bandwagon had begun to roll. With dazzling young society hostess Mrs Max McKenzie Smith in Scotland, her husband had been seen in an expensive restaurant in the West End of London sharing a table for two with Another Woman. The capital letters weren't actually there, but they might as well have been. In an adjoining column was an apparently unrelated picture of Naomi Merton.

Then there were photographs of the exquisite, distraught young leader of society, Mrs Max McKenzie Smith, with her two adorable sons in the grounds of Kirklaws, little Edward seated on the grass beside her, Frederick being dandled in her lap.

Tassie found this very curious. With grounds extending to three thousand perfectly private acres, why should young Mrs Max McKenzie Smith choose to be exquisite and distraught in such close proximity to the press photographers at the gates?

The press was solidly on Genny's side. She was, after all, prettier than Max.

Where he was concerned the reports became more imaginative and more scandalous by the day, and everything had a price tag. His cigars cost him a shilling a time, his suits fifty guineas. Kirklaws had recently been redecorated, at a cost of £10,000, with fountains and waterfalls in the (imaginary) conservatory. Max's nephew, Mr Monty Fitzalan, ran a gambling hell in Soho. One of his chief financial advisers, Mr Bruce Goudy, was known to have done business with a Chinese opium cartel.

A reporter even turned up at G.S. Advertising, looking for Tassie, but was sent firmly about his business by Mr Binns, of all people. Tassie herself happened to be with Norah in the visitors' gallery of the House of Commons at the time, listening angrily to a women's suffrage bill being talked out, lost by default, after a debate during which one MP declared that women had no sense of proportion.

The only paper in which not a word of all this appeared was the *Enterprise*.

4

Tassie had no firsthand knowledge of how Max was taking it. She hadn't seen him since his return from America, and didn't want to see him ever again. She knew, however, that he must be feeling savage. Having been the darling of the press for years, this was his first experience of bad publicity and it seemed increasingly unlikely that he would be able to charm his way out of it. It was all too nebulous – the taint of infidelity and immorality, the sickly smell of success gone rancid.

He didn't go into hiding. The newspapers had regular pictures of him at Lord's, at Henley, even at the Derby, which wasn't one of his usual stamping grounds. Nearly always, he was one of a group of people looking cheerful and convivial, but the groups no longer included other well-known faces. No minor royalty, no peers, no Cabinet ministers.

He didn't have the sense to bring Genny and the boys back from Kirklaws and demonstrate what a happy and united family they were. That, to him, would have amounted to an admission that he had been in the wrong.

Max being Max, Tassie reflected, shaking her head, he probably still thought he could get away with it.

5

Trying to ignore, trying to forget, she immersed herself in work. But it was no longer as absorbing as it had been. She had lost touch and lost interest. The events of

the last year had made her, not resentful, but bitterly
self-critical, so that her mind was constantly straying,
scanning everything that had happened, over and over,
wondering how much of it had been her fault, what
would have happened if she had behaved differently.

Even Norah's generosity in standing in for her at the
agency when she was in America contributed to her
unsettled feeling. It had worked very well in every sense
but one. It had deprived Tassie of the right to feel
proudly possessive of her clients. They weren't hers any
more. It was childish of her to be upset, but she couldn't
help it.

And Gus – dear Gus! – had become slightly but
unmistakably distant from her, as if they were communicating through a sheet of glass. Norah had scarcely
needed to tell her that, during the months of working
together, she and Gus had reached an understanding. It
was obvious in every look, every movement, when
they were together. Enviously, Tassie recognised what
a lovely, easy relationship it was – no strains, but a
warm, deep friendship that had developed an extra
dimension.

Norah had taken her own advice about knowing
before loving. The only problem that still faced her, she
said drily, was persuading her parents that a brash
American son of commerce was an acceptable match
for the eldest daughter of Sir Halford and Lady St John.
Hugo, of course, was being abominably sniffy about it.

The trouble was that, although Norah had returned
to her normal existence, wrapping herself up in the
WSPU and devoting her artistic labours to the suffrage
movement, Tassie knew that it was she, now, in whom
Gus confided. It was natural enough, of course,
especially when he had business problems and especially when his main business problem was Max
McKenzie Smith.

Soon after Max's return, he demanded Tassie's

presence for a consultation, and Tassie flatly refused to go. So Gus went instead and came back looking harassed. He didn't say anything to Tassie about it, as he would have done once. She felt left out and lonely and guilty.

If she gave up her job with G.S. Advertising, it would leave Gus with much more freedom of movement. But what could she do instead?

There was no one she could talk to freely, not even – especially not – her mother, now back at Graceholm. They spoke often on the telephone and Tassie, for the first time, was grateful that they had to guard their words even when there was no adenoidal breathing to warn them that one of the operators was eavesdropping.

Although Grace was disturbed by the newspaper speculation about Max and Genny, Tassie could tell that she wasn't surprised and not – or apparently not – seriously concerned. For herself, she said, it was tiresome having to put the local gossips in their place, but no more than that. Max and Genny would solve their own problems, or they wouldn't. No one else could help.

And then, one evening, she said hesitantly, 'There's some news I should pass on to you. Sad news, I'm afraid. You remember Mr Goudy, of course? I'm afraid he fell to his death on the castle rocks last week.'

It was over a year since Max had sacked him, and he hadn't found another job. After a long, shocked moment, Tassie asked, 'An accident?'

'They say so.'

'Did he have life insurance?'

'I believe so.'

With utter certainty, Tassie knew that Bruce Goudy had provided for Mistress Goudy and twelve little Goudies by dying – because he could no longer provide for them by living.

Max, Max!

She said, 'What are we going to do? Mother, *what are we going to do?*'

Her mother didn't pretend not to understand. With a sigh, she said, 'My dear, there is nothing we can do. Life and death make their own rules.'

6

On 8th July, Hugo took Tassie to Worple Road at Wimbledon for the finals of The Championships.

Privacy, for Hugo, was filled with inchoate emotional hazards. He had proposed to her, the first time, in a field, to the sound of traffic passing along the main London road, and the second time on Brighton beach, to the sound of distant voices and laughter. Now, he broke off their engagement in the presence of between six and seven thousand people, to the sound of 'Thirty, love', 'Forty, fifteen', 'Miss Douglass to serve', and 'Game, set and match to Miss Sutton.'

As they crunched over the gravel to the tea lawn, its title more gracious than the reality of trestle tables and coloured water from urns in the marquee, he said, 'You do understand, I hope. In my profession, I simply cannot afford to be associated with a family of ill repute.'

Tassie would have preferred to break it off herself, in her own time, but it was a relief just the same.

She said, 'According to my understanding, a man is innocent until he is proven guilty. He is certainly not proven guilty by spiteful scandals in the press. I would have expected you, as a barrister, to uphold that view. Nor is there anything criminal in marital infidelity.'

It made not the slightest dent in Hugo's armour. 'No, but as a barrister I am accustomed to assessing evidence and distinguishing truth from falsehood.'

'Nonsense. You're like everyone else. You'll believe anything, if it's scabrous enough and repeated often enough. It makes you feel superior, because you yourself haven't sinned – or the newspapers haven't caught you at it.'

Hugo was so offended that the two cups of tea he was carrying slopped in the saucers. 'Really, Tassie! That was a most improper thing to say.'

'It was, wasn't it? But you've just told me that I, personally, am guilty of impropriety by association. And you're afraid being engaged to me might tarnish your professional reputation. As it happens, I find your attitude ironic in a repellent kind of way. How many times, I wonder, have you mentioned to people – quite casually, of course –that your fiancée's brother is, of course, the millionaire industrialist Mr Max McKenzie Smith?'

His eyes flickered, but that was all.

Impatiently, she said, 'No, I don't think I really want that cup of tea, thank you. I'm leaving. You may come with me in the motorcar, unless you want to stay and see the Men's Final?'

'Well, you know, I think I will.' He was all too clearly grateful to be offered an escape route. 'With an American winning the Ladies', I should feel the better for seeing a good, sound Englishman like Laurie Doherty trounce that flashy Australian fellow, Brookes.'

Tassie's annoyance dissolved into honest laughter. There were times when Hugo was almost unbelievable.

7

The notice in the Social Announcements column didn't, of course, say who had jilted whom, but the gossip columns made up for it.

'Max McKenzie Smith's sister and Mr Hugo St John . . . informed sources . . . the lady's refusal to say anything to our reporter . . . living in the same house for the last three years . . . adds another layer to speculation about the family affairs of the man formerly known as The Great Max . . .'

It was highly offensive.

It also brought Max to the Bayswater Road in a fury.

Tassie heard what he had to say and, when he had finished shouting, remarked contemptuously that she did not regard him as a fit person to lecture her about morality and she would be obliged if he would leave, at once.

'Morality be damned! It's the scandal I'm worried about. The last thing I need is more scandal in the family. All this stuff in the press – and your friend Rivers is behind it, mark my words! – makes me look like a laughing stock. The entire structure of the McKenzie Smith corporation rests on the image I present to the world, on the fact that I'm popular, that people trust me. And now my idiot wife and her clever friends are doing their best to make me look a fool. Luckily, that Dakota deal's still fresh in the public memory, so they know I'm not. Otherwise, everything I've built up would be in danger of collapse.'

Tassie didn't believe he meant it, despite the wildness in his eyes, but was unable to think of anything other to say than, 'That doesn't sound like The Great Max!'

He took it for sarcasm, which in a way it was, and looked as if he were about to strike her. Instead, without another word, he turned and flung out of the house, leaving all the doors open behind him.

8

Things *must* get better, Tassie thought. But in whichever direction she looked she saw nothing but problems. Even the roof over her head had a question mark above it. Norah had said she must on no account leave the Bayswater Road merely because that nitwitted

433

brother of hers had broken off the engagement – one of the few things he had ever done that Norah found herself unequivocally able to applaud – but the fact was that she wasn't sure where she and Gus would live when they were married, and Tassie certainly couldn't remain at the St John house with only Hugo for company.

Nothing but problems, and no solutions.

And then a solution – or the possibility of one – came.

It had happened once before. Someone who admired her work had written to her out of the blue offering her a job just when she needed one; had helped her escape from a situation that was intolerable. It was that same job that, now, she needed to escape, not only for her own sake but to free Gus Silvermann from the awkwardness of being a no-man's-land between herself and her brother.

9

The offices of the new magazine were just round the corner from Fleet Street. There was no name on the downstairs door, only a number, but the brass plate on the first floor said, 'À la Mode. Editor, D. Macbeth.'

The cheerful, shirt-sleeved young man who shook her hand said, 'Not that Macbeth, so no jokes, please.'

'I wouldn't dream of it.' It seemed a very long time since Tassie had met anyone so instantly likeable and she smiled at him with a warmth that, as he was later to remark to his backer, knocked him for six.

'Sit down,' he said. 'You'll notice that I didn't rush to put my jacket on in your honour? We're very informal here.'

Tassie said politely, 'We?'

'The editorial "we". It means me. The reason you haven't previously heard of À la Mode is that it doesn't exist yet. Neither does its staff. But I live in hopes. Let me tell you about it.'

He was an enthusiast, so he didn't just say, 'I'm launching a quality fashion magazine. Would you like to do the drawings?' He was determined that she should understand the point of it all.

His fists doing a merry little drumroll on the desk, he said, 'I'm not going to waste time talking about black-and-white illustrations, either drawings or photographs. They're cheap and nasty and, be honest, have you ever seen a photograph of a new dress – even worn by Camille Clifford! – that's made you think, "I want that"?'

Obligingly, Tassie said, 'No.' It happened to be true.

'But you would agree that there's a huge potential market for a popular fashion magazine with illustrations in colour – good colour?'

'Yes, unquestionably.'

'Well, now, the main stumbling block to the expansion of the market for fashion magazines has always been the difficulties associated with colour reproduction. You know all about that,' said Mr Macbeth confidently. 'But you see the problem? It used to be so dashed expensive having every single picture in every single copy of the magazine coloured by hand that the fashion magazine cost more than the fashions themselves. So they didn't sell very many. Nowadays, of course, we can print in colour, but it's a specialist process. So instead of having a market that's limited by the price of the magazine, we have a market limited by the number of copies we can physically print. It's one thing for the fine art periodicals that wouldn't sell more than a few hundred copies anyway, mostly to institutions, but that kind of figure isn't commercial in the context of weekly or fortnightly publication for a popular readership.

'*However*,' he paused dramatically, 'I am now able to reveal to you – confidentially – that I have private, advance knowledge of a new type of colour printing, a stencil method, that will make it possible to print colour pictures relatively cheaply and in commercial numbers.'

He beamed. 'So, how would you feel about doing the illustrations? I've been admiring your figure drawings for a while, buried though they usually are in amongst furniture and household fittings. Your pretty girls are great. Naughty but nice.'

'Ugh! Please!'

'I mean it. You manage to get a glint of humour in their eyes that's really refreshing. And very much in the mood of the times. What do you think? Does the notion appeal to you? Fun, eh?'

He was like a large, sandy dog wagging his tail hopefully at her, and she couldn't resist patting him. Laughingly, she agreed, 'Yes. Fun!'

As she spoke, she heard the door open behind her. She was wondering whether she ought to turn when Mr Macbeth said cheerfully, 'Ah, here's my backer. The money man himself!'

For a terrible, heart-stopping moment, she thought, 'Max!'

But it wasn't. It was Francis Rivers.

10

'How's it going?' he said and then, without waiting for an answer, 'Make yourself scarce, Don, will you?'

'All right. I'll be in the composing room. Let out a yell when you've finished. I'd like my office back.'

'It may be a while.'

Mr Macbeth closed the door behind him, and Tassie said, 'It won't be a while. I can't think we have anything to say to each other.' She didn't know why she wasn't already jumping to her feet and gathering her belongings together.

Circumspectly, Francis walked round her and

perched on the edge of the desk. 'On the contrary, I have a great deal to say to you, and I should be surprised if you haven't quite a lot to say to me. Mostly in the ladylike equivalent of swear words.'

He was sufficiently near the mark for Tassie to feel a twinge of something that was almost amusement. But he had an air of the impersonal about him, a detachment that told her there was no possibility of her liking what he was going to say to her. 'I don't want to hear.'

'I don't suppose you do, but you're going to. That's why I've kidnapped you. Don Macbeth, by the way, is a young man with great ideas and not enough capital. I hope you won't let it weigh against him that I happen to have bought an interest in the new venture.'

Disbelievingly, she laughed. 'You can't think it's as simple as that!'

'Perhaps not.' He linked his hands over his knee and stared down at them. 'You can guess who I want to talk to you about.'

It didn't seem worth wasting her breath – which was temporarily in short supply – on answering him.

'That evening at Dunaird, I warned you about him. Very stupidly. It was neither the time nor the place, and I have regretted it ever since. I called him a cheat, a fraud, a liar and a good few other things besides.'

'Charlatan,' she said.

'What?' he looked up and then down again. 'Probably. I didn't succeed in convincing you – I don't remember whether I even tried – that my concern was largely for *you*. You probably thought then, and still think, that I was actuated by personal hatred of Max. All I can say is – and I beg you to believe me – that this whole appalling business started because my mother, for reasons that seemed to me comprehensible then, and still seem so now, wanted to know something about the circumstances of Max's birth. If you were aware of the full extent of her tragedy, I think you, too, might comprehend.'

Reluctantly, Tassie admitted, 'From what she told us, I can see why she hated my father.'

'Well, that's something. Later, having started looking into Max's background, I had to go on because it seemed to me there was something false about him. Nothing to put one's finger on. But my suspicions grew so that even being unable to prove or disprove them seemed only to confirm them. Do you understand?'

She understood. How well she understood.

'Yes,' she said after a moment. 'But I still don't want to hear.'

Frowning, he stared at her but, although there was a darkness in her eyes, her face told him nothing. And yet, in that moment, he could have sworn that she knew.

II

Restlessly, he rose to his feet and went to the window. 'In India and Australia my suspicions about him turned into hard fact. Your brother is careless, you know. He thinks he's cleverer than anyone else and doesn't, therefore, bother much about covering his tracks.'

As if the words were being dragged out of her, Tassie exclaimed, 'Oh, no. You're wrong. If you think that, it's probably because he's covered his tracks too well.' Then, with sudden intensity, she exclaimed, 'Oh, *God*!' and buried her face in her hands.

He was across the room in two steps and kneeling beside her. But he didn't touch her. 'Tassie?' She did know something, it seemed, or perhaps had only guessed. But he had no idea what.

She half turned away from him then, shaking her head, so he rose again and stepped back.

'Go on,' she said after a moment.

'In India,' he said, 'I found a simple business fraud,

very easy to detect if you happened to be on the spot, asking the right questions. You may not know that one of the commonest ways of siphoning money off from a business is to show expenditures that aren't real. A few years ago, McKenzie Smith supposedly acquired a jute plantation, which was described to the board and shown in the books as a major capital outlay. When supplies of jute began coming through to the parent company at a highly favourable rate, I have no doubt that his directors congratulated Max on having made such a good deal.

'Which, indeed, he had, at least where his own profit was concerned. He had not, of course, bought the plantation at all. Most of the "purchase money" went into his own pocket and the rest as a bribe to the zemindar, who agreed to charge McKenzie Smith an artificially low price for his crop in exchange for a guarantee that the firm would take the whole of the plantation's production, regardless of quality, for the next ten years.'

She had been listening carefully, despite her reluctance. 'But surely . . . Why did no one find out?'

'There was no reason for anyone to want to, or no one who mattered. The firm was getting its jute cheap, and that had been the object of the so-called purchase in the first place.'

'Yes. I see that. But it can't have been a matter just of cash changing hands, not with the sums that must have been involved? I know enough about accounts to know that the acquisition must have appeared somewhere, at some stage, and Max isn't a double-entry bookkeeper. Someone else in the firm must have known?'

'The chief accountant. It couldn't be anyone else.'

She had guessed even as she phrased her question. Bruce Goudy.

A 'frightened man', Max had said. And now, it seemed, with good reason to be frightened. Max had sacked him two months after the Whitaker Wright case, when the authorities were threatening to take a very much closer interest than before in the financial affairs of some of the bigger corporations.

She said nothing.

Francis had expected her to argue, to refuse to believe, to fight him all the way, but she didn't even seem very shocked. It was almost three years – three very long years – since their meeting at Dunaird, and in those years she had grown up from a lovely, emotional girl into a mature young woman. She was, it seemed, no longer Max's slave.

It was a relief, but it didn't make any easier the other, unacceptable things he had to tell her. Max was still her brother, must still matter to her.

12

Before he could go on, she asked, '*Why* are you telling me this? To prove you were right all along?'

He shook his head. 'If it were only that. No. I told you once that I was thinking of doing a full profile of Max, but it's never been done because all my research has been inhibited by his lies or withholding of information. If the profile was to be worthwhile, I had to be one hundred per cent sure of my ground, able to prove everything I said. I'm sure now, and I *can* prove it. Some time in the next few weeks the profile will be published.

'The reason I'm telling you is so that you will know what lies ahead. I am telling you because I love you, because you are Max's sister, and because publication may destroy him.'

For a moment, the silence in the room was a thing in itself, detached from the clatter and shouting in the street outside, from the rumble of presses within the building, running the feature pages of the next day's

Enterprise. It was strange, Francis thought, how closely allied the senses were. In the silence, he was aware for the first time of the light, fresh, floral scent Tassie was wearing.

He had kept his face and voice neutral as the light came to her eyes at his use of the word 'love', only to be extinguished by the other words that followed. Before anything else could happen between them, it was necessary for the shade of Max to be exorcised.

Feeling like a murderer, he said at length, 'Shall I go on?'

'If you must.' She had been so unprepared for any mention of love that she couldn't take it in, couldn't believe that the miracle had happened.

It was too dangerous to believe.

Francis said, 'People who cheat in their public lives very often cheat in private, too. And vice versa. It was my suspicions of the private Max that made me suspicious of the public one, and in Australia I discovered something about the private Max that . . . You're going to hate it, because it wasn't anything grandiose or stylish or even clever.

'Max said once that he'd made a modest pile as a gold digger at Coolgardie. I went to see the workings, thinking I'd write a story not about the miners who've struck it lucky but the ones who haven't. You'd be surprised how many there are who've been panning for ten or fifteen years, making barely enough to keep themselves alive. Almost by accident, I heard of one who'd known Max.

'His name was O'Donnell and I had to track him from Coolgardie to just outside Kalgoorlie. He told me that he *had* once struck it lucky, in 1893. But before he could profit from his good fortune, a fellow digger had stolen his hoard and decamped with it. A Scotsman called McKenzie. O'Donnell described him to me very precisely and with a good deal of feeling, and I'm sorry, but there's no doubt that it was Max.'

Not just a too-clever business tycoon. A cheap thief, as well.

She had believed that of him once before, in the matter of her jewel. There had been an explanation, of sorts, then. It didn't seem as if there could be any explanation now although Max, confronted, would no doubt think of one.

In a voice of unnatural clarity, she said, 'Max is very like my father. He doesn't have much consideration for other people, except those he loves.'

Which was one way, Francis thought, of putting it. But she had given him the opening he didn't want. It was with regret that he took it.

'Even those he loves,' he said quietly, 'don't always rate Max's consideration. How many years ago was it that he promised to rebuild Dunaird tower for your mother? Four, almost five? Last week, I sent my Inverness reporter to have a look. My darling, nothing has been done. Nothing at all. Not a blade of grass has been trodden since we were last there, together, three years ago.'

13

For all his perception, he hadn't realised quite how much it mattered.

She jumped to her feet. 'It's not true. That isn't true. There was a delay because they had to shore up the foundations, but everything's going very well now. Max told me. Your reporter must have gone to the wrong place.'

With clumsy hands she scooped up her purse and, with a jerk, freed the handle of the bright, flowery parasol from the back of her chair. 'No, Francis! I won't listen to any more of this. You're wrong. You're *wrong*!

I'll leave for Dunaird myself, tomorrow. And I'll find it almost finished. You'll see.'

He didn't try to stop her. He had done his best. And worst.

14

She went by train to Glasgow and on to Oban. After that, she sailed on the PS *Gael* to Gairloch. It was the longest, stormiest journey of the mind she had ever made.

Dunaird was the linchpin of everything. Max, for love of Grace, had made a promise, and the love and the promise had shone always in Tassie's mind, lightening every shadow that had come between them during the last four turbulent years. Because of them she could still find something to love in him. Because of them, she could still be loyal even though she knew, now, that he was weak and not strong.

She still believed that, without love, he *could* not have recognised Grace's longing, and without love, *would* not have made his promise. The promise that he must – must! – have kept.

If he had broken it, it would be the last and worst betrayal.

15

The sky was blue, and the sun was shining, and the sea birds were calling. There was scarcely a ripple in the molten silver of the sea, nor any footprint in the sand.

Tall, grey and austere, the tower stood on the grassy sward of the cliff top.

Unchanging. Unchanged.

CHAPTER THREE

I

St Andrews was no longer the quiet little backwater it
had been in Tassie's childhood, but development had
come gradually, modernity grafted gently onto the
familiar landmarks of castle and cathedral ruins, church
and college towers, the eyes of the little town continuing to turn outward to the wide, cold expanses of the
North Sea and its heartbeat remaining tuned to the
seasonal rhythms of university terms and golf
championships.

Soon after dawn, the streets began to fill, as they had
always done, with dairymen carrying milk still warm
from the cow, poultrywomen with eggs warm from the
hen, bakers with trays of steaming morning rolls. By
eight, the knife grinders were out, and the pan menders
and the fish sellers, and the cobbles were loud with
carriages, carts and drays.

Breakfast at Graceholm, too, appeared to be what it
had always been, a cosy prelude to a day of domesticity,
of shopping, visits to friends, and in the evening
perhaps a hand or two of bridge with some neighbours.
But the calm on this summer morning was deceptive,
because Tassie had arrived unheralded and straight
from Dunaird the previous evening and had told Grace
everything. Or almost everything. Her own and
Selina's most private encounters with Max were
subjects not to be spoken of to anyone, ever.

444

She had begun with Dunaird, thinking to get the worst over, but Grace had been less distressed than Tassie herself, saying after a few silent moments, 'I am disappointed, of course, but perhaps it was too much to hope for. If I have learned one thing from life, it is that you must wait until the bird is in your hand before you croon over it. And I have felt so dispossessed, being banished from Dunaird in these last years, that to be able to return will be a compensation in itself.'

She had been silent again for a while, her clear, mermaid's eyes staring into space. 'And, you know, perhaps it would be wrong to rebuild it. There was a poem of Mr Swinburne's, years ago, about a forsaken garden on the edge of the sea. I never quite understood it, but he seemed to be saying that it was right that the roses should fade and vanish while the sea and the rocks remained. Perhaps Dunaird is like the rose and should be permitted to die.'

' "For the foam flowers endure when the rose blossoms wither . . ." ' Tassie intoned, ' "And men that love lightly may die – but we?" I remember learning it at school. My teacher said it was all about worldly success being as perishable as the rose.'

Her voice ended on a strangled sound that was almost a chuckle, because it was so bizarre to compare Max with a rose destined to fade. He was more like a bomb destined to explode.

She had to go on with her story. 'It doesn't matter now, but do you remember I found signs of a surveyor having been at Dunaird three years ago? I think I know now what happened. You let drop to Max that I was going there and he sent Monty dashing up ahead of me to plant some evidence. The equivalent of salting a mine. He did it very cleverly. I was convinced. I still believed in Max, then.'

Her mother said, 'But no longer?'

For years, Grace had put her own continuing, faint

sense of disquiet about her son down to her lack of cleverness and the emotional distance between them that was a natural sequel to their long separation. His promise to rebuild Dunaird had touched her; had almost persuaded her that he did, after all, feel love and duty towards his mother. Almost. But she still didn't understand him. She didn't understand why he should have made such a promise if he had no intention of keeping it.

Tassie didn't answer her question directly. Instead, treading delicately through the minefield of Max's private affairs, she moved on to the problem of Genevieve, and Max's belief that Genevieve and her friends were doing their best to destroy him.

Grace said thoughtfully, 'I find it hard to imagine. It seems more likely that Max is dramatising things because his vanity is hurt. It was never a suitable or a happy marriage, but there have been unhappy marriages since the world began. The difficulty is that, nowadays, the newspapers always make bad worse.'

The newspapers.

It was then that Tassie broke it to her about Max's other sins, and Francis Rivers, and the profile, and the decision Grace herself had to make.

'We – you and I – must know the truth,' Tassie said. 'I don't think Francis knows the whole of it and neither do we. If Francis and I pooled our knowledge, we might arrive at it. But I don't think I could stop him from printing it – it's become almost a crusade for him – nor do I think I should.'

She paused, and sighed, and began again with difficulty. 'I've been fighting, for quite a long time now, against the suspicion that Max isn't – isn't a good man.' Despite everything, she couldn't bring herself to call him 'evil', a word she had always thought of as one to be thundered from the pulpit, not used seriously and rationally of real-life people. 'But he's not good. He's not even ordinarily, humanly bad. And he is dangerous. He hurts – even destroys – people for his own entertainment. Francis said to me once that he had to be stopped, before he could damage more lives. On the most rudimentary level, even if he's stopped tomorrow, many ordinary people who've sunk their savings into his companies will lose them. And the longer he is allowed to go on, the more losers there will be. Francis believes he can stop him, but he would be better equipped with our cooperation.

'That's why I'm here. I want your permission to tell Francis all we know. It isn't a great deal, really, but it might help to make sense of things. I won't do it, of course, unless you agree, and I will make Francis promise not to reveal the truth about Max's childhood.'

Grace stared out at the last fires of the sunset for ten long minutes before she said, 'What pain the world carries with it. I know it says in the Bible that the love of God passeth all understanding, but I have always thought it a most ill-advised policy. When one sees so few evidences of God's love, one would be more inclined to believe in its existence if one were granted at least an inkling of His reasons for giving or withholding it.'

'You're a pagan, mother.'

'Perhaps. I wish I knew more about the old religions. Oh, Tassie! Tassie! How has it all happened? How did my lovely, lost baby with his pink, screwed-up little face and his tiny, waving fists grow into a man who has to be stopped "because he is dangerous"? Would it all be different if he had never been taken from me? Or was it written into his soul from the moment he was conceived?'

Her own eyes shimmering with tears, Tassie said, 'All criminals were babies once, and only a handful of all the world's babies grow up to be criminals. It was Max's destiny to become what he has become, and nothing you could have done would have changed it.'

'Thank you, my dear. But that is too easy an answer.'

Quietly, Tassie asked, 'What shall I do?'

'There must be an end. Tell Mr Rivers whatever you wish, and whatever he needs to know.'

Tassie hadn't slept and neither had Grace. But nothing was said at breakfast to alter the decision of the evening before.

Within hours, Tassie was on her way back to London.

2

When the telephone rang on his desk, Francis was presiding over the midday news meeting and, impatient at the interruption, snapped, 'Yes?' Then he said, 'Ah,' hoping the change in his voice wasn't too instructively obvious to his staff.

Through the crackle on the line, Tassie said, 'You were right about Dunaird. Perhaps we could meet on Saturday? I would prefer neutral territory and I'd thought of Maidenhead?'

It was a pleasant enough place to think of, if not too easy to get to. Francis said, 'Fine. Where precisely, and when?'

'The tea garden of the Ray Mead Hotel? At about two?'

3

There were cypresses and a laburnum bordering the lawn, which was enclosed on three sides by the two-storeyed white buildings of the hotel with their bright window-boxes and hanging baskets. There were small white tables set out on the grass, not too close together, and all the ladies had their parasols up, which made it difficult for them to stare either at other ladies, or their gentlemen escorts. Although it was a fashionable haunt, there was little likelihood of either Tassie or Francis meeting anyone they knew.

She was there before him, already seated.

'A good choice,' he said. 'How did you come? By train?'

She smiled at him and he had to take a firm grip on himself, because it was a smile he had scarcely dared hope to see. 'I came in my motor,' she said mischievously. 'Do *you* have a motor, sir?'

'How very dashing of you! No, I don't.'

'Then you may drive back to London with me, if you dare. If we are still on speaking terms, of course.'

'That, my darling, is for you to decide.'

She drew in her breath sharply. 'No, you mustn't.'

He had been about to take her hand and crush it in his. As far as he was aware, there was no law against it. 'Mustn't what?'

'Don't call me "darling".'

'All right. What would you prefer? My beloved? My adored one? My dearest? – no, that's rather feeble. My angel?'

'Any of them, all of them. But Francis, you can't. What about Lucia?'

'Dear God,' he said blankly. 'What do you mean, "What about Lucia?" How do you know about Lucia?'

'Something your brother Jonny said at the suffrage meeting in Glasgow. I'd always known that you had either a mistress or a wife, but from what Jonny said it seemed that it must be a wife. It did explain a lot about how you'd behaved to me, but it hurt terribly, above all because you hadn't told me. It still does. And Francis, I do love you – dreadfully – but I cannot, I will not, be responsible for stealing another woman's husband. So don't call me "darling", please, however much I want you to. I've learned to resign myself, and . . .'

'Then you can damned well un-resign yourself. Lucia died last year. And she wasn't my wife. She was my sister.'

4

Tassie stammered, 'But . . . But why . . . But . . .'

Leaning over, he removed the parasol from her lax hand, saying, 'The sun's gone in.' She was looking deeply and desirably attractive in a high-necked white blouse under a cream linen bolero jacket and one of the new, slimmer skirts, her glowing hair drawn loosely back from a centre parting to a knot at the nape of her neck. Ignoring the social niceties, she had removed her veiled motoring hat, which lay on the seat beside her, flat-crowned, ruthlessly practical and looking like a large and disconsolate muffin.

'If you were in doubt, why didn't you ask?'

'Francis, I couldn't. I mean, how could I?'

'It's quite easy, really,' he said amiably. 'You just say, "Francis, would you please tell me . . ." '

She gave a gasp of laughter, feeling as if she were floating high in the sky on some fluffy sunlit cloud. Beatifically, she said, 'Why didn't you tell me anyway?'

His smile faded. 'Pour the tea. It's a long story, and it's my mother's story as much as Lucia's.'

Taking a moment to marshal his thoughts, he began, 'You know that my mother's twin, Simon, committed suicide?'

'Yes.'

'He and my mother had always been very close. I suspect that Simon depended far too much on her, while she thought of him as the weaker half of herself and protected him like a tiger protecting her cub. That was, and is, her nature. She does nothing by halves. But there came a time when she couldn't protect him, not only because he was in America and out of reach, but because she herself was almost at death's door. Her husband had died in a railway accident when she was six months pregnant with her first child. All that would have been bad enough, but it seems also to have been a very hard pregnancy. And then came the suicide of the person she loved most in the world.'

Tassie didn't speak, but there was nothing artificial, nothing forced about the sorrow, sympathy and shock on her face. She stretched out her hand and Francis took it and held it.

He said, 'You do see, don't you? It was too much even for Abigail. Her child was born before its time. It was a long labour and although – against everyone's expectation – the baby lived, she had sustained incurable damage to her brain. Poor Lucia. Mental deficiency isn't the kind of thing we're tolerant of even today, but in the 1860s the public attitude was appallingly prejudiced. There was a morality campaign building up at the time . . .'

He hesitated because, not even now in thoroughly modern 1905, was it possible to explain about syphilis to an innocent girl. 'It was directed,' he went on carefully, 'against a way of life that brought certain diseases in its wake, diseases whose symptoms were very recognisable. One result was that people made often unjustified assumptions. A child who, like Lucia, was weak in mind and trembling of limb, was often thought of as paying the price of immorality at second hand. "The sins of the fathers", and that kind of thing.'

'How *awful*!' Tassie said almost disbelievingly.

'There are few things more frightening in this life, my dearest, than morality on the warpath. However, you've met my mother. Not even three tragedies in a row could destroy her. They strengthened her, I think. She was far too proud to tolerate the social stigma of Lucia's condition, so she kept the child in complete seclusion. I think it was wrong of her, but then I have never been an almost penniless young widow alone with a mentally and physically sick child in a harsh and unforgiving world.'

Tassie shuddered violently. 'What a dreadful story. How did she survive?'

With a dry chuckle, Francis said, 'By being Abigail. By sheer force of personality, she squeezed some money out of the bank and set about making what she could out of the remnants of the business. I remember saying, once, that I thought it very brave of her and being told not to talk such fustian. "One does what one must". By the time she married my father – poor man! – she had the bit well between her teeth and there was no possibility of her ever relapsing into domesticity.

'I am reliably informed that the birth of three sons in rapid succession made not the slightest difference to her working habits. She shocked everyone by continuing to go her office until the very last minute in each case, and was back two weeks after we let out our first rousing squalls.'

The sky was clouding over. Tassie said, 'Oh, bother. It's just as well I put the cover over the motor. With our climate, I do think it's time the manufacturers put lids on the things.'

'Some of them do.'

'Yes, limousines,' she said scornfully. 'And the Sunbeam has a kind of awning that may, I suppose, serve some purpose if the rain's coming down vertically and you don't want to do anything rash, like going anywhere.'

'Better than nothing.'

She giggled. 'It's only sour grapes. I couldn't afford it. Anyway, go on.'

'Not much more. It's Lucia's story now, and mine. As you may guess, Abigail had no time for her children. David, Jonny and I, being boys and bursting with rude health, had a normal childhood at boarding school. But

452

Lucia, poor love, was a virtual prisoner with her nurse in her own rooms. The worst thing was that mother, for as far back as I can remember, always frightened her. She was too decisive, too impatient to be gentle, and gentleness was what Lucia needed above all. She sensed, I think, that my mother would have preferred her to have died at birth.'

'No, Francis! What a dreadful thing to say! Think of the memories Lucia must have brought back every time your mother saw her!'

'You may be right. I didn't recognise it when I was younger. I always felt very protective towards Lucia and when I was about sixteen I had a major row with my mother about it. She maintained that Lucia was as happy as it possible for her to be, but I was convinced that, if she was aware of nothing else, Lucia was aware of being unloved. I swore that, the minute it was practicable, I was going to set up house on my own and take Lucia into my care.

'It's the kind of idiotic thing one says at a crusading sixteen, but I meant it and I did it. I didn't realise, until much later, that, if I were ever to marry, I would have to marry someone strong and mature, able to face the stresses and strains of living with Lucia.'

He smiled deep into her eyes. 'And then, human nature being what it is, I fell in love with you, nineteen and touchingly innocent.

'My darling, how *could* I have asked you to sacrifice yourself, to share me and our life and our home with my poor, mad sister?'

5

She swallowed hard. 'You're a fool, Francis Rivers. I would have done it.'

'That wasn't the question at issue.'

'I suppose not. But you can't imagine what dreadful

things I thought about you after Dunaird and then, later, when I heard about the feud and about Lucia. I thought I despised you.'

'And now you discover that I am a paragon, and you love me again. The fickleness of women!'

'Talking about fickleness, what was that you said to Norah once about your – er – romantic needs already being catered for?'

'Not my romantic needs. Just my physical ones.'

'A mistress?'

'Three, actually.'

'*What?*'

'Not all at once.'

Tassie, glancing sideways, said, 'That parasol at the next table is getting nearer. Do you suppose she's listening?'

'Who could blame her? Let's walk along the river bank and I can hold your hand properly.'

They had been walking for five minutes when he said, 'Tassie . . .' at precisely the moment when she said, 'Francis . . .'

6

The rain came on when they were halfway home, and they ran dripping up the long stairs to the attic he had rented on top of a warehouse near Queenhithe Dock, an easy walk from the office.

Looking round the huge, sparsely furnished space with its wide vista over the bright, busy river, Tassie exclaimed, 'What a wonderful studio this would make!'

'Then we'll keep it, when we're married. What we both need, now, is a nice, warm bath.'

He didn't say, 'Together,' so she was surprised and momentarily selfconscious when the door opened and he came to her as she lay in the tranquil water gazing out, thoughtless with happiness, at the lights of the city.

454

But his own lack of embarrassment reassured her as he slipped into the bath beside her and took her in his arms. Some of the water slopped over and they both laughed breathlessly.

Being close to each other was enough at first, the water a caress as soft and sensual as his hands when at last they began to move. With seriousness, he said, 'The first time may not be what you hope, but I love you very much and if you love me, too, it will be all right. Will you trust me?'

She was too inexperienced to understand the care he was taking, to be aware that he could give her no more than the promise of something beautiful, that he was subduing the intensity of his own desire so that she might be protected from the consequences of it. All she knew was that this, at last, was love – and wonder, and joy, and gentleness.

She had been brought up according to the stern old Calvinist tradition that nothing was more important than discipline of the mind, which could master emotion and conquer even physical pain. It was a tradition in which there was much of value and much of truth, but she discovered now that, where love was, it had no meaning. In the transfiguring moment when Francis gathered her close in his arms, the separate passions of head, heart and body converged and the person deep inside Tassie Smith ceased to be a sum of parts and became a seamless whole.

When he saw from her eyes and knew from her breathing that the moment was right, he raised her hands to rest on the rim of the bath and placed his own hands over them. Then, smiling down into her dazed and dreaming eyes, he drew himself smoothly forward, guided by instinct, by magic, so that when they touched it was perfect and he slid inside her, gently and then more strongly, meeting the obstacle and feeling it yield, easily and willingly, the barrier waiting to be broken. She moaned, but it was with pleasure, not pain.

Like Ophelia she lay, her hair floating like copper seaweed on the water, her eyes locked with his as he moved inside her until, at last, they closed as she was swept away into darkness and delight.

When he dared no longer delay, he withdrew from her, but so smooth was the movement, so merciful the water, that she was left almost unknowing, absorbed in the mysteries that were taking possession of her.

When the time came, they would find a love together that was mutual and unconstrained. That time was not yet, but it must be soon.

'Come back to me,' Francis said. 'Come back.'

She opened her eyes and he had to turn away because he loved her too much.

He said, 'The water's getting cold. I'll make us an omelette. How soon will you marry me?'

7

When they parted, on a kiss that said more than words – more, in some ways, than their bodies had done – they had discussed nothing of what they had met to discuss. During supper and after, they had talked only of themselves. As they ate their omelette, Tassie said, 'I'm glad you can cook, because I'm not very good at it. Do you have something against housekeepers?'

'Not on principle. It's merely that I've never found one who appears to have any other object in life than to poison me. What kind of house shall we have? And where? Do you want a garden?'

They couldn't bear not to touch. Francis even ate one-handed, his other arm round Tassie's waist, so that she had to butter his bread for him and pour his wine. 'What an admirable wife you are going to make,' he said.

'Saturdays only,' she said. 'They'll be very special, won't they? With me working all day during the week, and you working all night? We aren't going to see much of each other.'

'The perfect recipe for a happy marriage. On second thoughts, you wouldn't fancy coming to work for the paper and sharing my office? I could install a sofa . . .'

But they had to talk seriously some time, soon, and without being distracted by their need for each other. In the end, Tassie agreed to meet Francis at the *Enterprise* at ten the next morning, which would give them, he said, two hours before he had to get down to work.

Norah took one look at Tassie when she reached home and said, 'You're glowing! I don't believe it. I *don't* believe it.'

Her gladness was so patent that it all became too much for Tassie.

'I'm so happy,' she wailed, the tears pouring like cataracts down her cheeks. 'I'm so happy. I've never been so happy in my life! Norah, will you be my bridesmaid?'

8

Francis had a large notebook on his desk. 'Are you sure you want to go through with this?'

'Yes. And mother agrees with me.'

His left hand tightened over hers. 'Good. I've sketched out Max's story as he himself tells it, with some addenda of my own. Let's check what you know against what I know.'

'All right.' Tassie sighed. 'Though I still hate it. Anyway . . . Your mother – shall I call her Abigail and my own mother Grace to avoid confusion? – told us you had found out that Max was conceived before my parents were married. You also know he was sent to the wet nurse in Ullapool. It's after that that the public and the true stories diverge.'

She coloured slightly. 'I know you've gone to a lot of trouble to find out about Jeannie and little Robbie, who was drowned, but the truth is that you couldn't find out anything about Robbie because he never existed. To protect Grace – and I still think it was both considerate and forgiving of him – Max had to explain away the fact that he'd been cut off from the family, so he invented the story of Robbie, and him being drowned, and Jeannie pretending it wasn't Robbie but Max who had been drowned.'

'Well, well,' Francis said satirically. 'What a very fertile imagination he has!'

'Yes. He thought it all up in a matter of minutes, too. I'd asked if he had any foster brothers or sisters, and he said no, but it was a dashed good idea. It all just developed from there.'

Francis studied her carefully. 'Are you trying to hoax me?'

'No, of course not.'

'My dearest love, what qualifications does a wet nurse need?'

She frowned. 'I don't know. Respectable character and being fond of children and – and – things?'

'The first qualification, Miss Innocence, is that she must have milk to feed the baby. That's what makes her a "wet" nurse. And human biology being what it is, no woman produces milk unless she has an infant of her own that needs feeding. So?'

'So Max *must* have had a foster brother or sister?' she said blankly. 'Heavens, how *stupid* of me. But why on earth . . .'

'Why on earth didn't he say so? We'll come back to that. I've found out something that might be relevant. Go on.'

'All right. The next divergence in the stories comes

with Max's upbringing. He always talks about his impoverished childhood in a Black House. He couldn't very well say anything else, once he had elected himself as Jeannie's "own" child according to the Robbie story . . .'

'From the publicity point of view, it sounded good, too.'

'Yes. But, in fact, my father sent money to Jeannie every year and on the strength of it, Jeannie moved away from Ullapool when Max was only a few months old, to a nice little house off the Inverness road. So Max's childhood wasn't luxurious, but there was never any danger of him starving or going without boots.'

Francis exhaled, feelingly. 'Which explains why I didn't find any records. I was looking in the wrong place and, for Highlanders, thirty miles takes you into a foreign country. I did, as it happens, find someone in Ullapool who had a vague memory of Jeannie and thought she'd "come into money and moved away" though he didn't know where. I rather dismissed it, because "coming into money" needn't have meant more than twenty pounds or so. This is most illuminating. Go on.'

'I don't think there's much more. Max grew up suspecting he was my father's illegitimate son, but papa had said the payments would stop instantly if he made any attempt to establish contact with the family. He ran away to join the Navy when he was about fifteen, just as he told you, but he hated it and jumped ship . . .'

'Yes, I put an enquiry in to the Admiralty about that, months ago, but I'm still waiting for an answer. I'd better chase it.'

'After that, the public and private stories tally until he came home to find his foster mother dying. My father's lawyers had written to her because my father was dying, too, so Max went to them and more or less said, "Who am I?" They wouldn't tell him at first, but my brother-in-law made such a fuss that it all came out. And that's about all.'

'I see. Have you any idea whether your father went on paying Jeannie during the years when Max was abroad?'

'I don't know. He might have. I mean, there's nothing unusual about fathers making their sons an allowance. Yes, I'm *sure* papa would have done that as a matter of duty, a kind of recompense, expecting Jeannie to forward it to Max, wherever he was.'

Francis finished writing, then, retrieving his spare hand from Tassie, said, 'We haven't much longer. I wish I'd known about the house on the Inverness road, because it might have answered a question that you, my love, hadn't even thought of until half an hour ago.'

She grimaced at him, half laughing and half mortified by her oversight. 'Foster brothers and sisters?'

'Yes. Or, at least, foster sister. My gold-prospecting friend O'Donnell told me that, a few days before "Mac" McKenzie stole his hoard, he had received a letter from his sister in Scotland . . .'

'*No!*'

'Yes. A letter telling him to return home urgently. O'Donnell knew about it because, before Max stole the money, he had been trying desperately to borrow it. O'Donnell apparently said, "Sure, an' what kind o' man wad take orders from a woman?" whereupon Max told him that his sister was a very special woman, rich and fashionable and living on the Riviera. O'Donnell thought he was just spinning a yarn, trying to convince him that he would be able to repay him, but it set me thinking.'

He surveyed his beloved amusedly, because she didn't seem to be making the obvious connection.

'Go on!' she exclaimed.

Provocatively, he said, 'Well, I *could* have started trying to trace the lady from the 1893 end, but I preferred to start at the 1905 end. Come on, my darling, think about it! If Max was really as close as that to his foster sister a dozen years ago, he's unlikely to have lost touch with her since. Isn't there one name that springs to mind?'

Her eyes were huge, and green as new grass. 'No. I don't believe it.'

'Try.'

'Naomi Merton?'

9

'It can't be anyone else,' Francis said. 'I'd already made some enquiries about her a few years ago, and I'd found out that, in about 1890, she'd appeared from nowhere as the mistress of an elderly gentleman called Merton, who lived at Nice. The "Mrs" was a courtesy title. It was rumoured that she'd been his servant when he'd lived in London, and later his housekeeper.

'He seems to have doted on her and left her comfortably off when he died. That was when she began appearing in London with traces of a French accent and in the rôle of his widow. She's a clever woman, but society has been deceived too often by ladies of her type and, though it accepted her on the strength of her money and her undoubted knowledge of jewellery, it kept her at arm's length.'

Tassie couldn't take it in at first. 'How extraordinary! Can you imagine her as a child running barefoot round a Highland fishing village? Because I can't. But she's certainly the only woman I've ever known Max defer to. It used to make me so cross when he listened to everything she had to say and paid no attention at all to what I said. Why do you suppose he never told us about her?'

'It wasn't an oversight; you can be sure of that! I'd guess he thought it would be safer to play his cards close to his chest when he first introduced himself into the family. He wouldn't know what kind of people you were or what kind of situation he was landing himself in.'

'Yes, and having denied her almost without thinking, he couldn't very well produce her later.' Tassie couldn't suppress the wicked twinkle in her eyes. 'And after all that fuss in the papers about Max and Another Woman! And poor Genny, getting so upset about Max having a mistress!'

Francis grinned back. 'She was entitled to be upset. She just chose the wrong woman to be upset about.'

He couldn't interpret the look that came to Tassie's face. 'Does Max have a mistress? Really?'

'If gossip is to be believed, there's hardly a good-looking woman he hasn't tried to lay – if you'll pardon the expression – at some time or other.'

'Oh.'

'Damn! Here comes my news editor. Can we continue tomorrow morning? At about 2 a.m? Or later, if you insist.'

She chuckled at him. 'I do insist. That's past my bedtime. *Francis!*' Blushing fierily, she went on, 'I don't think I can manage later, either, because it's Monday and I can't let Gus down without notice. He might let me have Tuesday morning off, though.'

'Can we live until then?'

'I don't know.'

10

Gus, having caught his artist murmuring sweet nothings into the telephone on four separate occasions during the course of that same Monday morning, said, 'Why don't I ask Norah to stand in for a day or two?'

'Would you really not mind?'

He shook his head, his dimples looking quite

paternal. 'I guess you'll tell me your plans when you're good and ready, but make it soon, huh? It's unnerving, this feeling that my artist's mind isn't on her job.'

'Is it so obvious?' she asked, stricken. 'Oh, Gus, you're being very good to me. I know I'm a nuisance, but it isn't all to do with being in love. I can't tell you any more but I'm afraid you'll find out quite soon, along with the rest of the world.' She thought for a moment. 'Gus, does my brother owe G.S. Advertising any money? Are there any outstanding invoices?'

'Some.'

She didn't say any more and neither did he, but the first thing he did when she left his office was start chivvying the McKenzie Smith International accounts department for payment.

11

It was love, Tassie supposed, that was responsible for all her emotions being thrown into a state of soft-hearted confusion. She worried about deserting Gus. She felt guilty about having let Hugo down. She even began to feel charitable towards Max, though not forgiving.

When she told Francis what she had learned from John Bell about the structure and finances of the McKenzie Smith corporation and Francis said that he knew most of it already, she blurted out, 'Must we go ahead with this? Must you expose him? I feel so bad about it. Max is my *brother*!'

Francis had been expecting something of the sort and was surprised it hadn't come sooner. He said seriously, 'If he had murdered someone, would you protect him?'

'No, of course not. Yes. I don't know.'

That, too, was what he had expected. 'It's a question the families of all criminals have to face, and they all feel as you do. But there are no excuses you can make for

Max. His whole life has been a lie in one sense or another, and nothing he has done has been for the benefit of anyone except himself. He is wholly self-serving. Even the relative deprivation of his childhood cannot possibly justify the lengths to which he has gone in pursuit of personal wealth.'

Tassie said, 'Not only wealth. The more I think about it, the more I think that power is what he wants and has always wanted.'

'The two go together. But whatever the case, my dearest, he has to be stopped.'

She sighed. 'I know. But – you won't tell everything about his early life, will you? My mother would be the one to suffer because no one would understand why she did what she did. The world has changed so much. Nowadays, people think they're in command of their own lives and forget that it wasn't always so. Acceptance and fatalism weren't always contemptible weaknesses. They were just a different way of surviving.'

She was so earnest, so anxious. She was also right about people's perceptions. Regardless of the half-glazed walls of his office, Francis took her in his arms. 'I have not the remotest intention of writing anything that would harm your mother. I'll puncture the Black House myth, that's all. Trust me?'

Speechlessly, she nodded.

'In another couple of weeks, the worst will be over,' he said. 'After that, let's be married as soon as we can arrange it. Quite apart from anything else, I want to make love to you properly.'

'But,' she raised her eyebrows questioningly and little shyly, 'you did, last Saturday. Wasn't that properly?'

When he found his voice again, he said, 'Not quite.'

The profile appeared on the front page and four inside pages of the *Enterprise* on the following Monday, and by the end of the week Max's empire was in ruins.

'Can a man who lies, lies and lies again about private matters be trusted to speak truthfully on public ones?' Francis began, and went on, sentence by sentence, to demolish the myth of the Black House, the poverty and the adventurous schoolboy running away to sea. 'He has admitted, disarmingly, that he did not like the Navy and ended by jumping ship. What he has not admitted, but which enquiries at the Admiralty have revealed, is that he jumped ship in the most cowardly way, deserting with a crony during the bombardment of Alexandria.' After that, there was a spell as a lowly clerk in a diamond office at Kimberley, with dismissal for petty pilfering, and after that the tale of O'Donnell's hoard.

It was a damning indictment.

'This, then, is the man who, since the new century dawned, has been one of Britain's most popular and successful businessmen and financiers.'

From there, Francis went on to the affairs of the McKenzie Smith corporation. There was much that he could do no more than hint at, because only Max – and, he suspected, Monty – knew the full extent of McKenzie Smith's huge spider's web of subsidiaries, some of them just a set of books, others providing the means by which paper loans could be transferred from one company to another to make balance sheets look good and attract new investors – investors with money that was real and spendable.

The corporation had needed real money, of course, to register subsidiaries, but once they were registered the money became available again. Francis was able to describe how Max and 'a close associate' had registered a company in Zurich with two cheques for half a million pounds each, and then used the same cheques, a few days later, to register another company in Liechtenstein. That having been done, 'the associate' withdrew all but £50,000 of the new company's capital 'to acquire weaving capacity in Poland and Czechoslovakia'. So, at a net cost of £50,000, they had established two companies whose only purpose was to funnel funds out of other companies and into Max's private pocket.

They had used nominees, too, notably one Mr Algernon Vale, lending him money to buy companies and accepting shares in those companies as surety for the loans. It meant the loans did not have to be repaid, while the shares could be used as collateral for other sham loans of the same kind. Every new company acquired was another money funnel into the pocket of Max McKenzie Smith and, to a lesser extent, his associates.

Such frauds, once in operation, had been easy to sustain for one reason above all – that normally sensible, reliable men had been perfectly prepared to take Max's unsupported word about transactions that, with benefit of hindsight, should have been questioned at every stage. The English auditors – who, in accordance with normal business practice, hadn't expected to be shown audited books for the foreign subsidiaries – had, time after time, obligingly written down the parent company's loans to the dummy companies as assets secured against trading profits that were in fact non-existent.

All of them had been blinkered by Max's personal charm and his success in attracting a consistently favourable press, although there had been sweeteners, too, of course, when they were needed – consultancies, investment opportunities, even contributions to charity.

And so it had gone on, with the tangle over the years

becoming almost impenetrable. The same assets had been entered in the books of several companies. One company had been credited, without another being debited. Borrowings had been omitted from balance sheets. Non-existent securities 'purchased' by one company were certified by another company as having been deposited with them.

The major McKenzie Smith companies were real enough and even profitable, but their true value bore no relation to the highly inflated value put on them in the balance sheets.

Too much of the McKenzie Smith corporation's success, Francis concluded, had been built on the personal magnetism of Max McKenzie Smith himself and the trust he inspired in bankers and public alike. Too many people had been seduced by the image of The Great Max into sinking their savings into his companies. It had taken only a whiff of scandal to send the corporation's shares into a mild downward slide and nothing could more clearly indicate the basic instability of the whole McKenzie Smith empire. The stock-market operated not on reason, but on hopes and fears.

The day of reckoning was bound to come and, in all probability, soon. It was indicative that Max had recently floated four new share issues. Could it be, Francis asked on a final, rhetorical flourish, that he needed the capital desperately, because he would otherwise be unable to pay the dividends due to shareholders whose capital he had already squandered – the small people, the ordinary people who had fallen for his charm, his zest, his initiative? Who had given him their life's savings because they thought he was one of them, a plain man at heart despite his rise from rags to riches. A man they could trust.

13

Max succeeded in shoring up the price of the shares with his own money, but only for two days. After that, they were worth so little that gentlemen in the City began using the certificates as spills for lighting their cigars. But there were many thousands of other people who couldn't afford to be so jaunty about it.

By the Thursday, every window of Max's office and the house in Audley Street had been smashed and the casino had been boarded up and was closed until further notice.

Francis spent the whole of the Friday with John Bell, summoned down from Dundee, and some high-powered gentlemen in the City, trying to work out a plan which might to some extent compensate the shareholders.

'From what you and Bell tell us, Mr Rivers,' said the distinguished accountant, 'it could take years to sort out the tangle.'

'I believe it will. However, the City failed to question McKenzie Smith's operations. In my view, if you had been doing your duty, he would never have got away with it. It seems to me that the banks and the leading auditors should do something to atone by setting up a fund, at once, to recompense those who have suffered. I should add that I propose to say so, repeatedly and at length, in the columns of the *Enterprise*, and I think this will be a case where every other newspaper in the country will be in agreement with me.'

'Blackmail, Mr Rivers?'

Francis smiled. 'Blackmail, Mr Decker.'

Afterwards, one of the bankers said, 'Glad you brought it all out in the open, dear chap. Never liked to say so, but I've had doubts about him for a while. You've saved my bank a lot of trouble, too. The fellow's been negotiating with us to set up a £15 million revolving credit facility for expansion at Dundee. Suppose he'd have finished up using it for one of his frauds, though.'

'If you're grateful, you know how to show it.'

'Mmmm. You set up the machinery for some kind of fund and I'll see what can be done.'

14

No one knew where Max was. No one saw him. No one heard from him. Every journalist in London, Dundee and the Borders was on his trail but he wasn't to be found.

15

Tassie, stitching industriously, said, 'I suppose there are advantages to Francis being busy every night. Otherwise, I'd never get my trousseau finished.'

'You hadn't thought of just going into a shop and buying it?' Norah enquired politely. An expert needlewoman herself, she regularly had to fight off the temptation to snatch something out of Tassie's hands, saying, 'Let me do it. Lord knows what Jessie Newbery would say if she saw you cobbling your seams like that.'

'I couldn't!' Tassie blushed. 'I have to make the nighties, at least.'

Resting her chin thoughtfully on her hand, Norah reviewed and rejected several possible replies, all of them calculated to make Tassie blush even more. In the end, she said merely, 'I'll do the embroidery for you. Call it an engagement present. Are you any further forward with your plans?'

'Francis wants to put a notice in the papers, announcing both the engagement and the wedding. We thought we'd hold an engagement party, too, in the office, and use the announcement to invite anyone who wants to come.'

'I didn't know Francis was setting up in business as a miser. Talk about economy! He'll be vetting your housekeeping bills before you know where you are.'

Tassie chuckled. 'He doesn't believe in wasting effort. And it's sensible, really. It means we don't have to send out dozens of invitations and finish up by offending umpteen people we've forgotten about. The office is quite a good idea, too, especially as Francis wants all his staff to share the champagne, and there's a local restaurant that can supply food and waiters and all the rest of it. I think it'll be a much jollier party than something more formal, besides being a whole lot less nerve-racking to organise. We've more or less settled on the first Saturday in September – the 2nd – and we're getting married on the 16th.'

Norah, a mother hen whose trusting and unworldly chick was on the verge of finding happiness at last, sniffed away a sentimental tear and said, 'Gosh! That doesn't leave you much time. You'd better give that stitchery to me!'

September 1905

CHAPTER FOUR

I

It was a magnificent party, and the most surprising number of people turned up. They were surprising people, too, some of them. Not just the entire staff of the national *Enterprise* from the deputy editor down to Albert, the copy boy, but several of the Glasgow staff as well. Not just everyone from G.S. Advertising but a making-the-best-of-it trio of Tassie's rejected suitors from the casino. Not just Abigail Rivers, half of Fleet Street and a goodly number of suffrage ladies, but Fra and Jessie Newbery, Bess Baird, and several other fellow students Tassie hadn't seen for years. Most surprising of all was the party from Dundee – John Bell and six uproarious mill girls, laughing and shouting and flaunting their best feather boas.

The most notable absentees were Hugo, Max, Monty and Genny.

Genny had spent the last two weeks barricaded into Kirklaws by reporters. Under Monty's guidance, she had used the newspapers to considerable effect, but now, when she didn't need them any more, they wouldn't go away.

Francis said, 'By the way, Tassie, you don't need to worry about Genny . . .'

'I'm not,' Tassie said.

'. . . because she's being guarded by the military.'

'What?'

'Believe it or not, Jonny has dragged five of his friends up there to spend their leave patrolling the grounds.'

'In full regimentals, I hope?' Half laughing, half sighing, she said, 'Genny's every bit as smitten as he is, you know. Oh, dear, I wonder what will happen?'

Francis put his arm round her. 'They'll have to work things out for themselves. There's nothing we can do.'

They were standing in Francis's office, apart from the others, looking out through the half-glazed walls at the chattering crowd of friends, the scurrying waiters, and the three-piece orchestra quietly plink-plonking and sawing away at the far end of the room.

'It's a good party, isn't it?' Francis remarked with satisfaction and then looked down when Tassie didn't reply.

Her eyes were riveted on the far door.

Max.

2

Silence fell in stages as the news spread, raised voices becoming first hesitant and then dropping in pitch, the strains of 'Wait till the sun shines, Nellie' beginning to falter, the clink of glasses ceasing. In the end, the room was full only of murmurings, broken by the pop of a belated champagne cork. Everyone jumped nervously.

And then Max's searching eyes discovered Francis and Tassie and he began pushing his way towards them, guests falling back out of his path. Only at that point did Francis and Tassie see that Naomi Merton was with him.

That's where he's been, Tassie thought. *He's been staying with her. That's why no one could find him.*

Francis said unnecessarily, 'Oh-oh! Trouble.'

Max, who had always made a fetish of being perfectly groomed, looked as if he hadn't shaved or changed his shirt for days. His suit hadn't been pressed and the buttons didn't meet. He had put on pounds in the last few weeks. He looked thoroughly slovenly.

He also looked murderous.

Tassie braced herself. With so many witnesses, he wasn't going to do anything physically violent, but words could be violent, too.

As he neared the door of the office, she saw her mother and John Bell and the mill girls converging in his wake – the people who had been close to him, in one way or another, for years. It didn't take any great powers of perception to guess that those who only knew him from a distance, or from his photographs in the papers, were thinking, 'Well, well! I wonder what he's doing here. Dashed bad form.'

As for the dozens of reporters present, there was no rush forward, only a gentle tidal flow, bringing them within hearing distance. Whatever The Great Max was going to say, it didn't look as if he was going to say it quietly.

3

Tassie gulped. 'Max,' she said. 'What a surprise. And Mrs Merton. Would you like some champagne?'

Naomi Merton shook her head. If there was any expression on her face, it was one of warning. Tassie frowned slightly, questioningly, but she only shook her head again.

Francis waited.

Max did, too. It was as if he were allowing his audience to settle, so that they shouldn't miss anything.

At last, his puffy, bloodshot eyes fixed on Francis, he said with great clarity, 'You scum. You cheap little rat. You think you've won but I'm here to tell you otherwise. You and your kind – all you arrogant, bloody leftovers from the past – you've always been

473

frightened of me because I'm the man of the future. You haven't the brains to make money yourselves, and you wouldn't dirty your hands at it anyway, so you're suspicious of anyone who does. I was too much for you. I was successful beyond your wildest dreams. So you hated me, you wanted to bring me down. All of you.' His voice rose in childish parody. 'Snap! snap! snap! and yap! yap! yap! round my heels. Everything was fine. I had everything under control. And you ruined it. But not for long.

'You only write headlines. I make them.' He spread his arms wide. 'Look at me. I came from nothing, and look what I've made of myself. And I can do it again. *I can do anything*.'

Quietly, meditatively, Francis echoed, 'Look at me – I'm a success. Look at me – I'm a millionaire. Look at me – I'm God.'

Max either didn't hear or didn't understand. 'You think you're clever,' he went on, shouting now, 'but you're only a pygmy. You think you've found out everything about me, but you don't know the half of it.'

Francis, aware of all the craning necks and pricked ears, considered the possibility of having Max removed bodily from the offices, but decided that it wouldn't solve anything. It would be better to let him talk himself out. Though not if he were to start airing the family's dirty linen.

'Don't delude yourself, Max,' he said, unaware of quite how supercilious he sounded. 'We know all we need to know.' He glanced at Naomi Merton. 'Not only about Max. About you, too.'

Max, suddenly maudlin, flung a protective arm around Naomi's shoulders. 'Only person I can trust in this world. Can' even trust my little Ginger any more. Hates me. Don' know why.'

'Oh, don't you?' snapped Tassie, as anxious as Francis to keep her brother's tongue under some kind of control. Stones and mortar seemed a safer subject than the human revelations she feared. 'You don't think your broken promises over Dunaird might have something to do with it?'

Blearily, Max stared at her as if her words had no meaning. Then his eyebrows rose a little. 'Is 'at all? That fucking li'l pile o' rocks? Better things to do with my time and money. Anyway, 's mine. Mummy transferred the deeds to me. I can do what I want with it.'

Tassie had forgotten. The ownership transferred to him – to facilitate the financing, he'd said. She felt sick. 'You *are* evil,' she gasped. 'Evil in private, evil in public. If I . . .'

'No, Tassie.' Francis stopped her. Then, while Max continued to frown at her uncomprehendingly, went on, 'Until a few years ago, we'd have called him a "moral imbecile", but now there's a new, scientific word for what ails him. He's a perfect specimen of a psychopath.

'Look at *me*, Max, not at Tassie! Power for you is a drug, and you've abused it long enough. You're not going to be allowed within reach of it again. Resign yourself, Max. It's over.'

Max threw back his head and laughed. 'Balls! Give it a year or two and everyone will have forgotten all this. I'll be back. Wars have ended without people noticing. But I'm not having you still around, making a career of reminding people . . .'

His hand went to his inside pocket in a gesture so long familiar that Tassie thought with relief, 'A cigar.' Something normal. Something reassuring.

But it wasn't his cigar case he brought out. It was a revolver.

'Time's up, Rivers,' he said.

There was the silence of total shock inside the office, because it wasn't an empty threat.

Francis, his brain racing, remembered two accidents that had nearly befallen him in the last few weeks, during the empty, early hours of the morning – the motorcar that had come careering towards him down one of the narrow alleys off Fleet Street, apparently out of control, and the two bruisers whose object, he had thought, had been to rob him but who hadn't been as quick on their feet as he was.

He had had some kind of chance, then.

One of the people clustering outside the glass gave a shout of horror. 'He's got a gun!'

Francis, the barrel not much more than a foot from his chest, saw that Grace Smith, her face stricken, was standing in the doorway, blocking the entrance. By the time any would-be saviour elbowed past her, it would be much too late.

There was a ripple of movement from outside that was enough to make Max, his back to the crowd, gesture with his revolver and shout thickly, 'Don't anyone try anything.'

It was Grace who responded, her voice light and calming as always. 'Max, my dear. This is really very silly of you, not like you at all. Do put it down, please.'

Instantly, rudely, sickeningly, he grunted, 'Stupid cow!' Then, his eyes unmoving but his upper lip lifting in a sneer, 'Don't tell me what to do, mother dear. Go back to your fucking tea cups.'

Tassie didn't – couldn't – wouldn't – believe what she had heard. She saw that her mother's face was as white as on the day, eleven years before, when her loved, lost son had come back to her.

Just before Grace spoke, she herself had been on the verge of stepping forward and saying, 'Max, for heaven's sake give me that gun. You know you're not going to use it.' But now she didn't dare. Max, her once adored Max, wasn't sane.

He was enjoying himself, scanning Francis's face, spinning the pleasure out, daring the world to contest the power of what he held in his hand, a power mightier even than money.

When Naomi, too, said, 'Max, my dear . . .' he shook his head in idiotic reproval. 'No, my love. This time I know better than you.'

Then, since Francis was spoiling it for him by showing no sign of fear, he lowered the barrel a couple of inches, as if the heart would be too clean and painless a kill.

The silence lay thick on the air, a silence that wasn't silence but a compound of tiny inchoate sounds, of rustlings, of whispers, of breaths held and breaths expelled.

Suddenly, it was shattered.

'Yah, boo!' yelled one of the mill girls. 'Yah, boo, The Great Max. Yah, boo, rotten bastard.' At once, the others joined in. 'Yah, *boo*, rotten *bast*ard! Yah, *boo*, rotten *bast*ard! Yah, *boo*, rotten *bast*ard! Yah, *boo*! Yah, *boo*! Yah, *boo*! . . .'

It was a loud, vulgar, living chant that went on and on, beating upon the ear drums, beating upon the brain. Tassie knew, and Max too, that the girls could keep it up for hours. When there was a strike at the mill, they chanted and chanted outside the gates, hour after hour, day after day, until those who were forced to listen thought they would go mad.

The effect on Max was electrifying. His eyes became suddenly wild and his hand began shaking. For an appalled moment, Tassie thought he was going to swing round and empty the gun into the group outside the door.

The group that was unobtrusively re-forming under cover of the chant.

Francis sent a swift, meaning glance towards Tassie and then said harshly above the uproar, 'Max! Never mind *them*, Max. Forget the girls. It's me you want, isn't it?'

Max's eyes came into focus again, and he tried to level the revolver, his teeth clamped over his lips in concentration, but his hand was still shaking and he was raising the other hand to steady it when John Bell came hurtling through the door in a tackle that would have broken every last rule on the rugby field.

At the self-same moment, Francis leapt aside and brought the edge of his hand down in a vicious chop against Max's wrist.

The gun went off.

5

Tassie, rising after a moment or two from her refuge on the floor, said weakly, 'Well, I'm glad the bullet parted the papers on your desk rather than the hair on my head. Goodness, what an exciting life we lead. I wonder if anyone's phoned for the police?'

Breathlessly, from his perch on the chest of the threshing Max, John Bell said, 'Miss St John did, as soon as we knew he had a gun.'

Which couldn't have been more than five minutes ago. Francis said, 'Tassie, cancel the call, will you? We don't want the police. There are charges enough against Max without this. He's ill and a cell isn't going to help.'

6

Tassie went to thank the girls, tears of reaction in her eyes and her voice unsteady. 'I don't know what we'd have done without you.'

Big, tough Aggie, half smothered in her embrace, winked. 'Aye, weel, we foun' oot years ago that yon

478

chantin' fair makes him squirm. I mind once I thocht he was gonny go aff the heid. Glad we came, now, Doris?'

'Aye,' said Doris, the glum one. 'Ah had ma doots, mind, though Mr Bell said Miss Tassie'd like us tae be here and the mill wud pay wur fare. But it wus great. Wouldny have missed it.'

From Doris, that was praise indeed, and Tassie began to feel almost cheerful again.

The number of people in the room had diminished noticeably, mainly owing to the hurried departure of reporters from the Sunday papers, scribbling as they went, so it didn't take Tassie long to exchange a few words with those who remained, playing down Max's madness as an unfortunate, drunken revel, and to ensure that the waiters had the champagne lavishly flowing again and there would be more warm food brought up shortly from the restaurant.

When Norah said, 'Sure you're all right?' she replied with worrying brightness, 'Yes, of course.'

7

The door of Francis's office was closed when she returned. Max was silent in the chair behind the desk with John Bell hovering close by; Naomi Merton standing by the window; and Grace occupying the visitor's chair with Abigail, of all people, standing beside her, a reassuring hand on her shoulder. Tassie smiled at her gratefully and Abigail inclined her head in return as if she were merely doing her duty and kindness didn't enter into it. Tassie knew, suddenly, that she and her intimidating mother-in-law-to-be were going to get on very well.

Francis was in his favourite position, perched on a corner of his desk. He was saying, 'I'm sorry if no one's in the mood for it, but this may be the only chance we have to talk, and explain, and perhaps change things. It's possible that Max won't understand what I'm going to say, because his own distorted sense of values seems perfectly normal and natural to him. He doesn't realise that his code of morality isn't the same as other people's. He doesn't realise that his feelings aren't the same as other people's. Other people, to him, are cardboard figures who don't *have* any real feelings and for whom he has no feeling himself. He simply cannot believe, when Grace there, or Tassie, says he has hurt them, that they truly mean it. And the same applies in a wider field.

'He is, however, intelligent and, on the remote chance that he might recognise himself and begin to see why he doesn't fit into normal human society, I want to explain what my medical informant told me about the psychopath.'

He glanced at Max, his eyes cool and clinical. 'Listen to me, Max. Normal, ordinary people don't need to be defined, but there is a pattern to the psychopath. If you see that pattern in yourself, you might understand where everything has gone wrong. It's even possible, I suppose, that with self-discipline you might be able to reform yourself.'

From her post by the window, Naomi Merton said unexpectedly, 'It is too late.'

She looked lined and exhausted. Tassie, who wouldn't have thought it possible, found herself feeling desperately sorry for the woman. The woman who had once been a child in a fishing village and had fought her way to money and style and a kind of success. Who had helped her foster brother to do the same.

Francis said, 'You may be right, but we have to try. Max may be ill, but he isn't mad, even if days or weeks of drinking have made him appear so, tonight. He is, and always has been, perfectly sane. Listen, please, and I'll check off the symptoms, one by one. First, personal secrecy, a genius for self-justification and an unusual ability to convince himself of his own lies.'

Tassie released her breath on a small gust of irony. 'Does this medical informant of yours know Max personally? It sounds as if he does.'

Francis shook his head. 'Secondly, the psychopath is a natural thief, but he doesn't necessarily steal things worth stealing in the ordinary sense. A miner's gold, yes. But he's more interested in things that have a sentimental or emotional value. Taking Dunaird away from Grace must have given him immense satisfaction.'

There was a momentary silence and then Tassie said slowly, 'And my necklace. He stole it and gave me a fake in exchange. I believed him when he shrugged it off as a joke gone wrong.'

'I didn't know about that, but it fits. There's vengefulness, too, which is often disproportionate. From the first day he and I met, he was convinced that I wasn't merely critical of him but persecuting him. He tried, unsuccessfully, to drive the Glasgow *Enterprise* into bankruptcy. And more recently, though I can't prove it, I believe he was twice responsible for trying to have me either killed or seriously damaged.'

'*Francis!*'

He smiled at her. 'Don't look so horrified. I'm still here.'

Max spoke for the first time, his voice slurred. 'You'd have done the same in my place.'

'No,' Francis said. 'That is where you've always gone wrong. A normal person doesn't react like that.'

Grace, who had shown little of her feelings until then, said, 'And poor Dudley. Dudley tried to knock him down once, and was very rude to him. Then Max recommended him to buy some shares and Dudley lost all his money.'

'But mother,' Tassie objected, 'that was years later.'

Shaking his head, Francis said, 'The psychopath knows how to wait.'

Tassie exclaimed suddenly, 'We used to play a kind of

game, years ago. Diamond cut diamond. Tit for tat. If ever he annoyed me, or I him, it was a matter of honour to get our own back. I thought it didn't mean anything, that it was just an amusing way of sharpening our wits and teaching us to be careful what we said. But . . . wait a moment . . .'

They waited, patient and undemanding, as she raced through her memories and said at last, 'I think that almost everything he has ever done to hurt mother or me has been an extension of that game. Mother refused to move from Graceholm to live at Kirklaws, and that very evening he set his sights on Dunaird. In my own case, he repaid me for forcing him to let me go to art school by forcing me to leave again, to work at the factory. And then I deserted the firm and found a job with Gus, and I refused to help him with the casino, and it was soon after that that he stole my necklace. And I threw a glass of wine at him once and criticised him publicly for neglecting Genny, and the next thing was that he gave the McKenzie Smith International contract to Gus and forced me into being at his beck and call again, and going to America with him.'

She shuddered and stopped. 'There were a dozen other things like that. Was it vengefulness – a punishment – every time?'

Max said carelessly, 'Of course.'

'I am afraid that nothing he has ever done to hurt you was done accidentally,' Francis said. 'And now – I don't want to prolong this, because I know it's a strain on you and Grace, but there's one more thing that needs to be explained, to put everything in perspective.

'The trait that is perhaps least comprehensible to ordinarily kindly human beings is the very real pleasure the psychopath takes in ruining anyone who has helped him on his way, even someone who has been foolish enough merely to show him a kindness. Poor old Sir Leoday was one of his victims. He had given Max social respectability by agreeing to join his board; Max, in return, sacked him in the shabbiest and most damaging way.'

'And Bruce Goudy,' John Bell intervened, his voice thick with anger. 'He was a decent man once. But he was feart of losing his job and fell in wi' what Max wanted and helped wi' his frauds. Maybe even suggested some o' them. Then Max sacked him, too, and from conscience and despair he killed himself.'

'Even Freddie,' Tassie said wonderingly. 'It seems very unimportant by comparison, but that must have been why he lost and went on losing at the casino. He'd helped Max, and Max fixed the roulette wheel.'

8

The light outdoors had faded, and Francis's office was lit only through the glass from the room where the party, now subdued, was still going on.

There seemed nothing more to say, or nothing useful. It was clear to everyone that Max had taken in what was said, but not the meaning or implications of it. There was no remorse, nor any sign of nightmare in his eyes.

Then, just as Francis was about to declare an end, Grace forestalled him. The half light drained the colour from her eyes, dulled the beautifully dressed hair that was now silver, not gold, showed up the lines in her once smooth skin. She had always looked younger than her years, but no more.

Almost reflectively, she said to Max, 'I have had many things to regret in my life but I never thought I should regret having a son to love. When you came back into my life, all my old guilt over losing you swept over me and I have tried ever since, in every way, to make things up to you. I have loved you as much as it is possible for a woman to love a son who has always held her at arm's length. I have never understood you. I still don't understand you. But I think it is time for you to go, Max. It is time for you to leave my life, and Tassie's. You came from nowhere, and the time has come when you should go back to nowhere.'

Rising, she went to the window, and Tassie followed, her heart full of tenderness and grief. Briefly, she noticed a curious expression on Naomi Merton's face, as if she were waiting for Max to say something, or do something.

But he only heaved himself to his feet and, looking at no one, crossed the room, opened the door and shouldered his way out through the remaining guests.

9

Unmoving, abstracted, the three women stood gazing down into the quiet street, each possessed by her own thoughts. There was little traffic on a Saturday evening, so that cheerful passing voices floated up to them, and the clop and clatter of a hansom, and the chugging of a motor omnibus.

Behind them, John Bell said, 'He'll come after you again, Francis,' but Francis said only, with a shrug in his voice, 'Perhaps.'

They saw Max emerge from the main entrance and stand by the kerb, waiting for the motor omnibus to pass.

Then they saw him step out in front of it.

10

There was an asthmatic screeching and grinding as the omnibus juddered to a halt, the horrified driver leaping out and passers-by already running to help.

Tassie wasn't even conscious of her own voice gasping, 'Max! Max!'

All she heard was the high, keening note of Grace's, 'My son!' a single wail followed by a blind turning away.

And then she became aware of Naomi Merton, rocking back and forward, her hand to her throat, moaning something that Tassie couldn't at first decipher.

Couldn't at first decipher, and then couldn't believe.

'Oh, Robbie! My Robbie!'

They had found out about all Max's lies, it seemed, except the greatest of them.

EPILOGUE

September

1905

September 1905

EPILOGUE

It was dawn by the time Francis and Tassie left the office to walk through the quiet streets to Francis's calm, white, airy flat.

Max's body had been taken away, long before, but the police had refused to allow anyone to accompany it. Mr McKenzie Smith was – had been – a famous man and they were determined that no fragment of evidence should escape them. Experience had taught them that, however accidental the death of such a man, it always raised questions, afterwards. Especially in the present case, where the law was already taking an interest.

They had been a long time about interviewing all the witnesses in the street before they turned their attention to those upstairs, but they had finished in the end, and Naomi Merton, née McKenzie, had been released to go in search of her brother's body, and mourn over it.

Norah, refusing to allow Grace or the silent Abigail to go back to their cold, impersonal hotels, had insisted that they spend what remained of the night at the Bayswater Road. Mrs Rivers could have the Blue Room, she said, and Grace could have Tassie's. No one asked where Tassie would sleep.

Grace had looked hesitant at first, but then Francis caught her eye and, after a moment, her slight, exhausted frown relaxed and she said, 'I understand. Yes, it would be best. To every thing there is a season, and a time to every purpose under the heaven.'

Francis took her up. 'A time to heal,' he agreed. 'A time to embrace.'

2

There had been opportunity enough, while they waited in Francis's office, for Naomi to tell them everything that mattered about the man who hadn't been Max.

Her false French accent gone, to be replaced by the lilt of the Highlands, she murmured, 'My fault. It was my fault,' and then went on, with occasional hesitations but few other signs of emotion, 'I was six years old and Robbie only a baby when our mother, Jeannie, was given little John – Max – to nurse. Robbie and I were both illegitimate, by different fathers, so it was natural for us to assume that our foster brother was illegitimate, too. We all grew up assuming that he was the un-acknowledged son of Josiah Smith.'

The annual allowance from Joss had permitted the whole family to live in comfort – or what passed for comfort by the spartan standards of Wester Ross. Max, the real Max, had even been permitted to share the tutor of the boys at the Big House, from which Jeannie took in washing. But learning had never appealed to him and, urged on by Robbie, who had always been the ringleader, he had finally joined him in running away to sea.

'I do not know whether I would, or could have stopped them,' Naomi said. 'But I myself had left home when I was twelve and gone into service with a family in Glasgow.

'The boys were used to running wild and hated naval discipline, so they decided to desert as soon as they had the chance. The chance came during the bombardment of Alexandria, and they took it, slipping down the side of the ship and swimming for the beach.' Naomi sighed. 'It was so like Robbie, not to consider the risks, but it was Max who paid for his foolishness. Just as he reached the shore, he was hit by a shell that fell short. It failed to explode, so Robbie was able to salvage Max's papers and pay book before he took to his heels.'

Grace had made a faint sound, then, and Naomi had emerged briefly from her absorption to glance at her surprisedly, almost irritably.

Tassie, gripping her mother's hand with all her strength, saw that Naomi either didn't recognise or didn't care that she had just, perfunctorily, told Grace the truth of how and when her son – her real son – had died. A victim, like so many others, of the man who hadn't been Max.

Absorbed again, Naomi had resumed her tale. Robbie had worked his way to South Africa and become a clerk at one of the mines, where he had learned some of the tricks of management and accounting, and afterwards he had gone to Australia.

At home, Jeannie had seen no reason to forego Joss's annual allowance merely because Joss's son was dead. With Naomi's help, she had continued to compile an annual report for the lawyers. 'Max' had left the Navy and, an adventurous youth, was wandering the globe, learning about other cultures, just as young men had done a hundred years before, making their ceremonial Grand Tour. No one had questioned.

It was when Joss fell ill that the crisis came. His lawyers had written to Jeannie, asking for current news of Max and she, cornered, had turned to her worldly-wise daughter for advice.

Naomi said, 'It was twelve years since Robbie had left Scotland. I was not sure, until he came hurrying home, whether my idea was practicable, but when I saw him, I knew that it was. Even I scarcely recognised him. The people in Ullapool had known him only as a baby, and none of our few neighbours at Fannich had ever known either of the boys well. The minister who certified the annual reports was old and almost blind.

'I can still remember Robbie saying, "It's hellish risky. Won't the lawyers ask questions?" And I said, "Why should they? They have been receiving annual reports about Max since the days of his infancy."

'Robbie had no polish, of course, but Max would have had none, either. I, on the other hand, had enough polish, and enough knowledge of society for both of us. I had made something of myself. I had persuaded people that, although I might not be quite a lady, at least I was acceptable. There was no reason why Robbie should not be equally successful.

'His time as a clerk had smoothed off the roughest edges and taught him how business worked, while two years in the Navy, even as a cabin boy, had given him some idea of how the gentry, the officers, spoke and acted. There had been one lieutenant, in particular, whom he had always admired. "A velvet-voiced bastard," he said. "He just had to look at a woman and she fell into bed with him!" He was good at mimicry and he had always been clever and sharp and quick to pick up anything that interested him. Josiah Smith & Co. interested him. Enthralled him. I remember him saying, time after time, "Just to *walk* into money! It's too good to be true."

'For three months I tutored him, hour after hour, day after day. Then I brought him to London, and clothed him, and took him to restaurants and theatres and shops and even, at the end, to one or two small, unimportant parties.

'And then he presented himself to the lawyers, as Max. And they found no reason to think he was anyone else.

'I have been so proud of him, my Robbie. What shall I do, now that he is gone?'

3

It explained so many things, Tassie thought, answered so many small questions that had never seemed important enough to ask, and others much larger. It made sense, too, of the man behind the psychopath, and some of the actions that no one other than Tassie knew about. Made sense of them, and even made them – almost – forgivable.

When he had forced himself on Selina, and on Tassie herself, he had known them to be only pretty, desirable girls. Not his sisters.

Even when, towards the end, he had come to believe in the lies he had been acting out for so long, the truth of that must have stayed with him.

Must have.

Despite everything, Tassie found that she wanted to remember him with at least a trace of kindness.

4

'Breakfast first,' Francis said and Tassie nodded dazedly.

They had crisp bacon and poached eggs, strong black coffee, and warm rolls straight from the bakery round the corner. They didn't say much, because there seemed little left to say except, on Tassie's part, and obsessively, 'What an *extraordinary* story!'

Francis, murmuring agreement whenever she seemed to expect it of him, consoled himself with thoughts that were irrelevant to the subject under discussion and very much more pleasing.

Tassie said, 'Why *did* he he kill himself? Because of what we had been saying? Because, instead of being unique, he had learned that he was just one of a category of people so common that their actions and even their ways of thought could be listed – predicted? That would have been awful for him. Or was it because the whole business had collapsed about his ears? Well, at least, he won't have to stand trial for it now. I wonder what will happen to Monty?'

'If they catch him, he may well find himself holding the baby. Do you mind?'

'I don't know. He seems to have been playing so many complicated games of his own. Selina and Dudley brought him up to think he had more entitlement than Max – Robbie – who *do* I mean? – to Josiah Smith & Co. And when Dudley was almost ruined, Bazz told me that he and Monty were going to get their own back. Then Monty became Max-Robbie's right-hand man and I thought they had forgotten about it.'

Francis said slowly, 'I see. It was Monty, you know, who was responsible for starting all the press speculation and scandal about Max personally, and keeping it going. He succeeded very cleverly in undermining Max's reputation. I didn't know why he'd done it until now.'

'Do you suppose he was hoping to get his hands on the business after all?'

'Perhaps. But I'm afraid he allowed himself to become too deeply involved in Max's frauds, and he'll be held liable. There's plenty of proof of his complicity.'

'Oh dear. Poor Selina.' Wryly, Tassie smiled. 'Although when she hears about it all, at least she'll be able to say, "I told you so". Because she was right about Max – Robbie – all along. And I was wrong. There something else I've just thought of. What will happen about Dunaird?'

'It'll be part of Max's personal estate, I suppose, if there's anything left of it when everything is eventually sorted out. The liquidators might try to sell it, but the valuation would probably be *de minimis*, no more than a token sum. Did Max – Robbie – make a Will?'

'I don't know. I shouldn't think so. He'd have hated the thought of giving anything away.'

'And refused to think about dying. In the case of an intestacy, everything would go to Genny and the boys. What a pretty widow she'll make!'

'Not for long!'

'No. If we can't retrieve Dunaird from her, somehow, I shall have some very harsh things to say to my brother.'

Tassie smiled. 'How *extraordinary* it's all been!'

'You're being boringly repetitive, my darling! The only truly extraordinary thing was the grandeur of the gamble. Naomi had the idea and Robbie played it for all it was worth, and brilliantly. He was lucky that he happened to have the right kind of mind for business, but apart from that . . .

'He might well have pulled it off, you know, if he hadn't insisted on being publicly acknowledged as Grace and Joss's son. He was too cocky to resist the temptation, but it was amateurish of him. If he'd simply remained a distant cousin, the press could have tried to trace his history until the heavens fell. Certainly, my mother – and I – would have had no particular interest in him. But his lies about himself led me to his lies about the business. He was good, though. The confidence trickster *par excellence*. Once he had made sure of you and Grace, he was well away. Did you never suspect?'

'No, of course not. He did make a few mistakes at the beginning but they were the kind of mistakes you would have expected.' She made a faint growling sound, deep in her throat. 'Isn't it sickening? – he had me exactly where he wanted me, on the very first day. He charmed me right out of my little buttoned boots, and now it turns out it wasn't him at all but an impersonation of some "velvet-voiced bastard" of a lieutenant. I've never been so deceived. And when I think how much time I spent teaching him all the things Naomi hadn't taught him! I still can't believe it.'

With relief, Francis saw that she was recovering. It would take a long time – weeks, months – before she sorted out the tangles in her mind and her emotions, before she could discern how much of the love she had given Max-Robbie had gone to him as a person and how much to the idea of him as a brother.

As if she had read his mind, she said, 'Oh, well, it's time for forgetting. I had no brother, and then I had a brother, and now I have no brother again. Isn't it sad? When mother and I gave him so much love!'

With a rueful grin, Francis said, 'Yes, I remember! I was the one who suffered. You had no love left for me.'

'That isn't true! I was being a virtuous, dutiful and loyal sister to him, and I *did* love him, but . . .'

5

Rising to his feet, he pulled her up after him and took her firmly in his arms.

'Hush, my dearest darling. It's over now. Come hell or high water, two weeks from today we will be man and wife. Must we wait, or will you come to bed with me? This minute? Because I don't think I can stand it any more. If I can't make love to you soon, properly, I won't answer for the consequences.'

Her hair was coming down, her dress was crumpled, and her eyes were huge and smudged with weariness. But she had never looked more desirable.

'Improperly, half properly, or properly,' she said. 'I don't care, as long as it's now.'